MW00987313

*small ceremonies*

# small ceremonies

a novel

## kyle edwards

Pantheon Books, New York

Pantheon Books and colophon are registered trademarks of
Penguin Random House LLC.

Library of Congress Cataloging-in-Publication Data
Names: Edwards, Kyle, author.
Title: Small ceremonies : a novel / Kyle Edwards.
Description: First edition. | New York : Pantheon Books, 2025.
Identifiers: LCCN 2024033709 (print) | LCCN 2024033710 (ebook) |
ISBN 9780593701515 (hardcover) | ISBN 9780593701508 (ebook)
Subjects: LCGFT: Bildungsromans. | Novels.
Classification: LCC PS3605.D8888 S63 2025 (print) |
LCC PS3605.D8888 (ebook) | DDC 813/.6—dc23/eng/20240724
LC record available at https://lccn.loc.gov/2024033709
LC ebook record available at https://lccn.loc.gov/2024033710

www.penguinrandomhouse.com | www.pantheonbooks.com

Jacket design and illustration by Kate Sinclair

Printed in the United States of America
First Edition
2 4 6 8 9 7 5 3 1

The authorized representative in the EU for product safety and compliance
is Penguin Random House Ireland, Morrison Chambers, 32 Nassau Street,
Dublin D02 YG68, Ireland, https://eu-contact.penguin.ie.

*for mom*

# dagwaagin

*game one*

IT STARTS WITH A RUMBLE, A HEARTBEAT, A POWWOW ON A GYM floor. All echo and thunder, a storm before the lightning, coming not from the sky but from the ice, rising above the glass and mesh meant for foul pucks and empty cans and trash and wrappers, the revenants of lost souls. Foot stomps and air horns. It's the sound of a beginning, a new longing, a new hockey season.

There's excitement in the air: it's growing, raising hearts and neck hair, and a residue of sadness. It starts before the players leave the dressing room, with the music turned up deafeningly high, all eighties rock and guitar solos, by a boy DJ not yet old enough to be in high school, operating from a stereo system in the box beside the score-keeper. There are fans, but only a few, mostly parents and friends and fellow students and girlfriends in jerseys with their boyfriend's name and number on the back in thick font, climbing aboard paint-chipped bleachers in what looks like single file, mining the seats for a place along the cracked wood and wobbly planks.

Outside the sky is big and blue, as endless as the prairies. The fall sun hangs on, casting lean shadows over the uneven sidewalks and dusty pavement. Inside Memorial Arena, a place where it's unclear what is being memorialized because all around there seems nothing worth remembering, the scoreboard counts down from fifteen minutes, at which point the puck will drop and a new campaign will begin. It's colder in the lobby by several degrees and the temperature drops even further behind the doors where the game is played. Each cold breath rises from the mouth and floats for a moment above toques and ball caps and then vanishes before the next one.

Boys, in groups of three or four, push their way to the front of the crowd, ahead of parents and elders. Local misfits and dropouts smile and laugh at nothing in particular, each holding something long and bottle-shaped inside their baggy sweaters and jackets, and in about four or five elegant leaps and a single breath, using muscles and tendons that could only be exercised by scaling beaten streets slant with danger and a certain beautiful misery, they reach the very top of the stands, where they will stand above the rest like it means something special to be there and where they shout a graphic litany of curses at the opposition and their supporters for the next three periods like prophets of a lost world. Some younger boys, a dozen in all, follow the pack nervously, careful to avoid the stern eyes and shaking heads of their grandmothers and aunties. Their movement is rough and forced, and the chants from the top only begin once all the boys assemble: "Fuck you, Bullfrogs! Fuck you, Bullfrogs! Fuck you, Bullfrogs!" And then the aunties turn around and hiss at the younger boys to smarten up and act civilized, but the older ones continue hurling their curses across the ice to the bleachers filled with the other team's supporters. In front of them, just behind the glass, elders escorted by adult grandchildren take their seats, and their laughter, when it comes, is high-pitched and with their bodies as much as their faces. They disappear into the crowd.

The first games always begin with faces halfway hopeful, because even in the North End, the soul of this young city, triumph is scary business. The game never changes—the pucks are made of hot rubber and a goal means the same and there is the constant mixture of dread and pleasure and suspense; a coming-together of a whole country's faith and passion and geography and the histories that hang from rafters and are carefully etched forever on trophies. For the Tigers, the outcome of the games doesn't seem to change either. But there's hope anyway. None of it changes but it's always changing.

Tommy sat in the dressing room rubbing the whites of his knuckles. Games always made him nervous, but there was something different about the first one of the season. Something different about the first and last and playoffs (maybe) games, which during his tenure they never, ever, qualified for. They felt like the exam, a test of their preparation and how far they've come as a team and as players and as men, if one ignored that few of them were actually raised by men and instead by women with dreams of something better. The first game of the season was their chance, *his chance,* to reap the rewards of all their hard work over the summer, all the weights lifted, all the miles run, all the whey protein shaken and consumed.

There was a breathable tension in the room, not much chatter. Most of the players bounced their heads in time to the music echoing through the walls. A whistle sounded in the distance, a referee trying out his silver. A scrawny eleventh grader pounded a fist on his naked chest and smiled with the enthusiasm of a bright-eyed rookie, then leaned toward Tommy and said shyly, "How'd you get so big, Tomahawk?"

Tommy worked on lacing his skate, flexing his biceps with each tight pull. "Water," he said, and immediately regretted trying to act good but continued getting dressed in silence.

"Water," the boy repeated. "Holy smokes." When their coaches came in for the pregame pep talk Tommy pulled on his jersey— black with orange stripes on the arms and shoulders and around the waist—and smoothed out the hissing face of an angry tiger stitched across his abdomen, while Coach Johnson took the locker room floor, his hands deep in the pockets of his track pants, his eyes fixated on nothing in particular. His speeches, which had become a pregame fixture ever since he took over the bench, had drifted more and more toward animal allegory.

"We're Tigers," he began, raising his head to observe the faces of his players. "They're Bullfrogs. If this was tigers versus frogs, and by that I mean tigers versus frogs in the wild, I know for damn sure which animal would come out on top." He cleared his throat and continued in a different vein: "Look, there are two types of sharks. Real-life sharks and the Hollywood myth of a shark. Real-life sharks are boring, they're actually quite smart, not easily fooled, they don't really care for human flesh, and really, they only ever attack humans when they're curious what we taste like. But the Hollywood Shark, the Hollywood Shark is a monster from hell, killing and eating anything in sight. Anyone see *Jaws*? The Hollywood shark takes names, has memory, exacts revenge on its enemies. He's a ferocious motherfucker. A complete badass. What I'm saying is, the Hollywood Shark mentality wins hockey games. We lost to these fucking frogs twice last year, don't forget that. We need to go out there and be hungry, hungry to win. Play for each other, play for Jonah, play for your school. Go out there and play like fucking sharks!" For a moment the room remained quiet. There was an air of confusion, but once Coach Johnson started circling the room to give each player a fist bump the room erupted with claps and cheers and high-pitched battle cries. They were Sharks, the Hollywood kind, but also Tigers.

Tommy didn't listen. The words were muffled in his ears. He tried to visualize his game, his reactions to both dangerous and opportunistic situations, the pass he'd make, the shot he'd take, and each time it ended getting knocked on his ass he smacked the side of his head with his palm. He came out of it as Coach Johnson, already sweating and screaming, the veins bulging from his neck, issued his final words, "Urgency, urgency, urgency, urgency!" The whole team cheered but not him. The graduating class before him didn't cheer either, they held it together. Or maybe they didn't care anymore, they'd accepted defeat because defeat was all they'd ever known and therefore they felt no more pressure to care about winning or their dimming window of success, which would close on all of them. He couldn't decide which version made more sense. His stomach fell into a crevice and his hands were damp and cold with sweat. Together they latched on their helmets, slipped on their gloves, clutched their two sticks, the preferred weapon and a spare, and marched toward the ice.

Jonah, their goaltender, stepped onto the ice first, and Tommy followed. Sometimes he was third, fourth or fifth, but rarely farther down the line. At the tail end of the order was Clinton, who always went last. He never wavered on this. He liked the feeling of seeing everything in front of him, the vision it gave him, like he could predict what was going to happen before it happened. Clinton searched the crowd for familiar faces and immediately recognized Jonah's auntie Maggie in her bright orange jacket with "Tigers" embroidered in big black letters that she had sewn on herself, whistling with two fingers and cheering them on like she always did, and then there was Tommy's koko Olga a few rows down to the left, who would remain cold and still until something more exciting happened, and beside her Tommy's sister Asemaa, who everyone except Olga referred to as Sam, holding a cup of something hot between her hands, and he often felt like he knew these people more than he actually did because of the kindness they showed him at hockey games. Clinton imagined his mother as if she were there, his brother Kelvin too, standing close to the glass so they could have something to thump on with their hands because neither of them knew how to whistle.

Tommy did a slow lap, testing the sharpness of his edges, knees high like a galloping horse. Floyd, their best player, skated fast until he felt a burning in his thighs, and then he parked at the red line and entered into a staring contest with players from the other team, which he won out of confusion alone. Jonah scraped the crease around his net with his blades. This he did to avoid sliding too far outside the blue paint when shit got heavy.

Being last to hop through the boards made the chaos of a game make more sense. Clinton could see all the pieces—the players, the coaches, the refs, the spectators, the girlfriends, the girlfriends that didn't know the other girlfriend was somewhere down the aisle, the moms, the absence of fathers, the rink manager with his nose almost touching the glass—and how they fit together like a perfect round of *Tetris*. It was its own thing, an ecosystem in which each person had a role to play and failure to perform that role meant the whole thing didn't work. Zamboni drivers needed ice and ice needed skates and skates needed feet and feet belonged to the human body, which sometimes took the form of a hockey player, and teams needed these players and these players needed parents, who largely made up a team's fan base, and these parents were relied upon in many cases to drive their hockey-playing children to each game, or at the very least retrieve them after the final horn rang, and when all the pieces worked together in harmony, that meant three periods of the game could be played and for the next two hours nothing else in the world mattered to Tommy and Clinton and Jonah and Floyd and the rest of the Tigers except the scoreboard.

Their opponents were the St. Norbert Bullfrogs, who in previous years achieved great regular-season success but ended the year with post-season disappointment. Coach Johnson's orders were simple: keep the puck away from their best, and only good, player.

Serhii. He dodged and weaved and dangled around opponents with deadly grace, and before you even noticed the puck sliding between your legs you were made temporarily blind by the glittering, fake diamond-studded Ukrainian trident dangling from his neck. And before you knew it, you were lost in his trance, puck-watching, awe-struck by the stick-handling moves of an ice-skating magician, and then you lost.

EARLIER, BEFORE THE START of the season, Tommy bet Clinton two burgers that by season's end he'd not be knocked over once by someone from the opposing team, any team. Tommy didn't have much but he had faith and hope in how big his quads got over the summer. They weren't just ripped, he told Koko, running downstairs to inform her what he'd just discovered in the mirror, but "jacked, like Tootoo's." He'd always been a skinny kid. Weak and lanky. And just when it seemed he'd made gains that only come with age he was always a step behind the other boys in the development ladder. Clothes were too short or hung awkwardly off his skinny body, and even though his calves and the rest of him were still not all that, he felt his newfound strength with every squat and stride on the ice and could trace the outline of his new muscles through his pants, like mountain ranges of manliness. Bruce Wayne in the bat suit. And like all great rolling hills and caped crusaders he couldn't be knocked down. Not this year. This year he'd finally live up to his name, the long version. The one thing his mother did right before she left them.

It was a name that instantly summoned attention, like Sitting Bull or Poundmaker, but any reverence evaporated when they realized he was a liability on the ice more than a sacred weapon. At hockey camp the summer before, Jordin Tootoo paused after reading Tommy's name during roll call. Mesmerized by it.

"Deadly," he said. He mouthed it silently—*Tomahawk Shields*—as if reciting a prayer, as if there was a hidden meaning. "Might be the deadliest name in the game." After he saw Tommy skate he never said it again.

The idea for the bet came to him after spotting his sister's tattoo as she reached for her stash of multivitamins and fish oils. In recent months she'd become health-obsessed, and Tommy reckoned it was because of all those social media posts that announced if you were Native you were either prediabetic or just diabetic. Those posts, which always began with the disclaimer "Personal News," came with their own kind of PTSD, and Tommy wondered from time to time whether the disease would eventually come for him. He likened it to an alien inside of him, hiding, waiting, lurking in his blood, and such anxiety heightened when he found himself with an unquenchable thirst. But the Shieldses were no strangers to amputated limbs. Regardless, Tommy saw Sam's new lifestyle as an opportunity. Her knowledge had become encyclopedic. She could cite a food's nutritional benefits offhand and had been fasting a daily sixteen hours long before The Rock made it cool. When she grabbed her krill tablets from the top shelf the phrase "Fall Down Seven Times Stand Up Eight" revealed itself in cursive near her ribs.

Sam made Tommy swear to secrecy. Koko considered tattoos a poor investment. He obliged because he needed her whey.

"Makes no sense," he said. He pictured the scene in his head, a man falling and getting back up, dusting himself off only to get swept off his feet again and again, and then explained the math. Falling down seven times meant you got up that same number.

"Not if you're already on the ground," she said.

"You're living off a scholarship funded by energy companies. Who's plotting against you?"

"This settler-colonial-white-supremacist-state called Canada. You'll learn."

The words of the tattoo still stuck. Tommy was tired of losing. Tired of falling and picking himself up. Tired of picking himself up eight times and falling down nine. On the ice and off. The city had a way of keeping boys like him down, big legs or no. And in the three years he'd been with the St. Croix Tigers they'd never won a game—no one knew the last time they'd tasted victory. It was a forgotten history, a forgettable history, a history you wanted to forget because the truth was so shameful, an erasure. The talent was raw but coachable, most of the kids new to the game, and Tommy knew that's where the problem started: the coaching staff. The coaches were teachers and teachers didn't last long in the hood, retreating to the other side of the tracks as soon as the opportunity presented itself.

He spent the summer before his final season lifting weights and staying up past eleven, something he had never done before. Like his sister, he was responsible, but without the grades to show for it. He was the definition of average. Not smart but not dumb either. But at least strong now. Strong-*er*.

The ice gave you superpowers. The ability to escape.

It kept the Tigers out of trouble. Most of them came from homes that broke them down, time machines that made them age faster than other boys, and for an hour each day, except weekends, they could vanish behind all that plastic armor and pretend.

The bet. Back to the bet. The bet is important. Because the bet changed Tommy's life.

Tommy had known Clinton since elementary school. They met, as most boys did in those days, on the playground, flicking marbles into a handmade hole in the ground with the finger of your choice. Like pool, each participant swapped turns if the marble didn't find its pocket. The first person to sink every marble kept all the marbles. Like chips down at the Club Regent casino, one second you could be on top of the world and the next there could be little separating you from a broke, deadbeat father with a gambling addiction. Rumor had it that the game originated from the rez, maybe Peguis or Sagkeeng or somewhere where there was a surplus of marbles and nothing to do. No one liked being out of marbles, the only real currency in those days, and so when Clinton took exception to Tommy removing a stray branch from the playing field the disagreement led to blows. Clinton picked up Tommy's biggest marble and chucked it far and high, landing somewhere on top of the school's roof. They shed their shirts like they'd seen their uncles do. They threw hooks. They rolled in the grass and exchanged expletives about the other's mother. The next day they joined forces.

After the final practice before the start of the season the two boys, both seventeen and having found themselves, ongoing genocide and all, in one piece, biked over to White's with their heavy gear bags slung over their shoulders for burgers and fries and soft serve. Tommy was due for a cheat meal. The place sponsored the team and offered its players the tenth burger free. Mr. White knew the Tigers' arena was a dump. The rink lacked the rounded corners of a traditional ice surface and its physics rendered any attempt to ring the puck around the boards futile, a feature that sometimes got them out of trouble. It was their Green Monster. It also lacked reliable showers, and Mr. White couldn't have any of the boys stinking up the joint after practice on days when the water wasn't flowing. He handed them their order and pointed toward the door. They grabbed their red trays and squeezed into a picnic table outside.

"I feel strong this year, my legs have that teardrop," Tommy said, observing Clinton's rituals, seen hundreds of times at school.

Clinton wiped his side of the table with a napkin, dusting away every observable speck, and then lined up his tray with the edge of the table. He treated all his belongings the same way: as if they deserved to last forever. Like Frodo and the ring. Every comic book he read looked like it hadn't been touched by a living soul, only a ghost. Any imperfection set off something in his head that Tommy didn't fully understand but he could tell when his friend had initiated his count by the subtle finger-tapping and eye-blinking. Somehow it relieved him of his worries. Waiting times varied when you spoke to Clinton, but you always knew he was listening, processing the information. A couple minutes passed and finally, as if snapping out of hypnosis, he said:

"That's good."

"What?" Tommy said.

"You said you feel strong."

"Oh. Right. Bro, that OCD shit is getting worse."

"Ms. Miller says I should see a psychiatrist."

"See a medicine man, *awsh*!"

Clinton nearly choked. "I seen one a few years ago outside the city, on some rez with a Robin's Donuts and a little strip mall, all sophisticated. Or at least I thought he was one. Seemed a little young maybe. We sat in a teepee out in his backyard and he told me bad spirits were following me. He asked if I ever seen strange things from the side of my eye. Said yeah, maybe. He said, 'Those are spirits, trying to lure you to the spirit world.' Scared the shit out of me, and the medicine didn't do shit. Looked like grass and tasted like ass."

The boys finished up and waved goodbye to Mr. White through the window, whose hands were full and so he raised his chin. They walked their bikes down Salter, taking up the entire concrete path, and paused outside a store that sold board games and Clinton's eyes widened at the selection. Boys from school called him "Old Man Clinton" because he'd rather play cribbage or Scrabble than shoot zombies and talk shit in chat rooms. He came from a rez that ran on dial-up and where you only got signal by leaving. A fly-in, winter road–type place. Board games were the Bush Man's entertainment, he'd say. A flood and an evacuation brought him and his mom and older brother to the city when he was eight and they lived in a Days Inn for eighteen months before they were told they couldn't go back. The ground was too soft. Graves filled with water as soon as shovels stabbed the earth. Refugees in their own land.

"How is that seventy bucks? Real games don't cost that much," Tommy said.

"Just as hard to make," Clinton said.

"I could make that with my bare hands."

"Okay, Schwarzenegger."

"Laugh now, but I'm going full enforcer this year. You'll see. I'll bet you anything I won't be put on my ass. Not once. Like actually laid out, making snow angels. I'll bet you that one there." He pointed toward a box illustrating an old steam train pulling up to white men and women in old-fashioned dress, top hats and corsets.

"Already have it." He scanned the selection for another option but thought better of it.

"Grow some *cojones.*" Tommy could hear Sam in the back of his mind saying, "Grow a vagina." According to Sam the vagina was the tougher genitalia.

"Make it two burgers," Clinton said, "I know you ain't going to have money to cough up when some fat kid lights you up a week from now."

They shook on it.

Clinton went his own way a couple blocks later, down a dusty street opposite his apartment block. Tommy asked where he was headed and didn't get an answer. Clinton said he'd see him Monday. Game Day.

IT WAS 2011 IN Canada, and Canadians were learning about them, about the originals, perhaps for the first time, because of something called Idle No More. Tommy didn't know much about it, didn't read or watch the news, didn't know precisely what his people were fighting for, but he'd heard the noise and hope and desperation all over their great city. He certainly felt Canadian, at times. Cheered for every Indian kid that cracked Team Canada and crossed seas and skies to defend their global prowess at their favorite game. But who he was, who he should be, who he should support, what he should believe in, about all of that he was not sure. Certainly he would side with his people, go with the flow of the migration, feel the powerful current and its pull, because it felt right. Not because he knew who he was or what he was supposed to be doing with his life.

On the first day of school that year, his senior year, Tommy was immediately drawn to the new maps pinned to the wall in every classroom, showing the locations of every tribe and First Nation and reservation throughout North America, their varying plots of land and territory, their uniquely Indigenous and anglicized names and languages and sometimes minuscule populations, and beside each map was another representing every single nook and cranny of the city they lived in. He could see his street, feel its pulse and spalling sidewalks. The homes there were old, had flaky paint and splitting plaster and broken screens, built during a time when the whole world was caught beneath the ribs of death, a destination for Jews, Ukrainians, Poles, Germans, Hungarians and others to start anew. They were bakers and shoemakers and barbers and grocery store owners and tinsmiths, a beautiful mosaic of the hardworking and the poor, which is to say they lived in poverty and hardship and squalor and prejudice then, too. As many of the new caretakers do now. They took the mantle, signed their lease to the neighborhood, forged it like hot iron, and made it their own. But much of the skeleton of the old North End remained intact, a cradle of Canadian socialism. Tommy ran a finger across familiar streets. There, he could get a bowl of borscht and a cup of coleslaw and, if he feared Jesus, take in a sermon at the onion-shaped Ukrainian Orthodox Cathedral that looked like it belonged in the heart of Kyiv. There, he could get a pair of hand-sewn moccasins for cheap and a book on some Indian shit and enjoy a breakfast of eggs and bacon and bannock all under one roof. There, beside those rust-brown tracks that separated them from the metropolis of steel and concrete and sky walking pedestrians and the American flare of Goldeyes baseball, he could get arrested just for being there, for existing. There, he had crazy cousins who left their toys and hockey sticks and balls in the front yard with reckless abandon. And there, on a filthy stretch of Main, he might offer some loving to a ghetto dog or ghetto cat or both and his uneaten lunch to a drifting man named Jerry, strays asleep in the sun, toiling in the hot streets, before checking out Eddie's Hobby Shoppy, a supplier of sports cards.

He studied the North America map again. On a macro level, Winnipeg was at the heart of the continent, situated at its dead center, perhaps the farthest major city from any ocean. He thought of Winnie-the-Pooh, the famous bear by A. A. Milne, who was named after a bear named Winnie, who was named after Winnipeg, the hometown of Lieutenant Harry Colebourn, a Canadian soldier who, while on his way to Quebec and then to France for World War I, purchased Winnie at a train station in White River from a hunter who had killed her mother and thus became the unofficial mascot of his troop. Clinton had once recounted the story for Tommy with a passion like he'd been there. Winnie went with Harry overseas, making a stop in England, where his regiment trained, and before his deployment to the battlefields of France—a trip Winnie was not allowed to make—the bear was loaned to the London Zoo on December 9, 1914, where she lived a life of celebrity and died at the age of twenty. Christopher Robin, Milne's son and a Winnie fanatic, would name his teddy bear Winnie-the-Pooh, which would also be the title of Milne's first book about the character. Tommy thought about the steps it took to make such things happen, from an orphaned bear in White River to a brown and furry luminary. But he never watched the cartoons or read the books, and at the time of Clinton's telling didn't understand the literary significance of the anthropomorphic protagonist and its friends.

Before lunch, Tommy and the rest of the senior class filed into the drama theater for a presentation called "Life After St. Croix: Adapting & Transitioning." The grimness of this title, projected in big letters behind the stage, both amused and worried Tommy. He knew the world outside offered its trials and tribulations, but for the time being he was convinced, with the help of inspirational YouTube videos, that with hard work anything can be achieved. Apart from the occasional performances that took place in the theater, Tommy had spent little time in the room. The theater felt colder than the rest of the school and everything—the floors, chairs and walls—was black except for the red curtain. Two tables were onstage, each with a banner for one of the local colleges behind it, and a woman sat at each one. They both wore thick glasses and quietly organized a stack of brochures. "It's a trap," someone whispered loud enough for the whole auditorium to hear.

Tommy hadn't thought much about university, or even whether it was a good or bad idea. The only person in his family to ever pursue a post-secondary education was Sam: probably walking the cobbled pathways at the University of Manitoba at that moment. Sam was studying computer engineering. She talked about becoming a software engineer and going on to design the microchips that go inside smartphones. "And soon humans," she said once, with a devious smirk. Tommy replied: "Why are you so committed to the extinction of the human race?" Sam gave a villainous laugh. "It is what it is." Tommy knew for certain that he'd be underprepared for the rigors and demands of university, a feeling that had been confirmed to him by his sister, who considered her four years at St. Croix a "complete and utter waste of the human experience." She lambasted the quality of the science labs, and decried that during her tenure at St. Croix she wrote every paper with a pencil and loose leaf because she was taught no other way. "The cafeteria's curly fries," she said exasperated, like a veteran telling stories of war, "almost made up for it." Still, Tommy knew that Sam had "it" despite a lifetime of academic austerity. And that it was those same intangible gifts that led her up the stage in front of him three years ago to collect the Governor General's award.

Principal Goodstock finally made his way onstage, lowering the volume of the students like he possessed two magic wands in his hands. He wore a suit, which he almost never did, and his facial hair, normally unkempt, appeared groomed.

"I'm going to do this without a microphone, so shout out if you can't hear me," he said, pausing a moment for any objecting students. "We're here today to talk about your futures as you prepare to embark on the next chapter of your lives after St. Croix. But you know the motto: 'Win, Lose or Tie, Tiger Till I Die'"—he turned and smiled at the two women sitting at opposite tables—"You'll always be a part of this family and this community. We're joined today by two admissions outreach officers: Jessica Chapman from the University of Winnipeg and Dolores Poole from the University of Manitoba. I'm going to give a brief PowerPoint presentation and then I'll hand the stage over to Jessica and Dolores."

The first slide showed a picture of a couple dozen students, each with wide, photogenic smiles and perfect teeth. The backdrop was the reddish, brick exterior of St. Croix. The photo had clearly been brightened and perhaps even photoshopped, because the grass around the school had never once looked that nice. The students, too, were immaculately dressed and stylish, despite being of an earlier generation where retro-looking jumpsuits and pants and shirts that looked far too roomy to be comfortable were trendy. This was the dream of St. Croix.

The next few slides showed portraits of students labeled "Success Stories." There was Feather Baptiste, Class of '01, who went on to become a lawyer. Ethan Greyeyes, Class of '95, ran his own car dealership and is credited with being one of the first to bring luxury vehicles to Winnipeg. Sisters Darla and Fancy Bushie, Class of '04 and '05, started their own physiotherapy practice and at one point worked as personal trainers for the Manitoba Moose. Rodney Ferland, Class of '06, was a conservation officer and part-time wilderness guide. With a hand pointed up at Rodney's smiling face, Principal Goodstock posed the question: "What do all these great people have in common?" Clinton, sitting beside Tommy, leaned over and whispered: "What about that guy who sells weed and cigarettes across the street?" Tommy replied: "J.J. is an icon. Our Jordan."

"They have all gone on to university and college," Principal Goodstock said after a long pause, frustrated and embarrassed that no one had answered. "Without their degrees or diplomas they wouldn't be up here. They wouldn't have been able to make such great lives for themselves and *thus* inspire our community." The next batch of slides compared life as a high school diploma holder versus life as someone with a bachelor's degree. There were charts and bar graphs that compared things like median household income, the types of jobs you can and can't get, the size of house one might be able to buy, encounters with the law and average financial debt, and the life expectancy of someone without a university degree (at this point in the presentation it had already been assumed that the rich and educated lived longer lives and had more fun). "Now," Principal Goodstock said, "not all of you will go on to graduate from university or college. That is statistically not likely to happen, that's just a fact. Nor do we as a society encourage everyone to pursue a post-secondary education. But we can all *try*. Life is about trying and failing and picking ourselves back up again." Eight times or nine times, or forever. Who knew?

St. Croix had a disturbing bluntness about these sort of conversations. In English class two years earlier, for no apparent reason, Mr. Dickinson paused from reading *The Outsiders* to talk about growing old. "Twenty years from now not all of you will be alive," he said, closing the tattered text without slipping in a bookmark. "Statistically speaking some of you will die. I hope we can all meet here again in twenty years, read this fabulous book, but I just don't see it." Then he kept reading.

After the presentation was over and the two university representatives gave their spiels, a few students walked up to the tables onstage, Tommy among them. He approached Dolores Poole only because Jessica Chapman at the other booth was busy fielding questions and handing out brochures and application instructions. Dolores stood as he removed his hands from his pockets and reached for a pamphlet.

"Considering university?" she said, with a smile.

"I don't know. Maybe."

"Do you mind if I ask what your average is?"

"About seventy I think."

"That's good. That's great. Do you have any particular interests?"

Tommy cleared his throat, feeling nervous by the question. "Biology is probably my best course. I'm also a fan of consumer math. The simple stuff."

"That's great. We have excellent science programs and brand-new lab facilities. They can lead to great careers in STEM." Dolores reached for one of the thicker university guidebooks, flipped through it, creased the top corner of a page, and handed it to Tommy. "You'll find all of our biology-related programs here."

"What's *STEM*?"

"It stands for science, technology, engineering and math." There was a brief silence, and then she added: "It's very white."

"Right."

Tommy noticed her face go red.

"But the university is hoping to change that." Dolores reached for another student guide and handed Tommy one for the Asper School of Business. "If you're into the business side of things, I might suggest considering Asper. Plenty of our grads, like Ethan Greyeyes, go on to do exceptional things in the world of business."

"I'll look into it. Thanks."

"One more thing," she said, reaching again for another item on the table and handing it to Tommy. "This is my card. Feel free to get a hold of me if you have any questions, or if you need help applying. It's my job."

Tommy thanked her and walked back to class.


AT NOON THE TIGERS filed into the team's pregame meeting room, a cramped space beneath the off-white, sneaker-scuffed floors of St. Croix filled with desks and chairs and a whiteboard. They ate spaghetti and meatballs; each year a referendum was held to decide between game day meals or Tiger apparel. The choice was easy. Coach Johnson came in last, appearing from the bright hallway like an eclipse. He was a short, stocky man with wavy dark hair and a dense stubble. He joined the team halfway through last season after the previous head coach left unexpectedly. No reason was given and there was no goodbye. Coach Johnson was in his mid-thirties and still fleet of foot. His enthusiasm commendable. By day he worked in the school's main office, filing paperwork and occasionally subbing in for the sick teacher and making the odd guest appearance on the morning announcements—"Let's get after it *TIE-GERRRSSS!*" blaring through the PA system. "He's willing to wear many hats," Sam once said about him. "That makes him indispensable around here." By afternoon he reminisced with wet eyes about his days playing junior and regularly dished out jokes about fucking his players' moms, sparing no one. Only once did it almost lead to a fight.

Coach Johnson stepped to the front of the room.

"Settle down, ladies," he said. "I come with shitty news, which we were going to wait until tomorrow to share, but I felt you deserved to know right away. Okay, here it is: this may very well be our last season. There's a petition floating around Hockey Manitoba. Parents from those fancy schools down south, mine included, are afraid of you boys"—he scanned the room like a comic after delivering the punch line—"They don't like coming up here. They say it's too far, too inconvenient, especially when this city starts looking like a Siberian Gulag and people start crashing into each other like bumper cars at the Ex. Some bullshit like that. Have they ever heard of winter tires? Long story short, they're trying to form a league that excludes schools in this part of town. Look, we know why they're really doing this, and we are going to fight it. Tooth and nail, with everything we have. We have your backs. This is unacceptable in this day and age, but unfortunately we live in Winnipeg for some reason. I don't have to tell y'all that."

The room fell quiet. Coach Johnson tried to lighten the mood with his signature japes. Then he introduced his own version of sports psychology, consisting of inspirational quotes from icons like Muhammad Ali and the motto of the Navy Seals, scrawled on the whiteboard in shabby marker: *The only easy day was yesterday.* But the boys were gutted.

Tommy looked around the room and watched his teammates slurp up their spaghetti like they'd just waltzed into the kitchen only to discover that there was no more cereal left, only spaghetti. This team was tough. But tough boys were only tough until adults came into the equation. Their scrappiness meant nothing then.

"Blacky's starting in net for us," Coach Johnson said, referring to Jonah Blackwood. The nickname, like many things that left Coach Johnson's mouth, was controversial. "Finish up, ladies. Then get your minds in the right place. Prepare for war. Prepare to collect our scalps."

"Wade."

"What's up?" Coach Johnson turned to the voice in the corner of the room, where assistant coach Dale Ducky and team manager Patti Klassen sat quietly, feet dangling from the edge of a pair of desks.

"Should we talk about press?" Patti said.

"Yes. We should do that. Double D, what do you think?"

Dale nodded. "Might be for the best."

"Klassy. Would you mind taking this one?"

Patti sprung off the top of the desk and stepped to the center of the room. "Okay," she said. "Let's briefly talk about the media, because I think for everyone here this might be a fairly new experience. We may—on occasion—come across a reporter or two from various newspapers or TV stations, and they're going to try to ask you questions about the league pushing us out. These people are different than the kids at the student paper. Your coaches and I feel that we should refrain from speaking out against the league harshly until we know more about the decision. An important thing to remember in all of this is that we have no power here, and the last thing we want is to start a fight in the papers about this shitty situation. Let the media do that for us. So, like I said, ignore these questions. Or don't speak to them at all. Questions?"

Tommy raised his hand. "What about student reporters. Should we talk to them?"

"Only about the game."

Floyd, the team captain, raised his hand and, before being called upon, said: "What's so bad about calling out the league anyway?"

Patti pinched her chin and gazed up at the ceiling, trying to conjure an answer. "The league has been around longer than we've all been alive. A few bad news articles isn't going to change that. At the end of the day the decision is theirs to make. It's a long season, you boys focus on winning. Let us handle the league."

Floyd nodded enthusiastically and looked around the room for any objectors. The boys were quiet, most of them with half-eaten plates of cold spaghetti. "This feels like ceremony," he said.

The Tigers finished eating and went to class.

NOW THEY WERE HOCKEY players, if only temporarily. If only till the end of the world.

There was no anthem. No ceremonial puck drop. They lined up at the center dot when the referee, a young man who could pass as about their age, motioned that it was time. They took their positions, feeling for the twitch in their legs like sprinters out of their blocks, their adolescent gazes trained not on each other but the dancing puck in the referee's hand. Floyd approached to take the draw, shouting spirited words at his teammates that carried an echo and went over their heads. Tommy, a reliable defenseman, a defender's defenseman, hovered just beyond the center circle. The buzz and rumble was draining if you were in it for too long, and he felt a numbness, first in his hands and then in his feet.

The puck dropped fast. Bounced.

Once. Twice. No more than that.

And was passed back to a Bullfrog defenseman who shoveled it ahead to a lonely winger. Tommy hesitated, balked and nearly stumbled. But he found his edges, pushed forward, felt all his weight and momentum and eloquence push him forward, and in one prolonged instant he lined up where the spiraling winger would be, where he would go next, the danger that awaited him, and Tommy knew, deep in his heart, that he had him, and delivered everything he ever wished to rinse from himself into the boy's chest, who went down winded and bounced to his feet and continued down the ice. Tommy wanted to say, "Stay down," but his point was made and everyone else had already moved on, back to chasing the game, the puck, keeping it close—a precious jewel with a violent fate.

Floyd was given the responsibility of trying to stop Serhii, and for a period and a half he did. Eventually though, Serhii found space and danced his way to the net and slid the puck past Jonah to give the Bullfrogs a 1–0 lead. After the play, Floyd strode to the bench noticeably dejected and slammed his stick against the boards. The bang was so loud that he replaced his stick before realizing it wasn't even broken.

Tommy patted Floyd on the shoulder as he squeezed onto the bench. "That was a very tigerlike play. We're sharks now, didn't you hear?"

Floyd's expression was unchanged. He didn't respond to the comment, and this made Tommy regret the joke.

On his next shift Floyd responded, accepting a onetime pass from Clinton and slapped it past the St. Norbert goalie to tie the game at one goal apiece. The two of them rejoiced and fell into each other's arms mid-air.

From the stands the game danced on the edge. At times soft and romantic and beautiful; at others brutal and unforgiving and disgraceful to watch. The crowd leaned and swayed to the left and right—reacting, doing their part, to flights of desperation and game-saving heroics—as the puck was passed, slapped, chipped, flipped, beaten, bruised, sometimes, occasionally, doing the bruising on parts of limbs that go unguarded, and chased again down the ice. By the end of the second Tommy returned to the dressing room feeling gassed, breathing fast, his face tense. Sweat burned his eyes and his legs felt heavy but never did he feel like they would buckle, or that he could be bucked by another player. He knew that he was moving faster than he'd ever moved before.

Coach Johnson came in and issued his final push: "This could be the last time we do this. This could be our last home opener ever."

Tommy looked around at his teammates. Even though this would be his last time, he couldn't let *this* be the last time. Three years ago he wasn't sure if any of them actually liked each other or got any enjoyment from playing the game. Now they were a breathing presence in his life.

The aggression of the game had been escalating all evening and at the beginning of the third period Tommy found himself in the middle of it. This was nothing new to the Tigers, who usually grew more hostile in the dying minutes of the game. But he'd already thrown more hits than he had his whole life. With his newfound strength he eagerly stepped into the role of enforcer. He became the agitator, the aggressor, the instigator, the guy who would fling his body around to get under the other team's skin. To begin the third period he dragged down two Bullfrog players at the same time and stood tall as the pair of Bullfrogs hung awkwardly off one of his legs. The Tigers bench celebrated, and this shifted the game's momentum.

But it wasn't enough. Serhii found the net two more times, and another Bullfrog player who clearly learned a few tricks from Serhii added another and then the game was over. They started the season in familiar fashion, caught in the gaze of cruel defeat, and as they slid through the doors and left the surface of the ice and as the rink manager came on to mop and scrape up the scene of the crime as if what had happened over the past sixty minutes had never happened at all, suddenly the world felt depressingly normal again.

Coach Johnson was red in the face, and his eyes were noticeably watery. The after-game routine, which never changed because losing was the only outcome the players had ever experienced in the Tiger uniform, involved a moment of silence until the coaches entered the room for a postgame debrief. Tommy braced himself, as did Clinton. Coach Johnson was a shouter. He shouted throughout every game, at players from his team and the other team, the officials and the fans. His high-volume rants usually carried into the locker room. At any moment any of them could be criticized as lazy, they needed to be better, work harder, skate cleaner. They were: bitch, cunt, loser, pussy, faggot, shitstick, fuckstick, cucksicle. But after the game, standing in the middle of that stinky dressing room, coach was emotional, not enraged. "That performance," Coach Johnson began, the words hoarse and strained. "Be proud of that performance. We were right there with them. All night. Right fucking there. It's going to happen for us. I believe this. Stick with it. Be proud of the work you put in tonight because this is the kind of shit you build on and learn from." Then he was out the door and the room was quiet again.

"Whoa," said Tommy.

"We're gonna get these guys," Floyd said, breaking the silence.

Jonah, who had already removed all of his gear and deposited it in his large bag and was fixing a cap around his hair, said:

"That European kid is their only good player."

"The Russian," Tommy said.

"Ukrainian," Clinton corrected, loosening the laces of his skates. "He's got that Ukrainian emblem around his neck."

"*Spacibo.*"

"Also Russian."

"Fuck whatever, that's the only word I remember from Folklorama," Tommy said. "So should we be calling ourselves the Tiger Sharks from now on?"

"Almost as dumb as Bullfrogs," Floyd said.

"Some Lord of the Rings shit," Jonah said.

"The tiger shark is a real fish," Clinton said.

Tommy wiped the slush off his skate blades before tossing both skates in his bag. "Real to you," he said, smiling big so as to show all his teeth and massaging one of his molars with his tongue. "I'll believe it when I'm lost in the big wide ocean swimming for my life."

THE NEXT MORNING TOMMY read the St. Croix student newspaper alone in an empty hallway. The excitement of a new academic year had already faded to the side. Even the teachers walked slower and without purpose and their depression depressed him. The Tigers' loss was on the second page:

## TIGERS DROP OPENER TO ST. NORBERT BULLFROGS, AS TEAM FACES UNCERTAIN FUTURE

### BY CLARISSA WALKMAN, STAFF REPORTER

The St. Croix Tigers lost their home opener by a score of 4–1 to the St. Norbert Bullfrogs on Monday. The Tigers, who were informed by the Southern Manitoba High School Hockey League earlier this month that they will be losing their spot in the league's Tier 3 Division at the end of the season, have not won a game in many years.

"Obviously, we played our hearts out tonight," Tigers head coach Wade Johnson told *The St. Croix Daily Drum*. "Obviously, we'll continue to fight both on and off the ice the rest of the season, because, obviously, we love having the opportunity to compete. Obviously."

Tigers starting goalie Jonah Blackwood stopped 39 of 43 shots. Blackwood, who is in his final year as a Tiger, held the Bullfrogs to one goal in the first two periods, before giving up three goals in the final frame.

"It's not the result we wanted, but we showed no quit," Blackwood said after the game. "We have a lot of young players this year and a lot to build on going forward."

Whether the Curse will be broken this season, Johnson said it's too early to tell. He said the team's main focus is improving their game as the season wears on.

"It's not something we think about to be honest," Johnson said. "We just try to have fun out there and make our school proud. But I think we have a great group of guys."

Community members say they would love to see the Tigers break the Curse. Darlene Loon, who graduated from St. Croix way back in 1966, said she can't remember the last time the Tigers won a game.

"I would love to see the team win a game soon," Loon said. "I know for sure it would mean a lot to the people around here."

Representatives from the Southern Manitoba High School Hockey League did not respond to multiple requests for comment.

The Tigers continue the season with a game next Thursday against the Sturgeon Vikings.

Tommy didn't dwell on the loss. He was good at pushing things out of his mind and forgetting, took pride in it, considered it one of his best qualities. One of his previous coaches at St. Croix used to tell him he was cool under pressure: "So calm you would make a good cop," he'd say. Whether cops were calm Tommy couldn't say, but nonetheless he appreciated the compliment and wore the words in his heart proudly, like a badge. If he took away anything positive from the game against the Bullfrogs, it was that he didn't get knocked over. He stood tall, and threw his body around like a wrecking ball, toppling the opposition like bowling pins. He collected eight hits on the stat sheet. His name was Tomahawk.

*tannyce shields*

or

*a wandering troubled woman*

BEFORE I BEGIN, I LOOK.

There's the two old ladies behind the help desk, both of them round and plump and short, one a brunette and the other with bright red hair. There's the young boy, younger than the rest who work here, with brown skin and brown hair that almost looks red when the sun catches him, just outside the front door smoking a cigarette, an intern maybe, or maybe just a lazy employee, or maybe he's a good employee who doesn't get paid enough to throw out his back hauling heavy books all day and can't be bothered. He's left a cart full of books beside me for like thirty minutes while he smokes and texts and occasionally smiles and looks back inside to see if anyone is watching him. After a while, when he does come back inside, the old ladies look at him all nasty. He doesn't talk to them and they don't talk to him, but when he turns away their eyes follow him all crazy and I wonder if that's the way they look at me, if they watch me when I'm not looking. I wonder who else watches me. On the other side of the room, where they keep all the books for kids, I hear a happy woman with a happy voice reading to happy children and every now and then they all laugh and clap together and the elders on the computers around me pause from squinting at their screens and look in their direction and shake their heads all annoyed, like they didn't see the sign by the entrance that says story time starts at one. The storyteller woman comes here every Wednesday and today we looked at each other for the first time. I wasn't sure what to do when our eyes made contact, so I offered a wide, exaggerated smile as she came through the main entrance and she looked at me quick with a friendly non-smile and a little wave before waving again to the redheaded librarian behind the desk. She's a beautiful woman with beauty marks all over her cheeks and nose and white teeth and a braid that reaches her lower back. She always arrives early for story time and greets each child with a unique smile and voice, each precious snowflake settling into their own patch of precious ground.

For the most part it's quiet. People have their heads buried in books, some in wrinkled magazines, a few others sinking deep in green armchairs, trying their best to sleep while pretending to read. Every once in a while a book slips and thumps on someone's chest and their head snaps up, awake and alert, their eyes red and tired but open. I don't like to read. I get lost and the words never make sense in my head.

It's my fifth time here and each time I've not been able to make progress. Littlefeather says I just need to sit down at a computer and the words will come. They'll arrive in my head once I start thinking about what it is I want to say—no, need to say, no, have to say—that people don't think the way we used to because of all the stuff we're doing on phones and computers. She says we're turning into computers, becoming one with them, one with machines, and that it's only the beginning. Soon we'll be no different than robots, under the control of someone else, they'll know where we are and what we think, and soon thinking won't be thinking anymore, it'll be knowing. There will be no more ignoring. Scary hey. But not much different than the way our people have been since Europeans arrived on our shores. No control over our own lives.

I'm in a chair, sitting, watching, but mostly waiting. Waiting for a spot to open up at one of the computers. I've come to learn that older people tend to type loudly with one or two fingers . . . clack . . . clack . . . clack . . . whereas younger people are able to write like they're playing piano or something. Me, I'm not sure I type well, not fast I mean, but I guess we'll see. An elderly woman at one of the computers is ready to leave. She's stuffing her travel mug inside her bag and places her glasses inside their case. She logs out and I stand and before the woman even rises to leave the spot, I'm no more than three feet behind her. She looks back at me annoyed, like maybe she thinks I've given her no space to make her exit but there's plenty. This I must do, be there ready to go, at the point of no return, because I've returned before, checked out, chickened out, and each time it was because I gave myself too much time to think.

I'm sitting, waiting, trying to think of what to say. Nothing. Nothing's there. Whatever's inside me is blank. A blank nothingness. I feel I should leave, yes, time to leave. I rise from the chair, the plastic armrest squeaks, but I stop halfway, like I'm squatting above the part where my ass is supposed to go and I wonder how many farts this ass-worn cushion has absorbed in its lifetime, because I notice that the plump blond librarian is walking in my direction and so I sit back down.

"Ma'am," the librarian says, "the computers are reserved for those who sign up at the front desk."

"Sorry," I say. "I forgot." I look at her with my kindest face. "I'll just be a minute."

I return my attention to the screen but for five seconds more I can feel the woman's eyes still on me before she turns and walks away. I look up as she sits down beside the redheaded librarian and they hunch over and share whispers and the blond woman's eyes shift back to me for an instant and then the redhead turns and looks over at me too. I look away and pretend to be busy doing something important and make tapping sounds on the keyboard but not fully pushing down on each letter . . . tap . . . tap . . . tap.

My email is open, the one Littlefeather helped me make. She said no one, not even the government, would be able to read my emails with this special account. It hides the messages, *encrypts* them she says, meaning that they're private and only I and the person on the other end can read them and that no outside person or thing can spy on me.

The redheaded librarian stands up from her chair behind the help desk and because of her plumpness you can see the effort it takes, like her joints and bones and muscles and organs and heart are crying for help and so is the chair, complaining loud enough for the whole library to hear.

"Ma'am," she says at least nine feet before reaching me. "This computer is reserved. I *have* to ask you to let this gentleman over here take over from you." She points to a man turned away from us, browsing a selection of DVDs in Chinese along the wall.

"I'll just be a minute," I say. "I'm sending an email to my son. It's important."

She sighs and her face turns red like her hair and she turns to look at the blond librarian behind the help desk and back to me. She's staring at me in a dirty way as if to say, *You again.* "Please be quick."

"I'll try my best." Yes me, why not me?

As she walks back to the help desk and slides through a gap in the counter I wonder if her hair is dyed red or if it's a wig, if she's pretending to be somebody else. Who is she really? Why choose to be seen? Why would you want to be picked out of a crowd so easily?

To my left the beautiful woman with the beauty marks is waving goodbye to a little girl in a flowery jacket who appears to be leaving story time early with her parents. Her smile is big and her teeth almost sparkle from the light flooding through the main entrance, and the little girl waves her little hand and I imagine that they both love each other for what they do for each other. I turn my attention back to the computer screen, back on the email I need to write before my time is up.

The words are coming to me now. I see them, unfurling in my mind like the credits after a movie. I see them. They're a light blue color, like the beads of my earrings. Like a small ceremony. And they sparkle and dance below my ears just like them too. They sing like birds. I want to say that I've always loved you, cared for you, still do, and that if we ever see each other again I'd say sorry and then shake your hand because a hug wouldn't feel right. Not after all this time. Would you think I'm fatter or slimmer than before? Everyone always says I'm too skinny. I want to say there's always been this piece of you deep inside me, in the center of my chest where you used to think the heart was, it's scarlet and bright and warm, and when I rest my hand on that spot suddenly the whole world breaks open and turns brighter but it doesn't last. Not until the next time. Now the words are vibrating. They're hummingbirds, yes, hummingbirds, and they hum and buzz . . . bzz . . . bzz . . . bzz . . . the same ones outside Koko's house hovering around the rosebush. They sing and dance, sing and dance, dance and sing, like they're moving to the beat of a drum. Maybe one day I'll say all this, just let it out. My fingertips are touching the keys now, warm from the lady that was here before me. And then I begin.

# *clinton whiteway*

KELVIN ONCE SAID THAT GANGSTERS START OUT LIKE VAMPIRES. They stay awake all night, learning to live with darkness, the real darkness. But they lean toward the brightness of TV screens, endless hours of shitty TV and first-person shooters, sucking the life from their faces. They thin out, become white, scared of the light, the crater beneath their cheekbones getting deeper and deeper. "Then you get used to it. Going outside," he said. "Kinda like Blade." Blade was on TV that night, slicing through bloodsuckers like it was an art form. It's not a bad metaphor. They become Daywalkers. Because the outside is where they eventually have to do their work, it's where the blood is spilled and taken and replaced with something worse, something you can't live with. Everyone around them bleeds out without dying. Eventually all die together, slowly, except there'll be a faint heartbeat in our place, baked into the concrete, waiting to be discovered. We'd become the undead. The undead undying.

My brother wasn't a vampire yet, but he was on his way. It started with his friends. They'd vanish one by one, and then suddenly return to the streets changed men. Meaner, and out for blood. Sometimes their own blood. Hardened by the brutality of whatever initiation they'd been through. It was the repeated nosebleeds that first caught my attention, along with the red, irritated nostrils, not so much his spurts of mania. He was always a little crazy, so crazy his teachers never knew what to do with him. But then I saw the powder under his fingernails. He'd come home, plop down on the couch, and scrape whatever it was from under his nails with the opposite finger and then suck hard. Scrape and suck. Scrape and suck. Mom saw it too. I know she did, but she never said anything. We were both witnessing the birth of a monster. I knew he'd officially been converted when he pulled back his sleeve one night to scratch his arm and there they were. The scabbed-over dots, like he'd recently donated blood. Like small fangs had pierced his veins, turning him, making him a vampire.

Still Mom said nothing about her vampire son. She didn't like confrontation, never liked to talk about the deep things, the real things. Shit only got deep when she spoke about our dad, but even then it wasn't much, didn't leave much to the imagination. Just that Kelvin was like our dad. Fucking crazy as him. "He was like Bigfoot," she said once. "He was seen and not seen, there and not there, and when he was there he was always playing tricks." I never met the man. Kelvin says he only has faded memories of him, or bits of a whole, as a child, the kind you can barely picture anymore, but who knows if that's true. Probably isn't. Sometimes when I walk through our neighborhood I try to imagine the man in the flesh, and wonder if the person coming toward me is my dad. Did he find a way to escape our community before it was drowned by floods? Or was he still there, floating among the other bodies? Guess I'll find out one day, do a DNA test or something. Confirm the other half of me.

Mom kept us straight for a long time. She even kept herself straight. Sobering up occasionally on our couch before disappearing into the night once more, the orange glow of streetlamps her new sun. Before The Fall she packed our lunches each morning, dropped us off at school, would be parked there at the curb running the engine before the final bell rang, took us to hockey practice and would sit and watch and check our homework before bed. She made all my games, watched and cheered and shouted my name the way mothers do. Made my teammates so jealous they started calling me Mamma's Boy, a testament to the motherlessness that plagued our roster. Mom always waited for me in the car and popped the trunk before I got there, and after depositing my gear we'd be on our way. She started missing games last season, or showing up late with a smell on her breath that scared you at first. She'd slur and swerve all over the road and sing out the window and call me her boy. The bags under her eyes got bigger, darker, until they eventually looked like they were about to sag and drop off her face.

One night I jumped in the back seat. A man named Chubby, her "friend" she called him, was sitting on the passenger's side. He was big and round and smiled with his whole face and I felt like I could see my reflection in his eyes, they were dark, black almost. He smelled like Mom and they passed a glass pipe back and forth, blasting old country music through the radio and singing all the lyrics. "This is my favorite boy," she said, handing the pipe back to Chubby and blowing the smoke out a small crack in the window. "Smarter than I ever was," she said. She turned down Mountain and said she needed to fill up before going out for the night. She drove fast, swerving from side to side, kissing the curb here and there. We all felt it as the car pulled into the gas station; like the engine went out and the tires stopped turning. The ice pulling us forward like a curling rock. "Frankie, look out!" Chubby screamed, gripping the handlebar above his head, bracing for impact. My head slammed against the roof of the car—our momentum halted by a steel post guarding the gas pumps. Mom and Chubby swapped seats, and he sped away before the cashier could run out and call the cops. They dropped me at home and drove off again without a farewell, leaving a wake of dirty snow in their path. My mother wasn't around the next day, or the next. A different kind of vampire.

Kelvin returned home from Headingley this summer, the summer before my last year of high school. Served eighteen months after attempting to rob a small bank by blowing a hole in the exterior and driving off with the safe in a stolen pickup. Stories of similar heists reverberated throughout the North End and its periphery neighborhoods, where more and more Neechis had begun spreading. Tales that passed the time, most of which I considered works of fiction, Hollywood rewrites. But Kelvin was determined to be remembered, and the money was a bonus. He didn't get past the first step: the blast nearly burned the building to the ground. Cameras caught him setting the charges, and he'd bragged about his plans to a resentful ex he'd spent the winter shacking up with, and to whom he promised the world, promised that he hadn't made other such promises to other

women, which turned out to be a broken promise. She offered pay-
back. He was in cuffs a day later, escorted by police in only his gitch,
his head lowered into the cop car by a constable's big palm. Gladue
rights softened the blow, but he was behind bars shortly thereafter.


WORD GOT AROUND QUICK: Kelvin had crawled back to his old posse
a week after promising to make sweeping life changes at his final
group circle, hours before the so-called House of Hate opened its
gates and spit him back out into the world. The elder smudged him
and he was a free man. I had just finished cleaning the fryers at White's
and was about to start on the soft-serve dispenser when a man with
a long dark braid somehow walked up to the cashier's counter, and
looking back now, I forgot to lock the door after Mr. White went
home for the evening. (Mr. White, who had actual cleaners come in
five days a week, tapped me over the summer to rid the restaurant
of errant grease spills and sticky messes that glazed tabletops and
kitchen appliances; it wasn't a real job, paid cash, presumably saved
Mr. White some money and me from the taxman, but I obliged.)
I walked over and noticed that the man had multiple scars below
his right eye, one along the socket where the soft skin meets sharp
bone, like he'd faced off with some wild beast, and another that ran
horizontal above his lip. "You open?" the man said.

"We're closed." I could see that he was studying me.

"You remind me of someone."

"I'm about to lock up."

"You sure you don't have any leftovers back there."

"I can check if you want." The man gave a thumbs-up. In the
kitchen I had a to-go box filled with fries and a few chicken fingers,
which I decided to part ways with. Anything to get the man to leave.
When I returned to the counter the man's face lit up when he saw the
box. I passed him the food and said it was on the house.

"I got you." He reached in his pocket and slapped a twenty on the
counter. "Keep the change."

"Thanks." I stuffed the bill in my pocket.

"You know," he said. "You really remind me of someone." He studied my face with the same concentration as before, and he was constantly on the brink of smiling.

"I should be locking up."

"Are you Kelvin's little brother?"

"Yeah. Why?" Somehow I felt busted for doing nothing.

"Knew it! I met your brother up there. He talked about you. Said you were smart. I can tell you got a good head on you. This is probably your dinner right here, am I right?"

I nodded.

"I hear he's not doing so well since he got out. Have you seen him?"

I shook my head. Truth was, I didn't know he was out.

"He's a character, that Kelvin. Liked to cross his fingers behind his back every time we prayed for the Creator to help us and when we made promises to each other and our communities to be better men. Thought it was funny."

"Sounds like him."

He started toward the door. "Thanks for the grub. If I see him I'll tell him he was right about you."


A DAY LATER I came home to find Kelvin sitting on a bench outside our building, waiting to get in. I'd spent the day restocking books at a nearby library; the old ladies there needed the muscle, and in return they waived late fees and thus gave me every reason to fill two backpacks with paperbacks. We said our hellos and for a while we sat there talking about all the good movies he missed while he was locked away. He said Headingley sometimes rolled out a projector and turned the prison cafeteria into a theater. I told him I despised remakes. I told him I thought about becoming a writer, maybe for the screen, but wasn't sure how. Kelvin said he was thinking about refrigeration. Business was apparently booming in The Pas. The conversation left me feeling disturbed. I felt wary by my brother's presence, and yet comfortable at the same time. He still felt like a big brother despite all he'd done.

Then the chat took a turn. Kelvin said he could get me some work

selling, which sounded more like an order than an offer. Both possibilities were frightening.

"You're old enough now to know what I do, hey little brother?"
Kelvin said.

I stared off, looked at my feet, looked at the sky, looked wherever.
Dirty white sneakers have a kind of character to them, a wisdom.
You can tell where they've been. Like cars they can only go so many
miles. They were the only belongings in my life that I allowed to be
imperfect, evidence of where I'd been, how far I'd gone. "I have an
idea."

"There's money to be made. We could use an educated man like
you."

"And all my zero diplomas."

"You know what I mean. Always reading. I was never like that.
The letters always jumped around on me like little fucking bugs."

"I don't think that life's for me."

Kelvin went quiet, and for a second he looked disappointed by
my response.

"What are you doing here, Kelvin?"

"I live here." He placed an arm on my shoulder. It felt heavy and
dead. "We're the men now. Men of the house." He undocked his arm
from my body and lit a smoke and balanced it between two fingers.
"We have to take care of Mom—of each other—make those ends
meet. Time you learned some responsibility, little brother."

"This is still Mom's house. She's going to be fine. Things are just
really difficult right now for her. Chubby doesn't help."

"Little brother." A short smile appeared on his face while the dart
was still pegged to his lips. "She's always been this way. Always had
her problems."

For a minute we sat there in a strange yet comfortable quiet.

Kelvin took a long drag. Then he rolled up his baggy shorts, revealing a circle-shaped scar on his thigh. It looked to be from a bullet,
the same way marks on the wrist made one think of self-harm. He
looked me in the eye and said that even after he got clipped he kept
charging, like a rhino fending off poachers. He beamed with pride.

## *kelvin whiteway comes home*

EVERYTHING WAS HOW HE LEFT IT. OR HOW HE REMEMBERED IT. OR how he thought it looked when he imagined it. Or how he dreamt it up during those long nights in his cell when he couldn't sleep, setting a miniature volleyball up toward the dark ceiling, disappearing for a moment and then returning. Always returning. It always came back to him. Or, perhaps, he imagined it so hard it became true, like a wish granted: the pile of dirty dishes in the kitchen sink, the couch with a mess of throw pillows and blankets, their shared bunk beds neatly made with the star quilts cut and sewn by a distant relative, his brother's growing bookshelf absorbing the light cast from the only window in their room. Or maybe it's just that feeling when something's familiar. Like how he sometimes dreamt of things that would become reality only when they actually happened. He wasn't gone that long, but he missed it, their home, even after convincing himself for a long time that he hated it. Back then it stunk like the elderly couple who lived and died there before they moved in and of the various lovers circulating in and out of Mom's bedroom on any given night. But he only noticed what he didn't smell, such as the withdrawal sweat of men.

Clinton walked into the apartment first, and Kelvin followed.

"You can have my key," Clinton said. "There's a spare around here somewhere."

Kelvin nodded. He wasn't expecting a tour and wasn't about to get one, he knew where everything was anyway, but some part of him wanted his younger brother to show him how things had changed when he was away. He wanted to keep their talking going.

Clinton slumped into the couch. "I took the bottom while you were gone."

Kelvin studied his kindergarten and junior high graduation photos framed on the wall above the couch, as if he were noticing them for the first time. Holding, with a crooked, artificial smile in both pictures, the only two diplomas he had to his name. He had fond memories of kindergarten, of the Head Start back on the rez, and so he assumed he was genuinely happy in that picture. In the other portrait he remembered his mom letting him gel his own hair that morning with disastrous results and the taunts of "human glitch" that followed for the rest of the day. "I prefer the top now anyways."

When he was young he wanted to be like Squanto. Not the real Squanto, the seventeenth-century Indian who was captured by English sailors and sold in Spain, but the actor who played Squanto in the movie *Squanto,* even though he could no longer remember the guy's name, only that he might be related to him through a distant cousin.

There was a period in his youth where the only thing he watched on TV was *Squanto.* After school and sometimes before. He nudged his friends and cousins when Squanto appeared on-screen, usually when Squanto is visited by a hawk, making hawk sounds with his voice to the bewilderment of a band of monks, banking and landing on Squanto's arm, and saying, "That's my cousin," to which his cousins and friends would reply, "Don't be a tuguy." He marveled at the actors, their skill and their beauty, and often wondered who they were for real. They made you believe in the lie, the fantasy, and he thought if he could do anything it might be acting. When he moved to the city his life became a sort of fantasy, one invented for him by elusive forces and which swallowed him whole. He pretended every time he left the house. Pretended not to see the eyes following him in stores, and instinctively brought the Native in his voice down when he said "Please," "Thank you" and "Have a good day" to throw them off. Convince them they had him all wrong. They got the wrong target. Until one day he decided he would act the part. He was tired of trying to convince the world he was good. Acting good. It felt, strangely, more natural than anything else. It felt more natural to be the worst kind of person. The role he was born to play.

They ordered pizza and chicken wings and poutine and together they ate in front of the TV, watching a replay of Game 7 of the Stanley Cup Final from earlier, after which pissed-off Vancouverites tore their city to pieces. Kelvin knew how it ended, but there was something euphoric about stuffing his face while watching the drama unfold.

"That's the pain and agony of defeat right there. You can see it on their faces. The crowd. Ready to fuck shit up. Punch a few riot police."

"Just no point," Clinton said between bites.

"There's always a point being made. Even back there the riots and the lockdowns always meant something."

"What's the point?"

"Power."

"Power?"

Kelvin put down his slice once Clinton looked at him. "Now, these idiots are mad they lost a hockey game. Sad, sure, but to those rioters, that's *their* city. It's not their fault the Sedin sisters became a couple girls that night, and as for the police, they have jobs because of those maniacs looting the streets. They sign their paychecks and give 'em too much if you ask me." He looked back up at the TV and dived into a chicken wing, and when he was done chewing, he wiped his mouth with a napkin and continued:

"Now, as for back there, as for those guards and shit when shit went down, all you need to understand is this: they were locked in there with *us,* not the other way around."

Clinton focused again on the game. "What was it like wearing a uniform? Sleeping in a cell all the time. Nowhere to go and stuff."

"Itchy." He laughed suddenly. "Like those raggedy overalls Koko used to make us wear when she'd make us dig out the rocks from her garden in the spring. Remember? Boy that woman. For a bush lady she always thought we had to look proper."

"Clean," Clinton added.

"Yeah." Kelvin grinned. "Could never have dirt under our nails."

They laughed. For Kelvin it was the first time in a long time that a laugh felt real. Effortless.

"I thought about her and Shoomis some days while I was over

there." His voice was low, like the words were only meant for him. The dim light from the kitchen cast shadows over his bumpy face, and below his sharp cheekbones was a small valley of darkness.

"What do you think they'd think about you being in there?"

"Little brother," Kelvin said, sitting back and spreading his arms across the top of the couch. "You might not think so, but I'm no idiot. I know if they were around still they wouldn't be happy with me. Mom's out there, no better than me, so I could care less what she thinks. I don't care what anyone thinks."

"Not even me?" Clinton smirked.

He knew Clinton was trying to inject some humor into the conversation, lighten the mood, but turned to him blank-faced and said sternly, "Not even you."

Clinton looked away. The players were back on the ice for the third period. After which Vancouver would be torn to pieces. Fires. Looting.

"What would you say to me. If you could say anything. If you had to be real with me. What would you say? Go ahead. Is there something you think I need to hear."

Clinton paused. He watched the game without looking away. "Nothing. I wouldn't say anything."

"Tell me. Tell me! This is your chance." He shook Clinton's shoulder, perhaps too hard, and felt committed to prying the words out of him. "I value your opinion. Over all others. You know that. Seriously. Let thy mouth speaketh thy truth."

Clinton gave an exaggerated sigh. "I would say it's your life. Do whatever you want with it."

Kelvin watched his brother begin playing with his food, doing weird, anxiety-induced maneuvers with his fingers. He forgot he did things like this and he felt sorry for pushing him.

Clinton cleared his throat. "But. But also I'd say. Even Dracula dies. Crumbles to dust in the end."

"Dracula? Like the cartoon?" Kelvin laughed. He swigged from a one-liter Pepsi and turned his attention to the game. "You read too much weird shit."

"Probably. It's not the right comparison."

For a few minutes they both stared at the TV without speaking, absorbed in the action. "What if Koko and Shoomis were still around, though? You were a little too young to see it, but they hated each other. Loved us though. We were probably the only thing keeping them together."

Kelvin observed Clinton, waiting for his words to settle in. He looked as if he'd just learned something he'd never known before and, Kelvin thought, perhaps felt stupid for not seeing it earlier. It felt good making his little brother feel stupid.

"Whether it was hockey or baseball or school they always thought I'd grow up to be some big thing. Even when it became obvious I sucked, when I couldn't skate or hit a fucking ball, when I started getting held back, in their eyes they were convinced I'd be a doctor or some fucking sports hero. They believed it so hard, especially Shoomis. Especially him. Fucking deadly guy. They'd literally tell all their friends. Tell them what I'd be. Fuck, for a while they even had *me* convinced I was special. But I was always too afraid to tell them otherwise. Me, I've always known where I stood. I never once lied to myself."

"Plenty of ex-criminals become successful after getting out." Clinton looked at Kelvin for the first time since the start of the third period.

"Nothing *ex* about me, boy!" He laughed loud but his cheeriness quickly subsided. "Anyways. I guess I wondered when I was over there whether they'd still think the same about me. But when I think about them I can't think of them any other way. Annoyingly fucking positive always."

The phone rang as the seconds ran down on the game clock. Kelvin stood and grabbed the phone and answered it in the kitchen.

"We're downstairs, bro," Moose said.

"Okay, bro. Be down in a minute."

He met Moose and Hurricane outside on a small patch of grass next to the quiet street. They exchanged hugs and bags of drugs.

"That should hold you over for a few days," Hurricane said, pointing to the bags. "More coming."

Kelvin nodded.

"How's the little bro?"

"He's good." Kelvin could see the balcony of their fourth-floor apartment and the light from their living room window from where they stood and thought he saw Clinton staring down at them, presumably, quietly, objecting to his life as he always did, before disappearing to some other part of the apartment.

"He should be riding with us," Moose said. "Pretty much a man already."

"Soon," Kelvin said. "He knows." He could see that his two friends were high, eyes red and big, but decided against joining them. He wanted to be clear when he watched highlights of the postgame riot.

Moose cleared his throat in a loud and obnoxious way and spat on the grass. "X wants us to start recruiting. Fresh blood makes a difference."

Kelvin nodded without saying anything. The order had been passed down.

"He keeps talking about expansion. Go after the young ones. Boys in school, high school. Even younger if they're promising."

"The little brother meets the criteria," Hurricane said, with a sinister grin.

"I guess so," Kelvin said.

The lights were off when he got back upstairs, as was the TV. The couch was tidied and the remaining pizza and wings and poutine was stowed away in the fridge. He washed the dirty dishes by hand and swept the kitchen floor of crumbs and debris. When he finished he went to their room and climbed the top bunk in only his underwear. "Clinton," he said, looking up at the ceiling, and Clinton replied, "What?" He hesitated, unsure how to phrase it, but eventually said: "Think about what I said. About coming to work. With me." He didn't get a response, and so he slept, dreaming of the breakfast he would make in the morning, when he landed back on the floor.

## errol whitecloud sinclair

### SEPTEMBER 30, 2011

In a previous letter to you, which I've since discarded, I was locked away for doing a bad thing or two and maybe even deserved it for other bad things. These bad things hurt people, and hurt me in a similar way but perhaps not as much. I don't mean to sound like a victim of the crimes I committed but I suppose I deserve the pain they've caused me, the time I've lost because of them. As I say, after I wrote this previous letter I quickly disposed of it. I could see the sorrow on the elder's face when I did so, because he'd spent many hours every afternoon trying to help us overcome all the things that have made us feel like broken goods. After I'd torn the pages into many little pieces and sprinkled them in the trash bin, Art the Elder came up to me and said, "Keep trying. It will only help you better understand what it is you're carrying, what it is that's weighing you down." We all sat together in a circle, and you left this circle of chairs with armrest-tables for writing the same way you came in: through a single gap in the circle. It was the rule, for this was a sacred circle, a place of healing. But in that moment I broke the rule, leaping over the back of my chair and moving toward the trash.

I suppose I thought Art would get mad at me and embarrass me in front of all the guys, who were quietly jotting down words with pens and paper. But he wasn't angry. In fact, he never got angry at any of us despite all the times we disobeyed or ignored him. He just looked at me through his big, old-school glasses and I remember being glad that his vision was piss-poor, that even with helpers he couldn't make out our faces or comment on every shit-drawn tattoo on our skin. So he said. All the guards joked and laughed about him pulling our legs because, at the end of the day, Art would jump inside a white Chevy Avalanche and drive himself home with seemingly no trouble. Jamie, one of the guards who enjoyed talking shit, said once at the end of the session, "He's just pretending not to notice how ugly y'all are."

On Sundays, Art would take us inside the sweat lodge they'd put up on the grounds about a year after I arrived. It wasn't like the lodges you see in books or movies. Instead of an animal's hide, it was draped in thick yellow tarps that didn't do a good job of making the inside dark like they're supposed to. However, it was still supported by a skeleton of tree branches, woven together in a way that resembled the shell of a turtle. But even still, when the rocks were inside and laid down in the pit at the center of the lodge, glowing red from the fire, the whole lodge felt hot and suffocating. Art poured water with a ladle onto the rocks and the steam hit your face and hugged your body tight. He sprinkled medicines on the rocks and they danced like firecrackers all bright before disappearing. Each sweat was different in terms of temperature. Some days Art asked his Helper, who was usually another inmate he'd mentored, to help bring in a certain number of hot rocks at the beginning of every round, the number of which also varied, and it was always more or less than the previous sweat. If you learned to control your breathing, short inhalations through your nose, you could learn to endure the heat, no matter how many rocks Art called for.

Before my third time in the lodge, I went up to Art, which I'd never done before the beginning of a sweat. I reached out my hand and offered him a tobacco bundle that I'd made a day earlier in the sewing room, and asked: "How do you know how many rocks to bring in?"

He accepted the tobacco bundle and inserted it into his pocket. "It's just a feeling. Some days we hurt more and other days less, and I can sometimes see that on all of you when I walk in. In the lodge we hurt for the Creator. The more rocks we bring in the more we let go of."

In the semidarkness of the lodge Art would give the seven or eight of us in there with him a chance to talk to the Creator, to say whatever was on our minds. For many weeks I said nothing when my turn came. I just said, "I'm done," and nudged the person to my left to let him know it was his time to speak. Some of the men cried when it was their turn. Some of them screamed so loud it hurt my ears, and sometimes I cried quietly with them because their stories were just like mine. Eventually though, I started talking. Saying things I'd never told anyone before, things I'd never repeat outside of that lodge, not even on paper.

April 3, 2006, a few minutes before lunch. My bedsheets smelled stale and the bed itself was stiff and uncomfortable. They don't tell you that the excessive formaldehyde used to manufacture inmate uniforms burns the skin and leaves horrible rashes, and so for the first few nights I slept naked, which is something you should never do in a prison.

A cab picked me up to take me back to the city on the morning of June 1, 2011. I served five years, one month and twenty-nine days, or:

*naano-biboon, bezhigo-giizis, miinawaa niishtana-shi-zhaangaso-giizhik*

As I write this, now, in this moment, I've been back for exactly thirty days and two hours, or:

*nisimidana-giizhik miinawaa niizho-diba'igan*

Scratch that. I have my doubts I'll finish this in one sitting. I don't expect you to be patient with me, and I wouldn't ask that of you, but I am learning to be patient with myself.

I didn't know how much I missed the sun and the fish flies in the early morning dew and the taste of bottled water. One of the first things I did was skip rocks at Birds Hill and take in the smell of grill-cooked meat drifting around the park. The sun was unobstructed and nourishing. I started this letter there, on a park bench at Birds Hill, as the sun dipped below some trees, casting everything around me orange before purple and then blue took over the sky. I write this again because I realize now that I don't just owe you the truth, I owe you the whole muddy river.

## clinton whiteway leaves home

I WOKE UP TO THE SOUND AND SMELL OF BACON CRACKLING. I crawled out of bed, rubbing my fingers across my eyes until the image became clear: him, Kelvin, in front of the stove, a hand at his waist and the other steadily flipping eggs and sausage and bacon in multiple frying pans, shirtless. He must've gone out early to get groceries, because none of this was in the fridge before. He made fresh bannock in the oven, a talent he said he picked up while he was away. "Rise and shine," he said, without turning to look at me. "You drink coffee yet?" He pointed to the coffeepot with his spatula, which I hadn't seen used in ages, and I poured myself a cup. He laid everything on the table—eggs, bacon, sausages, bannock, a tub of butter, a box of cereal and a carton of lactose-free milk.

I sat down at the table and we ate. The butter became a wet pool on my bannock, and the eggs were done over easy, the way I liked them. The yoke erupted in an exquisite deluge. The bacon, in my opinion, had too much fat.

Growing up, Kelvin had always been a good cook. When it was just us three—me, him and Mom—I remember him cooking us more meals than the only adult in the house. It was a job, a responsibility, that fell on his shoulders and he ran with it, never complained. He fixed things, too. Got his first toolbox for Christmas before he turned ten. He made things work again.

I went out after breakfast, did my shift at the library and popped by White's to see if he needed me for the closing hours, which he didn't.

For dinner Kelvin made hamburger soup. Our koko, back on the rez, used to make this for us and passed on the recipe to Kelvin before she walked on. He chopped the potatoes and carrots and celery just like she did, in a consistent size and shape, perfectly uniform. An abnormal stray never made the cut. I slurped it up and polished my bowl clean with bannock.

His friends arrived shortly after dinner and for a while I stayed in our room, reading a book about the history of the Bering Strait, and how sperm whales, through sheer intelligence and observation, learned to evade whalers and their harpoons. Self-preservation at its finest. When I came out they all sat on the couch and none of them seemed to notice me except Kelvin. He pointed and ordered me to grab beer, one for him and one for me, and I did. I returned to the couch and pulled up a chair. Across from me two girls sat together, laughing among each other, in our beige recliner intended for a single person. Closest to me was a man named Moose, who greeted me with "Sup, bro?" and on the other end of the couch, beside the girls, was another man.

"You remember Hurricane?" Kelvin sat between both men on the couch. "This is the little bro."

I nodded.

Hurricane nodded back.

I recalled only passing glimpses of both men, none of which occurred within the confines of our apartment. I looked over at the girls, young and strikingly thin, about my age if I had to guess, but there was no introduction. In fact, no one talked to them.

Thick smoke, from various sources, hung in the air like clouds, like a natural feature of the hood. The music was loud, but not as loud as it could've been. The bass, however, made my temples throb. The men, including Kelvin, bent over, one after another, and snorted white powder from the table in front of them. They drew lines with it, perfect lines, and then they were gone. They showed confidence in such an unusual act. I felt like I was watching something go wrong, never to be undone. I drank and felt drunk quickly. I'd had beer before but something felt different. I swayed in my chair, losing balance. I trembled.

"Easy," Kelvin said, observing me, smiling like one would to an overeager child. "That's high percentage shit. None of that cheap shit allowed in here."

I resorted to small sips. I finished my can and opened another, and then, at the suggestion of Kelvin, opened another after that one.

The men kept going, bending over, like synchronized swimmers.

I stood and demanded my legs take me to the kitchen and they did, though I felt unsteady the entire way there. I took a few bites of something edible and returned to my chair. I decided I was drunk, and so I kept drinking.

I locked eyes with Hurricane. He smirked.

"Feeling it?" He laughed.

"A little bit," I said.

"Have some of this." He gestured toward the powder on the table. "Make you feel good."

Kelvin, who was having a rather serious conversation with Moose, leaned forward, looking at Hurricane, and piped: "Leave him."

Hurricane laughed.

I tried to smile.

"I heard you play hockey."

"You heard right." I worried about my choice of words as soon as I said them.

"Who do you think . . ." He paused. "Who do you think would win in a fight. Me or you."

I looked away, startled by the hypothetical question. No one heard what he said this time. I looked at him again. His legs, arguably made up of only skin and bone. He was about as thin as the two girls beside him. His face, gaunt and scarred. He would win. Surely he would win.

"Me," I said.

He was smiling. Licking his lips. Showing too much tongue.

"I'm fairly strong. I don't think it's close."

He was no longer smiling, but mean mugging. "I think I break both your hands first. Maybe a couple ribs in there too." His eyes were red and wet and I got the feeling he wanted this. "Before punching you out."

Kelvin leaned forward again. "Hurricane. Fucking chill out."

Hurricane, in an instant, unraveled into the couch and laughed.

The night carried on. Kelvin, at one point, wobbled out the door of the apartment, saying he had "business to attend to" and I was left briefly with Hurricane and Moose and the two girls.

"Kezzy's back," Moose stated, turning to me. He never smiled. Always had an intense look about him. "He's gonna take care of you."

I wasn't sure what to say, so I said nothing.

"He looks after his own," Hurricane added, grinning wide.

"Who does?" Kelvin had come back inside and was standing beside me.

"Just telling Clinton here that he's in good hands now," Moose said.

I felt Kelvin's arm wrap around me, resting on my shoulders.

"That's right. Smart man this one." Kelvin reached into his pocket and pulled out cash held together by an elastic. He pulled out several bills, hundreds, and handed them to me. "For hockey. Should cover it. Right?"

I accepted the money and nodded politely and stuffed the bills in my pocket. I guessed more than a thousand. More than enough to cover team fees. The money I made working for Mr. White went to playing hockey, and now this was a nice bonus.

"Stand up," Kelvin said. I could barely understand him when he spoke. He slurred his words and spoke faster than my ears were working. "Shake your big brother's hand."

I stood, shook his damp hand, and looked him in the eyes. They were pitch black. An endless dark pit. Vampire eyes. The room around him a blur.

"What do you say?"

"Thanks."

"Thank you, big brother."

"Thank you, big brother." I spoke slower, enunciated more.

He laughed and put his arm around me again and turned us to his friends. "Good man. Good fucking man." He turned to me again and gripped both my shoulders. "So you've scrapped on the ice? What's your record? Undefeated?"

I chose not to wipe the specks of saliva off my face and just let them dry.

"Hit me," he said, before I could answer his queries. "Hit me." He broke into shadow boxing, threw a few straights and hooks, bobbed and weaved, danced on his feet, and slapped his cheek before returning his attention to me. "Hit me. Give me your best shot. See what you got. Stoodis."

"Kel . . ."

"Just fucking hit me. Don't be a fucking pussy."

"I'm not . . ."

"Hit me!" He was shouting now. I could see the red in his eyes again, the veins. His smile, creases of laughter, dropped from his face. The room became less blurry.

I clenched a fist but let go.

"I thought you said you'd spark Hurricane." He looked over at his friends, laughing, and back at me. "Hit me. I'm not asking."

I shook my head and moved to sit back down, but before I got there I felt a sharp blow to the side of my face and it instantly became hot and heavy and for a moment it felt as though my mind, the control I had, thought I had, was removed from my body. I fell to the ground, a lamp and beer cans came with me.

"Too slow!"

Something else, something harder and with more force, dug deep into my abdomen. Then again. And again. I gasped for air, sucking whatever I could, which, for a moment, was nothing. I heard laughter. Mostly I heard Hurricane.

I felt Kelvin's palm around my head like a basketball.

"This ain't a slow life," he whispered, as if trying to impart wisdom. He pushed my face into the floor.

I WOKE UP THE next morning with a shiner and bruised stomach. I inspected myself in the bathroom and diagnosed the hurts as minor, and easily explained away. I'd say I hit my head on my bunk in the morning or I ran after the bus and tripped and there it was . . . an ill-placed fire hydrant. Or maybe I just got jumped on the way home, an unlucky victim of the streets. I thought about my options.

Goofy, a support worker I used to go to movies with during a period when Mom needed help keeping the family together, came by our place a few days before Kelvin showed up. He told me of a place I could stay, a place called the Haven. That Kelvin was coming home and things might be different. I wondered, in the bathroom, whether I was being dramatic. But I also knew, even before Goofy came by, that Kelvin would find some way to turn me too, make me something else I thought I could never be.

I packed the things I needed most and crept to the front door. Kelvin was on the couch, comatose, behind a wall of beer cans. I thought for a second about letting him know, giving him a gentle heads-up, but decided that would defeat the purpose of running away.

I opened the door. Locked it behind me. And then I left. I found refuge.

WHEN I WALKED INTO the Haven it was a hot and humid day. The sky was perfectly blue, like northern blue: thin.

The city was almost never that humid, mostly dry. Which made going outside on the sunny days generally more enjoyable than that day in particular. I could see a shape-shifting mirage down the sidewalk as I walked down Main and the asphalt patches felt sticky on my sneakers. Days like that always made me wish for the winter, for the minus-forty. Kelvin once told me that the city was so cold in the winter because the sky was always so blue, that there were no clouds to trap the sun's warmth, which meant that the UV rays would bounce off the snow and go back the way they came, back to the sun. The Haven looked like it was either a church or a barn in another life, but because of the absence of any crosses or livestock I couldn't be sure which one it might have been. I liked the idea of a barn, and all of us lost boys being like lost cows. Cows without mothers and fathers.

Eli and Kimmy met me at the door when I arrived, a small duffel with a change of clothes and my hockey bag in tow. "You're safe here," Kimmy said with a smile, her hands folded at her waist. Eli nodded. I could see beads of sweat forming on his forehead. We moved inside the church-barn hybrid, the lobby of which was a wide-open space with a pool table and a couple of desks with board games and a few stacks of ratty books. The walls were sky blue and light came through large loft-style windows high on the right side of the room, close to the ceiling. Such windows were probably impossible to clean, and judging by the bird shit smeared across them I believed this to be an accurate assumption. Kimmy pointed to a corner by the entrance and said, "You can park your bike here. Just wrap a lock around it if you have one."

They showed me to a room with two beds, one on each wall. One of the beds had a freshly folded blanket with a pillow from IKEA still in its plastic wrapping nestled on top and the other a boy reading a celebrity gossip magazine. "Dinner's at five o'clock," Eli said. "We'll let you get settled." I let my hockey gear thump on the floor and tossed my duffel on the bed and observed the room. It was clean, my allotted half better than the other. On the boy's side two different pairs of shoes were divorced and tipped over, clothes were scattered, unfolded. His tabloid rags were crumpled and bent at the corners. He wore his shoes on the bed and I wondered if that's why my bedsheet looked less than clean. I felt my heart race and my thoughts skip like an old film projector except the story it played made no sense. I counted, like I always did. One to thirty, eyes closed, imagining the shape of each number and only once I could see each digit's lines, curves and color did I move on to the next. *1, 2, 3, 4, 5, 6, 7, 8, 9, 10, 11, 12, 13, 14, 15, 16, 17, 18, 19, 20, 21, 22, 23, 24, 25, 26, 27, 28, 29, 30.* Such rituals offered me at least some relief in those moments, but not much. The point of a ritual is to do it again, and again, because like a lifelong migraine one ibuprofen will never be enough, and over the years my rituals—I had a number of them— had only become more relentless and the numbers I counted grew higher and higher. Multiple teachers over the years have given me their unprofessional diagnosis: that perhaps I have something called obsessive-compulsive disorder. It's serious, they'd tell me, worse than the way some type A freaks joke about it, that it can debilitate, turn your mind to some kind of mush. But out here you have to learn to live with the mush.

When I opened my eyes I could feel the boy watching me. I sat on my new bed and the metal frame ached loud and the boy finally lowered the gossip magazine from his face and sat up across from me. "Jakub," he said. "With a K and a U. Pronounced like Jacob."

"With a K and a U?"

"Yeah. Not the Jew way."

"I think it's still a Jewish name, regardless of how you spell it."

"Yeah but I'm not Jewish. My great-granddad was from Poland and that's how he spelled his name. Jakub." He had eyebrows that could change direction like a seesaw, and while he said this they pointed toward the bridge of his nose in a serious manner.

"Cool name."

"What's yours?"

"Clinton."

"Not bad. Don't think I've ever met a Clinton. Not many famous people named Clinton." He bent over and gently placed the magazine he was holding atop a stack of other celebrity gossip magazines on the floor beside his bed.

"Guess I'll be the first."

He chuckled and scooted up the bed so that his back rested on the wall. "What's your last name, Clinton?"

"Whiteway."

"Clinton Whiteway." He was genuinely satisfied with my name and that made me feel good. "That's a famous name for sure. You might have a shot."

"What about yours?"

"Chartrand. Lots of famous Chartrands. Don't think I'm related to any of them though."

"You could always do a DNA test."

"No need. I know where I come from." He scanned my belongings briefly and then returned his attention back to me. "So you're a hockey player?"

"Not a good one." In the corners opposite our beds there were two small plastic dressers with opaque drawers, possibly also from IKEA. I wondered if it might be rude to interrupt our conversation to begin unpacking the small number of items in my duffel. But I also began to wonder just how long I might stay here, sharing a room like Kelvin and I once did before his days at Headingley.

"I'm not much of a moving-sports kinda guy. You know. With actual running involved. Pool is my game. You play? We should play sometime. I could use a challenge. The kids around here suck."

I wasn't sure what was mild about that statement, there was nothing mild about sucking at something. But this time I didn't question it. "I can play."

"After dinner, then." He picked up the same gossip magazine he was holding before and went back to reading. I unpacked my duffel.

AT FIVE O'CLOCK JAKUB and I went down to the cafeteria for dinner. We filled our trays with fried chicken and mashed potatoes and a bowl of mushroom soup and a bread roll and sat beside each other at a long table. When it looked like everyone had taken their seats I counted fourteen kids, not including Jakub and me. Jakub got a kick out of calling us refugees, pondering whether a big celebrity would adopt any of us. Saying that it happened all the time: poor kids ending up in mansions in Hollywood with servants of their own. He laughed at his own joke. I could see Eli and Kimmy in the kitchen through a windowless opening in the wall, laughing about something with the kitchen staff. Among the refugees there wasn't much chatter. Most of us tucked our chins in and stuffed our faces. But I could also tell that it was a naturally quiet bunch, that this was one thing we had in common. We were observers, witnesses to the worst traits our city had to offer, prepared to spot danger before it spotted us, out of necessity.

Jakub asked me where I was from, and when he said this I could see the kids around us look up from their plates, eager to hear the answer. I told him I was from Pelican Lake First Nation.

A girl sitting across the table from me, who I learned later was named Celli, offered a follow-up: "Why they call it Pelican Lake?"

I didn't know why, there was no lake around our community called Pelican Lake, and that's what I told her. "But," I said, "apparently the place was a nesting colony for pelicans a long time ago, but whether this is true no one really knows, just a story people like to tell."

Another kid, this time a boy, a few spots down the table cleared his throat as if preparing a question of his own. He had short hair so thick it was helmet-shaped, defying gravity. "Why you here, then, in the city?" Eyes darted back at me.

I told my audience—sharing my glance with the room but careful not to zone in on any one person in particular—that my community was swallowed by a flood one spring, worse than ever before, that everyone was evacuated and spent months, too many to count for some, living in a Days Inn until we were told there was no going back, the land was condemned, homes were boarded up and left to rot with the corpses.

Jakub asked where my family was and how I ended up at the Haven, eating dry fried chicken and slurping mushroom soup aged in aluminum cans for who knows how many years. At this point I wasn't sure how forthcoming I should be, and figured there was nothing left for me to hide. I'd given this place my life. Trusted them with it. I explained it all: how my mom is a regular patron at The Stock, how my brother is a thug and dad a mystery, how my koko and shoomis walked on when I was little and how I had no other family to turn to.

"Okay, that's enough." Kimmy was standing at the door that led into the kitchen. "Let him eat. There will be time to get to know him."

Celli was smiling and poking at her food. She eventually came out with it: "Cats or dogs?"

"Cats. Dogs are bitches."

Jakub laughed loudly in my ear and probed further: "You ever see a moose?"

I nodded. "Majestic creatures."

"They're my favorite animal." He paused and I could tell he was trying to conjure another query. "Would you rather get jumped by a great white shark or chased to your death by a lion?"

I let my fork rest on the edge of my paper plate for this one. "I'll take the shark. I read once that humans are only taste tests for sharks, and that our bodies don't contain enough blubber to satisfy a great white. They usually take a bite, realize we taste awful and move on."

"Interesting." He stabbed his fried chicken with his fork and raised it and took a bite. Mid-chew, he said, "I'll take my chances on land."

Jakub didn't tell me much about his situation. His origin story. Only that he bounced around foster homes and for a while lived in a hotel downtown, because it was the only place CFS had for him. CFS watched him day and night, made sure he couldn't leave past curfew. He said it felt like prison, that all the kids housed there had an entire floor to themselves and that the hotel staff hated them, gave them dirty looks, embarrassed for their other clientele. Like secret girlfriends you didn't want your parents to see in the morning. Staff would divert guests' attention to ensure they didn't catch a glimpse of the ghosts that occupied the fifth floor if ever one of them strayed into the lobby, or else tell them that the top level was off-limits due to renovations. The workers assigned to watch over them and make sure they didn't leave the hotel unattended often didn't give a shit whether they left or not. They were employees for some third-party company hired by the province to watch foster kids placed in hotels, some of whom couldn't really speak English.

Every now and then he and three other kids from the hotel—he called them Tristan, Lisa and Brigette for the purposes of the story, saying that he didn't like to reveal the real names of the kids he met in the system without their consent—wandered the empty streets of downtown, slithered the banks of the Red River and skipped rocks along the darkness-cloaked water, which at night, he said, "looks like a gateway to another realm, with little bright specks from the stars." He could never see where the rocks ended up, nor could he hear the splash that should've come after each pebble took its final dive. "Like I said. A gateway. Lisa liked to say that if you jumped off the old train track bridge into the river at night you'd end up in the Spirit World." And every now and then someone pulled up in their car beside them as they walked those lonely streets, asking if they needed a ride. Jakub said he always kept an extra rock in his pocket for this reason, just in case he needed it for something other than skipping.

Jakub polished his plate and bowl clean and walked his tray over to the dish rack. When he sat back down, I finally said: "That's fucked up." He replied: "This place here feels more like family than any place I've been in a long time. Maybe ever."

BACK IN OUR ROOM Jakub asked me why I'm "so" clean.

"Just the way I am."

"I mean. I've known neat freaks. But this is next level."

I went on dusting the rails of my bed frame with a paper towel I brought from the cafeteria.

"Nothing wrong with getting your hands dirty. Both literally and figuratively," he continued.

"Wise words."

"Nothing wrong with being dirty. I embrace it. One set of foster parents I had back in the day wouldn't let me in the living room because they said I was too dirty. Went in there anyway, only TV in the house was in there. Paid like hell for it."

I didn't know what to say, and thought maybe he wanted to be comforted. I turned to look at him and said, "You're not dirty."

"I like being dirty."

This we didn't have in common.

The first time I was called dirty was in the city, during a peewee hockey game. About a year after being shipped off my rez in a school bus. I didn't know what the opposing player meant by it. He said it with a grin, like he knew the secret words that would cut me. What about me is dirty? I thought. The second time I was called dirty, also on the ice, there was another word tacked on at the end. Indian. Dirty Indian. Then I knew. My brown skin was the thing about me that was dirty. But the more I thought about it the more I realized there was more to it than that. Where I came from, the rez, the North End, whatever you want to call it, was dirty. My culture was dirty. My people, the Anishinaabe, were dirty. Our history, the one I never learned about in school, was dirty, a stain on the country this person claimed as his own. Dirty. All of it.

You know they're wrong. But you believe it anyway. You start seeing dirt on your skin where there isn't any.

I remember when my habits started. I remember shortly after hearing those words coming home from school and observing the dirt on my hands, the dark stains trapped in the creases and folds on my fingers, outlining my body like I were a character in a cartoon. I jumped in the shower and scrubbed myself pink with a loofah, until I could see little red dots on the surface of my skin. I did this again the next morning, and soon it became routine: a shower in the morning, skin pink and sensitive to touch from the rough fibers of the loofah, and again after school and one more time before bed. If I broke skin and drew blood, even better. Anything to feel clean.

But I also had to dress the part. I washed my clothes and folded my own laundry, never once donning an article of clothing a second time without a thorough clean. I ironed my shirts before school and packed my lunches to perfection. I walked with my head down, not out of shyness, but to make sure nothing overly offensive was jumping up from the sidewalk to blemish my pants or shoes or, even worse, my skin. On alert, always. Always on alert. Always on the lookout for anything that could potentially ruin my day, my week, my life. These routines became a way of surviving, a way to convince people I didn't know and didn't wish to know that I wasn't the thing they thought me to be. I refused to be dirty. I refuse, I refuse, I refuse. Say it again twenty-seven more times. Now say it while simultaneously blinking your eyes. Repeat until it feels right. Until everything feels normal. This was another ritual.

## pete mosienko

BEFORE YOU HEAD TO WORK—TO THAT PLACE YOU LOVE BUT ALSO hate and have spent all but two of the sixty-three years of your life inside on a daily basis—you open up your freezer, the one in the basement, and pull out a block of frozen deer fat and rest it on your kitchen counter, grab a knife, gently carve off a piece about an inch in length and width, and eat it with your cedar tea. It's your morning routine, shown to you by your grandpa, who was a Ukrainian immigrant from a place called Odesa, somewhere along the Black Sea, who arrived in the city poor and alone and young and was taken in by a woman whose kids had all been taken from her and so she raised him as her own and she said to him, If you're going to stay with me forever you're to refer to me as *nimaamaa*, and so he did. He grew up, called his new mom nimaamaa, cared for her until she eventually passed and never did meet her children who had been taken from her, all three of them, and so he kept the house she raised him in, the house you now live in, met a nice woman, the most beautiful he'd ever seen, and before he proposed he said to her, Are you sure you want to marry me, our kids won't be treaty and nor will you any longer, they won't have none of the rights you have, and she looked at him deep with her brown eyes into his big blues and said, It's not about that, and then with a cheeky smile said, It's about the house! and they laughed but the answer was always yes. But your grandpa kept some of his ways. He called it salo, but his was of pig and not of deer but he had it every morning and said it made him strong and ready to take on the day and when he showed it to you for the first time you hated the cold taste but you wanted to be strong too. You have it every day like a multivitamin. You hate meat, the texture of it, the way it slithers all gross down your throat, but you hunt anyway, you hunt only for the fat, for the strength. You cite and recite these family legends whenever someone asks where the name Mosienko comes from.

You're a Zamboni driver, a rink manager, a skate sharpener, a glorified janitor, anything the Memorial Arena needs you to be. Except you don't drive a Zamboni. That's just what you tell people to avoid the look they give you when you tell them the truth about how you keep your ice in shape, the kind of look that says you're fucking crazy for not owning a Zamboni. You're not exactly proud of any of these titles or what you do for a living, it's not something you bring up in conversation, but whenever someone asks, you tell them you come from a long line of Zamboni drivers, because it's true. You took over after your dad, who took over after the original Mosienko, who took over after a guy named Freddie asked your grandpa if he could cover his shift for the day and your grandpa, who needed the work, tipped his hat in approval and Freddie gave him the keys to the padlock out front and never came back. The smell of sweat, puke, piss and shit, sometimes all at once, had finally gotten to Freddie, that and the pay. They didn't have a Zamboni in those days either. Old Mosienko relied on shovels and a few pails of water to smooth out the lacerations, a laborious task that could take an hour or two to finish on his own, depending on how much salo, and its quality, he had in his possession. But Old Mosienko kept coming back, and soon your dad tagged along too, learning to keep that sheet of ice cold and smooth for as many months as they could, because once it died, transformed into a pool of slush, like a dying fire it meant things were hard again, at least until the next big freeze.

Eventually, though, the legs and back have nothing left. And so it was around this time when your father, now a man, just a couple years shy of accepting the baton of rink management, and Old Mosienko, who wasn't quite ready to hang his hat, heard about a man named Frank from some place in California who made a machine so incredible he named it after himself. It was the early fifties, and you were a baby, or at least gimaamaa still treated you as such even though you were new to walking and talking and learning to eat on your own, when your father came home and packed a bag and said he was going to see a Mr. Zamboni about his Zamboni and that it was like the arrival of horses on Turtle Island, and that if they didn't adapt to the changing times and thus tame the Zamboni like the wild horse it was then it would be the end of them, and gimaamaa, not having it, reminded him that he didn't know how to ride a horse. Your father and Old Mosienko were gone for a month. They spent their mornings at the Pasadena Winter Garden, observing the Zamboni in action, and by the end of week one your father was convinced they should place an order with Frank, and by the end of week four he finally convinced your grandpa to do away with his shovels and pails of water and back pain and knee pain but he never did climb aboard the Zamboni and take the reins.

Your own maamaa kept you away from the rink for the first two years of your life, fearing it would keep you from the possibilities of the world. Fearing also that the sounds of the crowd and cowbells and the puck snapping off glass, board and post for two hours straight would fuck up your hearing, but to this day your hearing is mostly fine. Your dad disagreed, respectfully, said the rink was a way of life, that it would sink its hooks in you the way it did him and that's good enough. But eventually your mom couldn't keep you from it. You played the game, sucked terribly, couldn't hit the back of the net with a beach ball, couldn't skate backward without putting your life at risk, but you stayed anyway, took up the family business and gimaamaa cried but you comforted her by saying it won't be forever and she made you promise and lock pinkies and you did. You speak English because she wanted you to learn it, and you know this and a part of you is resentful for it, but you also know that it means if you wanted to you could put this life behind you and pick up something else. It wasn't the game that kept you coming back each day, or the shit, puke, sweat or piss, but the smell, the smell of the ice, the freshness of it. The day starts and ends with it. Life, like regular life, isn't always so satisfying.

You arrive at the rink before the sky stops being navy and the ice is already clean and just ahead beyond the glass a cold smoke floats above its surface. You check the locker rooms and pick up any tape stuck to the rubber floors. You make sure the lights are working in every room and the toilets flush. They all do. You head into the pro shop, which is no bigger than a closet, and restock the tape, laces and spare blades on the hooks on every wall and then turn on the skate-sharpening machine to see if it's working, because sometimes it doesn't, but on this day it works, and then you blow on the grinder, the part that meets the blade of a skate, and a puff of silver dust and unwanted residue hangs in the air before disappearing onto the floor, lost between the cracks. It's old, it should be replaced, but you know you can't afford it, the city doesn't pay you enough for such expenses and most of what you make goes into other things that require upkeep, such as the roof above center ice that starts to leak once the snow begins to melt, but still the device is more reliable than the automated one by the vending machine. And yet you still welcome that inevitable day, so the papers say, when automation surpasses your unmatched talent (it's true, you're the best, they all say it, the plaque on the wall behind you, just below a framed GED certificate you earned two summers back, from your local MLA for exemplary community service proves it) for finely sharp edges, because that'll be one less hat to wear and the robots can have it.

You head on outside and smoke beside the front door, close enough to feel the warmth from inside. You watch the first group of kids file into the arena for practice and every once in a while one of them waves and says, Hey Petey! because your name is Pete but that's what they call you. You wave back and after a while you toss your butt on the ground and crunch it into the concrete and then use the broom and dustpan you pulled from the janitor's closet to collect other discarded butts because you read somewhere once that they take ten years to decompose.

You take your seat high on the bleachers and drink your coffee and watch the kids take the ice. It's the Tigers and they're absolutely terrible but you watch anyway because you were terrible too but you don't play anymore, your knees won't allow it, they lock up and make clicking sounds with each stride. Doctors suggested leg braces and you tried for a week but they made you feel broken. But, still, the boys down on the ice are beautiful, their formations a dance. They weave up and down the sheet in unison and there's a music to it, skates splicing through ice like horsehair on the strings of a violin, pucks bouncing off the boards like a drum. They zig. They zag. And when one piece isn't working the whole thing doesn't work but they try and try again until it looks right.

There's a skirmish in front of the net and you see two players fighting for position, a defenseman digs the shaft of his stick in the lower back of a forward, who hacks back and finds unprotected tissue along the defenseman's calves, and suddenly the forward goes down from another hard push and the whistle blows loudly and you see one of the coaches glide over and pat the standing boy on the shoulder for holding his ground. You hear the coach say, Atta boy, Shields! and you remember then that you once knew a woman with the surname Shields and wonder if that boy is related to her. Her name was Olga, but she wanted to be called Sunshine, and that's exactly what she was: bright and warm and sustaining. You dated briefly, years ago, when the skin on your face was tight and you could still impress the ladies with your skating ability, such as it was. She gave you that sick feeling one gets when they're starting to really like someone. It was brief, you were sad when she broke it off and you asked her why but she didn't say, and so seeing this boy on the ice reminds you what you should've said, perhaps what you should've fought for. You sip your coffee and pull a leg up on your thigh and feel the blood rushing to your cock. She had the best ass, you say to yourself. It was like sunshine.

You often think about all the women you've ever loved, which isn't hard because there weren't many, and whether you'll ever see any of them ever again, whether you'll spark something one final time before you leave this Earth. Mom died at sixty-seven, dad was sixty-two when he walked, so you already got the old man beat but you know your final days are likely just around the corner. We are in the third period. Those last fifteen minutes are coming, sooner or later Father Time comes for all of us. Sooner if you're from the North End. Later if you're not. And when you think about past lovers you always think about the shit they said to you before they left and never the good stuff, about how you're broke, how the only thing you've ever loved was the rink and what it gave you, how you can't fuck right because of a degenerative disc in your lower back, and about how you come home late at night smelling like piss, shit, puke and sweat and cheap booze.

You love the rink. You often say it saved your life when the world was meaner than usual and sometimes, when the hydro bills piled up and your power was shut off, it actually did. You'd unfold a cot in the refrigeration room and feel the warmth coming off the web of rust-brown pipes and steel machineries, running through the floors and walls of the Memorial Arena like blood in the vein, pumping the cold needed to make eight months of smooth, hard, regulation-approved ice possible. You love the rink and you always have and it's the only good and constant thing in your life, because you have no kids or cousins or nephews or nieces or aunties or friends or enemies or ex-lovers you still give love to occasionally or cousins who are not really cousins but you call them cousin anyway. You just have the ice.

That's probably why you spend too much time on Facebook, browsing the names of people you once knew. You think sometimes you might be achingly lonely, but then remind yourself that you have the rink, so how could that be? And though you don't like to admit it that feeling of loneliness is why you walked into the Pelican Institute two summers ago and sat through hours of bullshit you could barely understand as a kid and still barely understood then and got your GED. To be close to others, to feel close to others. You closed down the computer lab, made small talk with anyone who'd give you the time. But none of it helped, you were still picked last when it came time for group assignments, everyone did their best to avoid the old guy that smelled like deer fat. You pretended not to hear the jokes about you shacking up in the student lounge, the speculation that you lived there, moved in, that perhaps you were having an affair with one of the overnight cleaners who couldn't speak English. You almost quit, almost. You decided one morning, as you ate your salo and drank your tea, that you wanted more to your name than a crumbling hockey rink, you needed that piece of paper that said you didn't graduate high school but here's this instead and it's apparently just as good if not better, because it says you went through some fucking crazy shit but swam your way out of the fucking gutter, now please treat me as your equal.

The Turtle & Crane Institute wanted all their GED graduates to feel like they achieved something. But this also meant they wanted you to feel like a winner when you eventually completed the course by throwing a graduation ceremony for all the hard-earned students, gowns and mortarboards and all. This you hated. Not because you weren't proud to earn your certificate (you were) but because it was embarrassing. It was a watered-down version of what could've been. But you went anyway. The reception was held in a room no bigger than the classroom that housed your entire cohort. You wore the cap and gown and smiled for the camera when your instructor, Mrs. Desjarlais, gave you your certificate. They offered sparkling wine in plastic glasses and served cheese and crackers and platters of carrots and cucumber and celery and broccoli and cauliflower and cherry tomatoes and ranch dressing for dipping. You skipped the dairy and grabbed anything that wasn't green. You tried your best to not feel awkward about your age and tried on different smiles in the mirror after you took a piss, calculating that you were at least fifteen years older than the next-youngest person in the room. And so was your smile.

Mrs. Desjarlais approached you while you nibbled on carrots. She offered her congratulations again and asked you what you plan to do next. She topped up her glass from a nearby bottle. Is university or college on the horizon? she asked.

Probably just get married, have kids, start a family, you said.

She laughed. You laughed with her. Never too late, she said.

YOU'RE ON YOUR LAST clean of the evening. You always tell people, mostly curious kids, that scraping the ice is a delicate process. The quality of the ice affects the game more than people know, can make it slower or faster or simply intolerable as a player. The best rinks have the best ice and the best ice always has a good caretaker. You know this isn't the best ice. But you believe, probably more than anyone, that you're a good caretaker. Your father's Zamboni didn't last long, became a rusted skeleton long before you inherited the keys. You know a *new* Zamboni would make it better, but you prefer the old ways. You have mastered them, so much so that you can get the job done in less than an hour on a good day. You use a big-ass custom shovel with a wide-ass blade, and as you walk up and down the ice you sprinkle water from a jug with tiny holes drilled into the bottom. You feel it today. It's become a daily feeling: your age. The aches and pains. Both knees, lower back and neck and shoulders, with every move. You've never wanted a Zamboni, never cared how long and grueling the job was, because Indians were fine before horses crossed the ocean and made things easier. But near the final push you let yourself think it and you know it's true. You need a Zamboni. You *want* a Zamboni. You'll find a way, save some money between now and spring, buy a Zamboni, one of the newer ones, all shiny and shit like a Ferrari, and you'll get a Zamboni driver's license and you'll drive the fuck out of it, maybe take a nice lady out for a ride one evening on the Zamboni under a pretty pale moon, and be free, finally, of your pain and suffering and your earthly chains. You've always walked on water but now you'll drive on it. When you're done you grab a lighter shovel and pile the wet-sugar snow into a garbage bin before rolling the bin outside and dumping it out. You close the gateway in the boards and lower the latch to lock it shut and you take a minute to appreciate the fresh smell, breathing it in through your nose, before heading home.

You walk up your front steps and wonder how long till there's a ramp leading up to your small porch. Before you go to bed you sit at your computer and throw on your reading glasses and scroll through Facebook and you search for Olga Shields and after verifying a few profiles that come up, one from some unpronounceable place in India, a pictureless person from Grand Rapids, Michigan, a woman from Florida who claims to have attended the School of Hard Knocks, you find her. There she is. You creep her pictures and say to yourself, Age looks good on you. You scroll fast, paying no attention to the excessive number of landscape shots, and pause when you see an image of her with a young boy and a slightly older young girl. Her grandchildren, according to the caption. You keep scrolling. No man or boyfriend or husband, at least none that you can see, and that excites you. For a second the thought that she might be available creeps up on you but you don't let it come any closer, because it's impossible, because it's too late now, and because you were told once to never think about crazy shit at night because at night you're never thinking straight and so you stop and go to bed. The next morning, at the rink, you watch the Tigers practice again. This time you sit closer.

## *clinton whiteway*

THE MORNING AFTER OUR FIRST LOSS OF THE SEASON I STEPPED OUT of the Haven and into the cool air. There was a light breeze and it smelled of fall. I took a deep breath and admired the sky's royal shade, the calmness of the clouds, how they seemed to carry the first orange rays with them. I walked down Burrows and took a left on McGregor before stopping for a Gatorade at Cooley's Quickie Mart, which could almost pass for a flatiron-style building. I said this to every person who went to Cooley's with me, explaining that the Flatiron Building is a famous landmark in Manhattan, a borough of New York City, and that the Gooderham Building in Toronto, also a flatiron, is older than the one in New York. Almost everyone I share these facts with looks up and shrugs, unimpressed. I paid for the Gatorade in cash and kept the change from my toonie and kept walking up McGregor, passing herds of small children who attended the elementary school just around the corner from the Haven. When I hit Machray Park, a short jump from St. Croix, I stopped in the oval and squatted down on a yellow bench to drink. The park was beautiful and the grass smelled like it was mowed recently. Whoever groomed the grass at Machray clearly cared about their work. The lines from the lawn mower were even throughout the field and rarely were there any egregious overlaps.

I walked through the front doors of St. Croix, escorted by the joyous sounds of students reunited once again for what society considers the good kind of brainwashing, and headed straight for my locker to find my notebook for Native Studies.

"Clean locker you got there."

I looked over my shoulder quickly and from the side of my eye assessed that a girl was speaking to me.

"I'm Clarissa," she said. "Clarissa Walkman."

I snapped shut the lock to my locker and set the dial to zero and turned around. She had long, straight dark hair, and not because it had been straightened but because it was thick and heavy, like it could be used to make rope. She was wearing a red sweatshirt with a fist holding a feather displayed across the chest, an emblem I'd been seeing around more and more, the logo for some movement. She had dusty-rose lips, this again a natural physical feature, and a serious look on her face. She was objectively beautiful. I glanced at the clock on the wall above her. Class was about to start.

"From *The Daily Drum*," she added.

"I've read your stories."

She smiled and flipped open the small notepad she was holding in her hand. "I'm working on a story about the league's attempt to push out the Tigers hockey team. Would you be willing to speak about it?"

I could tell that my mouth was open but I couldn't find the words. This was the first time I'd ever spoken to Clarissa. First time I talked to a paper. They had no reason to question me before, no in-game heroics on my part to report on. "Sorry. I have to go," I said as I moved down the hall.

"Wait a second. How come no one from the Tigers wants to comment on this?"

"Can't speak for anyone else. Maybe they don't have time."

"Rumor is you've been muzzled by your white coaches."

I turned to her, trying my best to look less annoyed than I was. "Who's saying that?"

"Just what I've been hearing." She had a proud look on her face.

I stopped to fill up my bottle at the water fountain. I struggled to balance my notebook under my arm while pressing the fountain's button hard enough so that the water would arc at the appropriate height to land inside my bottle. Noticing this, Clarissa nudged my thumb over and replaced it with hers. She had the nicest cuticles I'd ever seen.

"Give me five minutes," she pressed.

"I can't. I'm sorry."

"Why? This is an important story. It needs to get out there. You know that."

I did know that. "Off the record. *We* can't."

Her eyes widened, like she just learned of something devastating. "I see."

"It is what it is."

She swung her bag in front of her and reached inside and pulled out a wrinkled piece of paper. "Well. At least sign this petition. I'm on the student council and when we reach a thousand signatures we're gonna send it to Hockey Manitoba and the league." She handed me the paper, adding, "It's not right, what's happening."

"Isn't this like some sort of violation of your journalistic integrity."

She removed some hair from her face in a delicate manner. She had that serious look again. "Objectivity is a myth created by someone else, and it's a privilege that I cannot afford. I plan on doing things differently when I'm a professional journalist."

I signed the petition and handed it back. "So, you want to be a reporter, then?"

"One day." She reached out her hand. "Can I see your notebook?"

I gave it to her and she opened it up to a page free of messy notes and random doodles and wrote down her number. She wrote her name in pretty cursive and before walking off, she said: "Just in case you change your mind. Staying idle is no longer worth it, never has been."


IN NATIVE STUDIES WE were learning about Louis Riel, the Métis leader who founded Manitoba. The course was elective, meaning optional, and the smallest class I'd ever been in since I first walked the halls of St. Croix. In my experience, classes like these rarely crossed racial lines, broke into the mainstream. And by that I mean such courses were not normally consumed by the segment of St. Croix's population that wasn't Native. Such classes occupied a special niche. A bunch of Native kids learning about what it meant to be Native. Ms. Judy—who wasn't Native, but had done more than enough to earn her respect around here—stood at the front of the blackboard, the words "Who was Louis Riel?" etched behind her in pink chalk. High on the wall above her hung a row of student-made dream catchers.

Louis Riel, depending on where you live in the country or which school you attended, is regarded as a villain who stood in the way of *Kanata* and its progress—Kanata, Ms. Judy said, writing it on the board for all of us to see, is where the word "Canada" comes from, a Huron-Haudenosaunee word for "village" or "settlement." "But he wasn't a villain," Ms. Judy said. "He led the Red River Rebellion and fought for the rights of Métis people. He stood up to Canada and this country's first prime minister, Sir John A. Macdonald, and set an example for the generations to come."

This much I knew.

What I didn't know was how he died. I'd seen the bronze Louis Riel statue, him all tall, fierce, outside the legislature building. I'd seen his grave in St. Boniface, his portrait engraved in the marble. For a while he was hiding out in the United States, in exile. And when he eventually came back to continue the fight he was captured, tried for treason, and put to his death. I didn't know that throughout his lifetime he was elected to the House of Commons three times, but, fearing for his life, never once took the seat the people had chosen him for.

I flipped through to the back of a graphic novel about Louis Riel's life Ms. Judy had assigned, and there he was: hanging, dead, the rope taut from the weight of his lifeless body, his executioner behind him. A sick feeling came over me. "A man named Mudeater—Irvin Mudeater—helped capture Louis Riel," Ms. Judy said.

Mudeater was the son of a Wyandot chief from Kansas and a buffalo hunter. A really good one. One summer he claimed to have killed more than sixteen hundred buffalo. In 1882, Mudeater moved to what is now Saskatchewan and took the name of Robert Armstrong and pretended to be white. "There's a reason we don't remember this man," Ms. Judy said. There was disgust in her voice, like the words made her sick. "But," she said, moving to the left of the board and taking a seat on the corner of her desk. She held the chalk up to her cheek, smudging her face. "What do you think makes Riel and Mudeater similar?" She scanned the classroom and everyone looked away in unison, as if her gaze could steal our souls like that ghoulish thing in Harry Potter.

Crickets. A couple mouth breathers heaved in the back row.

"They went about it differently," Ms. Judy eventually said. "They were both"—she paused, like she was having trouble reconciling with the words or ideas that were about to come out—"surviving in a world that didn't want them to exist."

At the end of class Ms. Judy assigned us to read the first section of the graphic novel by the next week and everyone wandered out into the hallway with little enthusiasm. I resented that my copy, supposedly brand new, was battered and bruised. I thought about Mudeater, and what he did to Riel. I thought about how one man (Riel) was infamous or legendary depending on your point of view, and the other (Mudeater) was forgotten. But this forgotten character completed the story, and I liked that Ms. Judy brought him up, because when I flipped through the graphic novel about Louis Riel's life, nowhere did it mention a man named Irvin Mudeater. The "hero" who caught the "famous traitor." Or the traitor who caught the hero. Depending.

I had a thought: I am Mudeater. Here were two men, one who rebelled against a system bent on removing his kind from the equation and another who followed the rules, obeyed, yielded to the establishment, white-faced. I followed the rules. It was my worst trait. I bent to authority. Maybe the second-worst. I walked the straight path, not out of fear of getting in trouble but because it made an already inconvenient life a little more convenient. My third sin. I never once accepted my promo for the five-finger discount, turning down offers from friends to storm the Dollarama and come out with ten dollars' worth of junk. All because that one security guard with dreams of being a Mountie harassed and followed one of our moms during a little evening shopping. I never cheated on a test, never looked over to the person beside me for the correct answer, never gave out my notes to help a fellow Neechi. Risk was never my forte.

As for the Tigers: we *were* muzzled, and I swore an oath with the rest of the team to abide by the rules. We were being booted out of the league, and our response was to agree that it was legitimate to get booted. To say nice things. To be nice kids from the hood. I refuse. I refuse. I refuse.

In the hall I found Clarissa's number in my notebook and punched the numbers in my phone and, after taking a deep breath, sent her a text:

*I'll do it.*

Her reply was prompt: *Yes! When can you chat?*

*Whenever.*

I saved Clarissa's name and number. I slid the keyboard on my cell back behind the screen and slipped it in my pocket. I could turn back, but knew I wouldn't. For the first time in a long time I felt dirty, and it felt good. It felt good to be messy. Lighter on my feet, like I could fly after a few hops. After school I stepped out into the sun. Save for the morning, it had been cloudy. I soaked it in.

## *tomahawk shields*

THE MESSAGE FROM DOLORES POOLE ARRIVED IN TOMMY'S INBOX the day after their fourth loss of the season. October first. They'd played well, by their standards. They kept it close. "Keep it close" had become Coach Johnson's pregame anthem. "If we keep it close we give ourselves a chance," he'd say. "If we keep it close anything can happen." The words had been said so often in recent weeks that Tommy found himself dreaming about Coach Johnson, red-faced with veins bursting from his forehead, spewing saliva-infused words of rage in the locker room between periods. The Tigers trailed by two going into the third but the Tyndall Park Hounds pulled away in the last eight minutes by adding three more. Tommy thought about this loss more than he liked, annoyed that a player from the other team, one of their weaker members, had the courage to say to him, in the game's final seconds, "You fucking suck." He'd received worse jabs in life, possibly far worse. He couldn't explain why this one stung. Not that there was anyone to explain it *to*. It hurt his pride, it hurt his quads, it hurt because of the work he'd put in. That's what he would have said.

He'd called the number on Dolores's card the day after he met her. He left a message and two days later she called back. "Tomahawk, it's for you," Koko said, offering him the phone. Tommy told Dolores that he'd been thinking more about university, and she offered him a campus tour to see what it was all about. He said yes and she booked him into a time slot. There was a brief silence between them, and then Dolores said, "Tomahawk. That's a great name." Tommy thanked her and said: "My mom gave it to me."

Tommy hadn't checked his email in months. Dolores said she'd send him an email with the date and time of his tour at the University of Manitoba. He stowed this information in the back of his mind until he remembered that surely the tour was coming up and decided that he'd go and get a ride back home from Sam. The only computer in the house was in the dining room, next to a bookshelf of unused CDs and DVDs. He pressed the power button on the tower and the display on the chunky monitor lit up blue. The icons for each application popped up as slow as the city buses in the North End. He let the computer hum loudly for a few minutes—Koko always said it wouldn't work properly if it didn't have time to warm up, like a car in the winter—and then he logged in to his account. The email from Dolores said that he needed to be on campus at nine o'clock in the morning, two weeks away, and that there would be a person in the center of the quad holding a green sign that read "Campus Tour." He scrolled through his old messages, a blank white desert with only a handful of emails that dated back years. One of the earliest was from Clinton, around the time Tommy's email account was created, and offered only a subject line: "Welcome to the 21st century. Go fuck yourself." He checked his spam and scanned the phish swimming along in his inbox as Shoppers Drug Mart promotions and lottery notifications he'd supposedly won. If only. A million for Sam, a million for Koko, disappear with the rest, somewhere with a turquoise beach with an ocean floor made flat and smooth by human engineering and exported white sand. At the top corner of his screen he noticed the number beside the inbox tab change from zero to one and he quickly clicked to see what new transmission he'd received. The subject was "My Boy!" and it was from his mother.

Aaniin. My boy.
    I woke up the other day and remembered I still remember your email address and thought to myself that maybe I should go down to the library and send you this letter because maybe it might make you feel good to know that I still remember the small things like this. That's where I am right now as I write to you—the library—and right now people are looking at me all weird like I shouldn't be here

and about a minute ago a blonde woman with a face that
made it easy to imagine what she would look like in old age
came up to me to tell me I took her place and that there is a
sign up form at the front desk to use the computers and now
the whole place—everyone—is giving me dirty looks like I
shouldn't be here but it's okay I told her, because I won't be
here long and all I want to do is send an email to my boy
back home who I haven't seen in a long while and then she
walked off all angry and the ladies who work behind the
desk looked at me and then whispered some things to each
other I couldn't hear. Anyway: How is Koko? How is my
big baby girl? How is school? Are you still playing hockey?
When do you think you're going to graduate? Vancouver is
a nice city, very pretty and doesn't get too cold and the trees
and mountains are pretty and look like crystals on the cold
days. Me, I get by. I live in the DTES—maybe you've heard
of it—they say it's not a safe place for women. Me, I've been
okay. Sometimes people watch me, follow me, bug the places
I've been. Spy on me. Me, I'm okay. But lots of women, of
all kinds, go missing out here and there's this highway up
north—they call it something special, something to do with
tears and sadness—they tell you not to go down because
many women who do are never seen again.

Tommy stopped reading. His heart was racing and he questioned
the reality of the email, whether it was really from his mom. Or
another lottery notification. Another phish. Virus-laden pornog-
raphy had destroyed their previous computer—Dwayne down the
street who was good with computers said it had reached the point
of no return, that their antivirus software had more than met its
match—two days before Sam was to submit an important assignment and she had never forgiven Tommy for his moment of sex-
ual exploration. Then he remembered when his email account was
created.

He was a young boy, young enough for a mullet, his mom was
still around then. Sam and her friends had made their first email
accounts and she came home after school one day excited to show

Tommy how it was done, that if he made a virtual friend playing games on the computer he could message them even if they live on the other side of the world. "You'll be pen pals," she said, grinning. The three of them lived in a small two-bedroom apartment; Sam and Tommy shared a bunk. The only computer in the apartment was kept in the corner of their bedroom, near a blue trunk full of toys that had been getting used less and less. It was Sam who helped him set up his account as he peered over her shoulder. She suggested a username—tommy was taken—so they settled on tommyhawk.

Mom had short hair then, and as he read her email Tommy wondered if it was still short. Back when he set up the account she came into the bedroom as Tommy played a game that had to do with penguins. Tommy looked over and excitedly said: "Look what Sam did for me." He turned his body away from the computer and opened the inbox page for his new email account.

Mom's eyes widened, and for a moment she appeared hysterical. "What's this?" She bent over the computer screen and then turned to look at Tommy, her face close to his.

Tommy could feel his spine curl and his shoulders drop. "Sam helped me make an email. She said I could use it to chat with friends."

"No no no. You're too young for this. You do not need this right now. We don't need this in this house."

"It's just an email."

"Delete it."

"Why?"

She raised a hand near her face and briefly closed her eyes, like this would prevent further protest, it usually did. Tommy positioned himself back in front of the computer, and as his mom turned to leave the room she said again: "Delete it."

Tommy didn't delete it and he knew that she knew that he hadn't listened.

Tommy, calmer now, reopened the message and kept reading.

Now that I think about it people are definitely watching me. They're trying to track me down and hear me when I'm speaking and the other day I ripped apart my room to make sure nothing was planted there trying to get me. I tore apart the wood floors and got plenty of splinters doing so and then I emptied out all the furniture and slept on the blank floor in my pajamas. Do you remember when I took you to Grand Beach when you were younger? It was spring and the mornings were still chilly because winter had not yet left us and I remember waking up that first morning and there they were: hundreds, if not thousands, of worms littering the roads outside our cottage. When I look back on it I know now that they were placed there by someone trying to ruin my life, drive me away from my family, and they have been watching me ever since. It's the government. They have special devices everywhere and sometimes they buzz and try to scare us. They watch people, even their own people. This is to make sure we stay in line. My friend Littlefeather said the government has been trying to exterminate us women for hundreds of years and they're still trying to. Littlefeather was the first person I met out here in Vancouver. She's Woodlands Cree from Alberta. She was born a Freedom Baby, meaning her family saw to it that she didn't become a citizen. They didn't want her to become a slave to the system because it's not our ways because they hate our ways and because to be a citizen of this country is to be complicit in our genocide. That's what she says, and she's helping me write to the government to renounce my citizenship so that I will also be a Freedom Baby, or a Freedom Adult as Littlefeather likes to say, because it's never too late to stand up against the people who are watching us. Or else they will keep on with their spying. Anyway. I've been thinking about something long and hard. Not this but something else. About coming home to visit. I don't know when but soon and I suppose I wanted to let you know and now that you know I hope you will let Koko know as well. I don't know when but something tells me soon, or maybe next year. Who knows. More on that soon.

Take care,
Mom

TOMMY SHOWED SAM THE email when she got home that evening. She read the entire thing while covering her mouth with her palm. She sat back in the floral-patterned chair in front of the computer and scanned the note on the screen up and down with the wheel of the mouse. "She sounds paranoid," she said finally.

"So you don't think people are following her?"

"I doubt it. She sounds schizophrenic. I don't know. Psychosis maybe. I remember Grand Beach. It was summer, not spring. There's absolutely no way someone could plant that many worms on the ground. And for what?"

Tommy shrugged, unsure of what to say.

Sam placed her index finger on the computer screen and observed the domain name of the sender. "This is an encrypted email service. Some kids at the university like to brag about using this. Fancy."

Tommy didn't know what that meant. "Should we help her?"

"How?"

"Send her money or something." He stared off at nothing, a finger under his chin. "It could help her visit."

"We don't even know where she is. She could be in Victoria or Kamloops for all we know." The pitch in her voice grew higher and she was starting to look irritated. "She could have been living in the fucking attic all these years. We don't know if she even has a bank account."

"We need to try something." Tommy's voice deepened, like he was on a serious phone call with a stranger. "Renouncing your citizenship sounds like a fucking terrible idea. And . . ."

"And what?"

"She wants to visit."

Sam sneered, eyes hot. "You believe that?"

Tommy wanted to, but changed the subject. "Should I tell Koko about this?"

"Don't tell her."

"Why? What if she gets deported or something?"

"Because Koko has enough to worry about, and we don't even know if this is really her."

"Only Mom would know my email address." He tried to think of other things to say but couldn't.

Sam stood up and moved toward the bottom of the stairs. "Do me a favor," she said, refusing eye contact. "If she writes back don't tell me about it."

TOMMY SPENT THE NEXT morning googling ways to help someone from afar, even if you didn't know where they were. He typed "schizophrenia" in the search bar and found a help guide for people dealing with a relative who is schizophrenic or delusional. It said you shouldn't challenge the person or tell them their delusions are wrong, but you also shouldn't agree with them.

He emailed a mental health center, where patients lived and received treatment. He explained the situation and asked them for advice on how to proceed. About thirty minutes later the center responded with a brief note and five more PDF guides.

Good Morning Tommy,

Unfortunately, for legal reasons, we can't provide advice or guidance on what to do in your situation. As well, legally you cannot force a family member into treatment, as everyone has the protected right to decide if they wish to seek it. Please let us know if you require further assistance.

Regards,
Engagement Staff

AT SCHOOL HIS MOTHER was all Tommy could think about. Tannyce, out there, seeing and hearing things that weren't real. Then again maybe they were. He found it difficult to appreciate his chemistry teacher's monologue on acid rain after a couple of students, who were well versed in their teacher's tendency to go off on long, confusing tangents, saw an opportunity to kill twenty minutes of class. He took almost no pleasure in watching his media studies teacher tear into a rebellious pupil over the use of the phrase "bros before hoes."

"Women shouldn't be called hoes."

"All I mean is friends before women. Male friends. It's like a man code thing."

"Still. I think many women, including in this class, would find that phrase offensive. It implies that women have no value to men. In the eyes of the bros women are seen as just objects and unequal and undeserving of our attention."

"What if some women *are* hoes."

"Darnell, you're being a prick!" The teacher's face went red and his eyes, now watery and mean, seemed to squeeze out of their sockets.

The student didn't respond, his mouth hanging open. The whole class gasped and hid their faces, laughing nervously and whispering. Tommy admired the teacher's gutsiness. The class was held in St. Croix's only computer lab, a classroom dedicated to the desktop PC. Numerous computers and their swiveling thrones lined all four walls of the room and eight more workstations filled the open floor in two-by-two squares, and like most classrooms throughout the school the space felt small and cramped and oddly glum even on the sunniest days. Tommy normally occupied a spot closer to the teacher's whiteboard for no other reason than his vision was bad from far away. But on this day when he entered the room he went straight to the back close to the windows, figuring that the glare from the light outside might hide all his Google searches from those around him.

After it was determined that one of their fellow classmates was a prick, the class had the rest of the hour to research ideas for an upcoming presentation in which each student would examine a current affairs topic that had been widely discussed in the media and how it was represented. "If you think it's been depicted in a good or bad way you must explain why," the teacher had said. "If it's good explain all the reasons why and how you think this was achieved. If it's bad tell us why the portrayal could be potentially harmful to the people at the intersection of the issue or to society as a whole." Tommy didn't read the news, he'd never picked up a newspaper or thought about the words, whether what was happening on the page was actually happening out there in the world. The most news he consumed was with Koko, when she'd turn on the local FM station to play radio bingo and hear the latest updates around town.

The teacher left the room. Tommy turned his back to the whiteboard and faced the screen of his computer. He typed "Sad high-way in British Columbia" into Google and second from the top of the search results was the Wikipedia page for something called the "Highway of Tears." It was a 450-mile road from Prince Rupert to Prince George somewhere north of Vancouver. Numerous women, an *uncounted* number of women, a number the people and the police couldn't agree on, had vanished along this stretch of pavement. Many of them Indigenous. There were signs along the highway for the missing, their portraits blown up big for the passersby, and others that warned women not to hitchhike. Many of the photos were old, because many of the cases themselves were old, and of poor quality. There was talk of serial killers, and a lack of urgency on the part of the police to investigate. Tannyce was right. There was such a high-way in British Columbia. A horror story. The stuff of nightmares.

"What's that there, Tommy?" The teacher put his hand on the back of Tommy's chair, bending its plastic.

Tommy quickly minimized his browser and glanced back, looking up at his teacher's face. "Just researching, Mr. Klimenko."

"What about?" The teacher pushed his glasses higher up his nose.

"A road."

"A road?"

"I mean it's a highway."

"Where is this highway?"

"It's called the Highway of Tears. In B.C."

"Interesting." The teacher circled around, found an empty chair at one of the desks and rolled it over to Tommy. He sat down and leaned heavy on the armrest. "What's it about?"

Tommy cleared his throat. He thought about opening the mini-mized browser again. "It's a place where a lot of people, specifically women, have gone missing."

"Fascinating. I don't think I've ever heard about this. Maybe I have. I can't recall. Strong maybe."

"I just heard about it now."

"During your research?" The teacher raised a hand and pointed with his index finger toward the computer screen as if surprised to find a student working.

Tommy nodded.

"So these women." The teacher paused and leaned back in the chair. His expression changed to something more serious. "I take it that many of them are, let's say, vulnerable?"

Tommy wasn't sure what to say. Instead he said: "I guess."

"Because this sort of thing is usually what happens to vulnerable women, and vulnerable people in general. They put themselves at greater risk to be preyed upon by bad people."

Tommy nodded. The teacher's words didn't sound right. He knew Sam would've yelled at him for nodding, so he stopped. "I read somewhere that people are pretty angry that the cops aren't doing much." He braced himself for a rebuttal.

"The police would never *not* look into a crime. Remember that," the teacher said, looking Tommy in the eye and then in an instant the mood in his voice became cheerier. "It's important to be fair, especially during your presentation."

Tommy gave a single nod, stopping himself before the second.

"Interesting topic." The teacher stood and repositioned the chair back under a desk. "Looking forward to seeing how it turns out. If you need anything you know where to find me."


TOMMY STAYED ON THE computer after class ended and the room was nearly empty. He scrolled and browsed aimlessly, wondering whether now was the time to respond to the person who was likely his mother.

"Tomahawk!"

Tommy turned around. It was Floyd.

Floyd strode into the computer lab energetically: half-bounce and half-waddle. He threw himself into a chair beside Tommy and bumped into the desk so hard it made all the monitors along the wall sway back and forth, and Tommy's mind briefly flashed to presenting the bill from St. Croix to Koko. The image faded away once the screens caught their balance. "What's up, Big Weapon?"

"Nothing much," Tommy said, forcing a smile.

Floyd was easily the Tigers' best player. An Afro-Indigenous boy who looked more Black than Native, but talked more Native than the rest of the team, perhaps because he didn't look like the rest of them, or maybe it was more to do with the North End. Tommy favored the latter. Floyd was known at St. Croix for overdoing it with the word "sacred." Everything was, as he liked to say, "sacred as fuck."

"You alright?" Floyd leaned in to get a better view of Tommy's face.

Tommy continued to stare absently at the computer screen. "I'm alright," he said.

Floyd recoiled. "Talk to me."

"It's nothing."

"Lady troubles?" Floyd smiled, as if the thought of talking about girls, or a lack thereof, had excited him.

Tommy laughed. He searched his mind, he assessed the various tabs open in his browser, he glanced out the window at a flock of geese tilling a small patch of grass with their beaks, anything to get him out of what had the budding potential to be a deep conversation about feelings. Feelings were off-limits to boys his age. It was an unspoken law of the universe. But not to Floyd. *Sacred as fuck.* "No. It's not that."

Floyd nodded slowly, and then followed Tommy's eyes outside toward the geese.

"It's more fucked up than that," Tommy said, the words barely loud enough to leave his personal space.

"Talk to me."

"I have this cousin whose mom I'm not really close with. Which I guess makes her my auntie. I think. I don't know if that's how it works but she's family. Anyway, my auntie is having some problems. Some mental problems. She's apparently hiding from the family, leaves for days at a time, and my cousin doesn't really know how to help her. Says her mom doesn't want to get help. So I'm here just wondering what I can do to help out my cousin."

Floyd crossed his legs in a way that might be considered more feminine than masculine. He struck this pose with regularity and Tommy had the utmost respect for it. "They in the city?"

"Brandon."

"Never been. That's a tough deal. Want my suggestion? Ask some adults. They sometimes know how shit works."

Clinton walked into the classroom as the two boys spoke and Tommy regarded him with a friendly nod.

"We all have to take care of our mothers," Floyd said, swiveling his chair to greet Clinton. "Ain't that right, C?"

Clinton leaned the back of his thighs on a nearby desk; his eyes went large and suddenly reflective. "What are you talking about?"

"Big Weapon's cousin's mom is going through some shit."

"That sucks. Is everything okay?"

"It'll figure itself out somehow. We're working on it." Tommy offered an awkward thumbs-up.

Another group of students began pouring into the room and the three boys stopped talking and went to their next classes. They didn't have another conversation about Tommy's fake cousin and fake crazy auntie again. It was the law of the universe.

THE WOODEN BENCH IN the waiting area was covered in ancient markings, some older than others. Engraved in the pine were hearts, initials, figures like in the cliff paintings east of the lake. They ranged in their complexity from simple to intricate, and Tommy imagined that each design told a story about the artist—stories of boredom and anxiety disorders and struggles with childhood emotional neglect. Tommy wasn't one for vandalism, but he admired the confidence it took to believe one's work was worthy of immortality, or at least until the school bought a new bench. Am I next? he thought. He'd been waiting for the guidance counselor to swing open her door and call him into her office for ten minutes.

The secretary appeared sincerely apologetic about the wait, and each time she finished fielding an incoming call—"one moment please, transferring you now"—she tried to find something else to put Tommy's mind at ease. "So sorry about the long wait," she said, and with a proud smile added: "Have you seen our new student guidebook? You'll find a bunch of great stuff in there about all the new programs we've added this year." Tommy shook his head and reassured her again that the wait wasn't a problem. "Well, then," she said, rising from the big, blue exercise ball she'd been balancing on and pulling a copy of the guidebook off her desk and reaching across her wide welcome counter to hand it to Tommy.

"Thanks," he said.

"Don't mention it."

"Does that thing help?" Tommy pointed ahead with his chin.

"What thing?"

"The big ball you're sitting on."

"Sure does. I'm down four pounds!"

"That's good."

Tommy examined the guidebook, the cover of which featured a photo of a sleepy tiger glaring into the camera. "Doesn't it remind you of *National Geographic*?" the secretary said, poking her head above the counter for a brief moment. "Very realistic," Tommy replied quietly, admiring but also feeling sad for the majestic beast, who was clearly caged away in a zoo somewhere, lazy from captivity, homesick for its natural habitat. "Principal Goodstock took the picture himself while in Africa this summer," the secretary explained, never mind that tigers never lived in wild Africa, before returning to her exercise ball. The words "Tiger Pride," squeezed between quotation marks, shown in orange at the top of the cover, as if the words themselves had to be attributed to someone else. At the bottom of the cover, below the tiger, and also in quotes, were the words "A Thriving Community." As Tommy flipped through the guidebook he came across this adjective multiple times, a word he had seen before but never truly understood what it meant. Everything was supposedly *thriving*. Every student apparently wanted to *thrive*. Tommy noticed a dictionary on the table beside him and he grabbed it and looked up the word's definition: "To grow vigorously; to gain in wealth or possessions; to progress toward or realize a goal despite or because of circumstances—often used with *on*." According to Merriam-Webster, his quadriceps were thriving. But he wasn't so sure about the rest of him. He wasn't so sure that was thriving because he didn't have any goals, literal or otherwise.

Light from the greyness outside finally flooded through the guidance counselor's office door. "Tom-*ma*-hawk? Come on in," she said, emphasizing the *ma* in Tomahawk.

"Tommy is good."

"Good to know. I'm Trina. The new academic advisor."

The office contained a few unopened boxes, and the shelf behind her was mostly vacant, save for two framed bachelor's diplomas from the University of Winnipeg—one for arts and another for education. Four more years for that? he thought.

"Sit sit." She turned her attention to the computer monitor beside her and pulled the reading glasses down from her scalp to the front of her eyes. She wore a wide shawl that looked like it was designed by an Indigenous artist on the West Coast. "I was just going through your file. How's Sam? How's Olga? I hear your sister is quite the star."

He wondered if his mom's name was on there, and for an instant he was angry, angry that it wasn't. She was erased from his life. "They're good," he said. "Thriving."

She nodded, and appeared eager to hear more but Tommy looked away anxiously. "Well. It looks like you should be able to graduate, but you're missing a compulsory credit—grade eleven history. I'll enroll you into the course that's already started, so that you're all set to accept your diploma come June. Sound good?"

"Sounds good."

"How's everything else?"

"You know. Doing my best to thrive."

She smiled and leaned forward, elbows planted on a cluster of scattered papers. "As you should. Do you have a plan for next year? Have you given any thought about university? Your grades are good enough for U of M and U of W."

"I haven't really."

"Why's that."

"I'm not sure it's for me."

"Well. What's your favorite thing to do here at St. Croix?"

"I'm on the hockey team. I like playing hockey."

Trina leaned back in her chair and gently rocked back and forth. "That's good. But hockey doesn't last forever. Even professionals retire eventually. I heard we may not even be able to field a team next year." She paused and a look of concentration appeared on her face as she observed Tommy. "That must not feel good."

"Nope. I guess it sucks for the younger guys."

"So if you're not thinking about university next year. What else are you looking forward to?"

Suddenly Tommy felt like he was being coerced into deciding his future, or at least making one up for himself, there in a little room with a woman he'd only just met. His face and his throat tightened and he thought for a second about saying nothing, because he worried nothing would come out of his mouth but dead air. "It's my draft year." He gripped the arms of his chair like it were of the electric variety and these were his last words.

"That's good. But I wouldn't put all my eggs in one basket. The NHL doesn't call everyone. What about things other than hockey."

"I don't know."

Tommy knew it was a long shot. More like nearly impossible. He knew that for most of his life he and the game simply didn't get along, that it was an unhealthy, one-sided relationship. But despite all the chirps and ridicule, from teammates and friends alike, he still held out hope, hope that someone was up there in the bleachers watching him, seeing how hard he worked, willing to give him his shot. Because one shot was all he needed to prove everyone wrong.

When their meeting was over he walked out the door—not sure about college, not sure about himself, and doubly not sure if hockey would ever call him back.


KOKO FELL ASLEEP ON the couch watching a rerun of *Law & Order: Special Victims Unit*. Mohawk detective Chester Lake, played by local hero Adam Beach who wasn't Mohawk but Anishinaabe from a place called Dog Creek, cracked the case, identified the bad guys, and on cue, as the episode transitioned to mundane courtroom scenes and toned-down legal jargon, Koko was snoring. The light from the TV cast large shadows behind her.

Tommy found her like this when he came downstairs. He moved to the dining room and turned on the light and then turned on the computer. He listened to the machine's rhythmic hum and patiently waited until it felt right to proceed. Then he began to type.

Hi Mom,

It's nice to hear from you. I'm glad you're doing okay. Koko and Sam are good. Koko still watches Law & Order and Sam is killing it like always. School is good and hockey is also going okay but we're pretty terrible. Vancouver sounds nice, would like to visit one day. Looking forward to when you come out here too. If you ever need anything from us please let me know what number to reach you at and where I can find you.

P.S. Freedom babies. Interesting concept!

Tommy

Tommy read over the draft and hovered the mouse. He was confident that nothing in the email directly contradicted anything in Mom's original letter. He also felt sure that he didn't affirm any of the wild details she described, particularly the stuff about government surveillance. He read it over again, this time in a whisper. Then he pressed Send, logged out and shut down the computer. He turned off the dining room light and moved quietly into the living room to turn off the TV. The credits were rolling.

But something didn't feel right. Even before he received his mom's message something hadn't felt quite right. He was worried about the future, and about the Tigers and whatever would become of them. He was stricken by a profound disappointment but couldn't pinpoint the root. His quads maybe. His new body had been feeling increasingly worthless. He returned to the computer and booted it up and opened his email and started typing.

I need you back here.

And without thinking he clicked hard on Send and quickly shut down everything again, as if he was hiding evidence. He went upstairs and lay in bed. It was dark outside. It was probably still daylight in Vancouver. He fell asleep thinking about the mountains. He dreamed of avalanches.

## *clarissa walkman*

CLARISSA FOUND A LONE TABLE IN A LONELY SECTION OF THE MIL-
lennium Library, the biggest public library in the city. There were
windows all around. Outside it was grey and cold and that made
everything in the small clearing look grey as well. It was mid-
October. There were no bookshelves nearby, only a few soft chairs
with colorful ottomans perched near them. It looked like a place to
put your feet up and rest. To Clarissa the nook was the only appropriate area throughout the library to conduct an interview. She dragged
a chair over and placed it directly across from where she'd be sitting
at the table and then pulled out from her bag a small notepad, two
pens and a Sony recorder she'd gotten as a gift from her mother last
Christmas. She sipped a coffee that she'd let get too cold and dated
the page she'd scribble notes on and then texted Clinton:

*I'm here. Second floor. Sort of near the washroom.*

Clinton replied a couple minutes later:

*There in five.*

Clarissa didn't like to prepare questions, preferring to let the conversation flow naturally. And though her journalism education was
limited because St. Croix offered no such classes, she'd read enough
articles on the internet to know that this wasn't uncommon. The
consensus was that preparing too many questions might prevent
the interviewer from listening to what was being said. But she had
prepared five questions at a coffee place down the street. Each started
with *what, why* or *how,* because the internet also said open-ended
questions are best, and that this tactic would avoid yes-or-no answers.

Clarissa couldn't remember when she became interested in journalism. It wasn't the writing that interested her or the idea of it being a job that let you travel and go places and witness important events. She didn't like to admit that she didn't like her writing and that it was bad. Or almost bad. But not good. She wasn't sure how to end a sentence or begin the next one and as such her sentences were often wildly long and looked like paragraphs and when she read them aloud they took the breath out of her and not in a good way.

More than anything she was curious and liked to talk. Her mom told people she was chatty as a child, always needed to be heard and always wanted to be in the know of things. She needed to understand everything around her and why things were the way they were. After being curious she'd become angry, because the answers about her life and others around her didn't satisfy her. One article on the internet said journalists had to be impartial, that they couldn't be angry or driven by emotion or bias, and after reading that she wondered if maybe journalism wasn't for her, the same way some kids want to be pilots before they realize they're afraid of heights. But when she told her mother about it, the morning she'd unwrapped her Sony recorder, her mother said to her:

"That just means there isn't enough angry reporters."

When Clinton arrived, he was wearing the same outfit she'd seen him in at school: blue jeans faded around the knees and a plaid quilt jacket covering a red sweatshirt and dirty white sneakers and a beanie with the Tigers logo displayed just above his brow. He looked tired and anxious and had large bags under his eyes, and for a second this worried her. She wondered if this was her doing, in her role as reporter. She still wasn't used to making others uncomfortable.

"Hey!" she called out.

When he sat down, he took off the beanie and spent a long while combing his fingers through his hair and plucking debris and lint off his sweatshirt. After what felt like an unreasonably long time he said finally:

"How's it going?"

"I'm good."

"Good." Clinton hadn't made eye contact. Clarissa knew he was quiet and shy, and it made her uncomfortable as well and she decided to look away from him and around their empty section of the library.

"Well. Thanks for doing this, and for not changing your mind. Like I've said a hundred times already, I think this is an important story. What the league is doing to the Tigers is horrible. In my opinion, the school and the team should be doing more to get the story out there."

"I'm glad to help. Can't say I've ever been at the center of a 'splosive story like this."

She smiled. "That's the goal. Do you mind if I record?" She held up her Sony recorder.

"Go for it."

Clarissa pressed the red Record button on her device and then gripped her pen and, before speaking, straightened her back and cleared her throat.

"So," she began. "Just to give you a little bit of an idea what this'll look like. This will be your basic news article, maybe five or six hundred words, something around that range. But before we start can you just tell me your name, your nation, and where you're from. Or whatever you're comfortable with sharing."

"Full name?"

"That's right."

"Clinton Whiteway. One word. I'm Anishinaabe from the Pelican Lake First Nation."

"Perfect. Good. Got it." She jotted notes frantically, almost excitedly. She wanted to smile and to keep smiling continuously but believed it wouldn't be professional on her part. "How long have you been on the Tigers? Have you played the game long?"

"Two winless seasons before this one. I started playing pretty young. We haven't won in a long time, but I guess we do it because it's mostly fun. Not to be cheesy or anything. That's not to say we don't *want* to win games, but obviously we're not the most experienced group out there. Obviously."

Clarissa's expression became more intense. Now that the softballs were out of the way she could transition to something more serious, the whole reason why they were talking in the first place. It was a skill she had total command of, like turning a light switch on and off. It was also something she believed she was born with, that they were all born with in their neighborhood, where shit could be good one second and bad the next, the line between them brittle. "How do you feel about this being possibly the last season for the Tigers hockey team? Must be hard to swallow."

Clinton wasted no time answering. "It sucks. We feel as though we are being deliberately targeted for who we are. It's completely unfair."

"Has the league given a proper explanation?"

"None that we're satisfied with. I mean, I don't know much about the decision. You might want to get someone else to comment on this. But the idea is that many of the southern schools are forming their own league, leaving us out here hanging. They said travel distance was a big concern for them, or something like that. But the next closest school to us is twenty minutes down Main and they're included in this new league. So . . ."

"I see." Clarissa made a star in her notepad next to the barely legible words she took down regarding this new information, and then peeked over at her recorder and noted the time it was said for future reference.

"So . . . what's the team—your coaches, St. Croix—planning on doing about this? I assume they're going to fight it somehow."

"You'd have to ask them. They said they'd fight it, but they're trying not to start a whole war over it."

"So they don't piss off the league."

"Guess so."

"How do you feel about that approach?" She'd not prepared this question and she immediately felt as though it might come across as instigative.

"On one hand maybe it's smart, because if you're not white this game can be cruel, ruthless even. We all know that. On the other, I don't know. Fights give you at least a chance."

"But if the opponent is too strong."

"Then you're fucked." He laughed. Clarissa felt glad to make him laugh, or at the very least help set up the joke. "Don't use that. That's off the record."

She nodded. "So . . . what do you think it means for St. Croix to have a hockey team? Like, how big of a hole would that leave in our community if there wasn't one."

"Good question." Clinton paused and appeared to lack confidence for the first time since the interview began. "I've never known any Native kid who didn't play hockey, or at least try it once. It gives us a chance to do something outside of school. Keeps some of us out of trouble too, I guess. Keeps us out of places we don't want to be."

Clarissa raised her eyebrows and instantly regretted it because of how it might come across. "What do you mean by that? Places you don't want to be."

"Like maybe bad situations at home. Some of our players don't have it easy."

"What about for you?"

Clinton's face flushed and Clarissa noticed it, but it needed to be asked. "Me? Sure. Maybe. Hobbies are good for everyone."

There was a long silence in which neither of them looked at each other. Clinton was lost in thought. Clarissa reminded herself that silence, in an interview, was sometimes a good thing, because it allowed the subject to reflect on something they should have said and maybe will say amid the awkward void. Sun had broken through the clouds and rays cut through the windows. An older woman pushing a hamper with wheels full of books sat down on one of the nearby soft chairs and began peeling an orange. She eventually gave up trying to remove all the pith, tearing the orange in half.

"I guess it's good for the community too," Clinton said. "To have a hockey team. We want to make people proud. Clearly we haven't been doing that with winning, but maybe this will."

"What will?"

"Speaking about what's happening. Fighting for our place in this league."

"Right." She made another star in her notepad.

There was another long pause, longer than the previous one. This time the silence felt comfortable. Clarissa watched Clinton as he observed the woman eating her orange while she flipped through several of the books she had piled into her hamper. Juice from the orange dripped on the pages, and seeing this, Clinton appeared to be irritated.

"Where are you from by the way?" Clinton finally asked.

"Sorry?"

"You asked me earlier where I was from."

"Oh. It's just a thing reporters do before they start an interview."

"Why's that?" He smiled shyly.

"I suppose it's out of respect. We're not a monolithic people, like some believe. We're from all over, speak different languages, practice different traditions, think different things."

"I didn't mean to hijack the interview. Was just curious."

Clarissa felt her face get warm and it was now red. "Now I feel like I have to give an answer." She offered a laugh to let him know she wasn't serious.

"I'll show you my status card if you show me yours." Clinton laughed, and she smiled despite herself.

"I'm not status," she said. The words felt like revealing a dirty secret. "Not really sure why. My mom said she gave up trying to get it a long time ago."

Clinton nodded and looked at the woman again, now finished with her orange. Her sticky fingers blemishing the pages of various books. Clarissa, too, noticed that the woman turned pages loudly.

"I'm from nowhere. I'm from here. Ojibwe, Cree, Métis, Scottish. We got it all."

Clinton looked back at Clarissa. "What's it like being from here? Sorry. I mean, what's it like having grown up here?"

"Normal I guess. Normal to me. Some people call it an urban rez." She had forgotten that her recorder was still on and made another time stamp in her notepad before asking something she was genuinely curious about. "You're not from here, right? I'd heard something about your community being condemned. I don't mean to sound harsh."

"No, you're right. There had always been floods after the snow melts. Then when I was younger there was a melt that was really bad. Made it so we couldn't go back, and so my mom and brother and me came out here."

"That must've been hard."

"Yeah." He said this slowly and then smiled like he thought of something funny. "You know, when I was younger, on the rez, I used to only think white people and Native people existed in this country. Then you come out here and see every type of person there is pretty much."

Clarissa laughed. "Were you raised by wolves or what?"

They both laughed. "Don't underestimate the wolf. They're smart as shit. If humans died off they'd be in the mix to reign supreme. Fun fact for you."

"I'll be sure to note that you're a wolf enthusiast." Clarissa was enjoying the banter, but she could feel that she was losing control of the interview. It was a feeling she hated, and so a change in tone of voice was necessary; she needed her reporter voice. She'd used up all her prepared questions and now had to come up with something on the spot. "So . . . do you plan on ever returning to your rez? How possible is it at this point?"

"One day. Hopefully soon." Clinton's voice had changed to something more serious and deep as well, perhaps noticing the altered mood of their conversation. "Is any of this going to be helpful? This stuff about where I'm from."

"Definitely. It helps to understand you and your story." She glanced from her notepad to Clinton so seriously that he looked uncomfortable and so he quickly looked over to where the woman, now gone, had been sitting. "You're an honor roll student, aren't you? What are some of your favorite classes? What do you hope to do after you graduate?"

"Sure." He paused and gazed upward. "I'm a fan of the woodworking workshop. English too. As for the future, I don't have a clue. Being a carpenter sounds cool."

"Really? Carpenter. That's a noble profession." The sarcasm was transparent. Clarissa did not know what it was like to live without ambition, and she couldn't understand people who had no clue about where their lives were heading or what they wanted to do with them. "I heard you got the best score on the English exam last year."

"I didn't know that. Where did you find that out?"

"I asked around." This was true. The idea of being the best at something was one of the things she liked most about school, and if she wasn't at the top of the class then she wanted to know who was. She thought of it as a competition, which she believed could be said about most things in life, academic or not.

"I like writing."

"Have you ever thought about becoming a writer, then?"

"Sure I have. But I wouldn't even know where to begin or how to get started in that."

"You know," she said, with a big smile to suggest she was joking, "there's these things called computers. Failing that, there's this stuff called paper and these precious tools called pencils."

Clinton wasn't amused. "I don't mean that. I mean the business aspect of it I guess, like how writers even get their work on the shelves, how they even find people to turn their words into books."

"I think I have everything I need." Clarissa reached over the table to press the red button on her recorder, stopping the recording. "This was great. Thanks again for coming down here."

Clinton's face fell, disappointed by the abrupt finish. He half-nodded and glanced down at the table and then at his hands, watching Clarissa remove the device that had been between them.

"I think you should just write and see what comes out," Clarissa said. She could sense that their muscles had relaxed and the tone in both their voices had become less formal than they were when the recorder was there. "Don't worry about all that other stuff."

"You make it sound simple."

"Isn't it?"

"Seems like a fucking pain. I tried maybe once or twice and it's like I ran brain-first into a brick wall. Concussed."

"What's that thing sporty people like yourself always say? What is it? No pain no gain? There actually might be a bit of truth in it. When it comes to some things. Probably less so for head trauma."

"I don't think I'd describe myself as sporty. But yes. That is something our coach would say."

It occurred to Clarissa that she was doing something her mom told her was a horrible habit: telling others what they should do, like she knew better than they did. It was uncouth according to her mother. But she continued. "I read somewhere that writers need crazy experiences to be good writers. Maybe you need a near-death experience or something."

"Escaping a drowned rez not good enough?"

"Nope, that ain't it."

"How so?" Clinton appeared offended, but it became clear that he was only pretending. "Talking out of your ass."

"Did anyone die in this flood of yours?"

"We only die when we come to the city."

She hesitated an instant, conscious of his seriousness, but carried on. "Then that ain't it! It has to be worse than a harmless natural disaster." She questioned her usage of "harmless," whether it might be too much.

"So then what's a deadly experience in your book? I'm open to suggestions. How should I go about nearly killing myself for the sake of art?"

"Get beat up by some cops. Now that's something we'd be talking about for decades. Better yet, get beat up while protesting something. Remember Oka? We're still talking about it. Waneek Horn-Miller took a soldier's bayonet to the heart for her people, and lived to tell the tale."

"Are you suggesting I take a sword to the chest, try not to die, and then write about it?"

"Couldn't hurt. The stab wound, sure. That would suck. But on the other hand, your career would blossom." She forced a smile to convey she was mostly joking. "Why do you think journalists go to horrible places? It's not because they care or because they believe the world needs to know. It's because they're thinking two steps ahead, at book deals and the prizes they'll win. And the fame. So no. It's not because they care. Besides the news anchors you know who gets the most screen time?" She paused, wanting Clinton to guess the correct answer.

"Wait. They're not the only ones on-screen? I never watch the news."

"The fucking weatherman! The fucker who tells you whether or not you should wear a jacket when you go outside."

"Hold up. How would I be any different from these people if I went out and got stabbed just for the sake of being stabbed? To try and make a name for myself."

"Because you actually care." The tone in her voice when she said this surprised her. It was warm and calm. For someone so used to reacting to everything around her she rarely ever spoke this way to people other than her mother. "You being here. You care. Waneek gave a shit too, and that's why they tried to take out her heart with a bayonet."

Clinton nodded, as if to say he was unsure whether he was receiving a compliment. "Is the stabbing mandatory?"

"Yes." They laughed.

They were quiet for a long beat, and for the first time since they both sat down Clarissa felt the silence unbearable.

"I should probably get going. Again. This was great." Clinton appeared disappointed after she said this, and this made Clarissa feel good.

"Yeah. I should too."

She began packing all her things in her bag and pulled her coat from behind her chair and slipped her arms through each side. "You know, we're starting another movement. It's already happening. They're saying gatherings are being planned all over the country, and around the world. Blockades even. There's already been some round dances here in the city."

Clinton pulled his jacket over his lap and let it rest there like a blanket. "What are we protesting?"

"Everything. It goes beyond Bill C-45 even. This country is still trying to destroy us and everything that gives us life. You know, there's going to be a big gathering next month. The biggest round dance this city has ever seen. We'll be taking over Portage and Main. You should come with. I'm part of the group that's organizing."

"I'm not so sure . . ."

"Have you ever been to a rally before?"

"I'll be honest. I've never been much of a fist-in-the-air person."

"Exactly! You should come. We need all hands on deck. I can't promise you'll be stabbed, but who knows. You may get lucky."

"What should I wear?" Clarissa could tell he was serious.

"War paint, some feathers sticking out of your hair. If you're feeling deadly." She laughed hard at the thought of Clinton draped in chicken feathers and paint smeared across his face, beating a drum and shouting, Aho! every few minutes. "Dress warm. But also like you're trying to survive the apocalypse."

Clarissa stood up and went in for a hug. Clinton didn't pull away. She could feel the muscles on his back, the sturdiness of his torso, the broadness of his shoulders. He felt solid, planted in the earth, and she imagined all the labor he must've done in his past life, before the city, to acquire such country strength. She could tell he wasn't prepared to be hugged, because he had nearly fully extended his arm for a handshake before she had her arms around him. He was taller than her but not by much.

She was the first to leave. Clinton stayed behind to browse the library. He agreed to go to the Idle No More gathering at the end of the month.

Before Clarissa walked down the stairs to the ground level, she turned around and called out:

"Bring your asemaa!"

Clinton was puzzled by her request, and Clarissa knew, knew because she'd seen that face before on other people, that it was because he didn't know what "asemaa" meant. He just smiled and walked down the aisles, looking at books, and before long he was out of sight.

## *clinton whiteway*

ON MY FOUR-MONTH ANNIVERSARY AT THE HAVEN, JAKUB STOLE four pieces of heart-shaped bannock from the kitchen and told me to keep them in the dresser by my bed in a Tupperware. "You know the bannock's free, right?" I said. He looked at me all offended and said, "You'll thank me later." He was right, I knew he was right, but a part of me didn't want to believe that I'd been staying at the Haven for that long, because the bannock, when warm and fresh, was gone within minutes. Many of us took second, third or fourth helpings, and kept them somewhere in our rooms. But I didn't care much. I hated other people's bannock apart from Kelvin's, because his was never too dry, never like biting into a rock. He cracked the recipe as a child, got it just right, and thus no one else's could measure up. But I appreciated the gesture. Food was generally forbidden in our rooms because of mice and cockroaches and ants. It was worth the risk though. Jakub often warned that stress will make you hungrier than you ever thought you'd be, the stress of life. And we were all stressed.

I was surprised by how comfortable I'd been feeling at the Haven. It had been feeling more and more like a sort of home, but still a home you wouldn't mind leaving for good, and I couldn't remember anymore how my bed at home felt, where Kelvin lived.

The other kids became like weird friends, like distant relatives, and Kimmy and Eli were like mother and father. Some of us lost boys and girls, the ones who'd been around for a long time, even called them Mom and Dad, which Jakub diagnosed as a symptom of childhood trauma. I told him that I couldn't imagine calling Eli Dad and Kimmy Mom. "It's because they never had any real ma and pa, so the chemicals in their brains are telling 'em that's your ma and pa, even though y'all look nothing alike. Fucked up as it is, it's the truth," he said.

On Thursdays Jakub spent the entire afternoon and evening with a CFS support worker whom he described as his "big brother." They weren't even close to being siblings—Jakub wasn't shy to admit that he too was prone to chemical imbalances in the brain—but I got the sense, just by the way he spoke of this pseudo big brother of his, that he was too shy to say he adored him. After spending time, Jakub would arrive back at the Haven elated, eyes wide and pupils dilated, with stories of all the shops at The Forks, walks through Assiniboine Park and trips to the movie theater.

On the day he gave me four pieces of bannock, Jakub asked me, "Do you want to come out with me and Joey tomorrow? I'm sure he'd have no problem with it. He asks about my friends here all the time."

Jakub and I were friends. Apart from Tommy he had probably jumped the line to become my second-closest friend by virtue of sleeping next to me. He snored loud, so loud and violent that I was concerned about his health at times. My sleep was often terrible as a result. But I'd come to appreciate that he was there beside me. Just the fact of it. "Why not," I said. "I need to see what all the hype is."

THE NEXT DAY I skipped woodworking workshop for the first time in all my years at St. Croix to be back at the Haven by two-thirty and felt sad to be ending the streak but excited to learn that Joey would be taking Jakub and me to the movies. I told Mr. Geoffrey that I had an appointment with the dentist, that I would receive a crown despite my efforts to brush my teeth before bed and after lunch, that it would cost a lot of money and that my insurance would not cover it. He gave me a puzzled look and said, "Are you asking to borrow some pliers or something? They're over there. Just don't tell anyone." He pointed to a rack behind one of the big saws across the shop where various tools hang. "I won't," I said, and walked out of class.

Joey was thirty minutes late and arrived at three o'clock instead of two-thirty and during the time we waited in the lobby, rolling balls into the pockets of the pool table with our hands, Jakub kept going on about the zombie movie we were about to go see. Joey had a friend who worked at the fanciest movie theater in the city, somewhere down south, where the chairs were big and made of leather, and reclined for optimal comfort. This friend of his shared free movie passes with all his friends and family and Joey would be using these passes to get us into the movie.

Joey rolled up in front of the Haven in a white sedan that was strikingly clean. The word *KITNAGEEN* was decaled in big white letters at the top of the rear window.

Joey was younger than I expected, I would guess no older than thirty, which made sense as to why Jakub considered him something of a big brother. And this also reflected how Joey carried himself, because he was more concerned about the dirt on his wide, chrome rims and the person on the other end of his text conversation than about being late. Jakub didn't care. They bumped fists and referred to each other as "bro." I tried my best to hide my irritation by smiling big and shaking his hand. If I'd known he'd be running late I could have finished sanding the legs of the dining room table I was making in workshop. The inside of the car stank of something called Royal Pine, which dangled below the mirror in the shape of a fir tree. We were moving before Jakub and I had a chance to fasten our seat belts.

The movie was gross. Zombies leapt out of dark corners, smothering, spreading the virus. They moved together in large packs like hordes of mutilated insects. My chair was the only one of our three that didn't recline and for the inconvenience the manager gave us a free large popcorn. I tried to turn it down, saying I was comfortable, but Joey interjected to request that the popcorn have layered butter throughout the bag.

It was, though, a strangely thoughtful take on the apocalypse. It reflected all our fears—of famines and floods and military oppression. Things people like me already experience. Humans were more dangerous than the zombies—they were bandits and flesh-hungry cannibals—because deep down, no matter what we believe, we're all just beasts doing whatever we can to survive. Society, with all its laws, is just a temporary cage, rusting, ready to break.

The characters never said what they truly wanted to say to each other. It wasn't until the final act, that do-or-die moment, that they acted with urgency. The truth came out. The unlikely heroes saved the day—it's always those people who grow the most in stories, who learn to act out in ways that defy their DNA. They showed up when no one, not even themselves, expected them to, when all hope seemed lost. They gave their lives for it, for humanity. And they made the difference. A vaccine was eventually discovered, spreading hope instead of fear across the land. Joey roared and exclaimed at the movie's jumpy moments, and when it was over he stood up and clapped as the credits scrolled. Jakub spent nearly all the film covering his eyes with his sweatshirt. When it was over, we applauded with Joey, howling together in an empty theater.

The movie was a call to action. *Don't be a bystander. Face your fears.* I left the auditorium wanting to be someone else, someone like the white man on-screen. Except Anishinaabe. The Indian version. Just once in my life I wanted the chance to do the brave, big thing.

Joey ushered Jakub and me over to the arcade. At the sight of all the flashing lights Jakub caught a second wind after a torturous two-hour roller coaster, bopping around on his toes like a boxer.

"Wait here," Joey said. "Look at the games. I'll just be a minute."

I watched Joey as he lumbered over to one of the tables and chairs near a concession stand selling frozen yogurt and he sat down beside a man who I assumed to be his friend. The friend dressed differently than the other employees. Instead of a collared blue shirt with lighter blue patterns along the sides and a similarly designed cap, this friend of his wore a cheap, wrinkled business suit, faintly pinstriped, that I took to mean he held a position of power at the theater over the kids scooping popcorn into paper bags. They talked for a long time, longer than just a minute, and bent over in laughter.

I was staring. Mom always told me not to stare, said it was a rude thing to do and that people might think I'm looking to steal something. And when I made to move, I felt the resistance from the sticky floors, as if my feet were suction cups, and this, combined with Joey wasting our time, made me irritated.

Jakub hailed me, motioning for me to come over to the air hockey table. He stood on the Team USA side and I on the Team Canada side. We had no money to drop into the machine to release the plastic puck and blow air through the holes, so we each held a paddle and pretended there was a puck between us. Jakub claimed he scored after I imagined I did, to tie it up. We went into OT, tied at five goals apiece, and after some back and forth, swinging at nothing but air, Jakub asked me:

"Can I win it?"

"Sure," I said. "Thanks for asking." I meant it.

Jakub darted from side to side, as if he were making big saves, screaming so loud with each return that I had to look around just to see who would be staring at us and there was no one, the theater was nearly empty. Joey was still talking with his friend. Then Jakub whipped his arm back and shot it forward, and as the imaginary puck slid past into the pocket, I let my head hang low and pretended to dwell over an agonizing defeat.

"Tigers win! Tigers win! Tigers win!" Jakub shouted, as he ran around the table, arms high.

I looked around again to see who was watching and could see Joey approaching us, stopping about halfway from where he was sitting. He put a finger to his mouth and like an angry father he exhaled a big "Shhh!" and then turned around to be with his friend.

Jakub and I looked at each other and laughed, and then vacated the air hockey table to sit in the chairs of a car racing game.

"Does he always leave you alone like this?" I asked.

"Sometimes. He's got a lot of friends." He shifted the gears and turned the wheel even though nothing was happening on the screen, just a request for four tokens to be deposited in the slots below.

"Doesn't it bother you? Is he always late for shit?"

"You're still hung up on that? He's going to make up for it. I think he said we're going for ice cream after this. It's all good."

After about ten minutes of pretending to drive a race car Joey appeared, a hand on the shoulder of both our racing chairs.

"Shall we bust a move? You bros ready?"

Jakub and I jumped out of our chairs and walked with Joey out the door. I could see why Jakub was infatuated with this man. He had a charm to him, and perhaps that was one of the requirements for his job. Make others like you. He was nothing like Kelvin, he knew how to move through the world, and he did so with confidence, confidence that came from humor. Humor was his trick. He constantly made silly jokes. I wondered if he was always this funny and cool, even at home, when he put his feet up and turned on the TV. Or was it only for when he left the house. He seemed to never grow tired.

The ice cream shop was next to the Red River and beside it was an old rail bridge that appeared to be no longer in use and overgrown with weeds. Joey parked the car in a gravel parking lot and we walked over to the order window.

"What do you bros want? It's on me."

Jakub's eyes went big and so did mine. I wasn't sure whether Joey knew we had no money or not and during the drive over here I wondered whether we'd be resigned to watching other people enjoying ice cream the same way we watched others play the games at the theater's arcade.

"I told you!" Jakub said, turning to me all excited. "Thanks, bro. You know Clinton here just celebrated his four-month anniversary at the shelter yesterday."

Joey looked over at me. It was a look of surprise, if not pity. I was embarrassed, because it wasn't exactly worthy of celebration, but only slightly, because even though I told no one at school I was at the Haven I no longer felt weird about it, and if someone found out tomorrow, I wouldn't care. I thank Jakub for that. I could tell Joey wasn't sure what to say and he made a couple quick sounds to suggest he might begin a sentence, and then he finally said:

"That's . . . that's nice to hear." He swiftly returned his attention to the expansive menu above the window.

"I'll take that first one. At the top there." Jakub pointed up at the menu. It was the first item on the running list.

"I'll have a Swirl Cone," I said. I scanned the menu one more time to make sure I was content with my choice and I was. "Thanks, Joey."

"No worries at all, my man." Joey turned to the woman in the window to give our order. "I'll have the Epic Banana Split, Cookie Monster and a Swirl Cone."

"That'll be twenty-two seventy-five."

"Do you take card?"

"Cash only."

Joey opened up his wallet and pulled out two bills and handed them through the narrow gap in the window and said:

"I'll get my receipt as well." The woman in the window obliged.

When our order was ready, we each took our ice cream and walked across the bridge. It was getting cold, the sun was setting below the neighborhood houses, reflecting off the murky water below us. For early November it was mild. Jakub walked ahead of Joey and me and for the first time all evening he was quiet and noticeably deflated. I was the only one to finish my treat. Jakub got through about half of his Cookie Monster before it was a sugary pool in his bowl. Joey tossed his banana split in the river, the banana was too bruised for his liking and he admired the splash it made. Jakub, to my surprise, didn't find joy in this.

The car ride back to the Haven was also quiet. Jakub rested his head against the window and Joey played no music, but still tapped his index fingers on the steering wheel as if he were playing drums, like there was a song playing in his head.

"Did you bros have a good time?" He said this looking at Jakub, who didn't look back. He went on looking out the window.

Jakub said nothing. I decided that I needed to intervene. "I had a great time. Thanks again."

After this it was quiet again. We were driving down Main and I could tell we were close to the Haven. There were Native people everywhere, the only people out there, walking lonely and staggered along the sidewalks. It was like they were the only ones that went anywhere on their feet, or maybe it was because none of them had cars to take them places. I wondered if that would be me in the future. I wondered if I'd one day own a car.

"Why do you always keep receipts?" Jakub said sharply through the silence. He removed his head from the window but didn't look at Joey.

Joey continued staring ahead at the road. "Just something our bosses tell us to do."

"Does that mean you're not my friend?"

Joey's face was saturated in the stoplight's red glow. "Of course we're friends. Why would you say something like that?"

Jakub didn't say anything further, and neither did Joey. A few minutes later we were in front of the Haven and Joey reached back toward me and we bumped fists. He then turned to Jakub and said,

"You okay?" and Jakub said, "We're good" and they each offered a fist. But I could see something was still wrong. Jakub didn't talk for the rest of the evening, and during dinner he didn't eat much.

Back in our room after dinner we lay in our beds. The room was dark but objects around the room were still partially visible. Jakub liked having the curtain open, because the streetlamp just outside our only window cast shards of orange light into the room, but it wasn't enough to prevent you from falling asleep.

"You know," he said in a steady voice. "I never had a brother. I don't even have much of a family. You might be my only friend. We're friends, right?"

"Sure we are," I said, questioning whether this sounded sincere enough.

"Good."

I could hear him turn over. He usually slept facing the wall. I turned over too.

Jakub was never around again on Thursday evenings. He'd leave the Haven before noon and return after dinner. Some of the other kids said that for a while Joey kept showing up, looking for Jakub, asking when he'd be back, but then eventually he stopped coming by. I guess he stopped caring, didn't believe in their friendship after all. I could never work up the courage to ask Jakub why he cut ties with the man.

He eventually left the Haven for good, a month and a couple weeks after our trip to the movies. I saw him at breakfast, he polished his plate. He hugged me before I left for school, which wasn't unusual because we occasionally shared a hug, and told me he wished for us Tigers to win the game we had that night but we didn't. And when I came back home he was gone.

## *errol whitecloud sinclair*

### OCTOBER 4, 2011

There was a moment, Kelvin, after you were born, when I thought about running away. Go somewhere warm maybe, someplace where your little eyes could never see me. I'd watched this movie about a guy who gets caught up with the law and he escapes to Mexico and lives on a small boat where nobody can find him. I thought maybe that's what I'd do after your mother had you. But I didn't have a boat and back then I couldn't tell you where Mexico was.

I was just a boy, you see, barely sixteen, barely old enough to hold a baby let alone father one of my own. I was around during your early years. Your mom and I tried to be a couple, even had your little brother, but it didn't work out. We fought and yelled, often with you around to witness it, and we did this a lot, up until I left. You could walk and talk and were at that age where you could remember and think for yourself when I left. You could even skate. I remember your mom and I teaching you how to skate using a chair at the old rink, before it burned down. Do you remember the rink? How cold it was in the winter, colder than outside even. You held on for your life as I pulled you across the ice and you fell down maybe seven times at most before you were gliding and striding on your own, all on your first day. These rinks in the city just don't compare. On the rez you could skate any time and any day and as long as you wanted. Can't do that out here.

I wish I could say that we had some sort of special goodbye, but there was nothing of the sort. The last thing I saw you doing was playing with action figures in front of the TV. It was daytime. *Jeop-*

*ardy!* was on mute. You were wearing that pinstriped baseball shirt we'd picked out at Giant Tiger that time we'd driven the ice road to the city to go to the movies and eat fried chicken. You made punching sounds with your toys and screamed with joy, and I remember feeling happy watching you play, and I remember, just as the *Jeopardy!* credits were rolling, you looked at me in this serious way and I believed you knew. You saw me for who I was. For what I was. I look back on this often. You were too young to understand what was happening or what was to come, but there you were, like a young boy version of your mom all steady and hurting me with just a simple look, asking me to explain myself.

I remember the moment I walked out the door, too. It was at night, five to three, your mother was asleep, and I was picked up by someone along the road and let off at your koko and shoomis's house, my mom and dad's. My uncles were there, as they always were. I sat next to them around the table and I recall noticing their sour stench for the first time since I was a young boy, about the age you were then. I was surprised because I thought I'd gotten used to it after all those years of coming home to them around the table with your koko and shoomis. And we drank, all of us, Mom and Dad too. And I forgot about everything that happened to me in the years before, or tried to.

Your mom came around a lot back then, asking for my help. She didn't want money, she was always too proud to ask for anything financial. She didn't care about presents on Christmas or twenty bucks for Pampers, never anything like that. She never once tried to convince me to come back, because she was too proud for that, too. After all the times I walked out on her—this wasn't the first time, though it would be the last—she'd never asked me to come back. Nope. The help she wanted was purely physical. *Take the kids for the weekend. Have them for the evening. Pick them up from Head Start.* That sort of thing.

"Have you been drinking?" she'd say.

She said this a lot back then. My answer was usually, if not always, a lie.

Eventually I got so sick of it all. The lying. Seeing your mother around and then lying my way out of doing things for you boys. So

I decided to leave, and I did so well before I learned that the whole place was being evacuated. I spent some years on another rez shacking up with another woman before she showed me the door. I spent a few more years on a small piece of land out in the country with a white woman who inherited a big old house from her parents. Her name was Debbie and she was the last person I was with before I made my way to the city. Debbie didn't like me much, I'm pretty sure about that. She didn't like being seen with me in town, as I was not only jobless but looked like it. But I think she needed me, at least for a little while. She wanted to maintain the land she'd inherited, build a life out there in the middle of nowhere, and she needed a man's help and I served and accepted that role for a time. I mowed the lawn, whacked the weeds, planted spruce seedlings to eventually shield the house from prairie wind and made a big garden for growing potatoes and carrots and when they were ready to harvest we picked and cleaned and ate them together. I think about those days a lot. It was one of the only times in my life where I sat and waited for anything. I liked watching them grow. I wish I'd done the same for you.

## clarissa walkman

THE SKY WAS BLUE AND HOLY. WARM FOR A SUNDAY IN NOVEMBER. She pressed browned leaves into the ground on her way to the bus stop and watched them float from their branches on the ride. She got off early, wanted to walk the rest of the way and took off her scarf when she became too warm. She watched clouds drift behind tall buildings and then come out the other side different, altered by the breeze, never the same. Geese departed the city in formation. When she was small, she thought they migrated to Africa, somewhere warm and humid, and then returned for the city's dry seasons. In fact, she still doesn't know where they go. As she got closer to Portage and Main, she found herself alongside more and more people, each of them heading to the same place.

The gatherers had already stopped traffic by the time she arrived. Some drivers honked, frustrated by the disruption to their commute. Others went around, three-point-turned, and searched for another way.

Overlooking the gathering were some of the city's tallest buildings. The intersection, a perfect circle, was split down the middle by sunlight, one half in the shadow of bankers and businessmen and the other blessed in a golden aura. She stood in the shade but soon they were all glowing.

She found Clinton and they hugged. It felt more natural than their last hug. They didn't talk much. She didn't feel like talking. It was as if her heart was talking, saying something to her that she couldn't quite hear, but she understood the spirit of the message.

The whole crowd converged to the steps of an old building with a grand façade, its towering columns like something out of ancient Roman times.

A woman stepped atop a concrete perch, megaphone in hand. She glowed. Defiant of shadows. She began, in her language. Calling White Thunderbird. Wolf Clan. Treaty to some faraway First Nation with a funny name that only elders found funny, but the hearty laugh of an elder had the effect of making others laugh, too. Clarissa knew her as Cindy Birch.

"I woke up this morning to a beautiful gift," Cindy blared. "You see, from the balcony of my home I have the most amazing view of the Assiniboine River and Red River, and where they meet. The waters move, never stop. They bring life with them, like slithering veins in the earth. And hope, hope for a better future. Me, too, I feel hope when I look upon those rivers each morning."

She paused for a second and the crowd howled and drums vibrated, sending shivers down Clarissa's spine.

"We want to thank everyone for coming and being here." She raised a fist in the air. "Canada is not a country!" She punched the air. "Canada is not a country. The Creator put us here as the original keepers of this land. And as long as the grasses grow and the rivers flow we will rise up and fight for our rights, for our rightful place as First Peoples, as the Creator intended us to be. This is our home. Our ancestors were born and fought and died here. They are with us here today, watching, looking down on us. I feel their strength. We will stand. We will fight. We will move forward, together. And we will not be idle no more!"

The crowd, thicker than before Cindy started preaching, erupted. Drums, dozens of them, boomed from every direction.

Clarissa felt like telling Clinton to walk up there and grab the megaphone and say something about the Tigers and what was being done to them. But she knew he wouldn't, and what would be the point of suggesting something when the outcome was obvious. Her heart was telling her no.

Multiple police cars arrived, lights flashing. Someone, a rambunctious man, shouting obscenities at a young officer, was taken down and arrested while bystanders hurled insults and pleas for mercy. Others paid them no mind.

When the crowd was ready Clarissa held Clinton's hand in hers. She felt his calluses against her palm, and she assumed them to be from his woodworking class. He admitted to her at school that he thought about becoming a carpenter. He wanted to build a home, rebuild *his* home, back home, on the rez. It was an idea that had clung to him for so long that he was now convinced it meant something. Pleading its case ever since he moved out of the Days Inn.

On her right she held the hand of an elder named Mars. Beside Mars was Big Wayne Monias, and beside Big Wayne was his nephew Chip, and beside Chip was eleven-year-old Brontë Williams, and beside Brontë was her mom Tina Williams, and beside Tina was Dennis from the gas bar, and beside Dennis was his best friend Monica, also from the gas bar, and beside Monica was a handsome boy named Skylar, and beside Skylar was a hulking boy named Todd, and beside Todd was a former soldier named Audrey, who picked up trash and needles around their neighborhood in her spare time, and beside Audrey was her mom Clarice. On the other side of Clinton was a female classmate named Prairie Jack, who clung to him after spotting him in the crowd, and beside Prairie Jack was her friend Jade Iron Standing, and beside Jade was an elder named Quill, and beside Quill was her granddaughter Kira Parenteau, and beside Kira was a local organizer named Jeremy, and beside Jeremy was his pregnant wife, Nancy, due any day now, and beside Nancy was a guy who liked to call himself Chief Lightning Bolt, even though he was chief of nothing and wasn't from anywhere, and beside Chief Lightning Bolt was Nenookaasi Carpenter, and beside Nenookaasi was Audrey's mom Clarice, who stood directly across from Clarissa.

Together they made a circle. Hands linked. More circles, made up of other people and hands, formed around them, as round as the bright sun. In the middle of them all, the pupil of an eye, were the drummers and singers, loud as can be.

Clarissa felt a gentle pull from Mars and she followed it, shuffling her feet to the beat, and she raised her arms up and down to the rhythm, but somehow her limbs felt slack, as if the movements required no energy on her part.

After the first rotation of their circle she looked at Clinton. He blinked hard several times trying to shake away the sunlight that reflected off the glass buildings. His face was empty at first, but then a smile bloomed and she felt his grip tighten. She was glad to see him enjoying himself. She didn't speak. Neither did he.

She scanned other faces around her: all joyous, all faces of celebration. Clarissa started to cry. At one point a pair of hands separated and then reconnected with those of another circle, braiding the dancers together, taking them to new parts of the intersection. She felt like liquid, like water.

Her heartbeat slowed and she relaxed more deeply, an order from the heart itself. For a moment she forgot about the future and school and the chemistry test the next morning, and she just danced, round and round.

## *tomahawk shields*

TOMMY FELT LIKE A KID WHO RETURNED FOR GRADE THIRTEEN IN his grade eleven history class. He felt old; embarrassed to be the oldest one. His presence there, at the back of the class, said something about him: that he'd made some sort of grand fuckup along the way. Worse than that, he didn't know any of the other students in the class. He'd seen some of them around, walked past them in the halls, walked similar paths home after school, but other than that none of them were friends or friends of friends or played hockey. They were strangers.

Ms. Damphousse was also a stranger, new to St. Croix. She struck Tommy as an elegant and fancy Frenchwoman. On the first day of class she showed up wearing a Canada Goose coat that nearly touched her ankles and over the course of the semester Tommy and others counted at least three other Canada Goose coats in rotation. And to Tommy nothing else communicated such high degrees of wealth and status than the small fortune it took to wear another animal's pelt for warmth. There was more: she drove a BMW sport utility always clean and shiny, the world caught in its reflection. There were rumors that Ms. Damphousse had a shady past, as if this explained why she was posted in the inner city. Either she slept with a student at a prestigious private school that previously employed her or she had connections to the Montreal mob and St. Croix hired her anyway. Tommy hadn't ruled out any possibilities.

On the first day of class, Ms. Damphousse, wearing a red merino turtleneck and flared checkered pants the color of mustard, said, "Call me Josée." Tommy did so without hesitation.

Tommy didn't know much about Canadian history and so he looked forward to learning something, but at St. Croix all one could do was hope. Sam always said that Sir John A. Macdonald was a one-man apocalypse. And as for his cronies, Duncan Campbell Scott and the like, they were the atomic bombs.

MS. DAMPHOUSSE WAS A SURPRISE that Tommy didn't see coming. Despite the white savior complex that Sam pinned on the new teacher, it was undeniable that Ms. Damphousse knew her stuff, and *wanted* to work at St. Croix. Rumor had it she had a PhD in colonial history and wrote her dissertation on the shattered pedagogical and familial structures of Indigenous peoples and instead of finding work in the academy found God instead, who told her to wrap her angel wings around some brown kids in the hood. Or she was in the mob. Tommy hadn't decided yet.

In late November, Tommy learned about the land on which he lived for the first time in his life. The city, Ms. Damphousse said, falls within Treaty No. 1 Territory—the lands of the Anishinaabe, Ininew, Oji-Cree, Dene and Dakota, and is the birthplace and homeland of the Métis Nation. The desks in the classroom were arranged in a semicircle, leaving an open space in the center of the room. When Ms. Damphousse walked in that morning she dropped a big stack of papers on Sage's desk and told her to pass the pages down. The packages each of them received were thick and stapled and full of old words he couldn't understand. He wondered whether human intelligence over the years had advanced or regressed.

"Everyone," Ms. Damphousse said once all her pupils got their pages. "Turn to page five for me. This is the actual text of Treaty 1, the lands on which we all live and learn and breathe." She paused to glance around the room and Tommy felt her gaze like a burn and quickly shuddered in his chair and looked away. "Tomahawk. Would you read us this first section."

He sighed and cleared his throat. "Okay. No problem, Ms. Damp-housse."

"Please. Please call me Josée."

He nodded. And then he read, read loud.

The Chippewa and Swampy Cree Tribes of Indians and all the other Indians inhabiting the district hereinafter described and defined do hereby cede, release, surrender and yield up to Her Majesty the Queen and successors forever all the lands included within the following limits, that is to say: Beginning at the international boundary line near its junction with the Lake of the Woods, at a point due north from the centre of Roseau Lake; thence to run due north to the centre of Roseau Lake; thence northward to the centre of White Mouth Lake, otherwise called White Mud Lake; thence by the middle of the lake and the middle of the river issuing therefrom to the mouth thereof in Winnipeg River; thence by the Winnipeg River to its mouth; thence westwardly, including all the islands near the south end of the lake, across the lake to the mouth of Drunken River; thence westwardly to a point on Lake Manitoba half-way between Oak Point and the mouth of Swan Creek; thence across Lake Manitoba in a line due west to its western shore; thence in a straight line to the crossing of the rapids on the Assiniboine; thence due south to the international boundary line; and thence eastwardly by the said line to the place of beginning. To have and to hold the same to Her said Majesty the Queen and Her successors forever; and Her Majesty the Queen hereby agrees and undertakes to lay aside and reserve for the sole and exclusive use of the Indians the following tracts of land, that is to say: For the use of the Indians belonging to the band of which Henry Prince, otherwise called Mis-koo-ke-new is the Chief, so much of land on both sides of the Red River, beginning at the south line of St. Peter's Parish, as will furnish one hundred and sixty acres for each family of five, or in that proportion for larger or smaller families; and for the use of the Indians of whom Na-sha-ke-penais, Na-na-wa-nanaw, Ke-we-tayash and Wa-ko-wush are the Chiefs, so much land on the Roseau River as will furnish one hundred and sixty acres for each family of five, or in that proportion for larger or smaller families, beginning from the mouth of the river; and for the use of the Indians of which Ka-ke-ka-penais is the Chief, so much land on the Winnipeg River above Fort Alexander as will furnish one hundred and sixty acres for each family of five, or in that proportion for larger or smaller families, beginning at a distance of a mile or thereabout above the Fort; and for the use of the Indians of whom Oo-za-we-kwun is Chief, so much land on the south and east side of the Assiniboine, about twenty miles above the Portage, as will furnish one hundred and sixty acres for each family of five, or in that proportion for larger or smaller families, reserving also a further tract enclosing said reserve to comprise an equivalent to twenty-five square miles of equal breadth, to be laid out round the reserve, it being understood, however, that if, at the date of the execution of this treaty, there are any settlers within the bounds of any lands reserved by any band, Her Majesty reserves the right to deal with such settlers as She shall deem just, so as not to diminish the extent of land allotted to the Indians.

THE FIRST TREATY WAS an agreement between Indigenous peoples and Queen Victoria, the monarch of Canada, to allow Canadians and their government the pursuit of settlement and the extraction of natural resources. It was negotiated at a place called Lower Fort Garry, now the city's downtown, beginning on July 27, 1871, and signed on August 3 of that year. Indians showed up at the door of Fort Garry, set up camp: men, women, children, a thousand in all, to witness what would come of their lands. Sir Adams George Archibald, one of the negotiators for the Crown, a Father of Confederation, the first Lieutenant-Governor of Manitoba, called the Queen "mother" and seemed to imply, over eight days of tense talks, that the Queen would now be the mother of Indians. Tommy scoffed. He kept flipping after Ms. Damphousse took over and was now talking, saying things he didn't understand. "The audacity," he mumbled to himself, a word new to his vocabulary.

"Your Great Mother, therefore, will lay aside for you 'lots' of land to be used by you and your children forever. She will not allow the white men to intrude upon these lots. She will make rules to keep them for you, so that as long as the sun shall shine, there shall be no

Indian who has not a place that he can call his home," Archibald was reported as saying.

How did they even communicate? he wondered. Was it like a game of charades? Did they sit around a fire and draw shapes on paper and contort their bodies in weird ways to get the message across? It made no sense to him. But he came to learn that it was via a Métis man named James McKay. The Métis. It's always the Métis. The fucking Métis. He hated playing against the punks down at Collège Louis-Riel.

He looked up at Ms. Damphousse, who was making a point of saying that some of these Indians were given whiskey at the signing of some of these numbered treaties in order to get them to accept less favorable deals, like chicks preyed on at a pub or frat party. He scoffed again. Scoffed at all of it, the same way Archibald scoffed at the offers of Indians, saying, "The Indians seem to have false ideas of the meaning of a reserve. They have been led to suppose that large tracts of ground were to be set aside for them as hunting grounds, including timber lands, of which they might sell the wood as if they were proprietors of the soil."

He came to learn that each of the signatories on the side of the Indians got something called a buggy, except for Yellow Quill. The braves and councillors of each chief also got a buggy, except for the squad behind Yellow Quill. What the fuck did they have against Yellow Quill? he wondered. Each chief also received a cow and a sow, and "in lieu of a yoke of oxen," each reserve received a bull, as well as a boar. But these animals weren't *theirs* according to the fine print: "these animals and their issue to be Government property, but to be allowed for the use of the Indians, under the superintendence and control of the Indian Commissioner."

It was a hustle. That's all Tommy could think. That was his takeaway. Treaty Day was just a day a few Anishinaabe and Muskegon Cree Indians got conned by a few Englishmen. Their names: Red Eagle (Mis-koo-ke-new, or Henry Prince); Bird For Ever (Ka-ke-ka-penais, or William Pennefather); Flying Down Bird (Na-sha-ke-penais); Centre of Bird's Tail (Na-na-wa-nanan); Flying Round (Ke-we-tay-ash); Whip-poor-will (Wa-ko-wush); and lest we forget, our boy Yellow Quill (Os-za-we-kwun), the man without a buggy. The other names: Sir Adams George Archibald; Major A. G. Irvine; Abraham Cowley; Donald Gunn; Thomas Howard; Henry Cochrane; James McArrister; Hugh McArrister; E. Alice Archibald; Henri Bouthillier; Indian Commissioner Wemyss M. Simpson. Perhaps they were drunk also, Tommy thought.

Before class ended, Ms. Damphousse said the two sides surely had a completely different understanding of what a treaty meant, what land ownership meant, what the concept of "surrender" meant. The white side broke the treaty before the ink even dried, and left it to the courts to decipher what exactly it all meant over the next century and some change. The Indian side believed they were cutting a deal in good faith. That in the end they would retain their autonomy, sovereign nations within a sovereign state, that the two sides would coexist peacefully, without genocide, and that the treaty would be everlasting: "As long as the sun shines, the grass grows and the river flows."

At the end of class Tommy had a headache. He pinched the bridge of his nose. He couldn't remember the last time he tried so hard to understand something whose meaning evaded him. Why couldn't all this damage be fixed? he wondered. Things that are broke can be fixed, unless someone wants them to stay broken. Before this day he never knew what a treaty even was. It was common to hear someone boastfully say, "I'm treaty," which just meant they had a card in their pocket with their face on it that said they were Indian. But he now realized they meant more than that. More than the five bucks they got every year from the federal government.

As everyone ruffled their papers and stuffed them into their bags, Ms. Damphousse said they would be focusing much of their energy on treaties until the end of term, and that they would be required to deliver a presentation on "what it meant to be a treaty person." This excited Tommy. He'd thought long and hard about what it meant to live in the city, why there was something inside him that constantly begged to be heard, to say he was doing something wrong by being born here and living his life here and knowing no other way to live but here. But it was Indigenous land after all, shared land, but still theirs. It was treaty land. A treaty city.

Tommy thought to himself: I may not be treaty, but I am a treaty person on treaty land and therefore I belong.

TOMMY ARRIVED ON THE University of Manitoba campus at nine a.m. Sam valued sleep, and refused to drive him to campus because she would get less than eight hours. Tommy suggested she try going to bed earlier. She refused. She didn't need to be on campus until the afternoon, when his official campus tour would be over, and when she promised to meet him for lunch to give him the "Neechi Tour," as she called it. He reluctantly agreed, even though she'd previously agreed to drive him when he first told her, weeks ago. Sam was stubborn, smart, but stubborn. But admitting she was stubborn also meant admitting he was stubborn, even he could see the similarities. "So fucking stubborn," he mumbled after she rejected his request for a ride. She responded, even though she heard clearly what was said, "What was that?"

This was a day earlier, and Koko didn't help his case.

"Koko, Sam won't drive me," he pleaded.

She didn't look up from reading *The Sun,* the Sunshine Girl section hiding somewhere in his room under three articles of clothing for maximum privacy. "Boy, it's her car. Asemaa's a grown woman," she said. "It's out of my hands. Like page fifty-eight of this paper. Missing, once again. Strange how that happens so often."

His face flushed, and just like that the fight was over. He went into the dining room and purged the belly of a goose piggy bank that sat on the counter of a china cabinet for next day's bus fare.

THE CITY BUS, AS Koko liked to say, was like your typical member of band council. Ineffective, never on time, costing you more money every couple years. Her jokes tended to fuse her gripes with rez leadership with her list of grievances regarding local city planning into one large dissatisfaction. Tommy was embarrassed by how funny he found them, though he didn't quite fully understand the references. If there was one thing that he and everyone else that looked like him had in common, it's that they enjoyed laughing about their problems when they were the ones telling the joke.

He would need to travel the length of the city. At seven in the morning he boarded the thirty-eight and landed at The Forks half an hour later. The BLUE bus to University of Manitoba idled a short walk from his stop, and when he got there a pack of young bookish people huddled around or near the glass shelter to protect themselves from the wind. There were perhaps thirty in total. Their numbers combined with their ages made Tommy feel insecure. They looked far too big and mature to be able to fit inside the bus. But when the driver returned and made himself comfortable in his chair, a process that seemed to never end, Tommy was easily able to find an open seat. He watched the city drift by all greys, blues and browns. When the bus crossed the bridge over the Red River he paid closer attention to the changing environment: the bigger houses, the cleaner streets, the fancier cars and the whiter people. He knew nothing about the southern neighborhoods of the city other than that's where richer people lived, and that's where the university was. He wasn't sure of the statistics, for all he knew he was wrong, but he was pretty sure nobody like him lived out here, they were only visitors made to feel welcome.

The road into campus was lined with homes with big yards, and he wondered what it would have been like to grow up in one, so close to so much knowledge and information. In this daydream he was white, as were his mom and dad and two sisters and dog, because it was the only way it made sense. In the summers they lived in a cabin by a sparkling lake somewhere where only other white people lived, and in the winters, they vacationed in Costa Rica or Mexico and complained about the high mounds of snow when they came back to the city. I'd be smarter than Sam, he thought. Deadly smart.

The bus stopped in front of the quad, which he learned was basically a park with sidewalks that took you around campus. He wasn't sure what he'd been expecting. When everyone exited the bus they sped up, like they were late for something important and they were just as important as where they were headed. For nearly fifteen minutes he walked around aimlessly, observing the old buildings and manicured bushes and gardens and cobbled paths. It was beautiful, something out of a movie. The students walked with purpose, spoke as if they knew all the answers to the questions of the world, and wore hoodies that showed the school's name in block letters.

He found his way back to the edge of the quad and saw a woman holding a sign that read "Campus Tour" in the center of the park. There were only five others that appeared around his age and now him. Two of them were chaperoned by two separate pairs of pale and tired parents, none of whom appeared enthusiastic about the walk ahead.

The tour guide was young and blond and pretty, and the energy she injected into every word she spoke intimidated him. He guessed a student. She wore a bright green sweatshirt underneath her coat that had more block letters. Block letters were everywhere, on everything. And he found them overly aggressive, like texting someone in all caps.

"Are you here for the tour?" she said, as he approached the fountain around which they were gathered.

"I am," he said.

"Cool! I'm Emily! I'll be showing you our beautiful campus. We'll be on our way in a few short minutes."

TOMMY SAT DOWN ON the edge of the fountain and watched the students pass by. Emily passed around glossy booklets about the university and the courses and programs. After a few minutes Tommy noticed Emily fold her hands together and straighten her posture. Everyone else noticed this too, because they all turned their attention toward her. Her mouth opened wide before she spoke.

"Hello, everyone! For those of you just joining us, my name is Emily. I'm a third-year here at U of M studying biochemistry, with the hope of pursuing the DMD program after graduation—Doctor of Dental Medicine. Thank you for being here. I'll be your guide to our beautiful campus this morning."

The group of visitors crowded around Emily so that he could no longer see her, but he remained seated, watching passersby and listening to her voice.

"So," she said. "This is actually one of our two main campuses, known as the Fort Garry campus. The other is Bannatyne, located closer to downtown. And the place we're standing in right now is called the Duckworth Quadrangle, but we just call it the Quad! If you look around us you'll see some of the oldest buildings on campus, such as the Administration Building—built in 1912—just behind you over there, and to your left the Tier Building, which opened in 1932. U of M was founded a bit earlier, in 1877, and is the oldest university in western Canada."

Tommy looked over at both buildings she pointed out. They looked like castles, like something from Europe. The tour group had been slowly inching away, and he was now straining to hear Emily's voice, but he remained seated.

He flipped open the booklet Emily had given him and glanced at some of the courses and descriptions, including one called Dumpster on Fire: Global Pollution and Environmental Catastrophe. He read it over and over, as if it would help him understand the words better.

This course looks at pollution in the modern period through the lens of energy and resource use, focusing on four major categories of resources: coal, oil, nuclear power, and metals. Key themes and topics, including colonialism, exploitation, disposability, sustainability, and environmental racism and human rights, will be explored through the use of archival documents, newspaper articles, maps and multimedia. We will examine the histories of pollution worldwide and their legacies today.

A couple minutes passed, and the tour group began flowing across the quad. Tommy stayed where he was until he could only recognize the tone and sound of Emily's voice but not the words. Then she herded her followers down a narrow path and they were out of sight.

Tommy remained seated at the fountain for a while, watching, wondering whether he was creeping people out. He struggled to see himself among them. Finally, he stood up and walked slowly across the quad toward the tallest building he could see. He crossed the street where he had gotten off the bus and walked down a shorter, quieter street that had an energy plant with skyscraping cylinders exhaling smoke into the sky. The tall building was a student residence. He waited, like he did when he visited Clinton, for someone to come out and when they did he grabbed the door before it closed and let himself inside. The interior was clean, sleek, mostly grey. He pushed the button for the elevator and once inside he pressed the button for the highest floor. He felt like a spy in a movie, evading capture, using his street smarts and training to get by. The elevator door opened up to floor-to-ceiling windows and beyond them was a magnificent view of the city's southern reaches, lush with leafless trees and open fields. Cutting through it all was the Red River, a few steps from the residence hall, slithering across the land. He had never seen the river from this high before, never fully grasped its size and beauty, how it appeared to be alive. He wondered where it began and why it was coming all this way and where it would take him.

TOMMY WALKED A SHORT distance to one of the university's many cafeterias and ordered a pizza slice and found a spot at an empty blue table. The cafeteria was loud and every now and then the sizzling of a food item being cooked climbed above the clamor. He couldn't understand how the students were able to read or type at the surrounding tables and not be distracted by everything around them. He felt a vibration in his pocket and pulled out his phone. It was a text from Sam. It was a picture of him in mid-bite at the very spot he was sitting, alongside a message that said:

*You're looking at about 416 cals. That'll take you an hour to burn off. The saturated fat will cause cholesterol buildup in your arteries. Heart disease. Stroke. Early death. Etc. FYI.*

In a subsequent text, she added:

*Your posture is poor also. Be there in a min.*

Tommy looked around his shoulders like a woman in a horror movie searching for her predator but couldn't find his sister. It was true, his posture was bad. He replied:

*Weirdo.*

Sam sat down across from him five minutes later with a bowl that contained every available superfood on the planet, and she ate it so obnoxiously, with satisfied moans and nods, that she had even him convinced it was delicious.

"How was the tour?"

"It was . . ." Tommy wasn't sure what he was trying to say or wanted to say.

"Was what?"

"Not bad I guess." He went in for another bite of his pizza slice.

"Did it awaken your inner scholar?" she pressed, with a hint of sarcasm.

"I don't know. I don't know yet."

"Well, then. It was a bad sell job."

They went on eating. Tommy knew he looked out of place in the cafeteria.

"I was thinking about that teacher of yours," Sam said. "The fancy Frenchwoman."

"Damphousse," Tommy offered.

"Right. Her."

Tommy chewed slowly, watching Sam poke at her superfood with a plastic fork, anticipating another verbal beatdown of his history teacher.

"You know, every kid you see in here will go through their four or five years at school without having been required to learn about the history of these lands. They don't know about treaties or what this country did to us or have never even cared to know about the other side of this country's history."

Tommy looked around the cafeteria again. It felt like they were gossiping.

"They won't ever be taught that before the treaties were signed, government surveyors went out and confirmed that the land they planned to give as reserves were basically useless. Lifeless! Fuck, they won't even learn about the Pass System, which prevented Indians on the prairies from leaving their reserves without permission from the Indian Agent. The Starlight Tours! They won't even learn about the Starlight Tours. Residential Schools! The Sixties Scoop! Sharon McIvor! They won't learn about how the Indian Act fucked over generations of women."

Sam put her fork down and rested her elbows on the table. She was built like a brick wall on the outside, born that way. But all of a sudden she appeared tired—tired and sad—exhausted by the scrolls she'd just unfurled. And Tommy knew it was true, she *was* disappointed, if not worried. She was thinking about the years ahead, about her life and those of so many others. But when she pulled her hair back behind her ear to dangle behind her shoulder the look of concern was gone. She was made of stone again.

"So I guess it's cool she's making sure you know this stuff. Or at least some of it."

Tommy nodded and wiped his mouth with a napkin. He wouldn't bother with the crust of his pizza slice.

"So look. I can take you over to the Indigenous House, but apart from that I have to get going a little early today. I promised Koko I'd make dinner."

"Fine with me. I've had enough walking."


THE PATH TO THE Indigenous House was beautiful. Tommy was consistently impressed by how immaculately maintained everything was. Clean things always seemed like a performance to him. Even the smiles were fake. He was, after all, from the dirty part of town. He knew that's what people who didn't live there thought of his neighborhood, and the people in it. But it didn't bother him. Perhaps it did long ago, but like a horrible wound the nerves no longer registered to touch. At least it was transparent about what it was. It told a truth, and there was a truth here that this place was trying to conceal. But what it was hiding he didn't yet know. He wanted to find out.

They came upon a shorter structure made of beige stone tiles, some of which were uncut, looked rough on the surface and glittered softly in the sun.

"In there," Sam pointed. "This is where all us Neechis hide out. Cry and celebrate and get angry about all the shit they do to us here. Our safe space."

When they walked in the doors Tommy was taken aback again by how kempt the space was. It felt like a place designed by an architect who gave a damn about what the House would mean to its occupants in a spiritual and cultural and personal sense. That is to say, it looked like the child of a study hall and a museum devoted to Indigenous things. Complete with Morrisseau-esque paintings on the walls, artifacts protected behind glass, and every floral and star pattern that could be found in his koko's bedroom. They stopped walking just past the welcome rug, and Sam took the opportunity to point out areas of interest.

"This is it," she said. "You can study here. Eat here. As I said, you can also cry here. Scream here. Lose your shit here. Fart here. I recommend the farting, as this is a dairy-heavy campus and you know how it is. Maybe even fight here. There might be a Fight Club somewhere in the basement. Just kidding." She paused to turn and face a separate room with big windows. "Oh! There's a computer lab there. With printers. And just back there, down that hall is a kitchen, where you can store a lunch and heat it up in the micro. You could probably also live here without getting caught. Some of these kids actually sleep here during exams."

"It's nice," Tommy said. "So this is where you fart all the time. Just holding it in, saving it for here."

She laughed. "Just nice? Trust me. When you go here it'll be your lifesaver!"

"*If* I go here."

She appeared irritated by his ambiguity. "What else would you do?"

"There's Red River."

"Don't do college. You're better than that."

He wasn't sure that he was. Four years seemed like forever, and he had learned that apparently for some it took even longer to graduate.

He looked around the room. Some students at the tables were reading big books and taking notes simultaneously. He heard laughter coming from somewhere nearby, and noticed a large bowl against a wooden pillar that stood in the center of the room filled to the brim with condoms. The students were all bright and determined. They all looked like Sam.

Out of the hallway that led to the kitchen two girls emerged and greeted Sam cheerfully and approached them. They appeared about Sam's age and Tommy was struck by how confident they were. They spoke like Sam too, at a pace that wasn't definitively slow but sure of every word.

"This is my brother Tommy," Sam said. "Just showing him around." The two girls were standing in front of them and Tommy was now worried they were creating a hazard by crowding the main exit. If a fire broke out the fleeing frenzy would trip over them and become trapped inside. She pointed to the girl on the left. "This is Bea." Then on the right. "Lillian."

The girl named Lillian spoke:

"Tomahawk! We hear you've got the family brains. Will you be going here?"

Tommy was confused. Where did she hear that? It was the first time anyone other than Koko had suggested he had "brains." He looked over at Sam and her face was red, as if she were embarrassed. She was never embarrassed by anything.

"He's not sure yet," Sam said, before he could speak.

"Just seen the campus. Went on a tour." He slipped his hands in the pockets of his pants.

There was an awkward silence, and Tommy felt like they were waiting for him to say more, and so he said: "What do you both study?"

"I'm almost done with my BSW," Bea said.

"I'm premed," Lillian said.

"Lil's lying!" Sam interjected. "She just got into med school."

Sam's friends didn't stick around to talk for long, and mostly repeated and pointed out things about the Indigenous House that Sam had already mentioned.

"Seems like a good place to fart," Tommy said, patiently waiting for the perfect opportunity. "According to Sam. Her words not mine."

Lillian and Bea laughed loud with their whole faces, and simultaneously cried: "Err!"

"Don't act like you don't do it!" Sam shouted in defense. "Just like going on your phone on the toilet."

When the laughter settled Bea turned to Tommy and said:

"It's a big community here. Something like over twenty-five hundred Indigenous students. So it's a dope space, or at least it can be. The ISA—the Indigenous Students' Association—does a good job hosting events, like parties and gatherings and stuff, and they can get pretty wild! Sam knows! Anyways worth thinking about."

Bea was nearly halfway out the door with Lillian as she said this, and Tommy and Sam waved at them goodbye.

"Mind waiting here for a minute?" Sam said, like a worried parent leaving her child alone for the first time. "I have to run in and print something real quick."

"Sure."

Tommy was alone now, and moved toward the first thing on a far wall that caught his attention. It was a poster map of Manitoba showing all the First Nations in the province, most of which he'd never even heard of. There were dozens, and some of them had colorful pins stabbed into the dots marking their location, which he took to mean that someone who went to U of M was from there. Lake Manitoba, Ebb & Flow, Berens River, Sagkeeng, Waywayseecappo, Peguis. He'd heard these names before. He'd never been to any of them. He wasn't from any of them.

"Let's get the hell out of here," Sam said, rejoining him from behind and nudging her shoulder against his.

Before leaving Tommy grabbed a pin and stabbed it near the name of the city, offering his best guess as to where his house might be on the map.

"So," Sam said, while they were at a stop sign waiting for a handful of students to cross the street. "Was this a fruitful experience?"

"It was good," he said, looking out the window.

"What was good about it?"

He didn't respond. He kept on looking outside.

"Well, talk to me akittin."

He could sense that Sam was looking at him and so he turned to gaze ahead toward the crosswalk. "It was a very fertile opportunity, an enriching and absorbing moment of growth and enlightenment as a young adult. I shall tell grandmother all about it."

"Huzzah!"

They were moving again, and the houses along the winding campus road became smaller and smaller, the lawns shrinking. He thought about every one of them, their shapes, colors and numbers, and wondered whether their owners designed them themselves. He wanted to remember them, and so he imagined living in them, pretended to be their proprietor one last time, but this time as him and not anyone else, because he knew he would never be back here again.

## warriors at tigers

IT IS SIX O'CLOCK AND THE PUCK IS ABOUT TO BE DROPPED AND
*surely the Tigers don't stand a chance against the Maplewood War-*
*riors, the defending champions. The Tigers, though, have the benefit*
*of playing on home ice, the Memorial Arena, so . . . Can they pull off*
*an upset? Unlikely. But if hope lives anywhere it's in your home barn.*

*Maplewood wins the draw and their center, a small, tanky young*
*man, plays it back to a springy defenseman who rushes up ice, pierces*
*the Tigers' offensive zone easily and shoots! Save! Blackwood of the*
*Tigers does well there. An important moment and a big test passed.*

*The Tigers push ahead and, surprisingly, are able to find space in*
*the neutral zone. They seem to be keeping pace with Maplewood, but*
*they're not able to do much with it. RedHead has the puck now and he*
*looks dangerous and Maplewood, readying themselves, has two men*
*on him, pressuring him. He skates back into his own zone, takes his*
*time, wonderful patience. Maplewood continues to press but they can't*
*get him. He goes for a skate, winding up the ice, assessing his options.*
*Beautiful skill from RedHead to get past a pair of wingers and the*
*first defenseman and here he comes now with speed, drives to the net,*
*shoots, rebound, where is the puck? Another chance for the Tigers! And*
*another! Bouncing puck!*

*Maplewood clears, they have it now. The Tigers scramble to get back,*
*it's three Warriors against two Tigers. Drop pass! Shot! And denied.*
*Great save, Blackwood!*

*Back and forth they go. Shields knocks down his man. The partisans*
*here at the Memorial Arena like that.*

*The dying minutes of the first period. The game has settled. Both teams taking less risks. It's becoming a dump and chase game, a cycle game, a game of lucky bounces. Credit where credit is due. The Tigers are still in it. Holding their own. Blunting the attack of Maplewood. Staying aggressive. Playing with a calculated grit. Composure will be key.*

*1–0 Maplewood Warriors.*

*Nothing Blackwood could do there. He's been brilliant. Hung out to dry! It all started when the big defenseman Shields pinched low and laid out his man, which led to a two-on-one the other way and then the goal. He knew he screwed up, shook his head and slammed his stick in anger. Too hit-focused rather than worrying about his responsibilities, and he's hearing it now from his coach on the bench. There's a time when you just have to worry about making the right hockey play instead of lighting the guy up: there's always another time to be physical.*

*The second is all Maplewood so far. They have upped their tempo and the Tigers are deflated after letting in that late-period goal. Odd man rush for the Warriors! Racing back is Whiteway. He dives, takes out his man. Tripping call.*

*The Tigers' bench calls a timeout. Their coach is shouting, urging on his players, you can hear him from here.*

*The Tigers are being badly outshot. But they must be happy to be only down by one.*

*Maplewood wins the draw in the Tigers' zone. It's five-on-four for two minutes. The D-men exchange passes, trying to lull the penalty killers to sleep, another pass, a shot! Fans on it. They're throwing everything at Blackwood now, shots from all angles, looks like they know the next one has to be a mucky one with the way Blackwood is standing on his head. A scramble in front, the puck squirts out, Shields comes up with it, flying up ice, and he plays it through to a flanking RedHead and he has room, stick handles, nice move to beat the first man, showing his skills with the puck, and there's one more defenseman to get past, one-on-one, and he drives wide—what will he do?—he fakes a shot, the defender bites, more room to play with, now he shoots! Fluffs it straight at the goalie. Easy save. RedHead'll be disappointed with that rush. A waste of time and space.*

*The horn blows to end the second. The crowd can sense it. Something magical is in the air.*

*The start of the third period. Maplewood is getting creative now, slowing the game down. The Tigers continue to chase, unable to string more than one or two passes together. But they don't look deflated. They look indefatigable. They look finely coached.*

*Oh! It's in! 2–0 Maplewood Warriors. Blackwood will want that one back, a shot from the point with little traffic in front of him.*

*It's all Maplewood now. The Tigers are giving them too much space, collapsing too low in their own zone. The frustration is mounting! Some pushing and shoving after the whistle and a couple Maplewood players go down. Shields gets called for roughing. Soft call, in my opinion. Looked like a hockey play. Another whistle. Whiteway goes to the box for cross-checking, a careless, reckless play with seven minutes left. The Maplewood forward is still down, went into the boards dangerously, and is helped off the ice. His night is finished. The coaches on both sides exchange violent profanities, screaming with their arms as much as their lungs. The referee gives them a warning.*

*3–0 Maplewood Warriors. An easy tap-in on the five-on-three. The Tigers defenders were dead tired. As easy as they come.*

*That'll do it. The clock winds down. A less-than-convincing win for the Maplewood Warriors, who looked timid and vulnerable early. And another disappointing loss for the winless Tigers, in a game that, at times, probably could've gone the other way.*

# biboon

## *asemaa kimberly shields*

I'M SITTING IN LECTURE BORED AS FUCK. I'M TRYING TO THINK about what I should think about to distract myself from what the professor is *telling* me to think, telling the whole room to *ponder.* I wonder if boring teachers know they're boring, or whether they simply wake up the day after getting tenure and decide they no longer give a damn. Their lives over and they can now drift through the cosmos until they die. Is it a choice? If so, then, how did this boring woman get a job. Or are they just bad at communicating their knowledge to the world? Boring people shouldn't teach. They should take a test at their interview to see how many kids over the age of eighteen fall asleep over the course of their lecture. There should be laws against it. Lawsuits. Tenure revoked. A commission established to investigate how this teacher contributed to the academic capitalism rotting away the roots of for-profit education. How old is she? Without tenure, without her job at this university, she'd have retired long ago. I'm discriminating against the old now. Fuck. I'm bored as hell.

I'm thinking about how smart I am. I *am* smart. The smartest of this class without question. Smarter than this teacher was at twenty-one, my age now, that's for certain. That's not to say I go around bragging about my intelligence, but if hockey players can go around wearing leather-sleeved bomber jackets with their numbers and names on them and shaving their heads into mohawks for the playoffs then I feel I can wear my intelligence with a similar confidence. I'm smart. My GPA is 4.0, but technically 4.33 if you add the numbers right, though the university officially only recognizes as high as 4.0.

I'm so smart that in junior high I won a scholarship to study for a year at a private school on the other side of the city, and even there I was top of the class. The campus was big and beautiful, hidden behind a curved road. There were hockey rinks and tennis courts and swimming pools and residence halls. I bused from home every morning. The only downside was the ties and blazers and plaid skirts we were required to wear. It was there I adopted the name Sam, after my science teacher, Ms. Malenia, told me on the first day that Sam was easier to say than Asemaa, and from then on, I went with it. I was Sam to everyone except Koko.

I'll be honest. I didn't love my name growing up. Most of us are conditioned to believe that the white names are the best. We all wanted to be a Jessica or Ashley or Emily or Elizabeth or Sarah or Chloe. If you didn't, you're lying to yourself. I thought that way too for a long time. I complained to Koko too many times to count about the name Asemaa and its meaning and cried until I had no more tears left to give.

"Why this one?" I cried once. "Whose idea was this?"

"Mine," she told me. She was at her sewing machine, fixing a tear in my brother's jeans. She didn't look up and like she always does, even today, didn't care to elaborate further.

"But why? I'll never smoke. Never."

"Because tobacco is what we offer to the Creator, to Mother Earth, when we pray," she told me. "You're the medicine that gives us hope."

I felt better after that. Only slightly. I still didn't like being named after a key ingredient for cigarettes. I don't smoke. Not ever, not once. If a pipe goes around at ceremony, be it a feast or sweat, I'll accept the pipe and then rest the stem on my shoulder before passing it on to the next person, and even then I'm not exactly sure how inhaling works, how one allows a foreign vapor to breach their lungs.

I'm a computer engineering student. I want to be a software engineer at a place like Google or Apple, somewhere cool and morally suspect with a focus on artificial intelligence. Which is to say that I believe that singularity, the merging of humans with robots, is an inevitability. That's the kind of assimilation I'm here for, the next step in our human evolution, and I for one am ready to get on with it. I always joke to Koko: "The Digital Afterlife is the new Spirit World," and she says: "I have too many ancestors that miss me."

I'm in a class, an elective, called Social Identity and Citizenship and today we're talking about Indigeneity and how Indigenous citizenship is at odds with the idea of being Canadian. We are both of these things. I am Anishinaabekwe but I am also Canadian. This is true. But I will always be the former, and you will always hear me refer to myself as Kwe. Not because I hate this country, which I do, but because that was the agreement our ancestors made with the men who came here to start a country and instead signed treaties. This lecture in particular lacks nuance. The professor, a PhD in sociology who for some reason is teaching political science, is an older woman with impossibly thick and long grey hair and a seemingly endless collection of Nike sneakers. She could model as an older person in athleisure attire instead of clunky orthopedics. She constantly refers to us as "Indigenous Canadians," and is more inclined to convince the class that Indigenous people *are* Canadians than to offer explanations for Indigenous people's rejection of Canadian identity.

She stands behind a lectern and speaks softly into the microphone. She's commenting on pictures of dilapidated housing from various First Nations around the country, projected in large size behind her.

"Indigenous Canadians frequently find themselves in a state of *statelessness*," she says, emphasizing the word "statelessness" with a clever smile. "Let's take a break here until five after."

I USED TO RUN to campus from home every morning. Almost eighteen miles there and back. I don't like to run, but I became so good at it that I thought I'd one day do ultramarathons, the kind where you go for days and nights until you get to the end, until you nearly die from the punishment. Sometimes it feels like everyone around me, including my very own koko, suffers from diabetes. Or at the very least something life-shortening. I was in third grade when I quit bannock like cigarettes. I'm not sure about my mom, whether she's diabetic, whether she knows she has it. Maybe she does. Maybe she's already missing a foot and finger. I don't know about my dad either.

Tommy and I don't even know *who he* is, but we somehow know, through word of mouth, that he has a family and five kids. Anyways I stopped running due to stress fractures in my feet. The doctor said it could be hereditary. Now my only salvation is the weight room, the elliptical and occasionally the air bike. You can't run away from brittle bones.

I fill up my water bottle at the fountain, chug a liter, and then fill it up again. The smell of sweetgrass floods the hallway. It's coming from an adult education class that meets next door to my lecture hall every other week, where the handful of them all smudge before class. I stop by the door to where the smell is coming from just to watch students walk by with their noses all crooked, as if the smell is terrible, which it isn't. It's the most glorious of smells. I move into the lecture hall and find my seat and look around me at all the empty chairs that once had kids in them. It happens every week, every week at this time. I look over at the professor, who appears ready to begin again, and she looks up from the computer monitor on the lectern and I can tell she feels embarrassed that only eight of us remain but she clears her throat and moves on. How can anyone not be sad about not being loved? A reasonable person might ask us to come together a little closer, but instead we're scattered across the lecture hall and after every other sentence the mic screeches with feedback.

We're still looking at images of broken homes and buildings.

"Can anyone guess where this is?" She tilts her head and looks up at the projection and admires it like a mural in an art gallery.

No one responds.

"This is a slum in Nigeria." She clicks the mouse behind the monitor and it's another picture of another unlabeled ramshackle village.

"Any guesses?"

No one offers up an answer. I know it but I don't say it.

"Attawapiskat First Nation in northern Ontario."

I'm not sure how this lesson is supposed to help anyone. Comparing impoverished people to impoverished people. Our suffering has been allowed to happen, by her, by everyone, and even if you're not watching you're still watching, because refusing to watch is still watching, because you know it's there you just don't want to look. We died for the existence of this country, for the illusion of state, but no one calls us patriots. I often take issue with the word "patriot." More specifically, I take issue with calling half-brained high school graduates who sign up to wear camouflage and shoot guns and ride tanks and die for reasons they cannot fathom patriots. That reads more like xenophobia than patriotism. It's also a word that only ever applies to white people, but more specifically white men. Merriam-Webster says the word "patriot" arrived on the scene in the sixteenth century and for much of the seventeenth century it was used in Europe to describe someone who loved their country and agreed with government and the non-secular state of things; but in the eighteenth century it became both a negative—in Britain—and a positive—in America—thing to say, as it described colonists who resisted British rule, and from then on the notion of resistance, to perhaps a fault, has clung to the word's meaning. In 2005, a revision in the Oxford English Dictionary defined a patriot as, "An opponent of presumed intervention by federal government in the affairs of individuals, esp. with respect to gun and tax laws. Frequently in the names of right-wing libertarian political and militia groups." This language is old. It has changed. The debate around the word has mostly settled to describe love of country and usually falls on a brain-dead shell-shocked lover of war. But isn't it funny? The way some words only concern a few. By definition we're patriots too. Patriots to the land we walk on.

"How does something like this exist in Canada?" the professor asks. "Places like this, where suicide rates are high, where housing is substandard, and where residents can't drink water from their own tap because it's not safe, these places are Canada's Fourth World."

A hand goes up in the back row and I turn to look. The professor, noticeably pleased that someone is asking a question, directs her attention to the student. The student is a boy, and he exchanges a jokey smile with the boy next to him.

"A lot of Indigenous people don't even consider themselves Canadian. So I guess, like, how are we supposed to discuss Indigenous people and their political participation when, like, so many of them don't identify as Canadian?"

I can feel my feet tingle. They do that sometimes. Like the bones in my feet have their own kind of scar tissue. My heart races. I won't raise my hand. I never do. I refuse to let that become part of my identity, educating others. It's tiring.

"That's a great question. It's a complicated question. Does anyone want to weigh in?"

A girl raises her hand. She looks nervous. She has bleached-blond hair, bangs, glasses and an extraordinarily small nose. It's been several weeks of this class, and I've never heard her speak.

"I think that's an unfair statement." She turns to the boy in the back, and suddenly I respect her even more. "Indigenous people maybe don't think of themselves as Canadian because of how they've been historically treated by this country. Think of, like, police abuse. The Mounties are, like, supposed to be this big symbol. You see them everywhere, right? With the funny hats and boots. But if you look at something, like, the Starlight Tours in Saskatchewan, where they were literally picking up Indigenous people, stripping them naked, and dropping them off in the middle of nowhere in the cold to die, then it's understandable that they wouldn't see themselves as equal citizens, or even, like, accepted fully."

The girl is only a few seats to my left in the same row. The professor nodded with enthusiasm the whole way through her comment, and even said "exactly" at one point with delight.

"That is an excellent point. Any others?"

The boy in the back raises his hand again, but the other boy beside him also raises his hand soon after. The professor calls upon the other boy: "You on the left."

I've seen this boy before, but we've never spoken. He's wearing one of those leather-sleeved hockey jackets but it's not of the Bisons, the university team. He is very red in the face, different from his normally pale complexion, like someone you might find in Scotland or Ireland or a place with no sun.

"I'm sorry, but there's absolutely no way a police officer would ever do anything like that! It would never happen! These are cops. Professionals. There's a vetting process. What an absolutely ridiculous statement. I think we need to be careful about spreading lies like this."

"This happened!" the blond girl shouts back. "I don't think you know what you're talking about."

My feet feel like they're being poked with pins. My right leg is bopping up and down uncontrollably. The girl is right. The boy is wrong. But the Starlight Tours are more commonly associated with the Saskatoon Police Service than the Mounties. They picked up Indigenous men in the night and let them freeze to death. Men like Rodney Naistus, Lawrence Wegner, and Neil Stonechild. A pair of constables were convicted of some minor crime and served less than a year in prison in the early aughts. No cop had ever been convicted of doing any killing, which is hardly surprising.

Another girl closer to the boy turns toward him and without raising her hand says:

"That's very insensitive. Your comment reeks of privilege."

Another boy seated behind me shouts loud:

"Read a book! Pick up a newspaper! Educate yourself!"

"It would never happen! Cops don't go around killing people for no reason. There's always a reason."

"Oh my God." The girl closest to him rolls her eyes and head in unison and laughs hysterically.

The banter is loud now, and it's impossible to distinguish what any of them are yelling at each other.

"Everyone. Quiet! Quiet! Quiet!" the professor shouts, and the noise quickly diminishes.

"In case you didn't know I'm Jewish!" the boy says, throwing his hands in the air in comical frustration.

The whole classroom laughs at his attempt to deflect the criticism.

"Sure you are!" the girl with the bleached-blond bangs says.

"Okay that's enough. Quiet down." The professor turns to look at the girl with the bleached-blond hair. "I don't know exactly what you were referencing, but I do recall something about police picking up Indigenous people and leaving them in the cold. So I think there's some truth to that."

"Has anyone here ever actually been to a reserve?" the boy says with his hand raised.

I turn and look at him and raise my hand. I went to Berens River once on a school trip. I was one of a few students from St. Croix who got to go. We took a plane in the winter to meet young students and hopefully rub our city knowledge off on them for when they eventually make their way south for the schools.

The boy sees me and his eyes widen and he looks almost surprised to see someone raise their hand. "Yeah, they're not safe places. I played hockey on a reserve once and they don't like us being there. They basically drove us out with guns and shovels."

The professor nods uncomfortably and looks around. I realize my hand is still in the air and the professor, with raised eyebrows, gives me permission to speak. "Sam?"

"Oh it's nothing," I say. "It's already been said."

"Okay. Well. Let's stop here for today. See you all next week."

I look at the time on my phone. There should be thirty minutes left of class.

I stand quickly and walk out of the lecture hall first without looking back. I take a right down the hall to the quietest staircase in the building and pause on the steps to hyperventilate. My throat feels tight and painful and stiff, like knotted rubber cables. I sit down. My eyes are so watery I'm surprised they're not spilling over on my cheeks. I don't cry. I stopped crying a long time ago. Now my feet hurt.

Outside, it's mild for early December. I stop at the Indigenous House and print some worksheets for my class on Applied Computational Intelligence. When the pages are done, they are warm and perfectly smooth and the algorithms on the pages speak a language that calms me. I sit at a table in the main lobby and watch the slow falling snow outside a window and occasionally a person walks by and says hello and I gently wave back without looking. It's nearly dark by the time Peggy, one of the House's administrators, waddles over with the same unmaimed enthusiasm I've grown so used to seeing over the years.

"Sam! Mind if I sit?" she says, sitting across from me before I can respond. Her expression shifts suddenly when she sees my face up close. "Are you okay?"

"Rough day."

"You're almost there."

I nod, observing the colorfully beaded jewelry around her neck and chest and dangling from her ears.

"I have some news to share, but keep this between me and you, because the selection committee hasn't announced anything just yet. Okay?"

I nod again.

"It's sounding like you're going to be called in for a final interview."

"For the Rhodes?" My back straightens with excitement.

"That's right. Looks like you'll owe me a hundred bucks after all." She laughs with her hands around her belly, like she's pushing the air out.

I laugh too, remembering that we made a bet over the summer: me that I wouldn't get the Rhodes Scholarship and she that I would.

"Don't tell anyone yet. Just your koko." She stands and leaves.

I stay and smile out the window.

When I get to my car in the parking lot the sun is all the way down. The snowflakes drifting from the blank sky from seemingly nowhere are the only things absorbing the light from streetlamps, emitting a light of their own. Ash catching flame again. Now dull, now bright. I pop the trunk and throw my backpack inside and pull out a pair of battered running shoes. I slip off my black leather Chelsea boots and slide my feet into sneakers and tie them tightly. I shuffle my feet quick on the concrete to test how slippery it is from the melted snowflakes and it's fine enough. I throw my boots in the trunk and slam it shut, squat several times until my bum nearly touches the wet ground and then I start running in the direction of home, slow at first and then fast, and my feet, my feet feel free.

## floyd lewis redhead

THE MUSIC IS SO LOUD THE OTHERS AROUND HIM CAN HEAR IT. "Can't Stop" by the Chili Peppers. The same song Klitschko walks out to. So loud that when he eventually has to remove his favorite headphones, a Sony pair so old and so soaked in dried sweat and memories and baked in crusty earwax and tradition that not even his mother is allowed to take a wet cloth to them despite her pleas, it takes a moment for his ears to adjust to the nervous dressing room. He takes them off when it's time to tie his skates, because he needs to hear the subtle ache the fabric makes as he pulls on his wax-coated laces and increases the pressure on each foot. The harder he pulls the sharper the sound, and it's less the support around his ankles than the sharpness of the sound that lets him know when it's right. He looks around. Tommy is lost in a trance with his mouth open. Clinton looks like Clinton, ready to get this over with.

It's not the Tigers he's playing for, but a roster of NDN players from around the city assembled at the last possible minute. *Holy smokes we are truly of all nations, aho!* and laughs knowing how stupid he must look giggling away in the corner alone. They're full-bloods, half-breeds, brown-skinned, suspiciously dark-as-fuck-skinned, white-skinned, black-haired, brown-haired, straight-haired, Jewy-haired, brown-eyed, blue-eyed, grandfather is Sioux, great-great-grandmother was Cree, mom thinks she's Métis, dad thinks he's a quarter Sayisi Dene, and then there's him, the kid with the Anishinaabe mom and Jamaican dad.

They're huddled inside a tiny room at the Dakota Community Centre in a neighborhood called River Park South. And they're about to play in the final of the All Nations Winter Classic. After finishing with his skates, Floyd pulls his headphones over his ears again because he needs the additional hype, because for the first time in his young playing career he has a chance to go home with a medal and he wants it to be gold.

At last year's tournament he played for a team that just missed out on bronze. They were called the Eagles. This year, Tommy and Clinton joined the team as new recruits. As such it's been a tournament for retribution, at least that's how Floyd sees it. Which is why, when deciding on a team name, he rose to his feet and blurted out the only name appropriate for the occasion and the rest of them, including the coach, agreed. The Avengers, it was only right. And they are NDN.

FLOYD NEVER THOUGHT HE'D be a hockey player. His dad, Carl, was a tight end, played as high as the Bisons and was invited to try out with the Bombers until he blew out his knee and that was the end of it. Floyd's early years were football, but eventually he tired of it, wished the plays after the ball was snapped and in the quarterback's hands lasted longer than a few seconds. His mom, Carla, said, Why not try lacrosse? Indians started lacrosse and you're Indian, and he said, What about hockey? How many Indians play hockey? And then Mom said, How about basketball? Are you sure you don't like football? and he said, Do Indians plays hockey? Exasperated she said, Indians love hockey, but it doesn't love them back and you can be sure it won't love the other half of you either, my boy. He was on skates that winter, a day after turning nine.

He was a natural from the start. His hands and feet were fast, faster than the rest. He skated like he was running, knees high like an Olympic jumper, ready to take off, and still does it this way, the slashing of his blades on the ice so loud it frightens the other kids, because it means he's coming for you. He rose through the ranks quickly, wreaked havoc on the House League and the kids with feeble athletic gifts and then moved on to greater heights in only his second year of playing, cracking a AA squad before receiving the call to make the jump to AAA, where the best of the best get their chance to shine. And he was the best there, too. But it was when he settled atop the throne of youth minor hockey greatness that he realized no one wanted him there to begin with. He wasn't rich. His family wasn't middle class, and he wasn't of the dominant pigment.

"Go back to Africa," he remembers one boy saying.

"Monkeys don't play hockey," another boy said, arms splayed, mimicking a monkey.

They'll have to try harder than that. All he wanted to do was go out there and score. And he did. He scored every game and celebrated as hard as he could, arms in the air, fists off the glass, a roar to the crowd, to show he cared about the game just as much as anyone else. Sometimes, like he saw Teemu Selänne do, he'd throw his gloves in the air and aim down the shaft of his stick, the blade his stock, and make big kickback motions as if he were shooting down a flock of geese. It was after one such goal that he came back to the bench, and the coach, standing over him with a furious look in his eyes, said:

"Floyd, I've had enough of that nigger shit."

He was benched the rest of the game. His spirit crushed. In fact, he couldn't bring himself to play again for the next two years, until he arrived at St. Croix.

"I'm going to play this year," he told his dad before the first day of high school. "For the Tigers."

They were at Dollarama picking out school supplies. His dad was inspecting binders and tossed a green one and a red one in the cart in front of them. He looked at Floyd nervously. "You sure?"

Floyd nodded, inhaling deeply. "Most of the guys is NDN."

"You is not just Indian. Remember that. You look like me more than your mom." He raised his forearm and pulled back the sleeve of his sweatshirt. Floyd raised his naked arm too and they touched like a makeup palette showing all the different shades. Floyd a smidge lighter, less hair. "They don't see what's in there." He pressed a finger on his son's heart. "Only what's here." He vibrated his forearm as if to hammer home the point.

"I am both," Floyd said. He swapped the green binder for a black one.

OVER HIS YEARS AT St. Croix, Floyd felt nothing less than NDN. Sure, he leaned into it harder than most kids had to, felt they needed to, but Carla made sure he knew where he was from. She's from a place called Pinaymootang but everyone she's ever known now lives in the city. She taught herself to jingle dance and inherited a dress from an auntie and every Friday she'd dance in the kitchen to powwow music and little Floyd would sit there beside her, eyes fixed on the jingles bouncing up and down, creating a music of their own. He became a grass dancer the following summer, and besides hockey and his mom and dad and Koko and Shoomis and grandpa and grandma and aunties and cousins and kin he regards dancing as the thing he loves most. His colors are light blue, green, red and orange. His clan is turtle. On game days, and before the first beat of a powwow, he sits in the kitchen on a chair and behind him his mom braids his hair and the design and weave is never the same as the one before it, which is partly why everyone on the Tigers calls him Big Sexy.

FLOYD MET UP WITH Tommy and Clinton at the end of school. They were leaned up against a heater by the school entrance, hogging all the heated air on a chilly December day. It was the last day of classes before the start of winter break, and he wanted to know their plans over the holidays.

"Big Weapon, what's the plan of action this coming holiday season? You too, C. Fill me in. Merry Christmas in advance—sorry—holidays. My mom and dad are Christian, so you know how it be."

"Nothing," Tommy said. "Christmassy shit."

"Same," Clinton said. "Celebrating the birth of Christ."

"You?" Tommy asked.

"I have a proposal, and it's sacred as fuck." He noticed their attention shift from girls exiting the school doors to him. "The tournament at the All Nations Winterfest starts on Boxing Day, and my dad says we need some extra players. He's been calling around with the coach but everyone's got a team. I told him I'd ask you boys, because you're young and hearty and capable, and Big Weapon you're all of a sudden taller than Shaq. Damn."

The interest in their faces diminished, and Clinton went back to staring at passing girls.

"Hold on," Tommy said. "How . . ." He paused after catching a rare glimpse of Jasmine Courchene's backside, the finest of them all, normally shielded by a long parka but today, she chose to don a pink bomber instead. "What's the deal with this tournament?"

"The deal with what?"

"I mean, how good are these other guys. I'm not looking to get my ankles broken for a whole weekend."

"They're good. Lots of rez teams. They come from all over, even from Sask and Alberta and all that. Maybe a couple future draft picks but that's it. We'll be good too."

"How good?"

"Competitive. I think."

"I'm in," Clinton said.

"Sacred." He reached out and bumped Clinton's fist. "Maybe invite Clarissa so she can see us win for once."

"We're not dating. But sure."

"You in, Weapon?"

"Fuck it. I'll play. Clinton, this doesn't count toward the bet. I'll most likely be needing a ride from one of you."

"Okay."

"I got you." Floyd smiled wide. "Fuckin' sacred."


FLOYD WAS IN FRONT of Tommy's house at five o'clock sharp. His mom and dad sat in the front seats of the family truck. He could see Tommy pull back a window curtain before scrambling behind it again with a panicked look on his face, and after five minutes of waiting, he said:

"We're gonna be late."

"It'll be fine," Carl said, resting the back of his head on the driver's seat.

Three minutes later the front door of the house finally opened, spilling light on the snowy sidewalk leading toward the steps of the house, and Tommy emerged from it, taking great care not to slip. He moved toward their vehicle, hockey bag slung around his shoulder, and hoisted the bag into the truck bed behind Floyd.

"Sorry for making you wait," he said, once in the truck. "I had no idea you were coming this early."

"Weap—Tomahawk, I texted you we'd be coming."

"My phone died and I couldn't find my charger. I think Sam stole it off me."

"It's okay, Tomahawk," Carla said, turning her head to look at Floyd, Tommy seated directly behind her. "Boy, we'll be on time. Stop worrying. How's your koko doing?"

"You know I like to do a dry land warm-up," Floyd said, feeling annoyed, looking first at his mom and then at Tommy. His dad had started driving.

"She's good. Probably happy to have the house to herself."

"And Asemaa?"

"She's good."

"Is she still trying to take over the world. Make us all robots," Floyd said.

"Pretty much."

"How's C getting there by the way?"

Tommy shrugged. "He said he had a ride."

"We need him to show."

"He will."

"Tobacco down, prayers up."


WINTERFEST AT THE DAKOTA Community Centre was in full swing by the time they arrived. NDNs everywhere. Over the forthcoming weekend they'd come to take over the South End. Injecting millions into the local economy. Hotels booked solid. NDNs in the malls, restaurants, movie theaters, indoor swimming pools, casinos, everywhere you looked. Rich NDNs, poor NDNs, welfare NDNs, classy NDNs, city NDNs, rezzy loud NDNs, party NDNs, volleyball-playing NDNs. They would all show. At other nearby venues there'd be jigging, singing, square dancing, for some reason volleyball, and a powwow.

Floyd and Tommy marched through the crowded arena. A path opened up for them, as others instinctively cleared the way for their precious cargo. In the dressing room Clinton was already there mingling with the other players on the team. Neither of them knew then that Clinton had taken the bus all the way from the Haven, his equipment with him. Neither of them knew yet that that's where he'd been living all this time.

They narrowly won their first game. The opponent was a rez squad called the Shady Boyz, whom you could spot easily throughout the Dakota Community Centre because of their bright orange tracksuits and matching sunglasses. Floyd disliked the theatrics, but their unity made him envious. The Avengers had no tracksuits. They didn't wear aviators indoors. They were leftovers from around the city. Obnoxious NDNs, he thought, after finding himself trapped in a sea of orange in the lounge area of the community center after their game. He felt as though they were penning him in.

It was only Floyd's second time coming to Winterfest. He knew it was an annual gathering that happened, that existed, like the Festival du Voyageur and Folklorama, but there was a part of him that always felt outside of it, afraid to be seen as part of it. He has never danced at a powwow either. Truly danced. He's accepted the emcee's invitation for all to enter the circle in plain clothes and shuffle your feet alongside the real dancers for a few short minutes, but that's as far as his experience goes. For the longest time he only danced on Fridays in the kitchen with his mom, her in her jingle dress and him in his regalia with barely enough room to spin. But this year Carla convinced him, saying now is the time to move to the beat of a real drum, not just an old Northern Cree CD in the kitchen stereo, and so on Sunday, immediately after the championship game, he and she plan to dance at the festival-closing powwow.

On Saturday, Floyd and Tommy roamed the halls of a nearby convention center in between hockey games. They ordered bannock dogs and mini donuts from a nearby concession stand set up by an elderly lady and her granddaughter. Bannock was everywhere and a side to everything: the replacement for a hot dog and burger bun, the base of your Indian taco, the dough of choice for your fried Klik.

They ate while they walked the hall, which bustled with NDNs watching volleyball, and paused at the door of another large gym. A band inside crashed through a Johnny Cash tune. They found a spot on the bleachers pulled out from the wall and for two hours they watched the talent show. The bleachers roared with NDNs. NDNs who enjoyed music over sports. Eventually the show transitioned into something else, the jiggers jigged out, and behind them a man with a fiddle sliced the chords like a swordsman. Their knees moved up and down in a mad flurry, their feet carefully brushing all parts of the gym floor, their torsos taut and steady. And after that came troupes of square dancers, which Floyd had never seen before in action. The men and boys wore bright satin shirts and the women and girls twirled around in matching skirts, tapping away, tap tap tapping, creating music with just their feet, and the fiddler helping them along to something called the Red River Jig.

When it was time to leave, to take to the ice again, they walked down a busy hall lined with vendors selling various NDN crafts and art and jewelry. They stopped at one that was mostly free of other shoppers, and behind the table was a man slumped so deep in a lawn chair that he seemed incapable of getting out of it without a helping hand. He didn't greet them but watched them intently.

"Put your weed in there," Tommy said, holding up a turtle rattle with a deer foot handle to Floyd. "Keep it safe." He tilted the rattle upside down and inspected the bottom of the hoof.

Floyd laughed. "I'm not trying to get killed by my mama."

"If tomorrow we start puffing Mary Jane's wacky tobaccy you'll regret not getting it."

Quickly, the man behind the table stood up from his lawn chair and grabbed the rattle from Tommy before flopping back down.

"This isn't a toy," he said sternly. "This isn't for your weed, or your wacky tobaccy."

Tommy's face went red. Floyd looked at the man for the first time since arriving at the booth. He was wearing a deerskin vest and a cowboy hat and a beaded medallion swung like a war shield over his chest. Behind his ears were strands of partially greyed hair, which led Floyd to believe he was sporting a mullet.

"What's it for?" Floyd said.

"It's for dancers. The dancer carries it in their right hand during ceremony. The foot represents the swiftness of the deer, while the shell the longevity of the turtle. Are you a dancer?"

"I'm a grass dancer."

"What about you?" The man turned to Tommy.

"Me? Nah."

"You don't look like one. Not much grace in your walk. I could tell your friend is one straightaway, once I saw him coming over. Lots of grace there." The man looked back at Floyd, who was suddenly feeling an overwhelming sense of pride. "It's perfect for you, then."

"How much?"

The man had to look at the sticker on the belly of the turtle shell. "Eighty."

Floyd quickly pulled out his wallet, a Velcro piece from his koko, though he already knew he was short. His dad had given him a fifty for the day when he dropped them off in the morning and he already spent ten of it on bannock dogs and mini donuts. "Damn. I can't swing it."

"What do you have?"

"Just forty."

"Tell you what. Just give me what you have and it's yours."

"Really?" Floyd was naturally suspicious. He didn't believe in concessions. Concessions were never just concessions, because even concessions had a price, at least that's what his dad always said.

"Yes really. Maybe it'll bring you some luck tomorrow at the powwow."

Floyd couldn't hide his elation. He handed over the money and the man slipped the bills inside his pocket without counting. Quickly, the man wrapped the rattle in brown paper and placed it inside a brown paper bag and Floyd reached out and accepted it.

IN THE DRESSING ROOM Floyd pulls his dank sweater over his head and over the shoulders of his pads. It's a black and yellow number with a poorly printed eagle on the front. They may not have matching tracksuits but at least they're all wearing the same jersey, he thought, save for all the mismatched socks. He pulls out his phone from his pants to check the time. It's five minutes until puck drop, but he finds it curious that their coach, a man named Chris who's the father of the team goalie named Christian, hasn't come into the room yet to offer an encouraging speech and game plan. He looks around the room. Worries settle deep in his stomach, but no one else seems worried.

A couple minutes later Chris, who looks like a fully grown high school nerd, comes through the door, fixing his glasses on the bridge of his nose.

"Fellas," he says, and Floyd takes solace in seeing that the coach himself is slightly agitated, his wet forehead glistening under white lights. "We're running a little behind here. They're sorting out some things before the start of the game. It'll be a few more minutes." Then he leaves the room.

Floyd searches his bag for nothing in particular. There's a can of dip in a small pocket on the side of the bag and he reaches in there and pulls out the tobacco and opens it and even though the smell disgusts him he pinches a large piece between his thumb and two fingers and inserts it under his bottom lip and as he does he remembers the first time he dipped, how he didn't know not to swallow and vomited soon after and swore to never open the can again, but in this moment it feels right. The initiation after the initiation. He sucks hard to ensure it's covered well in saliva and spits in a water bottle.

Chris opens the door again but stops until only his torso is inside the room, looking more sweaty than before.

"Floyd, can you come out here for a second," he says.

Floyd doesn't respond, getting up and walking over and pushing the door open with his skates tightly bound around his feet. He follows Chris down a long hall with floors made of blue rubber. They stop near a water fountain. Echoes of NDNs filling the stands.

"What's going on?"

"So listen," Chris says, looking down at the scratched floor. "They're . . ." He looks up to meet Floyd's eyes. "They're protesting."

He feels a heavy tug in his gut, like a spirit below is pulling him closer to the surface of the floor. "Protesting what?"

"They're. They're protesting you."

He can see that Chris is waiting for him to say something, but he gives a short nod.

"They're saying you're not Aboriginal."

"I'm NDN."

"I've told them. But they're crying to the organizers that you're a ringer."

He feels a wobble in his legs and so he places a hand on the wall. Chris steps forward and rests a hand on his shoulder and Floyd notices how much darker his hand is than Chris's. "They can't be real. They can't actually be fucking with this."

"I've told them about your mom and dad. I told them your mom's from Fairford. They said they wanted to see a status card or letter from your band. I told them your mom's side of the family isn't status, and so now they're . . . they're escalating it."

"They say my mom looks fucking white? Shit shouldn't matter."

"No, it doesn't matter."

"I'm NDN."

Chris squeezes his shoulder. He has that face one has just before they burst out crying but he doesn't cry.

"So what, then?"

"The organizers are saying if we have enough guys we should play."

"But without me."

Chris nods gently.

"Or we forfeit."

Chris continues nodding.

Floyd moves toward the fountain and spits. His head feels light, and he wonders for a moment if it's the dip making him feel unsteady.

"We're not going to play," Chris says. "It's not worth it. It can't be handled this way. We're not going to sit you out and pretend it's okay."

"Fuck no. Play. Y'all should play. Coach, if you don't make the guys play, I'm gonna be more pissed at you than with this shit." He's telling a lie.

Chris removes his hand from his shoulder and no longer looks on the verge of crying.

"Just play."

There's silence between them. Chris sighs loudly. And then says:

"I'll go tell them we're playing."

Floyd walks back to the dressing room and takes his seat. A few minutes pass. Tommy, beside him, leans over and asks what coach wanted him for and then asks him if he's okay. Floyd says he'll tell him about it later and then the door swings open again and Chris, his forehead dry, says:

"We're ready to go, fellas. Ice is ready. Let's get out there. I just spoke with Floyd and he's going to sit this one out. He's fine, nothing serious. I'll explain later. But they need us out there right away."

Helmets and gloves go on around the room, and one by one the Avengers walk out the door and down the hall and onto the ice. Floyd turns to Tommy, who now looks worried. "I'll tell you later." He looks to Clinton, who also looks worried. "It's no big deal."

HE'S ALONE IN THE dressing room and he takes his time undressing. He rolls his sock tape into a ball and airs the trash bin. He maneuvers his tongue around the inside of his bottom lip and swallows, clearing his mouth of the dip that had been there and which he had forgotten about. He washes it down with water and waits, waits to vomit. But he doesn't. He rushes to the toilet and drops down on his knees and inserts two fingers deep inside his mouth and gags over and over but the only thing that leaves his body is tears. When he's ready, he lifts his bag over his shoulder and grabs his two sticks and shuffles down the hall into the raucous lobby. It feels like everyone is staring at him, taking notice of his dark complexion, of his abnormal braids, but they're not. His mom and dad are there, waiting by the doors. They wrap their arms around him.

FLOYD IS SITTING IN the gym bleachers in his regalia. It's almost time. The Winterfest powwow takes place where he and Tommy watched singers and jiggers and square dancers. Powwow dancers are everywhere, in every color. They sparkle and jingle and float in their feathers and moccasins. Some of them wear paint on their faces. Floyd does not. He's been here since leaving the Dakota Community Centre more than two hours ago. He thinks, *This is what it all means, this is beautiful, aho!* He checks the time on his phone. The championship game has likely ended by now. He texts Tommy:

*Let me know when you're done over there, my dad will pick you up.*

In a separate text, he adds, *I don't want to know the result of the game. So don't tell me. Miigwech.*

Tommy replies:

*Effin dead. Tell your dad not to worry. Heading home with Clinton. Got a ride. Have fun out there, brother! Break your legs!*

*Sacred. Get home safe, Big Weapon. Gwetch to you both for coming out.*

A NEW HOUR, ON the money. He forgets that in this same day he was at the rink, feeling dejected, rejected, that if things were different, he could still be there, racing over in his desperate postgame funk to catch this first beat, feeling the momentum of each pulsing thump in his veins, on his skin, coming alive, vibrating within him, until the rhythm steadies like a heartbeat. The drums, they pound. The strained vocals of each singer fill the air, blaring out from large speakers. It's Grand Entry. The colors are dizzying. All the dancers dance their way into the gym. Floyd is there, dancing the way he would in the kitchen with his mom, Northern Cree on the stereo. He moves beautifully. He's a natural. It comes naturally. That's what his mom would always tell him too, that he's been blessed with a gift from the Creator. The Creator, and also God, because she's from a God-fearing rez, blessed him with this gift because they wanted to see beautiful dancing from that place beyond the clouds. When all the dancers are there, in the powwow circle in the gym, the music stops. But then it continues, round after round, for hours, drum group to drum group, through the afternoon and early evening.

Floyd's eighteenth birthday was on Christmas, so he's resigned to dancing in the Men's Grass Special. There's a lot of waiting and watching and eating, and every now and then the emcee invites everyone to come into the circle and dance to a couple songs, which he does happily. He's sitting in a lawn chair just outside the circle with his mom and dad, and when the emcee finally calls upon his category he looks to his parents and both his mom and dad give him encouraging smiles. He finds his place in the circle. It's not a competition dance, but still he's nervous. The other dancers are older and more experienced, and somehow their colors seem brighter than his but he can't be sure. Maybe it's the lighting. The emcee, a big man with a fedora and two braids dangling along both sides of his chest, brings up a small woman to the stage where the band used to be, where he is.

"This is Colleen," he says. "Colleen is from Opaskwayak Cree Nation." He lets out a high-pitch whoop. "She's kindly offered to help me with a very special prize for one of these dancers. Colleen's going to pick a spot somewhere there on the floor and whichever dancer lands on that spot, or is closest, by the time the song is over wins the prize. So Colleen. Please have your spot ready. And no changing! If any of you see Colleen at the slots tonight, you tell me!" He laughs. "Eagle Spirit Singers take it away!"

The drumbeat starts, then the singing. Floyd leans his torso forward, elbows high, and he moves, shaking his new rattle to the beat. He remembers what his mom used to tell him about the grass dance, how when NDN peoples roamed the lands, moved camps, they relied on their grass dancers to enter first and dance in their beautiful way to flatten the high grass. He loved hearing the story, and so he came to believe that everything begins first by flattening the grass, no matter who you are or where you come from. He imagines he's no longer dancing on a gym floor but a grassy plain, high and green and swaying to a light breeze, and each stomp is one step closer to making room for his mom and dad and relatives and kin and himself. He's making the grass flat.

He's still moving by the time the drum stops, and the crowd cheers at his efforts and the emcee says, "Howah! Give it up for this young man! Holding it down for all the ancestors watching with us today." He catches a glimpse of the other dancers, bent over catching their breath, and realizes it's over. He stops and stands still, remembering there's a prize to be given, and glances over at the other side of the circle where he started his dance.

The emcee hands Colleen an envelope and instructs her to give it to the dancer closest to the spot she had chosen and so she makes her descent from the stage. She's far from him. There's many other dancers between him and her. She walks past the first two dancers, and then a third and fourth. She passes two more. Her step slows and she fakes out an older dancer and they share a big laugh like they know each other. The crowd laughs with them. She's getting closer. His heart races. It started racing as soon as she leapt onto the gym floor. She's close now. He thinks she might be looking in his direction. But it doesn't matter, won't matter. The work is done. She's walking on flattened grass.

## *clinton whiteway*

BAGOSENDAM. HOPE. HE/SHE WISHES. HE/SHE HOPES. PUH-GOH-send-uhm. Mbagosendam (nim-bagosendam). I am hoping.

Sometime in the middle of December, a speaker came to the Haven to teach us about hope and what it means to have it and what we should do if we don't. I don't know if I've ever thought about the meaning of hope before. I also wasn't sure I lacked hope, but then I considered my current circumstances. The speaker, a philosophy professor with a whispery voice who we were told became famous for posting Anishinaabemowin videos on YouTube, called hope a building block for courage and confidence. He said Hobbes considered hope a complex "pleasure of the mind" that comes from *thinking* not *feeling,* and that Descartes believed it to be a weaker form of confidence, coupled with anxiety. He said that hope implies an absence in our hearts, communities and the cultural parts of us. Then he said a return to the land is essential to building hope, to having it, as if tomorrow we could wander into the woods and graze with bears and deer and wolves.

As I say, I'm not sure I have hope. Or if I believe in the belief that hope is real and if it is real I'm not sure if anything I hope for is justified. I guess you could say that hope sprung up on me the day we played in the finals at Winterfest. I *hoped* we'd win. Because when things seem possible, that is when I feel I have the most hope. I felt more hope after the game. Twice in one day. It was when Tommy approached me in the lobby of the arena, fresh from the shower, his hair with a shine to it.

"What's going on with you?" he said, as serious as I've ever seen him.

I was tapping each of my fingers with my thumbs, thinking maybe he'd forget about me but he waited patiently for me to finish. I said, "What do you mean?"

"All this sneaking around. I went to your house the other day. Just to see how you're doing. See if you wanted to do something. Kelvin was there. He said he didn't know where you were."

I felt trapped like a buffalo at the edge of a cliff with nothing to do but fall.

"I'm at a shelter."

I looked away. I could see Tommy trying to find my eyes.

"Why?"

"Because I can't live there anymore."

He looked away, like he regretted asking. Then he said:

"Come stay with us."

I wanted to say, "Are you sure?" and lead the way to Tommy's house, but I said what I *really* wanted to say: "You don't need to take care of me. I can take care of myself."

He looked shaken. "We're friends."

*Friends.* Jakub, my friend, sometimes called me his brother and I liked the feeling it gave me, a sudden good feeling, a soundless eruption. Buckled, I said: "I'll come over."

He didn't respond. He called a taxi. Then he started texting.

"Who are you texting?"

"The guy who drove me here and then abandoned me."

"Floyd?"

"We'll split it. The cab. We'll split it." He continued typing.

"Cheap guy," I said, trying to lighten the mood. But there was another thing I needed to say. I cleared my throat. "There's something I need you to do for me."

He looked up from his phone. "What is it?"

"I need some things from home." I looked away all shy.

"You can borrow whatever you want at my place."

"No," I said. "I can't do that."

He looked at me for what felt like a long time, and then said:

"Okay."

I think I felt hope then. It's hard to say. Hard to say what it actually felt like. In that moment it was a bright, warm, golden feeling, like the medals that hung from our necks. Turned over there was an engraving of a special word that indicated a possible outcome, a belief, a desire, a likely possibility, even if in the beginning it was improbable. The word etched there was "champions."

## *errol whitecloud sinclair*

### DECEMBER 16, 2011

I don't drink anymore. I found a way to make coffee and carbonated water feel like suitable substitutions, even though they taste like shit separately. But sometimes when I crave the feeling that booze gave me I go out to see what drinking-people look like and I'm reminded that I enjoy and appreciate the feeling of waking up clearheaded in the morning. The other day I went out for the first time in two weeks. It was karaoke night at the bar near where I live and so I walked there. A disco ball hung from the pub's ceiling and sprayed rainbow colors across the dance floor. The dancers swayed and spun clumsily. I sat alone at the bar under the purple light of neon words that reminded you of where you were in case you forgot: The Stock.

I ordered a club soda and then a Diet Coke. Nobody cared that I was alone and sober, sober and alone. I turned around and watched the groups of people coming through the door and then looked over at the small stage where two mics and two TVs were set up for brave singers, and behind them the lyrics were projected for the rest of the bar to see and sing along with. I sang quietly, in a way that only I could hear, when Nancy Sinatra's "These Boots Are Made for Walkin'" started playing. The woman onstage dipped the mic like it was a dance partner and nearly tripped over some cords. It's not the number I would have chosen. Such a song would have brought out the jigger in me. The woman was drunk, but the raspy sound in her voice was beautiful and she swayed and bent the muscles in her neck in a way that could only be described as free. She was like cattail in the wind. I knew right away that it was your mother, and before the song ended I turned back to face the bar again and initially planned on finishing my Diet Coke and then leaving.

But I stayed. I waited after the song ended before standing up and making my way through the dance floor. I found her at a high table with a big man who wouldn't stop smiling, and this made it hard to see what his eyes looked like and even now I can't imagine what his face looks like when it's not bent and creased. She noticed me, and suddenly that free expression was stripped from her face and she looked more alert and guarded, like something had frightened her.

"Judy," I said. "How you been?" I didn't go in for a hug or nothing.

"Fine," she said. The big man beside her leaned over, noticing that something about her mood had changed, and said something to her but it was too loud for me to make out what it was. When he sat back straight and adjusted his posture he was no longer smiling like before.

"How are the boys?"

"Fine." She sipped her beer, and then said, "What do you want?"

"I'd like to see them."

There was a silence, and for a moment I thought I was being ignored and took it as a signal for me to leave. But just as I shifted my body, giving the impression that I was about to turn around and walk away, your mother responded.

"After all this time, huh? Then go see them. Not sure they'll want to see you. They probably think you're dead."

"Is that what you told them?"

"I haven't told them anything. Didn't need to."

"Look . . ." I took a small step closer to her table so I could hear better, and the big man quickly reached out with his hand to stop me.

"Hold up," he said. Judy made him put his arm down.

Looking at your mother, I said, "I'm trying."

"How's Tamara?" she said, referring to a woman I used to be with back on the rez we come from. "Or was Tamara before Bathsheba?" Bathsheba was another. For the sake of transparency and honesty: there were a number of women, some of whom I struggle to remember clearly. I am not proud of it but feel I should admit it right here.

"Ancient history."

There was another longer pause, but during this time your mother didn't take her eyes off me. She stared me down intensely and didn't blink or look away, not even when she sipped her drink. She always did love a fight.

"Heard you just got out," she said.

"Two weeks ago."

"Huh." She kept on looking me in the eyes. "Didn't seem like very long. Considering."

"Time moves slower in there."

"Not out here." She broke eye contact, taking a look around the bar before locking onto me again. "Nope. Not out here. That's for sure."

We didn't talk much longer. She told me where to find you and your brother, told me that you were messing around again with bad people and bad things. I'd heard, through the grapevine, that you were in for something too, robbery or something or other, and had been released around the time I was. I'll admit that it was nice talking to someone for a change, even though she stabbed me up a bit. I waited until there was another awkward quiet between us, with nothing else to fill it with, before saying, "I'm going."

Before I left I could see that the smile had returned to the big man's face but not your mother's, and as I turned to leave I heard him say, "Cool braid."

*pete mosienko*

YOU'RE RUNNING LATE. IT'S LATE AFTERNOON, THIRTY MINUTES before three, and you know this won't give you much time to scrape the ice clean and sharpen the row of skates that's bound to run the whole width of the counter in your pro shop before the Tigers game at four-thirty. You cuss out the doctor for making you late, for the forty minutes you spent waiting in the lobby of the clinic, despite you showing up and filling out the paperwork a whole fifteen minutes before showtime. You cuss him out and spit in the snow as you struggle to get out of your car in the parking lot of the Memorial Arena, grabbing and pulling the handle above you and then the door and then the roof of your old sedan, moaning and willing yourself out of the car. You cuss him out because once you were finally called into his office, he gave you the same bad news he always gives you: that the muscles around your knees, neck, and lower back look weak and appear smaller than they should for a man your age. Then the new bad news: you have arthritis that is somewhere in the ballpark of stage two and three, which means you have little cartilage left in those painful areas, and that it's a miracle you find the strength to shovel the ice several times a day. It's a bloody miracle, the doctor said, in his English accent. You're told to keep active and maintain a regular exercise routine and a decent weight, which you find confusing and funny at the same time, because your work at the rink, your version of the gym, is the very thing that is at once killing you and keeping you alive. You cuss out your bones and joints and muscles for crumbling on you, failing you, and for the health care system for only covering a microscopic portion of the costs of monthly treatment. But more than anything, you cuss out that being late meant buying a two-dollar cup of coffee rather than going home and brewing your own. You check your bank account online multiple times a day and stare at the balance for too long, calculating in your head, as if the zeros and commas will grow the longer you stare, an unhealthy habit you think may also be contributing to your demise. You're saving up for the Zamboni, and every day that goes by without spending a penny is a victory, because once you step out of the house everything costs something, even being with—and nurtured by—nature, but today you're late, you lost, and it's killing you.

You shuffle to the doors of the Memorial Arena slightly bent, legs not fully extended, because it takes a few minutes for your body to unfold after long periods of sitting. You unlock the door and clip your keys onto your belt and proceed to go from room to room turning on all the lights, everywhere except the dressing rooms. The players can do that themselves. You think about maybe installing new lights in the restrooms, the kind with sensors that turn on when they detect movement and then off when nobody's around, anything to save on hydro. But you worry about the potential lawsuits, the accidents that could occur from piss-covered floors in an unlit room. You head to the refrigeration room, which can be found below the scoreboard at the furthest end of the rink, where only you're allowed to be, where you sometimes sit or lay on your cot during games when you're tired of the noise, relaxing to the hum and music and warmth of the arteries pumping life into your facility, breathing life and meaning into the game, because without everything in that room there's nothing to give light to, no roar of a raucous crowd, no puck to drop, no ice to skate on—there's no point in your existence. No point to you. There, you use another key to open your circuit breaker and flip the switches that turn on the lights above the playing surface and so you leave the room and for a minute or two you watch the giant bulbs hanging from the ceiling change from blue to bright white, and when they do it's time to scrape.

But before you do you notice something. In the lobby. You see a person standing there behind multiple sheets of glass, like they're looking for something, and you begin your walk toward them, rounding the curves of the boards, preparing to tell them this isn't a public restroom and they can fuck off, because you worked it out and you spend about seven hundred dollars a year on toilet flushes, and so your resolution this year is fewer shits and pisses in your toilets, which might mean throwing up an Out of Order sign every now and then, even when the plumbing is sound, which, morally, feels a little wrong, but asking others to hold it in isn't a crime.

As you get closer you see it's a man, on the younger side, in clothes that are too loose for your liking. You immediately assume he's no good. The kind of young man that looks like they've never worked hard their whole life but thinks they're owed everything.

You say, You lost.

It's Petey right, the man says, reaching out to shake your hand and his strong grip does a little to impress you. Name's Kelvin.

Are you lost?

He smiles but the enthusiasm disappears from his face and you can see you've annoyed him. I was wondering if you're hiring, he says.

You refrain from turning him down straightaway and say, Who said I was hiring.

My buddy. Hurricane. He comes around here to watch the games. Said you might be looking for some help.

You know who he's talking about because there aren't many who come to see the Tigers play who aren't parents or grandparents or aunties. He stands while everyone else sits and calls you Petey like the players do, because maybe he was a player back when the team showed a bit more pride in the absence of wins, and he speaks to you the way most people who come in here speak to you, like he knows you and you're friends, but really he doesn't.

I'll do whatever you need me to do, Kelvin says.

You don't turn him down because you could use the help. You think of the pain in your knees, lower back and neck, and you feel it again. You're able to stow away the pain like a memory, but it's always there. You think of your arthritis. The missing cartilage in your body. You check your watch and see that you're running out of time. You say, Have you ever worked in an arena before.

He shakes his head.

Have you ever scraped ice before. We're getting a Zamboni. Soon. But for now we scrape the ice by hand when it needs to be cleaned.

No, he says. But I learn fast.

You run a hand through your hair, thinking of the hit this will have on your bank account, your savings. You don't believe in credit cards or credit lines or loans or the prison of debt, which is why, when you have enough, you'll pay for the Zamboni in cash, in full. You say, thinking you already know the answer, Have you ever worked before.

He shakes his head and drops eye contact with you, as if he's embarrassed of his admission.

You say, I can't pay you the minimum wage. Whatever it is.

I'll take anything, he says. Looking for the experience.

You say without even thinking or wanting to, Call me Pete. And then you turn and gesture at him to follow, Come this way.

You take Kelvin to the indoor garage just beyond the corner boards of the rink that once stored the Memorial Arena's previous Zamboni, where you'll keep the new one, and say, This is where we keep the shovels.

He nods as he looks around.

You grab the widest shovel there is and hold it out for him and he accepts it with a smile. You explain the importance of spattering water from the jug as you move up and down the ice, as if you're watering a plant, and then look down at his tattered black sneakers, and explain the importance of wearing slip-resistant boots to avoid a nasty fall. He nods along to every word and you're impressed by how well he's listening, the earnestness in his eyes, which you find a little crazy-looking, and then you say, with an authority you never knew you had, Start cleaning.

You leave him to do the work and proceed to open the pro shop, and, an hour and a half before game time, the pairs of skates start lining up before you, begging to be made sharp by your hand. You take it one blade at a time, brushing it against the machine and each stroke sounds like a miter saw penetrating wood, and every so often you raise the skate to eye level to assess the sharpness and the bite, and then you pull down your face mask, which you wear so as not to inhale steel dust, and you run a finger along the edges to feel for any dullness, but usually there isn't any. And as you do this work you feel a sense of relief in not having to pull your body up and down the ice with a shovel. You might call it happiness, and it's overwhelming.

After a short time Kelvin walks into the lobby and stands before you at the counter of the pro shop. On his dark shirt there's a Rorschach of sweat marks around his armpits and chest.

All done, he says.

You glance at your watch. You left him no more than forty minutes ago. You pull down your mask and think he mustn't have understood what the job was, and so you come out from behind the counter and swing through the rink doors and Kelvin follows you, and there, beyond the glass, is a clean sheet of ice, a gentle fog floating above it, as good a job as you could've done in half the time.

Good job, you say, and you mean it. Now empty the trash cans and take the garbage bags to the bins out back. And throw in fresh plastic.

You're in the pro shop when the first of the Tigers players arrive for the game, wearing suits and ties and shined shoes. Then there's Kelvin, dusting his hands on his pants as he comes through the front doors before sitting down on one of the benches in the lobby, and he looks over at you, nods upward and smiles, and you smile from inside your face mask.

You notice Kelvin stand when a player opens the door to the arena and comes in wearing a track jacket over his shirt and tie instead of a blazer, emblazoned with a Tiger head on the chest. The boy pauses when he sees Kelvin, and then, after a second, they both slowly make their approach.

The boy quietly says something to Kelvin.

Over the drone of the skate-sharpening machine you think you hear Kelvin say, I'm working here now. Hearing that makes you feel proud.

You hear the boy say something else, but it's difficult to piece together, like he's sharing secrets.

You sense a separation, a distance between them. But also something that draws them together. There hasn't been any eye contact and you wish you could go over there and tell them to love each other.

You pull down your mask and blow on another blade, and you see the boy inching away from Kelvin.

You hear Kelvin say, Things are going to be different. I promise.

The boy doesn't say anything. His hands are moving around in his jacket pockets, but you take that to mean he's nervous. Now you're nervous. He continues moving farther away in small steps, and there's a moment during this where you think he's about to say something but it never comes and you consider that a shame, and when he's far enough he turns away and strides down the hall and inside one of the locker rooms.

You close the pro shop once the game starts. You watch for a while. Until the opposition runs up the scoreboard and the contest becomes less exciting.

During the third period you lean back in a chair in the garage. Sometimes being here, eyes closed, away from everything, is better than being out there. You like the sounds hockey makes. The clacks, the bangs, the fan horns, the goal horn, the whistling, the shouting, the high-pitched screaming, the swearing, the arguments, the joy and the absurd panic of it all. You enjoy it until Kelvin walks in and leans against the stone wall across from you.

Had enough, you say, tilting forward in your chair.

It's a bloodbath, he says. They always this bad?

We've been bad for a long time. But we won't have to suffer much longer.

What do you mean, he says. Being sold or what. Relocating somewhere richer and nicer.

You chuckle because you know he's not making a joke. Doesn't work that way at this level, you say. Let's just say the league is reconfiguring and we won't be part of its final form.

*We,* he says, laughing. I take it you used to be a player.

What makes you say that, you say.

Only people that say *we* like that are players or parents or girlfriends . . . or boyfriends. He laughs at this last part.

It's true. You played for the Tigers in your younger days, before you quit school to work full-time at the rink, and back then you didn't win games either. I wasn't much of a player, you say, which is a modest statement.

Kelvin yawns big and looks tired and you're going to feel bad for telling him to clean the ice before he heads home. But he's impressed you more than you thought he would. There's something about his youth, his energy, that's inspired you, and you think that's what your dad must've felt watching you take over for the first time. Makes you want to keep going.

Who was that boy, you say. Whiteway. You're referring to the name on the back of his jersey, after seeing him take the ice.

My brother, he says.

He's always around here, you say, which sounds dumb, and so you continue and instantly regret saying, Is he always so sheepish.

He removes his back from the wall like he's uncomfortable and says, I don't know.

Deciding you need to change the subject and because you haven't said it yet, you say, The job's yours if you want it. Helping me out. Monday to Friday.

He nods looking pleased and leans back again and for a moment there's silence.

I'm not a good brother, Kelvin says.

You hear the final horn and some clapping and cheering and whistling. You point to the shovel hanging from a couple nails in the corner of the garage and he grabs it with both hands.

You say, It's never too late.

## *maggie mary taken alive*

HERE IS AN AUNTIE.

Maggie Mary Taken Alive, the daughter of a gambler who lost everything, was sitting at a wide table inside a community hall playing bingo. It was humid, the air was thick with cigarette smoke, and she held the cap of her dabber tightly in the palm of her hand, fearing that if she rested it on the table her numbers wouldn't be called.

Maggie believed in her superstitions. She hadn't planned on playing on that cloudy spring day, years ago, but then two things happened. First, she found a spider in her sink and carried it to a bush outside her porch. Then, she spilled salt all over her counter and quickly hurled some of it over her shoulder. Two things in one day had never happened before, and so later that evening, without thinking twice, she packed her purse and dabbers and walked the twenty minutes or so it took to get to the bingo hall.

Tim, a manager at a grocery store that sold Indian foods and who lived a few doors down from Maggie, sat across from her at the opposite end of the table. He sighed loud enough for Maggie to hear and rested his dabber on the table and rotated his wrist.

"I just can't win anything!" he said. "It's always political. The cousins are the ones always winning around here. I don't think I've ever called out bingo once. And it's supposed to rain this evening, so that's two bad things in one night. Either that or I just have awful luck."

Maggie, irritated by seeing the cap of his dabber upside down, yelled out:

"Go home, then! You're not helping me here. At least try to do the right things."

Tim continued mumbling. Maggie tried not to pay attention. She told herself not to move and stopped herself from standing up to find another seat somewhere far from him. She told herself that doing so could potentially interfere with her own luck, and that maybe Tim's misfortunes would somehow benefit her. She liked looking at Tim. He slicked his hair back like Elvis and spoke in a calm, smooth voice that made him seem gentle, and she found it adorable the way he threw his arms up in the air in frustration when he didn't bingo.

She had been getting closer and closer each round, and Tim was getting closer and closer to her. When her final number bopped and popped out of the machine onstage, like it had been waiting all these years to finally get to her, she dabbed her card so hard it left a puddle of red ink on her card, and for a second she feared the card reader may not be able to read it.

"Bingo!" she shouted, arms in the air. Tim raised his arms as well.

The card reader hurried over to verify the result, and before long they shouted back to the caller onstage:

"Good bingo!"

"Ladies and gentlemen, we got us a good bingo!"

She had won the jackpot. Fifty-one thousand dollars. It was the most money she'd ever had in her life. She was convinced that Tim was her lucky charm and she loved him for it. She wanted to marry him and have children. She convinced herself that she would grow to love the whiskers on his face that he considered a mustache and didn't mind so much that she was taller than him. He walked her home in the rain and he made her eyes wet from laughter and sadness because sometimes he enjoyed talking about the horrible things that happened to him in the fourteen foster homes he'd lived in. By the end of their walk she knew for certain. She loved him, and she felt his love for her. Something inside her had woken again.

Maggie had always wanted to be an auntie. Her sister Theresa had a son, her godson, whom she cherished. She was Auntie Maggie. Her nephew would crawl all over her like a jungle gym and hold on to her leg like a tree trunk as she walked. But more than anything she wanted to be a mother. She dreamt of marrying a man, a good man, and raising five children. She yearned to be loved by them, and to share the love she would pass on through generations.

But she would never have children, would never open herself up to men. She was afraid. Not of love, but of dying. Because love meant death. It was destined, a fate she couldn't avoid. A destined death. When they were teenagers her sister Theresa ran through the front door of their family home with a horrible look of terror on her face. She huffed like a tired dog, having run home from school. Her eyes were big and her clothes were heavy from sweat. She had a vision in the park. She saw Maggie lying in a hospital bed holding a newborn baby, but there was fear on her face, and sadness, and Theresa felt it like a cold sweat. There was blood. She was dying, dying after becoming a mother. Maggie looked her sister up and down, and though she could be a jokester she knew she was serious.

And so she went through life avoiding men like an auntie of hers avoided the sun, afraid it would boil her skin. She hid from the urges of motherhood. She ran away from love, from being loved, from the advances of men across the city. She would run into the arms of her nieces and nephews instead. And for years she took the insults from men—bitch, dyke, cunt—on the chin because of it.

Tim felt different. He washed his dishes and cooked her breakfast. His house was clean and his laundry was folded; he even rolled his underwear neatly and called it a Gitch Sausage. She felt safe. She listened to him talk for hours into the night. They imagined their lives together and named each of their future children. She moved into his house, leaving behind her family home, and with her bingo winnings they renovated the floors, roof and kitchen and added flowery wallpaper throughout. Tim was glad to have a woman in the house.

By next spring he proposed and they were married. She took the name Taken Alive. And on their wedding day, as they drove away from the church, he said to her:

"This is the best day of my life."

And for the next six months she was the happiest she'd ever been.

She and Tim went to bingo every Saturday and sat in the exact same spots as the night she won the jackpot. Maggie helped out Tim almost daily at the store. She admired his way of speaking at work; his tone was deep and commanding, different than the way he spoke at home. She was good at math and so Tim assigned her to looking after the books. She was also good at painting and drawing, and so he asked if she would paint something beautiful on the store's blank brown façade so that the customers had something nice to look at when they parked their cars. She agreed.

It was June. Trash went skidding through the city streets. On the wall outside the store, she painted a woman and her young son, who she imagined to be her husband as a young boy. To the left the boy is missing his heart, and to the right the mother is holding the bloody organ in her hands, stitching it back together using the sinew of a dream catcher. They are both smiling.

When she finished Tim looked upon the mural blankly, confused by what it meant. She believed he hated it and didn't bring it up further.

Bad things started happening to Maggie. That summer Tim said to her that he wasn't ready for children.

"I'm ready to become a mother," she said.

"I need more time," he said.

"Time for what?"

"Time to get things in order." Tim couldn't say to her, say aloud, that the store was failing, but this she already knew because she looked after the books.

That fall, Maggie's parents passed away two days apart. They were both in poor health and it was to be expected. After their funeral, she went back to the mural and behind the son and mother she painted the spirits of an elderly man and elderly woman looking down upon them. They were her parents, and she knew it made no sense in the context of the painting but to her it meant something. Somehow, there, they lived.

Days later Theresa was diagnosed with breast cancer. Her husband, John, who was from a reservation in Oklahoma, sickened by her diagnosis, hopped in his truck and drove through the prairies for several days and nights and returned one evening, five days later, ready to be a husband and father again, after everyone feared he'd gone to kill himself.

The next bad thing to happen was when Tim went north for work. He said something about potential investors for the store and that he needed Maggie to take care of things in the city. He would drive, take the winter road, thick and stable that time of year, and the last time they saw each other they smiled and waved as he ducked into the door of his truck.

She didn't hear from him for a week. She was in the back office of the store when she heard the jingles near the front entrance. It was January, a Monday. She moved out of the office and walked down a short aisle to find two police officers who first asked for her name, which she gave, and then told her that Tim had died.

"His vehicle fell through the winter road," the younger officer said.

"It appears he went off the normal path," the older officer added.

She nearly sobbed in front of them. "Did he get lost?" she asked.

"We've not been able to determine that. It's possible that this could have been a suicide."

She didn't say anything more. The why didn't matter. She'd never find an answer.

There was a funeral. Tim was buried next to her parents because he had never known his mom and dad and never spoke fondly of his many foster parents. The store closed. The new leaseholders turned the place into a fabric supplier, but they agreed to keep her mural. She kept Tim's house and at night slept in the smallest room, perfect for a small child. For months she mourned, and when she was ready she turned the master bedroom into an office space for her beading.

Five years passed, and Maggie never married, never thought again about children. She was still an auntie to her godson Jonah. She tried to pass on wisdom. Auntie wisdom. Like how to bead and sew and illegally download pirated movies and burn them on CDs. But mostly he was a student of swear words and perfecting the art of the middle finger. As he grew, he brought a kind of happiness she only felt with Tim. Where he belonged, she belonged too.

She watched over Jonah while her sister Theresa lay in the hospital, sick from the cancer. Fighting. The phone rang at three in the morning, filling her with a sudden terror. She was on the couch, Jonah in her small bedroom. It was Theresa's husband John and he spoke sedately.

"She's gone," he said. "It was peaceful."

"Should I wait for you to tell Jonah?"

"Can you tell him for me?"

"I will."

"Tell him I'll see him soon."

John came home two days later. He had been driving aimlessly again, listening to nothing but the wind. Theresa had always described John as dependable. Emotional. But he always came back.

Several weeks after Theresa's funeral John asked Maggie for her help. He worked for an Interlake construction company, which meant he left the city early in the morning and returned late in the evening. He offered her a room in his house, the house he shared with Theresa, and asked that she keep an eye on Jonah, see that he didn't get into any trouble. She agreed.

And it went this way for a time, all three of them under one roof. Jonah was about to start high school. He called her Auntie Mag. She loved being close to Jonah and didn't mind living with John. He woke at five in the morning, earlier than her, and brewed coffee for her and him. He returned late and slept late, often without dinner. Which she didn't like, because it was she who made sure Jonah had his dinner. He claimed to have a gene that allowed him to sleep four hours a night and be completely okay.

They spent Sundays together. First, they took Jonah to hockey, which was either a game or practice, and in the evening, they played bingo at the community hall. She enjoyed this time with John. He made her laugh, teary-eyed, sometimes she cried, from the slackest jokes, and whenever something didn't go right he'd say, "You gotta sweep before you can mop." Which also amused her. He sat where Tim once sat, honoring her request, and held his dabber and cap the way she wanted him to. They'd walk home together in the dark, and his height and broad stature made her feel safe.

One night, after bingo, under the orange of a streetlamp, he asked her, "Do you think we could ever be a real family? Would you want that?"

It was bright enough to see her face. She couldn't hide her sudden joy. Because she'd always found him attractive. She liked the grey in his hair, and often joked that he looked like a brown George Clooney.

He spoke like a cowboy, or what she thought a cowboy sounded like. She liked the deep scar between his brow, from a skipped rock that found his face as a kid. His beaten, bruised hands were about the only thing that disgusted her about him. That and him calling his dabbers "tools."

"Is that wrong?" she said.

"I don't know."

"Something about it sounds incestuous. You think it's incest?"

"Don't know. We're not related really."

"Would I still be Jonah's auntie? Or would I be his mother?"

He reached for her hand and held it in hers. "What's the difference."

"There's a difference."

She held his cheek in her hand and raised herself on her toes and kissed him gently on the other cheek and then kept walking. He followed her, and at the house they went to sleep in their separate rooms. Neither of them raised the issue again.

At night she dreamed of her sister Theresa. They were in the bush somewhere, looking for a pit to swim in. Along the way they picked and ate saskatoons and she warned Theresa of the poisonous options in front of them. When they found the pit, the water was deep and dark in the center and Theresa cautioned about the snakes that swam below. The sky was blue and bright. Maggie pulled at her arm, screaming for her not to jump but she always did, always with a big smile as she cannoned into the murky pit. She woke up before going after her.

One night, instead of bingo she had John take her to the mural. The lights of his truck washed over the wall of the store as she painted. She borrowed a ladder from him. She added her sister, in the back with her parents, smiling the way she did in her dreams.

In the truck, she asked, "What do you think?"

"Not bad. Maybe you should sell some art."

"Beading is an art."

"I mean, like, paintings or drawings. Something that goes up in museums."

Jonah was a week from starting high school when John left and didn't come back. He told Maggie that he was going back to Oklahoma to visit family, that he would be driving there. She woke up before him, made him coffee for the first time, and he didn't look back when she stood on the porch and watched him drive away. He sometimes messaged her on Facebook, asking, "How's Jonah? Miss him . . ." To which she'd say, "He's doing good. Skips class lots."

Jonah didn't ask much about his father, didn't ask much about anything, and Maggie sometimes found that odd, but figured he was a naturally shy boy now dealing with the loss of two parents. The day before his first day of high school, he said, "Auntie, is my dad ever coming back?"

"Yes," she said. "He's just in Oklahoma visiting."

And when they were forced to move back into Tim's old place, Maggie's house, Jonah didn't question it. He lifted more boxes than anyone. He took the small room, and she the master.

It went like this for several years. Just the two of them. Maggie continued beading from her bedroom, and made sure Jonah made it to school. Some days she walked with him, half the way, claiming she needed to pick something up from the fabric store. A lie. She kept her distance behind him, to confirm that he arrived at St. Croix. She knew that Jonah knew this, because he did that thing people do when they look off to the side to see what's behind them.

Secretly Maggie hoped John wouldn't come back. She loved Jonah more than anything. She would give her whole life for him. She packed him lunches, which she knew he threw out, waited at the window in the afternoon for him to come home, baked warm bannock in the morning, made sure he finished his homework. At hockey games when parents asked her, "Which boy is yours?" she pointed with pride, brimming with love, to the goalie in the orange Tigers jersey, his body covered by heavy padding.

"I'm his auntie," she'd say.

THE BENCH IS COLD when she sits back down. The third period is about to start. Jonah is in front of his net, scraping the ice with his edges, wearing a bright pink jersey. The Tigers are wearing pink uniforms for breast cancer awareness and she is wearing a matching sweatshirt, the only piece of clothing she owns that is pink. She blows on her coffee and feels the steam touch her cold cheeks. She makes it to every game, and it's around this time that she tries to think of something positive to say to Jonah when it's over, something to cheer him up. They haven't won a game all season, zero wins, twelve losses, and they're losing now, they'll lose again.

She looks over at a couple in the front row below her, a man and woman, parents of a boy on the other team, and imagines what might happen if she were to lob her coffee near them. Not that she'd do it. But if she did, it would have to be a perfect throw to be seen as an accident, as if they were just caught within the splash radius. She'd offer an apology, but she wouldn't mean it.

She first noticed the couple at the canteen in the arena lobby. They were in front of her in line. The game between the Tigers and Voyageurs had been senselessly rough all evening. You could hear the players and coaches chirping at each other like birds. The tension made its way into the stands.

"Gosh, it's getting nasty out there," the woman said to the man.

"Worse than bush league," the man replied.

"Everyone'll be thrilled when this team isn't around next year."

"You bet."

She didn't say anything. She didn't like confrontation, and there were times when she didn't like that this quality may have rubbed off on Jonah. On the ice especially he was no stranger to standing up for himself, but he was always nice about it. Nice Jonah. She ordered a coffee and returned to her seat.

The puck almost never leaves the Tigers' zone. It's dumped, chased, wedged in the corner by Voyageur forwards, killing time before the inevitable. The Tigers scramble to fish it out of their end, turn it over before they can make something happen, and then the process is repeated once more, over and over, like it's being rehearsed.

When there's a whistle, that's when the whole show gets dicey. The two sides bicker and test each other. They slash, poke, shove, anything to instigate conflict. Her stomach sinks, heart rate rises. Her hands tremble and her coffee spills over the rim and onto her hands. She hates this game, but Jonah loves it. She thinks, Where are the damn penalties? Isn't instigating two minutes in the box? It is. But the referee, a tired delivery driver, doesn't care.

With two minutes left there's more wrestling in front of Jonah's net. Parents around her are shouting things, including the couple below her, making gestures with their hands, but she's not sure what they're saying. She just hears sounds. Jonah skates above his crease and begins barking at the Voyageur goalie who's made his way to center ice.

"C'mon then," she hears Jonah say. "Friggin' white piece of trash."

The whole arena hears it. Parents of the other team gasp. She feels the glares of parents who know her personally, moms and dads and kokos, like a bug on your skin that's not there. Jonah doesn't swear, doesn't like the feeling curse words give him, not even when things get heated. She's proud of him for not swearing, but embarrassed that the whole place heard it. Everyone knows she's his auntie.

Nothing comes of it. No fists thrown. The final horn is meaningless. Another defeat. The two teams are ushered off the ice without shaking hands, fearing another outburst.

In the restroom she runs cold water over her coffee burns.

"It'll come," she tells Jonah in the car. "Be patient."

THEY'RE AT THE DINNER table eating macaroni soup and bannock. One of her favorite things to do is to watch people eat the food she makes, but this especially applies to her nephew because she cooks for him most. He cleans his plate, finishes everything put in front of him. He also has good manners. Rarely does he burp in front of her, excusing himself if he does, and when it comes to soup he doesn't slurp loudly from his spoon. And when he's finished, he takes his dishes to the kitchen sink.

"The school called again today," she says quietly.

"I was late. By only like a few minutes." He slices open a piece of bannock and lathers butter on the two soft sides.

"They're saying you're getting close to auto-failing three classes if this keeps up."

His mouth is full.

"We both know you need to get your act together. Or we can kiss graduating this summer bye bye. Is that what you want? You're so close."

"I'm telling you it was only by a few minutes."

She could see him becoming irritated, but she told herself today to put her foot down. "And last week it was because you apparently rolled your ankle in gym. And yet you still went to hockey after school. The week before it was because you traded hats with Tommy."

"What's with you right now?" He rests his fork on his plate.

"I'm trying to get you to understand. You're so close. You need to smarten up."

"What. You saying you don't believe me now? I made it this far."

She sighs and takes a sip of water. "I'm saying what the school is saying. They don't give a damn if you don't make it out of there. I do. They're not going to drag you by your arms and legs to class, kicking and screaming. I'm trying to do my job. To get you to see the big picture. To stop skipping and get your butt to class."

"What job?" He moves back in his chair and stands. "You're not my mom. You ain't my dad either. You're . . ."

"Your auntie. I'm your auntie."

He turns and walks, calmly, down the hall and she hears his bedroom door close shut.

THERESA IS THERE AGAIN at the edge of the pit. The water lately has been clearer and she can see that there are no snakes lurking below. Theresa jumps, goes under, and Maggie can see her swimming, laughing. But she doesn't go with her. Something always holds her back.

She wakes from the dream to the vibration of her phone. Messages from John.

*Why aren't you replying???*

*Please . . .*

*Thinking of him . . . of you both . . .*

*How is he?*

*How you been? I'm living, breathing . . .*

*Is everything okay? Please say something . . .*

It's four in the morning. She thinks to write back telling him to go to bed but her thumbs don't budge. It's true. She hasn't been responding. Hasn't been for a long time now. She taps on his profile, takes a moment to familiarize herself with his profile picture. A shot of him with a woman that isn't Theresa from the year before. She goes back, finger scrolls down, hits Block. She closes her eyes and soon she's at the pit again, cold, shaking, slowly adjusting, wading through the ripples of her splash. Swimming.

## *errol whitecloud sinclair*

### DECEMBER 31, 2011

I don't mean this letter to be some long ramble about how I've changed, or how I'm a better man than I used to be. I've come to accept that that's not for me to decide, and I'm at peace with this, more so than years past. But I haven't mentioned my braid, which is probably the biggest noticeable difference about me since you last saw me. It's dark and thick, but perhaps not as long as I'd hoped. My ends tend to break at a certain length and I'm told there's nothing you can do about that. Simply genetics.

I grew my hair in prison. I was never one for long hair before that. Never liked the way it felt on my skin after a shower, like a dripping wet mop that never dried. But the more you put up with it the more you get used to it, and the more your pride and love for it grows and then you can't see yourself with anything but long hair. You see, son (can I call you that?), the braid is your strength. It's your connection to the Creator and your relations. We cut it only when we grieve a great loss, offering it to the Creator for that spirit's safe passage to the next world. But in a more personal sense, the braid is a symbol of cultural pride, as not long ago we Indians were forbidden from wearing our beautiful hair down to our waists (I have come across some men who have grown it even further!), and so it means a great deal to many to reclaim their hair. There's also something soothing about the daily ritual that is braiding, or learning to braid. It requires patience and care. It's an act of loving, or learning to love, one's self the way the Creator does. But mostly I think it makes me look like one deadly fucking Indian. When I told Art that I'd grow my hair for the first time in my life, he said to me, "That's beautiful. It's like flipping the bird to the people who told us no. Make sure to condition your ends well, leave it in there for a few minutes before washing it out. Argan oil for when it's damp."

You didn't know my parents well, and that's not your fault. They're both gone now. We didn't speak as much as we probably should've after I left the rez and that's something I'll always regret. Dad was a drunk, as I've said. I loved him, but my memories of him when his eyes weren't glossy are sparse. Mom was a spectator of sorts. She did her share of the drinking but mostly she refereed the festivities, ensured the safety of others. I loved her more than him, because I learned more from her and because she was more approving of me leaving than he was. She'd say, "Errol, you gotta go and do something useful, wherever that is." I appreciated this each time she said it, even though I knew why she offered such words.

My mom wasn't from the rez, but a nearby Métis village. Used to say her grandfather could only speak French. She prayed at night by her bed to Jesus and tried to teach me how to pray too but it didn't stick. Life was never easy for her. Even today my memories of her leave me in awe. She was always at peace with herself and the world around her, even though it was obvious how much my father had worn on her. He died on the rez, at an age that the rest of the world would consider a young man. Heart failure at thirty-nine. She didn't touch a bottle or can after that, didn't care to, said it wouldn't bring him back. She passed on a couple years later, at forty-three, from cancer. That and a broken heart. But how would I know that?

Dad didn't believe in nothing spiritual or religious, though I wonder now how his opinions may have changed if he had the chance to meet someone like Art. An atheist probably not, because he had that one ghost story, which was about the only thing he truly believed in, that he repeated (with never-before-heard details sprinkled in here and there) when the topic of drunk conversation with my uncles turned to supernatural and unexplained phenomena.

Art taught me a lot about our ways and teachings. I became his helper for a time, and was charged with carrying the grandfathers into the lodge. He gave me my Indian name, which I won't say here so as to be mindful that I am fortunate to have this blessing and believe this time now is not the appropriate time. However, he did tell me that I am a member of the Bear Clan, and so you are too. Being a clan member, as you may know, comes with a set of important responsibilities. As Bear Clan, we are the protectors and guardians of our communities, and we are also privileged to be able to become healers and carriers of medicines. I never knew which clan I belonged to before Art. But of course he taught us other things as well when he could, such as some Anishinaabemowin. He prefaced this one afternoon in the sacred circle by saying the demands to teach all of us who wished to learn Anishinaabemowin would simply be too much for him to take on, and so he mainly taught us how to count. Art said that learning numbers would be most useful to us in the short term, and encouraged us to push the prison staff to introduce language classes, but they never did. Because in there you're always counting—the minutes, the hours, the days, the months and the years and if you're fortunate enough the seconds, until that door finally opens.

## *olga shields*

I'm going out tonight to look for Shadow. Which is to say, I'm leaving the house at around five o'clock, but by then it will be close to dark. I like it when twilight turns the snow blue.

The boys are in the kitchen making tomorrow's dinner. When they got home they came through the door looking scared. Like the life had been drained from their eyes. Sunken and pale. It's moments like that that make me wonder whether my grandson and grand-daughter are afraid of me. Afraid of what I might say. Afraid of me judging them. They'd come to me in the store as little kids asking for something and I'd turn away and say no and they'd walk away all sad. If they are afraid of me then I suppose that's a good thing, better that way. I'm not their mother. I'm their koko, and as far as I'm concerned the only job I've been tasked with is to raise them right. Tomahawk told me his friend needed a place to stay, and in return he promised he would cook more often, and I looked over at Clinton and said:

"What about you?"

"I can do the dishes," he said.

"He'll do the dishes," Tomahawk repeated.

"Mm-hmm. How's your mom doing?"

"Not good."

"Mm-hmm. What does she call you?"

He looked at Tomahawk confused.

I said, "For example. He's Tomahawk. Asemaa is Asemaa, though some call her Sam. Does your mom call you anything?"

"When I was small she called me Klik. Because I loved eating Klik."

"Do you still love eating Klik?"

"Sometimes."

"Then I'll call you Klik."

I sit on the couch and turn on the weather channel. There's a wind chill warning tonight and tomorrow. I can see Tomahawk just standing around, less of a cook than a supervisor. Clinton—Klik—said he learned how to cook a turkey at the shelter he was living at over Thanksgiving. He went out this morning and brought back a Butterball turkey and put out the breadcrumbs to dry overnight. He's off to a good start. He's telling Tommy to get started on the macaroni salad, but Tommy won't listen—he's breaking the deal he'd made with me already. I handled the lemon pies, date cake, and peanut butter confetti cake earlier, because I like them a certain way. And tomorrow I'll do the ham and meatballs while the boys say they'll take care of the mashed potatoes. But I'm sure that'll fall on me too.

When it's time to leave I grab my purse from atop the fridge beside the cereal. Nimaamaa used to do it this way, always afraid someone was trying to steal from her. I pack the whistle the trainer gave me. I pack my spare change and dollar bills, which I keep in a leather pouch Nimaamaa gave me when I was a little girl, in case of bus fare. The pouch still smells like cow, like the coat she used to wear on cold days just like this. I wrap my favorite patterned scarf around my neck and slip on the ankle-length parka Asemaa got me as a birthday present. I hug the boys. I tell them I might be home a little late, but I'll be back to wish them Happy New Year.

It's not the first time Shadow hasn't come home. He's a free man. Likes to run with the squirrels, perhaps sometimes forgets he's a dog. He's a black Lab, dark as night. Shadow. He's always been this way, likes to take off and roam the city streets, but he always comes back home. He knows where home is. But I suppose he's this way because of me. His free-spiritedness, I mean. I've allowed him to come and go as he pleases ever since he could tough the urban wilderness. It's how I've always let my dogs be.

I'll admit, though, that lately it's gotten me in some trouble. But I blame that as much on the city changing as myself, because that's not always how it used to be. Nevertheless, people from around the neighborhood have been coming to my door, saying Shadow has been in their backyards, leaving yellow in their snow, sometimes a number two, chewing their shovel handles, scaring their kids. I try to tell them he's a good boy, as friendly as they come. But as I say, this whole place is changing. There's less tolerance but also more rules for us, but not anyone else.

Animal Services came by over the summer saying there'd been complaints, threatening to take Shadow from me. I told them he's neutered and that I don't believe in collars or dog tags either, and was about to shut the door on the young man before Asemaa marched over from the living room to reassure the man that we'd take Shadow to a trainer. And so that's how I got this whistle.

I start by walking east down my street, peering down the sidewalks of houses that usually run into their backyards, where you can partially see what's back there. Nothing. No sounds. Yellow lights from the main windows of houses. Everyone has Christmas lights on, swollen and pretty. There's a park a few blocks ahead that I know he likes to hang around at. The kids during this time of year build igloos and tunnels out of the snow and I've found him there on more than one occasion curled up like a donut in one of those shelters, eating the snow for the heck of it.

Shadow has been gone now for a full week. Back before I made it so that he could only go as far as our backyard, he'd come home every other day or two to eat some food, cuddle up on the couch and then be gone again.

I'm worried. Scared even. I'll admit that's how I'm feeling, and if something terrible happens to my Shadow I guess it will be my fault for always forgetting to close the gate to the backyard.

Back on the rez, dogs seen as troublesome, the way some have described Shadow, are shot for going around plucking carrots and potatoes from gardens. I know because I had one such troublesome dog, a mutt really.

And that's because I didn't always live in the city. I was a rez girl before I became a city woman. But this mutt was beautiful, as handsome as any mutt you'd ever seen, so much so that people mistook him for a purebred German shepherd. He was my first dog and his name was Burnie and he saved my life. But in doing so he showed me something else too. He showed me the magic, the sacredness, blurred and forgotten, behind the place that I called home.

Nimaamaa had me at an unadvisable age. But once I showed no signs of poor health, my father, who died when I was little, called me his lucky charm, and so for a large chunk of my childhood my nickname was Charm. After my dad died I lived with Nimaamaa, my older sister Rosie and older cousin Katia in the house my father built for Nimaamaa and just across the dirt road was Uncle, my father's cousin.

Burnie had been missing for a week, the same amount of time as Shadow. I couldn't remember the last time I rubbed him behind the ears, kissed him on the nose and told him I loved him. I just knew he was missing and I needed to find him.

Uncle was a mystery, a shadowy figure. Technically, Uncle was my father's uncle, but in my family, great aunties were kokos, and somewhere throughout our history someone decided that Uncle would be an uncle, despite traditional definitions. My *cousin* Malcolm for instance, about my age, was by definition my uncle. I didn't question these labels, didn't think twice about them, considered them a quirk that came with being Indian, the same way all Indians like to think of themselves as related to that one kid who became a movie star.

I was, as a girl, petrified of Uncle. He was no different to me than the bogeyman, and many times I cried on the walk from our house to Uncle's to deliver supper, and on many more occasions I accused Nimaamaa of using my fear as a form of punishment. "You're going to wish you spent more time with him. He used to be hilarious when I was a kid," Nimaamaa would say. But in my mind, Uncle only existed as a dark silhouette hiding in the shadows, peering out his living room window, his glowing eyes following me as I approached his door with a bowl of soup and warm bannock.

Nimaamaa had suggested that I ask Uncle if he'd seen Burnie. There was a calmness in her voice, like she knew he would eventually come back. Burnie, like most rez dogs, spent his days outdoors, unchained. He had his own doghouse, stuffed with hay like a plush to protect him from the cold and came and went as he pleased.

"He might know where to look at least," she said. She paused to finish folding the towel in front of her and then deposited it in the hamper next to her with the rest of the organized laundry. "He knows all about this place. Every nook and cranny in the bush. Ask him."

"What do I even say?" I said. "Burnie's lost, do you know the mating locations of dogs around here? Any idea where they fuck?"

"Language."

"Sorry."

"Take the food on the stove when you go over there. Tell him we're out of cedar. I'm going picking tomorrow."

Later that day I crossed the lawn behind our house to Uncle's. It was an old place, with a sagging roof that looked like it could cave at any moment. With its recent paint job—a light grey—the house reminded me of an old English cottage if its builders ran out of bricks. Uncle had lived there forever, no one was certain how long. As for when the house was built, well, that was another mystery. I knocked three times and after what felt like a long time Uncle opened the door and waved me through the screen door. Boy if Asemaa and Tomahawk could have walked through that old man's doors back then they'd wonder what planet they're on, because he, like my family, did things the old ways. To the right of the entrance was a room with a station for washing laundry by hand and at the back of the home was a kitchenette with appliances that looked like they belonged in a museum. I reached out my arms and offered Uncle a plate of food covered with tin foil.

"Miigwech," Uncle said, directing me to the living area.

I kicked off my outdoor slippers and sat down on a brown sofa, the fabric of which looked like corduroy. Uncle sat across from me on a rickety rocking chair with a flowery cushion. I hadn't looked at Uncle directly yet. Uncle, I seen, had light brown eyes and when the sun occasionally caught his face they looked like honey. His hair was short and grey and there were patches of white on his hands in various places. He looked like a nice man but he wasn't old enough to look so old. I looked away again and studied a pink paper pterodactyl hanging from a lampshade.

"Rosie made me that," Uncle said. "She learned about dinosaurs."

"I have one too," I said. "Mine's red."

He clapped his hands and said, "So your dog's missing, at least that's what your mom said when she was here last. Good cook your mom, better than her mom anyway. And that's saying something."

I nodded. "He's a pretty brown mutt with ears that perk up like a wolf's. Can't miss him. His name is Burnie, in case you didn't know that already. Two years old. Any idea where I should—"

"I used to have a bunch of dogs. Nothing like yours though. Ugly ones mostly. We used to call them rez breeds. Mixed-breeds and half-breeds. But every now and then one comes along that's gifted with beauty. Me, I was always good at training them. One of my boys, Buddy his name was, was so good at herding the cows and making sure the horses didn't wander too far into the bush, because there were wolves in the area in those days, picking off the horses. Not so much anymore."

"I hate most of the mutts around here. This one time I was walking home alone—"

"Lots of places to hide around here you know. The bush is thick and the bogs have gotten worse over the years, with all the flooding and such. If you go too deep you could get stuck and no one will ever be able to find you out there. I used to go for my morning walk just out back here but don't do that anymore because everywhere there seems to be a new swamp. Does Burnie like playing in the bush? In this country you ain't gonna find someone who doesn't want to be found."

A kettle in the kitchen started whistling and noticing the noise, Uncle looked over his shoulder.

"Would you like some tea?" he said, turning to me.

I nodded.

Uncle stood up and walked slowly to the kitchen. A few moments later he returned to the living room couch with two mugs, some sugar packets, and a French press filled with steaming hot water, the loose black tea floating at the surface. He placed the press on a coaster and after a moment he pushed the top of the plunger down so that the tip of the metal rod met with the steel lid, and then he poured the tea into the two mugs. I found many things strange about Uncle's small bungalow, such as the old-smelling decor, but it was this French press that I found most odd. Where did he get it? And who taught him how to use it?

"So," Uncle said, "has your mom or dad ever told you how they came up with the name for this reserve?"

"Reserve?" I said.

"Rez, reservation, Indian band. Grass prison. Whatever the kids are calling it these days."

"No, I don't think they have. I think they said there used to be a bunch of dogs around here back in the day. In the days of teepees and loincloths."

"Not just dogs, but a creek of wild dogs! They would live and survive off the creek. Off the land, like in the old days. Like we used to. All the kids, your mother and father and I, would go out trying to find this dog creek, this creek of dogs. We had to see it. See if it was real. I dreamt about your dad recently, gosh I miss him so much! We were walking around, I was a kid but your father and mother were fully grown. They were on both sides of me, holding my hands. We weren't that far apart in age you know. We were pretty much siblings. Anyway, we were out looking for the creek. They kept saying, 'It's not real, it's not real.' But I kept telling them that I know it's real, I know it's real, because I came close once to finding it and I started telling them the story of how I almost found the creek, the dog creek. But I woke up before I could finish telling the story. It was a good dream.

"It was a damn good story, too. I hope you don't mind I share it with you. I don't like to admit it but I'm getting old, and when you get to my age you realize that stories are the only thing you really have to offer the world. Us Indians were the first storytellers on these lands. They love old stories everywhere else in the world except here it seems. When I was a young man—or boy shall we say, because I still feel like a young man—your dad's family took care of me when my mom and dad were not around. Your koko and shoomis loved us, and they especially adored your father. They called him their 'Little Star' because of his Indian name, which translates to: *The First Star You See*—so next time you see him up there say a prayer. It was because of them that we didn't get dragged off to those schools far away. We heard all the stories: the violence, the torture, how you weren't allowed to speak Indian. English wasn't our first language, you see, so your father and I would have been really in for it if his mom and dad let them take us away. But they kept us safe. Each time the Indian Agent, the priest and those two nuns came to our house to round us up and take us to the school to live there with them, your father's parents made us hide, me and him. 'The boys are hunting,' your father's mom would tell them. A lie. Some lies are good. They came for us four or five times one winter, and they would wait for hours for us to come back home but we never did. Not until your shoomis came to find us to tell us it was safe. Your shoomis built us a tree house, high in a really old tree, far in the bush. He lined the outside of it with birch bark so that it would blend with the snow and the clouds, and he put hay in there so that we'd be warm while we waited for the Indian Agent, the priest and the nuns to leave.

"But one day we waited in the tree house for hours, hours longer than we normally did. 'What if they forgot about us,' your father said, 'what if they arrested them.' I kept telling him it'd be okay, that your shoomis and koko will come for us soon. But then he started going crazy, losing it, jumping around, freaking out. The fear of being kidnapped had been making him scared. 'Calm down, calm down, they'll hear us,' I said to him. But he just kept jumping around, grabbing his head, trying to catch his breath. Gasping for air. I didn't know what to do. I tried holding him down, but he was strong, stronger than me. Then I heard a loud sound, like the snap of wood. And the next thing I knew your father and me were falling through the air, we'd broken through the floor.

"I woke up covered in fresh snow. Your father was gone. He told me later that he was scared your shoomis would get mad at him for destroying the secret tree house. He was right about that. Our tracks were covered with new snow. I had no idea where I was or which way was home. I walked and walked, looking for marks in the trees that looked familiar. Nothing. No one. But then I heard a sound: the gushing of water. The creek! I thought. This was it. And looking back now I know it was, it had to have been. I had never heard a sound like that around here before. There's only lakes and swamps. I followed the sound and it kept getting closer. But then another sound. I turned around and there they were: five or six mutts with snow sprinkled all over their faces and bodies. I put my hand out but each one greeted me with sharp teeth. I was only a boy, but even at that age I'd learned to recognize when an animal wants to hurt you. So I ran and I didn't stop, even when I knew they'd stopped chasing me. I got home. When I walked through the door, your koko and shoomis looked at me with great surprise. Their eyes were red and wet. Like they'd been crying. I never got to tell your father this story before they took him away. And even when I tried to tell him about it, years later when he was back home again, he didn't care much to hear it."

Uncle sipped his tea. He looked at his hands and inspected his cuticles, like they communicated information only he could see. For a man who apparently worked in a garage for many years they were in remarkable shape. "I'm rambling."

"I knew dad went to Sandy Bay, but I never asked him about it."

"He never liked to talk about it. Not even to me."

"Why you think?"

"I wish I had the courage to ask him that question. All I know is he left here a boy but did not return a man. They say they weren't raising children over there, but corrupting them, spoiling them, and not in the good way. That's what they should tell you kids in school."

I touched my mug against my lips and swallowed some tea. It was lukewarm. We sat in silence for a moment, which I didn't mind and neither did Uncle. A breeze came through the screen door. Grasshoppers vibrated outside.

"I'll tell you what," Uncle said, "you should find the creek. I bet that's where Burnie is. You don't think these dogs all know about it? It's the creek of dogs!"

I gave a barely audible sigh. "Where's this creek, then? Maybe I'll go check it out. I'll let you know what I find."

Uncle's eyes widened with excitement. "Back when this reserve was smaller, before they built all these rotten, cookie-cutter-shaped houses, most of us lived around the church, before it was boarded up. When them missionaries arrived to build that thing, they wanted to be in the dead center of all of us, easier for them to convert us! You know that old road behind the old church they say leads to nowhere? Follow it. Keep going. Keep going as far as you can. I never had the courage to go back there, but maybe them dogs are nicer these days."

I rested my chin on my fist, something Nimaamaa always did when she became impatient. "How is it that you're the only one around here talking about a secret creek?" I worried he thought I didn't believe him and I'm not sure I did. But more importantly I felt bad for possibly coming across as churlish.

"My niece," he said calmly. "This reserve wasn't always a reserve. These boundaries around us, holding us, restricting us, suffocating us, *killing* us, exist only up here." He tapped a finger on his temple. "Out there, down that old road, across that land, all over, that's where we come from. Out there."

I WAS UP BY dawn. I jumped up, the springs of my mattress launching me skyward like a rocket, and looked outside the window. The world was still blue, a light frost cloaked green grass, a dark line of smoke floated above Uncle's house next door. I tiptoed down the hallway to the living room, poking my head in Nimaamaa's room to make sure my soft steps didn't wake her. But as I suspected she wasn't there. She was never there, and for the longest time I thought it was maybe due to the comfort of her bed, but then years later Rosie would tell me that Nimaamaa felt cold and sad without my father.

I cracked the door to Rosie's room and there they were, Nimaamaa and sister snuggled together in a small bed. Nimaamaa always said that Rosie was named after koko Rosalie, but I had a good feeling that both of them were named after the rosebush out front, hiding during each harsh winter and blooming again bright pink come April, like a lost friend you were surprised to see once more before you die.

In the living room, I shook Katia awake. "Time to go," I said.

"You scared me," she said, squinting hard to shake the sleep from her.

Katia had lived with us for many years, and Nimaamaa enjoyed her help around the house. We were cousins, but I thought of her like a second sister, my closest friend.

In the kitchen I filled two thermoses with water, wrapped some cooked deer meat and bannock in foil and loaded everything into a knapsack. Next to the kitchen was a small eating area, where an old wooden gun cabinet stood in the corner of the room. Rosie always said that no one had touched anything inside it after our father died.

She was much older than me, and knew more about him than I did. I went over to the cabinet and observed the dusty rifles and the pretty designs on each stock, my father's initials carved into one of them. I heard the front door open and turned to see Katia's head poking through, awake.

"Are we doing this?" she said.

I turned to face the cabinet again and opened one of the drawers, pulling out a knife I'd seen Nimaamaa use to skin game after one of our relatives went hunting. It was about the only thing she still used that belonged to him and one day to me, she'd say, and so I packed it in my bag and was out the door.

WE SET OFF ON foot. The frost that was previously on the grass had melted, and now the rising sun reflected off wet lawns like a mirror. When we got to the old church, the sun was just coming up and you could see all the wear on the building's white paint, as if you could peel it off like the shell of a hard-boiled egg. Remove it of its whiteness. On one of the boarded-up windows someone had written "No God" in black spray paint.

"Did I ever tell you I was baptized here?" I said. "We're not even Christian."

"So was I," Katia said. "I don't think I ever went in there again after that."

I thought about her statement. I couldn't recall ever stepping foot inside the old church after my baptism either, before whoever was running the place left it to rot.

"I asked my mom once: why did you baptize me?" Katia continued. "She didn't really have a good answer. She said it's just what people did."

The road behind the old church was almost no longer a road, overgrown with weeds and a plant that I only knew as "hot-dog-on-a-stick." Rutted. We walked, looking across the boggy fields on both sides of the path, and I was certain none of this was here years before, long before worsening floods began wrapping our community in a blanket of water and bugs. Damn mosquitoes. Soon we were going uphill and the land turned from swamp to bush, where according to Uncle a bunch of dogs thrived near a gushing creek and where all sorts of creatures lurked, waiting to drain you of your humanity. Damn ticks.

We paused near a fallen tree that blocked the path. We didn't say a word to each other. I opened my knapsack and took a big bite of bannock and Katia eagerly leaned forward and took a mouthful while I held it in my hands. The bush hummed with life. I swigged some water and pulled out my father's knife and slipped it into the pocket of my coat. And then, without saying a word, we continued walking.

"Do you think this tree decided to die here on purpose?" Katia said, stepping over the fallen tree's soft corpse.

"What?" I said.

"Do you think this tree decided it would die here on purpose? To block this road. To protect the rest of this land from the likes of us."

"How is that possible?"

"Trees communicate you know. They talk, just like us. They share food, they give each other nutrients out of nothing more than the kindness of their hearts. When another tree is sick, they'll rally together to help that sick tree by giving it food, helping it get back on its feet. And they also help each other fend off pests."

"You learn something new every day."

"So maybe, maybe this tree died here to protect its sisters. Maybe it died here to protect this creek you're looking for. Maybe this was her last act of kindness."

"Are you saying they're all women?"

"Only women can be that kind."

"I suppose." I could tell she expected more from me.

"Isn't it crazy how this religion and the people behind it made so many people unhappy?" Katia said.

"Everyone seems unhappy. City people aren't happy either," I said.

"They made themselves unhappy. We didn't make any of this."

The tire tracks faded away, slimmer and slimmer until they were gone. The road we had been walking on was no longer a road. Each step was spongy and wet and it was darker in there, and cooler, too. I opened my knapsack and took another bite of bannock and handed the rest to Katia.

"So," Katia said, chewing. "Are you going to tell me why we're out here?"

"What do you mean?" I said. "For Burnie. What else?"

"This just seems sudden. I mean, all these rez dogs come home. Burnie'll get hungry and come running home. As filthy as can be. We both know that's what's going to happen."

"Maybe. Or maybe someone shoots him for picking their carrots."

"I'm pretty sure everyone knows who he belongs to."

"You never know."

Bannock brought out the worst in Katia. She almost became confrontational, and didn't mind interrogating others about their feelings. She always knew when people were bothered, had a natural instinct for it, like they had a language only she knew written all over their face and body. There were times at home when Nimaamaa would enter the room and Katia would ask, rather abruptly: "What's wrong?" But Nimaamaa always smiled and said: "It's nothing." But Katia was always right. There was a sadness inside Nimaamaa for much of my childhood, despite her best efforts to shut down Katia's intuition.

I suppose I am like Nimaamaa, as in I struggle to allow myself to feel my feelings, to share them with others. I, much like Nimaamaa did, pave over them like concrete and get lost along the road I create. Which is to say, I'm aware that I am a cold person. And for that I am sorry to Asemaa and Tomahawk, though I never say it.

I'll say this: at that age I never once considered my father's pain. Much like Uncle he was a mystery, living somehow through Nimaamaa, but I could never tell whether it was a good sadness or bad sadness or both. He was, according to Rosie, a gone again, back again human man. Broken and decommissioned. A prisoner of something somewhere that you could not see, but which he made felt on those around him. He drank, he fought, he yelled, and inflicted abuse on Nimaamaa and Rosie. When Rosie thought of the concept of anger she thought of our father slamming his large fists on the kitchen table and hot vegetable beef soup splashing on Nimaamaa. Nimaamaa didn't react, she didn't make a sound. She slowly removed each stray noodle from her arms and body and dabbed her face with a towel.

We were lost in the bush hunting down a lost dog. I took bites of deer meat as we walked, waving away the bugs. Katia tore a few blades of grass from the ground and tossed them in front of her to observe the direction of the wind but didn't care which way it was blowing. Suddenly she tapped me on the shoulder and pointed forward. A doe and two babies in the distance. Their heads in the grass.

"Should we feed them?" Katia said.

"Feed them what?" I said.

"The meat?"

"Feed the deer deer meat? Sounds like cannibalism. Deer cannibalism."

Katia cupped her mouth to prevent herself from laughing loudly.

We walked forward, slowly, trying not to make noise. It felt like the forest had gone silent. Like all the birds were watching us creep ahead. The doe's head perked up, as if it heard us coming. That's when I heard it too. Something ruffling in tall grass. I heard a branch snap behind us and we both turned around. The doe and its babies vanished. Seven brown mutts approached us in a semicircle, their heads crouched down like little wolves, growling.

"Oh no," I said.

"Get out of here!" Katia shouted. She took a small step forward, kicking the air. The dogs didn't flinch. She stepped back.

"What do we do?" I reached in my coat pocket and pulled out my father's knife. I pointed it toward the dogs, who inched forward.

"I don't know."

My heart pounded so hard it hurt. Wild rez dogs usually stopped, kept their distance. These dogs inched closer.

"Run on three," Katia said.

I looked at her and nodded.

"One. Two. Three."

We dashed. Between the two of us I'd been the slower one but adrenaline pushed me ahead of Katia. We ran the same line, the dogs nipping at our feet, trying to trip us up. We passed the spot where we had seen the doe and its babies and then Katia deviated toward a tree that looked climbable. "Over here!" she yelled. In one hop she pulled herself high and out of harm's way. I looked over in mid-stride and knew she was too far. I wouldn't make it. I kept running. Looking for anything that wasn't a birch tree, something to get me off the ground. The path had changed. I was running down a small hill. I thanked the Creator and Mother Earth. Thought: Trees, I could use your help. But then I felt teeth latch on to the heel of my shoe and I went tumbling and the world spun. A sharp pain climbed up my arm and over my shoulder.

On one knee I looked up. The dogs slowed. They knew they had me. I looked down at the grass, blood was everywhere, dripping like warm coffee. My father's knife had cut me deep across my palm, and I would later need many stitches. I felt oddly warm and calm. Hoka Hey: a good day to die according to the Dakota. Was this how I was to die? Mauled by ugly dogs. Would they find my body? Probably not. If that was to be my time, then I prayed they'd let the strays be. Mourn me without slaughtering them. It was their creek anyway.

I wailed in pain so loud that the dogs stopped in their tracks. I took off my coat and wrapped it around my hand and put the blade in the other and decided I would go out fighting. "C'mon then!" I screamed. My eyes swelled with tears. I thought death to be scary and boring and utterly tragic, and I feared the confines of coffins. But before I could stand, I felt a warmth and wetness on my cheek. A moist heat. Burnie was licking me.

"Burnie," I said, "baby."

Still the mutts marched forward. Burnie turned to them and bared his teeth and snapped forward to push them away. They performed this dance for a few minutes, Burnie refusing to yield, protecting a piece of meat he'd found in the forest and wanting it for himself. The mutts eventually conceded defeat and slunk away.

I leaned forward and put my hands around Burnie's ears, massaging him gently. I could feel my heart rate slowing and my vision became clearer. Like everything before had been a dream and I was awake. I finally stood up and looked up the hill, wondering whether Katia was still in the tree.

"Let's go home," I said, moving toward the hill and looking back.

Burnie didn't follow.

"Let's go," I repeated.

I went to pick him up, but before I could get close Burnie darted away, weaving around trees and bushes. I followed, trying my best to keep up, to stay within sight, but he was lost. A disappeared dog, again.

"Burnie!" I shouted. "Come back!"

I heard the sound when I caught my breath and could hear things other than my tired lungs. Water. Gushing water. The creek! I ran toward the sound, once turning back when it got thinner. This way. Over there. It grew louder and louder and I knew then that finding it was inevitable and so I slowed to a walk. I could see it, the brightness of it breaking through the foliage like the sun after a storm. I was up against a spruce tree and peeled back the needled cloak like a curtain.

It was true. Everything Uncle said was true. It was a creek of dogs. A sanctuary, and it was theirs. Dozens of them, damn mutts mostly, splashed and drank from a stream with stones large and small directing the flow. I wiped sweat off my forehead and disbelief from my eyes. The creek was still there. I thought against the idea of walking up to the stream and cupping some water to my lips. I'd had enough drama.

I sat there on the ground for a while, watching the dogs, and every now and then one would glance at me, disinterested. I was glad to be wrong about Uncle's tale. Still there was no sign of Burnie. I wondered whether Katia was walking back home or looking for me.

More dogs arrived on the other side of the creek and among the herd I spotted Burnie. He looked happy. He jumped in the water and took a long drink. The sun was disappearing behind the trees. It was time to go. I stood up and turned around and went back the way I came.

When I reached the top of the hill that I fell down, I saw Katia in the distance. She was inspecting something on the ground and didn't acknowledge me until I was a few feet in front of her, my coat soaked red.

"Jesus, they got you good," she said.

"I'm okay."

"Did you find Burnie at least?"

I shook my head. "I'm sure he'll come home eventually."

Katia returned her attention to the rotting wooden slabs on the ground. "Why would someone build a tree house way out here?" she said, prodding the ruins with her foot.

I looked up at the tree, presumably where the structure once stood, high off the ground, hidden in a sea of green leaves. In a few weeks they'd be orange and they'd fall to the ground as they always did, revealing all the secrets of this place. I hadn't told her this part of Uncle's story, the part about the tree house. There were thick pieces of wood nailed to the side of the tree, one on top of the other, a ladder. "Maybe it's for safety."

"Safety from what?"

"Crazy dogs."

Katia laughed. She went on poking the scraps with a long stick. When she was done, she breathed in deeply, looking up, and exhaled. I watched her and we exchanged closed smiles. It was getting cold and dark. Our breath trailed upward and evaporated above our heads, lost in the sky's first stars.

I'M IN THE PARK that Shadow likes to run around in and stop in my tracks when I notice what could be a clue. There's a yellow stain in the fresh snow, and everything else around it, around the park, is white and pure and untouched. It could be Shadow's pee, but it's hard to say, because around here he's not the only animal known to urinate in snow.

Asemaa and Tomahawk love their Auntie Katia. We moved together to the city when we could. Rosie stayed with Nimaamaa and Uncle till they passed, and then she too made her way south. Relatives back home tell me the rosebush outside our old home is still there, which always brings a smile to my face. They say Uncle's old abode is unoccupied, dissolving into the soil, and that a young family now lives in the house my father built for Nimaamaa, which I'm also glad to hear.

I'm home well before midnight. No luck finding Shadow. And when I get home Asemaa is on her way out to a friend's party. She hugs me and wishes me a Happy New Year and I do the same and tell her to be safe, but I know she will be. I find Tomahawk and Klik playing Scrabble at the dining room table and challenge our new guest to a game once he is finished with Tomahawk, because the best my grandson can come up with is "Weenuck." They giggle when I read it on the board, and I run a hand through Tomahawk's hair and give his head a gentle shake.

"Look who I found rummaging around my house, pissing and shitting in my snow," a familiar voice says.

I move into the living room and it's Katia, on the couch with Shadow. Smiling just proud. My heart feels ready to burst, like it could grow larger and fuller if my flesh would allow it, and as a result a greater capacity for loving the things I already do cherish, just more of it. More love. If it could grow, I would allow it, but it won't. It's just a feeling. I lunge for my boy and hold him. I hug Katia. At some point in the night I win at Scrabble. And when the clock approaches twelve we count the seconds.

## tomahawk shields

TOMMY HAD PUT OFF GOING TO KELVIN AND CLINTON'S APART-
ment, where only Kelvin lived now, for several days. The plan was
to go there around noon on New Year's Day, because the only places
not closed for the holiday around the city were usually hockey rinks,
because the game never stopped and because toddlers and immi-
grants learning to skate didn't care what day it was, and Kelvin would
presumably be working at the Memorial Arena at that time. Tommy
stayed hush about the whole thing, did his best to avoid broaching
the subject. The idea of sneaking around scared him. "Tomahawk,"
Clinton said, on the morning of 2012, shaking his head like an angry
mother. He surely picked up on the use of his full name from Koko,
even said it like her too, like there was always a problem, and if
he were to regret anything about the year he bunked with his best
friend, in his room, in his house, it would be Clinton calling him
Tomahawk. "You said you would do this for me."

"Fine," Tommy said, pausing the video game in front of him,
chucking the controller on the floor. His soldier's face was blown
off by a sniper.

In the kitchen, Koko and Sam were preparing a turkey dinner—
Koko handled the bird and the lemon and apple pies, and Sam made
everything else because she was tired of the boys botching a simple
mashed potato—and the smell drifted into the living room like
delicious clouds, and that would be his reward, for helping Clinton,
Tommy thought.

They threw on their jackets and left the house. They trudged through the year's inaugural snowfall and Clinton remained with Tommy until they were a block out from his apartment and there, he said, he would wait for his friend's return.

"What do you need again?" Tommy had asked this question a million times before.

Clinton sighed all annoyed. "Some clothes and my notebook, it's red, and my favorite shirt, it's grey with the San Jose Sharks logo on the front. They're not my team, I just like it." And like he had to explain himself further, he added: "I forgot them the first time around. Wasn't thinking."

"Right."

Tommy continued ahead. He didn't fully understand Clinton's plight, only that he was beaten up pretty bad the last time he and his brother were in that apartment together, and for Tommy that seemed a good reason to leave his home behind, to be afraid to go back.

The whole building was almost hidden by the falling white flakes. He unlocked the door to the main lobby with Clinton's key and climbed the stairs. When he reached the fourth floor he entered the apartment and moved swiftly. He hadn't been in there in a long time. He shook the snow off his boots and decided to keep them on, reasoning that the carpet that covered the floors looked like it had lived a thousand different lives.

In Clinton's room, which was surprisingly clean and tidy and perhaps even dusted, he found a suitable gym bag and began stuffing it with clothes. He found Clinton's notebook, which contained short stories written by hand, underneath his mattress like he said it was. But he couldn't find the grey shirt. All his shirts were grey, and Tommy knew it was because grey made dust and hair and lint and any other particles less visible. He searched everywhere—the bedroom, the bathroom, the living room, the bedroom closet. It was nowhere to be found. He started to doubt the sacredness of the shirt but remembered Clinton mentioning that it fit him better than any other crew neck he owned, a sentiment that spoke to him in a way he didn't foresee.

He kept searching, digging, throwing any manner of things behind him like his arms were two shovels until the dresser was completely empty.

Then he heard the front door slam, and then a cough. And before he had time to think or decide what to do next, briefly considering the window as a possible exit and the dark space beneath the bunk beds as a hiding spot, Kelvin was standing at the bedroom door. He wasn't afraid of Kelvin, because the man was an adult male pit bull he'd known since he was a mostly harmless puppy. But Tommy would put his hands up if he had to, and height was on his side.

"What are you doing here?" Kelvin said.

"Just getting some things for Clinton."

Kelvin looked squeamish.

"I'm looking for his Sharks shirt." Tommy slung the gym bag around his shoulder. "I can't find it."

Kelvin turned and walked away, down the hallway.

Tommy waited there for a moment, unsure if he should keep searching. It all felt wrong now. He stepped quietly into the hall. Then Kelvin emerged from another room, standing in front of him, blocking his route to the front door, and for a second Tommy thought this was it. Then he noticed the grey material in his hand.

"I washed it," Kelvin said, offering the drab shirt to Tommy.

"Thanks."

Kelvin shuffled his whole body awkwardly. He was always charismatic in a physically awkward way, and there was a time Tommy envied him, wanted to be like him. "How is he?"

"He's good."

Kelvin stepped aside, barely enough for Tommy to squeeze through, but Tommy scrambled for the door anyway and left the apartment and held the shirt in his hand as he skipped down the stairwell. He felt a rush of excitement. Mission accomplished.

Before he left the building he spread out the shirt before him with both hands. He had to see it, make sense of the fuss, of the menacing encounter with his friend's older sibling. But it was unremarkable, uninspiring. The logo was flaked and barely there. It had the texture of something old and gentled over, the material feel of unmeasured time. *It's just a shirt.* But despite this it was soft and felt nice to touch, probably comfortable to wear. And Clinton was right, it showed no lint or hair or dust and didn't crease. Nothing but dull grey fabric, a cheap cotton blend from Cambodia.

He folded the shirt and added it to the gym bag. He found Clinton a block away, in the same spot he left him. And together they went home, where they were surrounded by all the things that made them familiar, once again, to themselves.

## *errol whitecloud sinclair*

### JANUARY 6, 2012

I've been thinking as I write this what a shame it is that I write to you in English.

### JANUARY 10, 2012

After one Sunday sweat, I went up to Art and said, "How do I get to do what you do? Run the lodge and help people. Even after release." This was before he assigned me to helper.

He said, "The first principle is total respect and acceptance of the one to be taught."

He offered to mentor me. Then, he added, "We show respect for living the good life, *mino-bimaadiziwin,* by abstaining from drugs and alcohol prior to ceremony. This is the path you must take."

I nodded and said, "Then that's what I'll do."

### JANUARY 11, 2012

I saw your brother shortly after my release. Spoke to him even. I failed to mention it earlier because I felt embarrassed. Basically, I stalked him. Only this once. Despite telling myself I wouldn't lurk in the shadows, hiding from you boys.

He was cleaning the fryers and wiping down the counters at White's. It was near closing time but he let me in and gave me some chicken fingers. I know he didn't recognize me, he was barely a toddler by the time I was out of the picture. But it was like I knew him once I saw him, his skin slick from oil and sweat. He made the whole place immaculate, and I knew even then that he was nothing like me. I told him I knew you and that we'd been together up in Headingley, that we're friends. Lies of course, I was up in Stony Mountain. I didn't tell him who I was, I couldn't bring myself to do it even though I'd thought about it so many times. His face was new to me, too. It scared me. Perhaps I was taken aback by how beautiful he is, how warm and gentle his eyes are. I don't know. I chickened out. Something or other prevented me from saying, "I'm your dad." You know just by looking at some people that nothing you say will ever change things with them, they'll stick to their guns no matter what. Your mother was that way, still is, and your brother looked that way too. I figured he'd look me down and say something like, "Okay. What do you want?" In that moment I wasn't sure if I could handle it. I accepted the chicken strips and walked out the door and about halfway down the block I decided I'd go back and did, but when I got there he was no longer there. The place was closed.

I'm pretty sure my face scared him. It tends to do that these days. You see, son, I have these scars ever since the accident. From the glass that stuck to my face. I still have tiny shards of glass embedded in the skin, even now, years later. The doctor said once they're closer to the surface I should get them removed, but that hasn't happened yet and I'm not sure if it ever will. Maybe my face has given up on me. It's been numb so many times before maybe it just doesn't work the way it used to. Every now and then I feel my face tingle and when I smile I can feel exactly where those little bastards are, which is why I limit my smiling. I didn't smile at your brother that night, because I'd already used up all my smiles for the day. That may sound callous, but son, routine is everything.

## asemaa kimberly shields

LATELY, I THINK OF MYSELF AS HALF-DEVIL, HALF-CHILD. THIS helps me feel like a badass: scaring my enemies because I'm less than human; dumb and scary; horns and all, like Darth Maul. I know it shouldn't. But it does, for now at least.

Cecil Rhodes and his friends, I have come to learn (no, digest) were raging racists. To be clear, I've known this for a long time. Long before I even put pen to paper for the hundreds of drafts I needed to write to try to win, long before I ever applied for my school's endorsement, and before I was eventually named a Rhodes finalist. I knew some of it anyway. Looked it up.

Cecil Rhodes was an unwanted, unannounced, unnecessary man. And by that, I mean unnecessary for all of humanity, but chiefly unnecessary for African peoples and territories. He was a human asteroid, leaving a wake of dust and destruction and disfiguration in his path. A terrible, terrible man, Cecil Rhodes profited, no, thrived, off colonization and exploitation and became a millionaire on the diamond fields of South Africa before age thirty. Cecil Rhodes was a proud imperialist who believed it was the responsibility of brothers of his hue to conquer and civilize the lands and non-Anglo-Saxon people they stumbled upon. Cecil Rhodes founded De Beers, which has plundered Indigenous land in this very country. This, of course, is no great secret. But when you apply for the Rhodes, you'd think it was. The scholarship is about Cecil Rhodes the determined vision-ary, not Cecil Rhodes the ambassador of global white supremacy. Cecil Rhodes had a famous poet friend, Rudyard Kipling, who wrote the 1899 poem "The White Man's Burden," which would go on to become the anthem for American imperialism and progress at the expense of anybody not white, domestically and abroad. And in one particular stanza of the poem, Rudyard Kipling describes non-whites as "half-devil and half-child."

The Rhodes Scholarship, as its name suggests, is funded by the estate of Cecil Rhodes. Which, for reasons I can't explain and at this time don't wish to, I desperately want to win.

THE INTERVIEW FOR THE Rhodes is at a hotel conference center near the airport. I wondered why there, instead of some ritzy place downtown, but my best guess is that our judges, the people who will decide our worthiness, don't care to see the city where some of us (I counted eight) come from. I had this unrealistic hope, an impossible fantasy, that they would tour each of our homes and streets like a jury visiting a crime scene, and thus they would each share a greater appreciation for my story, the improbability of it.

The day before the official interview, a fancy party was held at the hotel for distinguished finalists and esteemed judges, a panel made up of business titans, grey-haired scholars, a judge, a lawyer on his way to becoming a judge, a lawyer who became a human rights investigator at the United Nations, and a law school graduate who became a military pilot instead of a lawyer and then went on to be a doctor and then an astronaut.

Our inquisitors were an impressive bunch, and I was intimidated. But more than that it was the party itself that left my hands and feet clammy and my nose and armpits moist, because I'd never been to anything so fancy, so illustrious. I wore a black skirt and black blazer and a button-down shirt with little tigers all over it because it might spark conversation. I wore two necklaces, five rings, a pair of earrings that belonged to Koko before me, and a shoe with a bit of heel. I let my hair down, wore makeup for once, which partially brightened the tone of my skin. Before I left home Koko gave me a mint, having noticed my reluctance to eat all day, which was part nervousness, part bloaty anxiety.

The party was held in the finest hotel suite like ever. The light was dim and everything—the floors, walls, cabinets, chairs, marble counters, tables, decor, faucets in the kitchen and bathroom—was glossy and reflective. There were butlers, walking around serving fancy cheeses and appetizers I couldn't name.

When I arrived, a cheery young man in a bow tie took my coat. The suite was bigger than any "home" I'd ever been in. I stood around, alone, while the rest mingled in pairs and for a while I went unnoticed. I ate two small things that looked like burgers but instead of a patty it was something crunchy and buglike. Like a deep-fried cockroach. And for a moment I could imagine the rich and powerful turning roaches into some fancy hors d'oeuvre. I raised my hand too high when I turned down a glass of champagne, like one does when they see alcohol after a heavy night, and behind the server I noticed a tall woman take notice of me. She ended a conversation with a young man, another finalist with dreams of solving climate change, and approached me.

"Please feel free to take in a cocktail," she said. "We won't hold it against you."

"No thanks," I said shyly. "I actually don't drink."

"Oh," she said, as if regretting coming over. "Did you have a problem? I understand alcoholism is an epidemic in *Aboriginal* communities."

I was used to the question, though it usually came from plucky university students. The harmful stereotype was an interesting twist. "No," I said. "I just prefer not to drink."

Her confidence held firm. "I'm Pamela," she said. "Pamela Chipman."

We shook hands. "Asemaa Shields. But you can call me Sam."

"Where are you coming from, Sam?"

Her attention shifted to a server hovering at my rear, and so I turned around and was offered a can of sparkling water, which I graciously accepted. "I'm from here," I said, snapping the can open. "I grew up in the North End. With my koko—my grandmother—and younger brother."

"Interesting," she said. "That's fascinating. Do you know your parents?"

"Not well," I said, sipping my water. "They've not been in my life for a very long time. I was raised by my grandmother." I'd answered this question and others like it so many times before both orally and in writing that my answer was almost always the same, vague enough to represent something close to the truth. "Are you from here as well?"

"Mississauga is home for me, and then much of my childhood was in Toronto. But I've been here now for close to twenty years. You can probably tell by my sunburn that I came from somewhere much warmer than this." She laughed. "I was in Costa Rica just yesterday, where my husband and I like to spend the colder months. As much as possible anyway. I imagine that when we both retire, we'll be full-time Costa Ricans." She laughed again like she told a joke.

I'd noticed the redness on her face, the subtle sunspots, and the sun-bleached strands of blond hair framing her cheeks. "What brought you west?" I asked.

"My career," she said, and explained that she was the first woman to be named CEO of a popular potato chip company. "My daughters are in private school here as well. My son plays hockey for a prep school just over the border in North Dakota, so we try to be close. Are you from any particular First Nation?"

"No," I said. "I've spent my whole life here. My koko, though, grew up on reserve. Dog Creek, they call it."

"We have a cottage in The Narrows!" Her eyes lit up, thrilled by the mutual connection. "We're basically neighbors."

"Small world."

"You know," she said, in an almost-whisper. "James Gandolfini used to be our neighbor until we purchased a property further away from the touristy parts. What a wonderful man. Brilliant artist."

I finished my water, and within seconds a server had a fresh can in my hand.

"But what delightful cottage country it is up there. We love spend-ing our summers there, boating and wakeboarding and such. The kids absolutely love it. Do you ever get up there?"

"Once," I said. "When I was friends with a rich kid."

"Oh. What happened to your friendship with this . . . *rich* kid?"

I downed the remainder of my canned water in three big gulps, questioning where I'd taken this conversation, wondering how the hell we got here. Or did she take us here? I wasn't sure. I knew, obviously, this could potentially ruin my chances of winning the Rhodes. This soirée was the interview before the interview. Surely. The judges of our fates would get their first impressions of us—to judge us before we'd be officially judged. I worried I might be dismissed as radical, as the young woman who couldn't keep a rich friend, who couldn't keep her mother around. Because when it comes down to it, white people don't like hearing about how fucked up they are. I gulped nervously, and then thought, Fuck it, I don't owe this woman and my former friend anything.

"This rich friend told her other friends she met me in the forest," I said.

"I see," she said, accepting another glass of champagne. "And I take it that's not where you two met?"

"We met at private school. It was a joke at my expense."

"I take it you're interested in artificial intelligence. Automation hasn't quite disrupted my industry as it has other sectors—"

"The potato chip industry," I interrupted.

She smiled thinly. "Everything from accounting to sales to, say, delivery of our goods. I'd go as far as to say that our company still operates much the same ways since it was started more than fifty years ago. Where do you see the evolution of AI taking us in the future? And by *us* I don't mean my company specifically or any for that matter, but us broadly, our world. Where will it take us as a people?"

I felt heat in my ears and under my eyes, as if I'd been slapped across the face. I thought about saying I don't know. I imagined myself walking away without saying a word, something I've always dreamt of doing, and I would feel no shame about it. My capacity for awkwardness overshadowed any pride. A server appeared beside me, from nowhere, and offered another water and I exchanged it for my empty can and cracked it open, took a long shot and exhaled. "It has the potential, the certainty rather, of stripping us of our humanity. Which, could be argued, is a good thing. To remove human selfishness, personal politics, greed, from the decision-making processes regarding the most seminal problems of our time—climate change, armed conflict, global pollution, water rights, human rights, the wealth divide, you name it—would mean a more calculated, rational response to these challenges. Once we, as a species, learn to rely fully on AI, which we already do, it's in your pocket after all, it will have the ironic effect of restoring the *value* of humanity, that is, caring for others and other life rather than just ourselves. The result would be progress."

I could see her interest in me suddenly wane. "Interesting," she said, puckering her lips. "It's been a pleasure, Sam. You'll have to excuse me now. I look forward to speaking again tomorrow."

She moved past me and I was alone again.

I left the party earlier than I expected to, but made sure I wasn't the first to go. I mingled awhile after speaking to Pamela. I met the judge, a professor of philosophy and the astronaut, who surprisingly encouraged me to keep the Canadian space program on my radar and I nodded with the feeling I'd just been complimented. I met some of my fellow finalists. There was a women's Quidditch world champion who by day is a master's student in biological sciences with a focus on aquatic ecosystems and who has a plan to save our oceans and sharks in the process. There was an eighteen-year-old prodigy committed to curing death, or at least making it easier on the human body—"Death is a disease," he said. "We just refuse to acknowledge it as such." And there was a child of refugees with dreams of furthering his study of public health in famine-prone nations who aspired to work in the foreign service. I said to each of them, with the feeling I should dream higher: "I'd like to work for Google or Apple or maybe a start-up."

I ARRIVE AT THE hotel, the day of the interview, in the same outfit I wore the night before, hoping nobody will notice. Though I felt confident knowing that Koko spent the morning ironing the entire ensemble until every visible crease had been removed. She combed my hair and refused to let me leave the house unless she gave me a braid and I agreed and then she made me smudge.

The interview is to take place in a conference room. The other fourteen finalists are already there when I arrive outside the door. I take a name tag on a lanyard from a woman behind a table draped in various accoutrements advertising the Rhodes Trust. Among the women, I'm the only one wearing a braid and I decide then to keep it, which wasn't my original plan, while every man has short hair, combed and gelled to either side of their heads. I take a seat and learn that we're moving alphabetically by last name. Each of us has twenty minutes with the judges and time seems to move quickly and exactly as described, no wasted seconds. I've wondered for a long time what they might ask me, imagined my responses. They'd ask me about my life and I'd tell them about my koko and how, before she retired from driving buses, she sacrificed promotions at transportation to be closer to me and Tommy. I'd tell them, in modest terms, how I want to be an inspiration for my community, that the Rhodes would not just be for me, but for Indigenous women working toward careers in STEM. A career is good, and yes, I want a good career, I want to be a success, I'd say. But I'd tell them how badly I want to change the world, the world *I* know, like when humans woke up one day and televisions were no longer grey but bright and colorful. And I'd hope they'd see me as worthy, worthy of Cecil Rhodes's vision.

A finalist with baggy suit pants with the last name Saint exits the conference room. His hands are shaky and legs unsteady. The woman at the table stands and for a brief moment enters the room herself and then comes back out to the waiting area.

"Shields," she says. "*Ah-Say-Ma* Shields." She pronounces my first name phonetically.

I'm up. I stand.

I open the door and before me is a long conference table flanked by black swivel chairs. The judges are there, taking notes, and it feels like none of them look up to notice me as I take my seat at the end of the table.

The room is bright, the sun coming through a big window to my left. All eyes are on me now. I see Pamela and smile, but she doesn't offer one back, instead returning to some pages in front of her. A small gold cross dangles from her neck, which I didn't notice yesterday.

"Asemaa Shields," Pamela says, studying what's in front of her. "How are you this morning?"

"I'm great," I say. "I'm excited. Sam is fine."

"That's right. Sam."

I nod, sensing we are not about to waste any time.

"To begin," Pamela begins, looking up at me and folding her arms on the table. "I'd like to ask a question about Indian band politics here in Canada. What do you think explains why there are so many First Nations chiefs earning more than one million dollars in annual salary?"

Fear and confusion come over me, but I don't waste time. "I think that's a misconception," I say. "One that is fueled by discrimination and double standards. There are no millionaire chiefs in this country. That much has been proven. In fact, many of these claims have been fabricated by the Harper government. The reality is that the average elected First Nation leader's salary is less than forty thousand dollars per year, with a few exceptions."

She ruffles around some of her papers. "By 'fabricated' I assume you're alluding to our government's Bill C-27, which would require First Nations to reveal their leadership's salaries, as well as submit to audited financial statements." She pauses and I'm left unsure whether to respond. "Then how do you explain the salary of, say, a chief of a band in or around Alberta's oil sands?"

I can feel my hands getting sweaty and so I rub them on my knees. "I should preface by saying that I don't claim to be an expert on financial matters, especially those pertaining to First Nation governments. Nor do I believe that I'm qualified to speak to every issue facing Indigenous peoples. But, and I know this much, the salaries you cited are largely generated by band-owned businesses, presumably related to resource extraction or similar, rather than funds from the federal government. There's a distinct difference. On the First Nations Financial Transparency Act, which you mentioned, I would argue that it's more of the same, only more paternalistic and driven by politics than previous federal Indian policy. By that I mean First Nation bands have been required to file audited financial statements for years—and to a fault. One could argue that they— Indian bands—face greater financial accountability than any local government, including our own federal, provincial and territorial governments. Missing in this narrative about the so-called 'corrupt chief,' which, as I've said, I believe to be fabricated to benefit certain people in power, is that First Nations across the country already file tens of thousands of financial reports each year to the federal government, which our Auditor General has harshly criticized. Falling behind on these reports can lead to a loss of federal funding, but it can also result in an enforced policy known as Third-Party Management. Which is exactly as it sounds."

I take a breath. Pamela takes notes, and then speaks:

"Are you saying that as a Canadian taxpayer I don't deserve the right to know how my tax dollars are being managed by federally supported bands? Are you concerned at all that these First Nations leaders don't pay taxes on their high salaries?"

"Financial transparency, as I mentioned, has existed on First Nations prior to this most recent legislation," I say. "To your second question. Would you say the same about your church? Many religious institutions, as well as some religious colonies, do not pay taxes."

Pamela smiles, the kind of smile she gave yesterday when we spoke of her potato chip company, but whether she's impressed or unimpressed I have no idea. She glances around the table, seeming to hand the reins over to another questioner.

For the next thirteen minutes I'm pressed about non-Indian topics, but which have nothing to do with me or my areas of interest. At one point I'm quizzed about how many seats there are in the British House of Commons, to which I say I have no idea but answer wrongly anyway and learn that it's six hundred and fifty. One of the judges, a lawyer in glittery cuff links and a collar that is a different color from the rest of his shirt, asks about Bach, no, rambles about Bach and how he lost both parents at age ten, and then asks me about the importance of facing adversity and my general thoughts about classical music. To which I preface by saying that I know little about classical music. "But both of my parents are also absent from my life," I say. "So I guess you could say I'm also like Bach, but with less musical talent." The judges laugh.

Near the end of the interview the astronaut jumps in, the first time he's said anything.

"I just have one final question if there's time," he says, looking around the table and receiving approval from his peers. "How would the Rhodes change your life?"

I pause for a moment at the question. A sudden boost of adrenaline runs through me as opposed to the nausea I've felt for the past eighteen minutes. This is it.

I take a breath. "It would change everything," I say, making sure I make eye contact with each of the judges. "More than just myself, it would change the life of my family, of my community." I pause for a moment and decide to leave it there. "Plus," I conclude, "it's tax-free." And everyone at the table, including Pamela, has a laugh.

When I stand and leave the conference room it feels as though I've been through a car accident or some dizzying amusement park ride, like my legs aren't under me, supporting me. I'm greeted outside the door by the table woman and she directs me to a special waiting room with beverages and platters of cheese and crackers and questionable vegetables. I take a seat closest to a window with a view of an empty parking lot and the baggy-panted finalist shuffles closer to me and introduces himself as Martin M. Saint. I introduce myself as Sam.

"How are you holding up after that?" he asks, while crushing a baby carrot in his mouth.

"Confused," I say.

"I think we're all feeling that way."

"But glad to have it over with."

He finishes his small plate of carrots, and then says:

"At one point they asked me about quantum mechanics and its potential to shape the internet of the future." He laughs and there's orange specks in his teeth. "My major is history."

"They asked me about Bach. I study computer engineering."

The hours go by. I lose track of time. Time loses meaning. At some point caterers roll in a late lunch but most of us are too anxious to fill our stomachs and instead nibble on bread buns and baklava for the sugar. I finally text my koko to tell her I had the interview and now I'm waiting for the committee to make their decision. Seconds later she responds:

*That's good my girl. Don't fret. Best not to worry about what you can't control.*

That's her classic line. Don't worry about what you can't control. I've heard it so many times throughout my life that it's almost instinctual. I know she'll be proud even if I don't win. I tell myself that over and over even though the disappointment of not winning would sting for an indefinite period of time.

At six o'clock—nine hours after my interview ended—we're finally called into the conference room. All of us. All the finalists. I've been wondering how celebratory I'd be if I were to win after all this time. Would I raise my hands in the air like at a track meet? The enthusiasm left the room ages ago. Phones died. Smiles disappeared. The laughter and joy among the finalists quieted. Before the long table is an even longer line of chairs, and one of the judges asks, no, orders us to take a seat and we do as we're told. And they're noticeably more comfortable than the ones in the waiting room. To soothe those of us who come away with nothing I assume.

"Thank you all for your incredible patience," the astronaut says, now sitting at the end of the table, the spot for bosses and chairmen. "We couldn't have asked for a better group of finalists, and I have no doubt that each of you will go on to achieve great things in your chosen paths regardless of today's outcome. Leaving a profound, indelible mark on our world, which is the very spirit, vision and intention of this life-changing opportunity." He clears his throat. "I will now announce the two recipients of this year's Rhodes Scholarship, as agreed upon by the judges of this committee. First . . . Ranni Chau, from the University of Winnipeg." Ranni gasps, hands over her mouth, to claps from other finalists. The astronaut clears his throat again, waiting for the room to settle. "Our next and final recipient is . . . Asemaa Shields, from the University of Manitoba."

There's a swell somewhere inside me, a release of some sort. It's just an award I think to myself. I could go to Oxford anytime I want on my own dime. Probably. I'm being dismissive. I always do this. I used to skip my own birthdays because I hated the attention. But maybe it's just the feeling of being overwhelmed by goodness when you're not used to good things. Joy now.

I shake an unknown number of hands for what feels like a long time. Hands of every color and shape and texture. From smooth and soft to rough and solid like coal. I give my thanks to the committee and when I come to the astronaut he says to me:

"I meant what I said about the space program."

I say, "Maybe when I'm done here on Earth."

He congratulates me again and departs and I do as well.

Outside, in my car, I call Koko. I say to her:

"I did it! I won the Rhodes. I'm going to have tea with the queen."

It's quiet on the other end, too quiet for her. "Oh, my girl," she finally says. There's another long pause. If she's crying she's hiding it. There's nothing to suggest that she is. I accept the silence for a short time, interrupted occasionally by a light static. I wonder what she's thinking about. Maybe she's scared I won't come back. This has crossed my mind before. I wonder if she's hung up.

"Koko," I eventually say. "You there?"

Nothing. Some static.

"Koko," I repeat.

"I'm here," she says softly.

There she is. She's there, and I go to her.

## *tomahawk shields*

IT HAD BEEN MONTHS SINCE TOMMY LAST HEARD FROM HIS MOTHER. He had largely forgotten about her email. Like it wasn't real, didn't truly happen. Memories of his mother existed as dreams do, fragmentary, flashes of moments that felt real, but were no longer reliable as fact.

He was passing all of his classes with relative ease and moderate enthusiasm, including the history credit he needed to ensure his graduation. He still stood tall on the ice, still yet to be knocked on his ass, despite the zero on the left side of their season record.

He cheesed his way to his first A in all his years at St. Croix, and did it at the end of last term in Ms. Damphousse's history class, a streak that would continue until the end of the school year. They spent the first half of the course learning about treaties and their final assignment was to deliver a class presentation on "what it meant to be a treaty person," in the words of Ms. Damphousse. It could be anything, she said, she welcomed creativity in any form. Mistakenly—as he'd done throughout the entirety of his high school career—he waited until the night before presentation day to sit at the small desk in his bedroom to do anything about it. First, he masturbated to mental images of a substitute cutie fresh out of her education degree who suggested he had the "soul of a poet" in the comments of his English paper, and then, once freed of further distraction, set out on a late-night journey to awaken his inner poet.

The next morning, before class, he watched videos on YouTube of poetry scholars and was mesmerized. They recited their poetry without once looking down at the page, the audience their partner, caught in a dance of beautiful words. And the movement, the movement too, the movement did something he couldn't quite explain or comprehend. The way they swayed and moved their hands, strained the muscles in their jaws, eyes serious and wet, jittery from the nerves or trauma or emotions they were revisiting, sharing with the world. Surely he didn't have time to rehearse in this way, to be as good as the professionals. But he could try. On the way to school he read his poem aloud over and over and over until it was glued in his mind like the old scar on his eyebrow from when, as a little boy, a goose went berserk for his bread. The doctor fixed him with glue.

In class everyone else had red or blue or green posters with big words and each one shared the same image of a medicine wheel. If anything, he thought, he would earn sympathy points for trying something different. When it was his turn he stood from his chair with a single piece of paper and appeared before the class at the front of the room. Ms. Damphousse sat on her desk, a hand on her chin. She wore her usual bright colors, clashing reds and blues on top and shades of pink and green and brown from the waist down, which would've made any other person look unserious, but she made it work.

"What do you have in store for us, Tommy?" she said, slightly confused by the lack of a poster.

"I," he said, "have a poem."

"Oh." She beamed.

He turned to the class. "I just wanted to write something that sort of, I guess, expresses how lucky we are to be surviving our ancestors, our relatives. My sister Sam always says we're living survivance documents, and after learning about treaties this term I sort of agree with that idea." He cleared his throat, kicking himself for saying "uh" too many times. "So here's my poem. It's called 'They Are Dead But Alive.'" And then, without looking at his paper, he recited:

> On cold dark winter nights
> they dance upon the stars;
> hand in hand they join
> as they look below us;
> They are dead, but alive
> somewhere beyond the blue;

where life is endless
where they'll one day send us
where life is true

He paused briefly after this last stanza, looked down at his single wrinkled page and then back up, and everyone was more or less aloof. It didn't bother him. He couldn't recount a single thing from the presentations that preceded his. Ms. Damphousse appeared on the verge of tears, like the young pupil before her was the result of her molding. He continued:

not a word of guilt
not a word of evil
They are dead, but alive
where flowers bloom, and waters flow
where there are no ebbs and flows
where their journey is endless
But we must never forget what they gave us
wherever we may go
Because even here;
the sweet smell of love is everywhere
as the warm summer winds blow

He sat back down to mild applause. He folded his paper. He heard someone hush the word "gay." Which didn't necessarily mean he was gay but was intended to be an insult. He didn't care. He'd be gay as shit if it meant a passing grade.

In her feedback Ms. Damphousse called his presentation "a brave, moving, ambitious, astonishing performance that at times misunderstood the assignment. It would have been worthwhile to incorporate the core themes and arguments from our selected readings. But I have a soft spot for the personal. THIS TIME ONLY. Grade: A."

The day after telling Koko about the A she bought him a cake from Safeway to celebrate. It was marble with white and green icing and a big red "A" drizzled on top.

"Tommy gets a cake?" Sam said, acting offended. "Where's my cake?"

"I'm not rich," Koko said. "I can't always be buying cakes for you two."

"Yeah," Tommy said. "We're not rich."

IN JANUARY, AT THE start of the new term, he was in the computer lab, skipping his morning classes, celebrating, in his mind, another defeat the night before in which he pulverized two unsuspecting forwards at center ice and scored his first goal of the season, a one-timer off a face-off, when he checked his email for the first time in almost three weeks. There, hiding among a barrage of phishing scams, was another email from his mother, which had arrived before the New Year.

My beautiful boy,

How are you? How is my beautiful daughter? How is Koko? The signs, as I said in my last message, are becoming more and more real and I am beginning to see them everywhere now, and, my boy, as I said, it's important that I renounce my citizenship soon for the sake of sovereignty, to be free from the shackles of this system trying to destroy us, all of us, including you and my girl and Koko, but more on that later. Littlefeather and me are still working to get that process going, it's slow but coming along. As I say, the messages are now everywhere, my boy, just the other month Littlefeather and me were down at the Walmart shopping—we bought ten big bags of the best candies, some of which included Kit Kat, Twizzlers, Hershey's, Snickers, Twix, Coffee Crisp, and small packs of Skittles, Gummies, and Rockets, and big cases of soda like Pepsi and Orange Crush because we wanted the women's centre to be the best place in the city to get candy and because we would use some of the candy for the Halloween party at the women's centre, and Littlefeather bought a big round mask with bulging and veiny eyes and bloody stitches and a screaming mouth because she said she wanted to look scary for the children, and me I went as a ghost, a happy ghost, like Casper, and so

I bought a cheap white sheet and cut out some eyeholes and drew a smile for the mouth; Littlefeather said Halloween is the one time of year where it's not weird or odd to not show your face, to dress incognito, because everyone just wants to dress like a crazy ghost—and at this Walmart we found ourselves at there was a guy honking at us in his big Ford F250, mad at us for driving slow and waiting for shoppers and their carts as we exited the parking lot, and so Littlefeather looked angry and annoyed and flipped him the bird, and seeing this the man in the truck pulled up next to us at the next red light and using his right hand like sign language ordered me to roll down the window, because I was driving and so I did, and Littlefeather, leaning on me and reaching her long arm out the driver's window flipped him off again and called him a "fat fuck" and reassured him that McDonald's wasn't closing anytime soon and that he had all the time in the world to "remain a fat ugly fuck." The man's face, now red and angry in a violent way, like that kind of anger that can only be relieved through punching something or someone else, you know the kind, my boy, he looked fierce, and for a moment I had a strange fear he might get out of his car and walk over to us but instead he shouted at us quickly before the red light changed to green: "You stupid retarded cunts! Stay off the road if you can't drive!" And then, pointing his finger at Littlefeather, which I took to mean he was directing these next words at her and not to me, he said: "Fuck you, you fucking ugly bitch!" Littlefeather looked at me with a big laugh and was like: "Holayyy! Fucking asshole! What a fucking piece of shit." Her face then went very serious and angry even, and this hurt me, seeing her like this, because she was neither an ugly bitch or a retarded cunt, and suddenly I was driving fast, flying, following the man's wide and high truck closely through every intersection and turn. The man didn't signal when he turned his big truck left or moved it into a left lane and only did so when he moved right and the cars around him appeared not to have signaled either and I took this to mean something, a sign maybe, but

I can't be sure, but there appeared to be a distinct pattern of the signals before us as we chased the man, and so I said "ho wa" once I noticed what was happening and turned to Littlefeather and said "are you seeing this or am I seeing things?" And there was a long pause so I kept following the lights and their movements and observing the signs, and the man swerved and sliced past cars like he was moving through a snaky road, and finally Littlefeather said "don't lose him." We followed him down East Hastings and the road seemed lined with all green lights, a sign, yes, it was another sign, and by the time we turned off the busy road we were no longer in Vancouver but in another city called Burnaby but it all feels like one big city that never ends! About five blocks down this quieter street where the houses all seemed to have driveways and lawns that all looked like they could use some water and the man's truck slowed and I noticed he had no brake lights, which might explain something, and I looked over at Littlefeather again and could see a grin appear on her face and her dimples rise high till they almost touched her cheekbones and so then I slowed down too. The truck pulled into a driveway and I observed many curious things about the man's one-story house, if it was indeed his house, but pay attention to this, my boy, it looked far too cheap and flimsy and small for a big shiny truck, with that same white horizontal paneling you always see back home where you are (you know the kind?) and it covered the lower half of the house while the rest of it was a burgundy stucco and the place sat on a small mound on the corner of the street and a row of short spruces almost made a fence along the sidewalk. I put the car in park but kept the engine running and before Littlefeather got out she looked at me all serious and said "wait here" but I had no intention of getting out anyways. As if! I thought. As if! But then I could feel my heart start beating quicker and quicker and for the first time in many days I felt scared for her and me. She grabbed the bottle of water she got at the store from the cup holder, which was still about halfways full, and opened her door and walked quickly around the front of the car and shouted "hey!" as the man was stepping out of his truck and the man looked over at her but didn't say a word, as he looked a little bit confused and surprised that we'd found him, and then Littlefeather cocked the water bottle just behind her ear and then released it as hard as she could, almost damn tripping over the sidewalk that Littlefeather, and it spun and spun and spun and struck the man's forehead and bounced on the roof of his truck and rolled down the windshield, and as it all happened, as if it were in slow motion, Littlefeather yelled, all red-faced and high-pitched, "go fuck yourself and your mother and your sister, you stupid prick!" Still nothing said from the man, even after this. He was just shrugging, palms pointed up at the sky, looking all confused and embarrassed. At one point he may have said "what?" but I was too busy focusing on Littlefeather, who ran back to the car, closed the door hard, looked in the mirror, fixed her hair, fastened her seatbelt, and told me to drive, and so I did before I could take a final look at the man. Ever crazy that Littlefeather, and that's what I told her, brave even, but I forgot to tell her that I also thought it was brave, but maybe more crazy than brave. I think bravery is one of the nicest things you can say about someone, it's one of our teachings. That's what they tell us at the centre. They tell us to spread love and truth, to keep moving forward even if the destination is unclear, even if you're moving at a turtle's pace. I've been thinking about what you said earlier, that you needed me. Well I'm coming, my boy. Littlefeather and me. She likes to say sometimes that I need other people that aren't her, and that it's my turn to be brave. I don't know when or how, can't give you a date or anything like that, but I think I'm ready to try.

Best wishes,<br>Mom

Tommy didn't respond. The messiness of the tale raised worries but also doubts about veracity. Still he had an inkling of hope, he wanted it to be true, for her to come home. But he could hear Sam's voice telling him that it was all bullshit, that she was crazy and that none of it was real. He closed his email and left the computer lab.

AT HOCKEY PRACTICE HE would forget the drills even after Coach Johnson explained them on the board. He found himself lost in various transitions, passing the puck to the wrong person. "Salvation! What the fuck are you doing! Get your head out of your pussy!" Coach Johnson shouted. Coach Johnson was the only person on the team and off it that called him Salvation as a nickname. Salvation as in the Salvation Army. The Salvation Army's logo is a red shield. The red shield as in his surname is Shields. As punishment the whole team was ordered to get down and do push-ups. "Salvation!" Coach Johnson barked. "You call that a push-up? You look like you're fucking your sister!"

At home Tommy wanted to tell Sam about the new email, but remembered she didn't want to be reminded of their mother's existence. He wanted to tell Koko, but Sam had also stressed that their koko didn't need to be reminded that her only daughter was somewhere out there going crazy and using the internet, a dangerous recipe in the modern age. The secret was now carrying an uncomfortable weight.

He slept on it, wondered throughout the night where his mother slept, whether she put her head down on a pillow or a concrete slab. He got out of bed before the sun had risen and threw on some clothes and his winter coat and every scarf he could find. He went to the backyard and shoveled some snow off a pair of small steps and laid there, resting his head on the concrete. It was cold and hard and unforgiving.

## *clarissa walkman*

CLARISSA ARRIVED AT THE DOWNTOWN OFFICE OF THE SOUTHERN
Manitoba High School Hockey League sweaty and out of breath, her
shoulders and toque covered in snowflakes that glistened under the
fluorescent lights before they melted. A snowstorm had disrupted
her bus route, and so she ran most of the way there, hoping to catch
the major players in her story returning from lunch. But there was
no one. She shook off the snow like dandruff and stomped her boots
into the carpet and approached the front desk. She cleared her throat.
"Hi."
The secretary paused from writing something in one of the squares
of her calendar that nearly covered the whole desk and looked to her
with a wide smile and kind eyes, and said, "How may I help you?"
"I'm here to see Fergus Fergusson."
She looked down at her calendar. "Do you have a meeting?"
Clarissa was embarrassed, and in that moment questioned her
decision to show up unannounced. And the running, which she
hoped would inject her with confidence by way of endorphins, was
having the opposite effect—she felt gross underneath her clothes.
"No, I don't," she stammered. "My name is Clarissa Walkman. I'm a
student reporter from St. Croix High School."
Michelle beamed. "Oh, Clarissa! Yes, yes, yes. Of course. It's so
good to see you." She stood. "Let me just go see if Fergy is available
to meet with you. Maybe he has a few minutes to spare right now.
Though I'm thinking he might not be back from lunch yet."
"Is his license plate 'FER FER'? It's out front." Clarissa shrugged.
Michelle smiled politely as she stepped around her desk and trot-

ted down a long hallway, which, in lieu of walls, was mostly made up of frosted glass and behind each window was the shallow figure of a man or woman typing away behind a desk.

The whole place was cold and lifeless. There was a small green plant on every surface to break up the office's grey color scheme. To her left, on the wall, hung portraits of the organization's board of directors. All men. Next to them, down an unfinished hallway, tall trophy cases stood empty next to buckets of paint, the words "Hall of Fame" on the wall above them.

Clarissa leaned over the high barrier that surrounded Michelle's desk and turned her head to get a better read of the calendar. Most of the days had something in them, words scribbled so small she couldn't make out what they read. But there were some days with nothing booked: next Thursday, the Monday and Tuesday after that. Clarissa had left eleven messages with Michelle intended for the league president, asking for an interview with the man she considered responsible for ousting the Tigers from next season and beyond. It wasn't just him. But, if anything, he was the judge who handed down the judgment, and, if he wanted to, could reverse it. Because, she thought, mistakes can be rectified. Either that or the public can will it into existence. But it starts with a story. She sent more than a dozen emails to both Fergus Fergusson's work and personal emails and received no response. On the twelfth time she called, Michelle answered with, "Clarissa! Hi!" Her voice quickly went quiet. "Honestly, I can probably get in some trouble for saying this, but maybe just come by the office one of these days and we'll see if Fergy has time for you."

When Michelle came back and saw Clarissa still standing in front of her desk she tilted her head and frowned dramatically.

"I'm so sorry," she said, clasping her hands. "He's in meetings all afternoon."

"That's okay," Clarissa said, trying not to show her frustration. "Can I wait here until the day is over?"

Michelle frowned. "Unfortunately no. Not unless you have an appointment."

Clarissa sighed. Louder than she wanted.

"Do you have a carrot I can borrow?"

"A carrot?"

"Yeah. Like the vegetable."

Michelle searched under her desk and came up with her lunch bag and from inside she pulled out a baggie of mini carrots. "How about these?" She held them out. "They're yours if you like."

Clarissa took the carrots.

Outside it had stopped snowing. She started with a snowball the size of her hand and rolled it until it became too heavy to push any longer. She rolled another one, slightly smaller than the one before, and with all her strength, careful not to blow out her back, raised it atop the bigger one. She then rolled another, the smallest of the three, and planted it above the first two. She grabbed two branches for arms and made eyes and a mouth with pebbles she found hidden under the snow. Finally, a mini carrot for the nose. She admired her creation, taller than her by at least a foot, munching on the remaining carrots.

She stood outside the office building for hours. She watched the cars skid across the fresh snow, the sun near its last, ready to sink behind the buildings ahead for good. She watched the downtown lights come on, adding a shade of orange to the twilight, burning bright, warming the city if only a little. She looked up, found the first star, then the Milky Way, then the Northern Lights, streaking north in beautiful bands of green.

Darkness had fully taken over by the time Fergus Fergusson walked out of the building. He trudged toward the parking lot and she made her approach.

He stopped just before his car, almost stumbling, looking appalled. "What the shit fuck?" He threw his hands in the air.

"I saw some kids do it."

She spoke calmly, crossed her arms.

Fergus Fergusson turned to her with a confused look, and then back at the large snowman blocking his car.

"I told her to buy a shovel," he groaned, pulling out his phone.

Clarissa took two steps closer.

"Fergus Fergusson?"

He didn't look up from his phone. "Yes. And you are?"

"I'm Clarissa Walkman. I'm a student reporter from St. Croix

High School. I've been trying to reach you about the St. Croix Tigers hockey team, and their exclusion from next—"

"Right. Yes. Look, it's out of my hands." He glanced at her briefly, pointing with his index finger like an upset parent. "And that's off the record."

"I'll help you get this snowman out of the way if you give me five minutes."

Fergus Fergusson's eyes darted at her suspiciously and then smiled, like someone accepting defeat for the first time. "Impressive," he said, turning back toward the office building. "Five minutes. But in my office."

She followed him inside and stomped her boots on the carpet. Michelle had gone home for the day, and most of the lights had been turned off, creating strange shadows and patches of darkness in every corner. He unlocked his office and held the door open for her—"After you"—waving her in, brushing his hand on her lower back as she entered. It was completely dark and a moment of panic set inside her as Fergus Fergusson fiddled with the light switch for what felt like an unreasonably long time.

When the lights were on, she waited for him to be seated at his desk before taking the chair across from him. He was a mustachioed man with a bright red nose and silver hair that she guessed was blond in a past life. In truth, he bore a striking resemblance to the snowman she made outside, but she assessed him to be a big man who could be nimble if he wanted to.

"So," he started, elbows planted. "What's your story about?"

"The Tigers."

"Oh, right. The inner-city school."

She nodded and pulled her notepad and recorder from her bag and rested them on her lap.

"Now, just to be clear, this isn't an interview. I haven't agreed to anything. Nor am I comfortable with you recording this. You should know that, being a journalist."

Nerves settled in. She glanced around the room quick: trophies with gold statues displayed on various shelves, one too many framed certificates that commended leadership and community service from various bodies, and two jerseys, also framed, on the wall to her right, complete with signed signatures. No pictures of a wife or children or anything personal, just accolades. "I've been calling your office and emailing you for weeks trying to get an interview."

"Well," he said, leaning back far in his chair, his arms on the rests, the brown leather speaking. "Things get busy this time of year. Tough schedules."

She was annoyed and thought about mentioning the calendar on Michelle's desk: the free Thursday next week and the following Monday and Tuesday. But she refrained. "Off the record, then?"

"Go right ahead, honey. But I'll hold you to that." He folded his hands and rested them on his bulging belly, and then added: "What's a pretty girl like you doing in print journalism. Don't all the pretty ones belong on TV? Talking to the athletes." He grinned. "But like I said, I better not see anything I say here printed anywhere. Journalists are supposed to have integrity. Otherwise, what is the media for? Certainly not to keep us informed."

She nodded, and let all that other stuff fly over her. It was the only way.

"Then shoot."

She put away her recorder. "Do you mind if I take notes?"

"I'd rather you not. For integrity's sake."

She put away her notepad and straightened her posture and looked him in the eyes. She tried to look mean, but also confident. "So why has the league decided to exclude the St. Croix Tigers from participation next season and presumably going forward? What was the reason behind this decision?"

"Look, the first thing you need to understand is how our game— and this goes for most sports in general—is played. It requires a lot of travel. And during this time of year, traveling, for many of our teams, becomes difficult and sometimes very dangerous. So, it was the decision of this league that, with this decision, we will alleviate the demands of travel on many of our teams. It makes for better scheduling, such as time and day of games, keeping in mind school nights, because education always comes first. Which also means better access for teams to and from games, whether they be at home or away. Makes for better sportsmanship, and, as you know and probably goes without saying, fosters fairer competition across the league.

It's easier on the players, coaches, team staff and, of course, the parents, who we can't do this without."

"But—"

He raised a finger. "Second, and this is important to understand, the Tigers are not the only team affected by this decision. There are two other high schools, aside from St. Croix, that have also been impacted. That's not to say these athletes are not allowed to play hockey next season or in the future. This is Canada. Hockey is everywhere. And there are plenty of opportunities."

"That's correct," Clarissa said, brushing strands of hair behind her ear. "St. Croix is not the only school expelled going forward. But the other schools, as you noted, are also centrally located."

"Centrally located?" He maintained the same grin.

"Inner city. Not in the suburbs."

"Okay . . ."

"So. So what about the optics of this decision. How does the league feel about excluding teams from these communities?"

His face went red, matching his nose, and his grin disappeared. "What are you alleging? That we restructured the league because these other teams from the suburbs no longer wanted to play in the North End?"

"Did you?" She kept eye contact.

He scoffed. "That's outrageous. Certainly not one I'd expect from a budding journalist."

"I'm only asking a question."

He looked away from her for the first time since sitting down, at his empty monitor, and then back at her.

"Others in our community are saying that this decision is unfair, unjust, that it's taking away an opportunity from the Tigers to participate in organized hockey. Sports can bring communities together, lift them up, and what it gives our youth is something special. People are also saying that the decision is fueled by racial discrimination. I mean, surely, you're aware of the outside perception that some have about our community. How would you respond to that?"

He smacked his palms on the table, hard enough for a cup of pens to rattle. "This is not an interview," he said, calmer than she anticipated. "This is not about racism. We condemn racism and any sort of prejudice. We believe in treating people equally regardless of race, class or gender. That's how this sport is, plain and simple. When I played junior hockey, back in the day when society was much simpler, we'd travel nine, ten, sometimes twelve hours for games on Native reserves. It was hard. We didn't like doing it. But we did it. Sucked it up. Were set up in a hotel. Ate a few Squaw Dogs. It's not so easy anymore. People like being close to civilization."

She hesitated, fearing another outburst, but said, "The travel issue goes both ways."

His face had returned to its normal pigment, though glossier now. "Maybe it does. Maybe you're right and the experts have it all wrong."

"I don't care about being right. I just want to understand what's happening here."

"I think you're looking for a story where there isn't one. Trying to stir the pot in the wrong direction. That's called bias. Remember that when you make it big."

His phone rang and he answered it and hung up immediately after saying, "Sounds good." When he returned his attention to her the grin was back on his face. "Well look, honey, your time is up. I have to end our conversation here."

They both stood. Clarissa pulled her bag over her shoulders and rushed out the office and down the hall to the lobby, where she waited for him, observing a colorful collection of scarves Michelle had hanging on a coatrack beside her desk.

Fergus Fergusson barreled from the dark hallway toward her, the outline of his body and face becoming more discernible as he approached the light. They shook hands, and his grip was so tight it left her palm feeling numb the whole way home.

"Thanks for your time, Mr. Fergusson."

"You too," he said, leading them out of the office building. "Remember, everything I said in there is off the record. But I'll have Shelby from PR reach out on Monday. She'll answer whatever she can in a written statement." He turned to her before getting in his car and looked surprisingly cheery. "Stay in school."

Smoke gusted out the back of his vehicle, and in one swift and elegant acceleration he bulldozed through her snowman and she felt a confused sadness watching it burst pathetically into a white plume, re-creating its own snowfall. She watched his lights fade away and went home with more doubts than she arrived with—about herself and the world.

AS PROMISED, SHELBY EMAILED her Monday and answered some of her questions with a careful vagueness that irritated her more than the conversation with Fergus Fergusson. But it was enough. She had done her due diligence, and the story would run. Out there to be read. For the whole world to see.

## *clinton whiteway*

THE WAY TO TOMMY'S HOUSE FROM SCHOOL IS DIFFERENT THAN the way to the Haven. They're in opposite directions, opposite ends of the hood. Sometimes I take the long way though, when there's time and when Tommy isn't with me, when I'm alone, loop around the neighborhood so I can catch a glimpse of the place I once sort of called home. I don't go inside. I don't see Kimmy and Eli, as I suspect the last thing they want to see is me walking back through those doors. I know I shouldn't wish for this but when I'm there, leaned up against a rusty newspaper dispenser, I hope to see Jakub. I wouldn't mind seeing Celli too. Or the big round guy with hair like a hedgehog who cleaned the kitchen and made us meals. But I don't. Each time I'm there it's like no one is coming and going, the doors rarely open, like the place is abandoned. Seeing Jakub would let me know he's okay, which I know would mean he's regressed, that he's back in that small room in that small bed and that life ain't good, which is the opposite of being okay. Not seeing him is better confirmation that he's doing fine, and yet seeing him in the flesh would let me know that he's alive. Still alive. But I haven't seen him.

I walk to school most mornings now. Walking to school at this time of year isn't advisable, and each time I leave the house Tommy's koko scolds me for not wearing a thick enough toque, claiming that my ears will literally fall off my head, and that when I'm older the cold I let penetrate my bones and joints in my youth will make me a stiff old man. Life, she says, usually making us bannock toast and eggs, will be unpleasant then, adding that she's "seen it happen." Tommy, meanwhile, takes the bus.

In late January I walked to school the day after a blizzard. I had class at ten. The sun was in my face, pressing on my nose and eyelashes, keeping them free of icicles. The sidewalk was covered in snow, snow was in my shoes, the whole city covered in a blanket of white. The only fresh path was the one I blazed with my numb legs and feet. It was cold. January cold. Which means cold as hell. If there is a hell then surely it's freezing cold, freezing like this. Maybe this is hell. Maybe I died at the Haven, choked to death on one of Jakub's too-thick peanut butter sandwiches and this is my hell. Hell is cold. It must be. A freezing hell is worse than flames and fire because in a cold hell you'll yearn for a warmth that will never come.

I arrived at school and put my hands to a heater. I felt my ears, took off my shoes and socks and inspected my toes, checking for signs of frostbite. I was in the clear, thawing slowly. I went to class with bare feet, which gave off a wet funk, and the teacher, presumably conscious of the rocky home lives of much of our student population, didn't say a word.

AT LUNCHTIME I WALKED by the student newspaper's office and beside the door was a blue rack carrying the latest issue and the front page story was written by Clarissa. It was about the Tigers, about me, about our shit season, about the league's plans to boot us out after our final game come May, about how our coaches and team manager requested from us not to talk to press, not even student press.

## CLINTON WHITEWAY: LEAGUE DECISION TO DROP TIGERS "COMPLETELY UNFAIR"

### BY CLARISSA WALKMAN, STAFF REPORTER

There's more hanging over the St. Croix Tigers this year than another winless season, as it seems the prevailing Curse will continue until at least next year. That depends, however, on whether there is a future for the popular sports club.

Last summer, the Southern Manitoba High School Hockey League informed St. Croix coaches and team staff that they would be losing their spot in the league's Tier 3 Division at the end of the upcoming season. The details behind that decision have not been made clear to the public until now.

"SMHSHL representatives voted unanimously last August to prioritize the safety for high school clubs in our southern regions, through a more efficient travel schedule that in the past has been described as burdensome for both sides involved," a spokesperson for the league told *The St. Croix Daily Drum* in a statement. "It is our hope that these incoming improved changes will make our great game more accessible for players, coaches, parents and supporters alike."

Asked whether the SMHSHL believed they were unfairly excluding inner-city hockey teams such as the St. Croix Tigers, the spokesperson said in a statement, "The SMHSHL strives to promote the game at each level in a host of different communities, and our goal every season is to encourage participation throughout Manitoba regardless of financial status."

Still, the decision to exclude St. Croix next season doesn't sit well with Tigers forward and graduating senior Clinton Whiteway.

"We feel as though we are being deliberately targeted for who we are," Whiteway said in an exclusive interview with *The Daily Drum*. "It's completely unfair."

Whiteway (Anishinaabe from the Pelican Lake First Nation) was informed by team coaches and staff in September, before the start of the season, of the league's intentions. He said he's unsatisfied with the reasoning behind their exclusion from next season.

"The idea is that many of the southern schools are forming their own league, leaving us out here hanging," he said. "They said travel distance was a big concern for them. But the next closest school to us is twenty minutes [south] down Main [Street] and they're supposedly included in this new league."

According to Whiteway, coaches and staff for the St. Croix Tigers are quietly fighting the league's decision, adding that, "They're trying not to start a whole war over it."

"If you're not white this game can be cruel, ruthless even," Whiteway said. "We all know that. On the other hand . . . Fights give you at least a chance."

The Tigers have yet to win a game this season. The Curse, which describes the Tigers' winless streak over many consecutive seasons, has reached mythic proportions, largely because no one seems to remember how far back the Curse goes.

Community members say they would love to see the Curse be broken. Speaking to *The Daily Drum* last fall, Darlene Loon (Class of '66) said she couldn't remember the last time the Tigers won a game.

"I would love to see the team win a game soon," Loon said. "I know for sure it would mean a lot to the people around here."

Tigers head coach Wade Johnson, assistant coach Dale Ducky and team manager Patti Klassen did not respond to multiple requests for comment.

Whiteway started playing hockey at a young age. He's played two winless seasons with the Tigers, in addition to the run the team is currently on.

He believes the absence of a Tigers hockey team next season would leave a big hole in the community.

"I've never known any [Indigenous] kid who didn't play hockey, or at least try it once," Whiteway said. "It gives us a chance to do something outside of school. Keeps some of us out of trouble too I guess. Keeps us out of places we don't want to be . . . Like maybe bad situations at home. Some of our players don't have it easy necessarily. Having a team can be sort of an escape from all that."

I placed the paper back into the rack after reading. It was surprisingly fair and balanced, with comments from both sides of the issue and yet the objectivity of it flustered me. One side was clearly in the wrong, and I knew it wasn't us. But I'd leave these types of decisions to the reporters. In a way I'd leave our lives in their hands after giving it to them. On the story, I thought: I can live with this.

I walked into the student newspaper's office and found Clarissa at a desk littered with papers, old newspapers and yellow sticky notes.

The room was dim, windows shuttered, visible only by the yellow light of desk lamps. There was a coffeepot on a counter with stale coffee I estimated to be toxic by now. She looked up and her eyes widened as she saw me coming toward her and she removed the earbuds connected to her recorder from her ears.

"Hey!" she said. "Did you see the story?"

"I did," I said, forcing a smile despite that it now felt strange seeing my name and words out there for the public to consume. "Took you long enough."

"A girl gets busy," she said, now standing, scribbling into a notepad. "It took a long time before anybody at the league would even talk to me. But I kept barking up the tree, the wrong one for them, but the right one for me. And then finally, a spokesperson reached out and agreed to answer some questions in a written statement. But hey, better than nothing."

"Wow," I said. "That's a good get."

"It absolutely is!" Her attention was on me now. "Especially considering their reasons for banishing you guys is total horseshit. It's unfair in every sense of the word. Like you said."

"Right."

There was an awkward pause, so I looked around and examined the general messiness of the room. I wondered if this is how most newsrooms operate. Random shit on the desks. Random shit on the floor. Random shit on the walls. The visuals stressed me. I started tapping my fingers with my thumb on one hand and the cap of a red pen on the other. I counted to twenty in my head, over and over until it felt right.

"Hey," she said. "Has anyone from the team approached you? I know they didn't want any of you speaking to the media."

"No," I said, first in a mumble and then repeated myself more clearly. "Not yet. We have practice after school, so we'll see I guess."

"Well. I hope it's okay. That it goes well. You're brave for doing this, talking to me. I don't know why anybody talks to me, or the media in general, and I mean that. I'm appreciative."

I nodded, and mumbled again, lost in my count, "Me too."

"Well," she said, "let me know how it goes. Text me even? I have to run and get some lunch before next class. I've been here all morning and my mom will kill me if she gets another call saying I skipped *another* full day of class. But I keep telling her I need this experience if I'm to get into journalism school."

"I thought we're pretty much past application deadlines at this point."

"Not for this fall," she said quickly. "I'm going for a bachelor's in Indigenous Studies, to first get real-world experience, *and then,* after that's done with, I'll maybe go for a master's in journalism. Ryerson maybe. Maybe Columbia. We'll see. I don't like thinking too far ahead. I try to remain in the present, grounded, as much as possible. Take it one step at a time."

"Wow," I said. "When you're a world-famous journalist don't forget about me, my story, my incredible tale of resilience and determination." I tried to wink but failed miserably.

She laughed. "I won't! I don't forget these things." And then she brushed past me.

AT PRACTICE LATER THAT day Coach Johnson made the entire team skate laps and suicides for the whole last thirty minutes. He shouted at the top of his lungs until his face turned red and swollen with rage: "Faster! Pick it up!" At the end of each skate, he'd come around and dig into the player brave enough to get down on one knee and then we'd go again. "Rest is for pussies! For winners! And so far this season you're a bunch of fuckin' losers! Cousin-fucking bush-league losers! You have to want it!" he roared.

I couldn't help but feel responsible somehow. That he saw Clarissa's story and was now punishing us for it. Near the end of practice, as we all stood in a line at the end of the ice, huffing, panting like tired dogs, exhaling fog into the cool air, he glided past us like a military sergeant, sneering at his tired soldiers. He stopped at me:

"Whitey," he said, his voice now hoarse from all the screaming. "I saw your mama at The Stock this weekend. Lookin' wiry these days. But still flirty as ever. One wild broad she is. Almost took her home for myself. Fuck me. Maybe you could use a manly presence in the house. A new daddy."

His words were daggers, except they were covered in poison, like the venomous frogs Indigenous peoples in South America used for their arrows, because I froze, became paralyzed. I didn't say anything. I didn't look at him. I wondered for a moment whether it could be true, what he said, and assumed it was. My mom, last I'd seen her, had gotten slim, she was suddenly a different person altogether, an alien in our own apartment. But she was still my mother, and I knew at the heart of her there was still something made of steel, that it would always be there. He skated back down the line, and as he did so I said:

"Go fuck yourself."

He turned around with a wild grin. The eyes of my teammates darted at me. "What was that?" he said, and I knew full well he'd heard me. His grin turned quickly to fury.

"You heard me," I said.

"Everyone except Whiteway get some water," he declared. "He's skating for all of you. We're going to be here for a while."

I did. I accepted my punishment.

I TOOK THE LONG way home after practice. I left my gear in one of the arena's storage rooms because we had a game the next day, and when this was the case, Petey, the rink manager, often let us leave our bags overnight instead of hauling them back home. I left the rink before Tommy and didn't tell him where I was going. We were in the showers together but didn't say anything, nobody said anything to me, not even an apology or a friendly checkup after my exchange with Coach Johnson. Not that I expected anything. The accord we signed as kids, toddlers, or at least the one we were taught to believe, was that I made my bed, and I skated for it.

I stopped outside the Haven and watched the odd person come and go. Again, there was no sign of Jakub or Celli or the big round cook. I began to shiver and bounce on my toes from the cold. I thought seriously about going inside to get warm and giving my regards to Eli and Kimmy and imagined them greeting me again with open arms, assuring me that I'm always welcome, always a safe place. I would thank them and ask about Jakub and they would tell me he's staying with a long-lost relative and doing well. I'd leave and that would be the last time they saw me. But I started walking home instead.

As I trudged through the snowy sidewalk I felt like I was being followed. I kept seeing the same black car with obnoxiously tinted windows and loud exhaust. It slowed when it drove by me and at first it seemed like a lost driver trying to read house numbers. It went around the block and came up behind me again, moving slowly. I looked over my shoulder only once without stopping, trying to show I wasn't bothered. It drove past me again and around the block and this time pulled up beside me, moving at my pace, and so I stopped nervously and the car braked still too and I tried to peer through the dark windows but the only thing I could make out was a shadowy silhouette. I waved confused, thinking they might roll down the window and hoping it was just a lost person in need of directions, but nothing. The window stayed rolled up. Then, loudly, the car drove away until its blurry lights faded in the distance. The streetlamp above me went out then, and suddenly there was nothing left but darkness. I fixed my toque, which had been hurting my hair, pulled it down low, and kept walking until I reached home.

## *errol whitecloud sinclair*

### FEBRUARY 25, 2012

I'm still thinking about what your mom said, about you boys possibly thinking I'm dead. I've often wondered whether you boys wished I was. Whether that'd be somehow easier to explain than telling all your friends and girlfriends that your dad ran out on you. Or maybe you don't talk about me at all, pretend I'm not out there roaming the world. I think that's probably what I would do if I was you. Just pretend I don't exist, because in truth I never existed. I never *really* existed. I only drank. I'm not sure what you know about where I've been and why, but nonetheless I will do my best to explain it all in full. To lay it all out in the open.

First and foremost, I'm no thug and I'm no hardened criminal. I've been a piece of shit for much of my life but I never intended to hurt anybody. When I first moved to the city I couldn't find work, and so a buddy of mine taught me how to steal. And for the first year I spent in the city that's all I did to get by. I'd go into Polo or make the drive down to St. Vital and sometimes Northgate—never Portage Place; too many fools there to sell you out—and I'd steal, and sell, whatever I could. Overpriced leggings and sneakers, ball caps and colognes and perfumes, Jordan jackets and football jerseys. Anything. It all sold well, and it was easy to find people willing to pay for copped goods for cheap.

My buddy—I'll refer to him here as Dallas—was a computer whiz and as such he could often be found scavenging junkyards for spare parts, and specifically for something he called "rare earth magnets." They could be found in old computer hard drives, and a single one of these bad boys was strong enough to hold a thirty-pound dumb-bell off the ground with no problem and, if you were reckless, sticky enough to leave sheet metal looking like a razor-sharp weapon at the end of your pull. Dallas and I would head to the yard together and search for hours, usually to no avail, but every now and then, from a distance, I'd hear, "Sweet sweet neodymium!" and that's when I knew we scored big. You see, son, neodymium magnets are small, dis-creet, mighty tools that instantly remove plastic magnets attached to most valuable items found at the average mall. Anything less risked unwanted attention. Or else fresh ink splattered all over a fresh pair of Lululemons.

But as I say, I was a drunk. And you should never drink and steal.

It was a Monday morning. The best time and day for a thief. Places are usually quiet because everyone is at work. The weather channel said the coldest day of the past two years. I remember there being a layer of fresh ice everywhere, on the roads and sidewalks, and I swear you could have skated around the whole city that day. I hadn't slept. I only drank, and to this day I'm not sure when that bender started. I arrived at Polo and parked as close as I could near one of the mall's seven public entrances that weren't linked to any particular store. I knew there was an electronics store near this particular entrance, which would be my exit, and I knew the green-haired goth girl who worked at this store was more than likely to be working. This was good, because she was usually oblivious to everything around her in all the times I browsed the store's shelves. Her name was Georgia, name tag crooked and scuffed, work shirt untucked. She killed time texting and painting her nails black. Rarely stepped out from behind the counter along the left wall.

I'd never stolen from that store before. Electronics presented great risk, and so I most often performed my thieving in the changing rooms of unisex clothing brands.

I probably don't have to explain to you what drinking does to you. It makes you take risks that you probably shouldn't. It tricks you into believing something about yourself.

When I walked into the electronics store Georgia was there as I suspected, texting and painting her nails not black but a bright pink. Her hair was not green but a normal brown. I wouldn't have described her as goth then and she was more aware of me in the store than I expected her to be. I moved to the right of the store, away from the checkout counter along the left wall, to browse a selection of video games and DVD movies. I hate hats but I wore a big trucker hat as a sort of disguise, even though all malls and the stores in them had fairly short memories and every time you successfully stole from them capitalism carried on just fine. The task was straightforward: place as many games and DVDs as I could inside the backpack I'd brought with me, while making sure to scan the security strip with my neodymium magnet to avoid triggering the alarm as I left, and do so while making sure Georgia didn't become suspicious.

And so that's exactly what I did, demagnetizing and dropping each video game and DVD movie into the bag I'd placed on the floor, and after each successful drop I'd peer up to see where Georgia was. After about five drops, she was still there behind the counter, still texting, blowing on her pink nails. But then I started getting anxious. I was out in the open, and anybody who walked into the store would have been able to see what I was doing. So I began to pick up the pace. My bag had approached near full. On what would've been my last drop I stumbled, knocking two small boxes off the bottom shelf, and then the drunk in me missed the bag as I tossed a game called *Halo* toward the floor. I looked up quickly and Georgia was no longer at the counter; she was fixing a sign near the entrance advertising a big store sale. She turned and we locked gazes and she started toward me and I knew then that I was busted.

She was about six steps from me when she greeted me with "Can I . . ." and paused as she looked down toward my bag. For a moment her face was red and panicked but it quickly changed to composed, and I could see now that the name on her tag was not Georgia but Brooke and I blame this error on simply being a drunk. "Can I help you? You have to pay for those. I have to ask you to remove them from your bag. Store policy."

And then the drunk in me decided to make a run for it. I grabbed my bag from the floor and lunged past Brooke and out of the electronics store, and as I was running I could hear Brooke yelling, "Hey!

Come back here!" and I noticed straightaway that the mall was now bustling with passersby. But I kept on running toward the exit nearest my parked Corolla, and I couldn't help but remember that my car's old battery often failed in cold weather. As I passed through the mall's doors and the sharp cold hit my face I felt a strong hand on my shoulder. I turned and it was a security guard. He was young and clean-shaven, barely an adult. He tugged hard at my bag and said, "Give me that!" and I said, "This is my bag!" and for about a minute we tugged and pulled like it was a game. And then, well, I decided I needed to let go. But after I did this the young security guard slipped backward on the ice and to this day I can hear the cracking sound of his head hitting the ground, and as I darted toward my Corolla he stayed there, motionless and unconscious, and if I could do it differently today I believe I would stay there with him until help arrived. I have to believe it.

The Corolla started and I drove. The drunk in me drove like a drunk. The drunk in me didn't buckle up. I drove too fast and as I went through a red on St. James I clipped the rear of another vehicle moving across the intersection, and this collision was enough to send my vehicle into a streetlight post. I don't know what happened next. They told me I was lucky not to get flung around too bad. They said when they found me video games and DVD movies were everywhere, scattered all over the interior and some on the ground outside, and this surprised me when I first heard it, because it meant I went back for the bag, even as the young security guard lay there unmoving. They found more stolen goods in the trunk.

I was in the hospital for I don't know how long. The entire time I was there two different police officers exchanged turns outside my hospital room door. The doctor they had me seeing was very religious. He had Jesus on a cross hanging above the door in his office and a bumper sticker on the wall that said *FAITH IN GOD IS THE BEST MEDICINE.*

They told me the young security guard wasn't a security guard, but a volunteer for a neighborhood watch group that helped young dreamers get into the police academy. They told me he was in a coma for a time, and that it was likely he would never become a cop, let alone work a normal job for the rest of his life.

The religious doctor told me I was lucky to have my vision, given the damage to my face. "He must've wanted you to see something," he said, shining a bright light on my right eye.

"What do you think that is?"

"I'm sure you'll know it when you see it."

## tigers at rebels

IT'S NERVOUS TIME NOW! THE THIRD PERIOD IS ABOUT TO GET *underway. There was no flood between periods, so the ice is probably as bad as what you'd find over at Memorial Arena. The visitors tonight must be loving this, embracing a familiar environment.*

*It's 6–6 between the St. Croix Tigers and the Collège Louis-Riel Rebels. It's been an absolute shooting gallery! Between the two worst teams in the league no less. The Tigers: winless. The Rebels, meanwhile, have just one win and an overtime loss on their record this season. Both teams desperate. Both feisty, hungry.*

*Here we go! The Rebels win the draw, the puck now hurried up the boards by the Rebels captain René Peltier-Lévesque-LaFrenière and he can fly, looking for help, he's into the Tigers' zone, he tries a drop pass for Babineaux, wisely picked off by Whiteway, pass to RedHead and he's always dangerous, skates up the ice, into the offensive zone, around the net, finds Shields, and Shields spins to evade pressure from a winger, space to work with, shoots, it's tipped, and the Tigers score! Deflected off the stick of Whiteway.*

*The Tigers lead 7–6 with eighteen remaining in the third. It's elation on the Tigers bench. Can they hold on now? We're about to find out.*

*Relentless pressure from Louis-Riel. At a glance they are the faster team, but size has been the difference so far in this one. The Tigers are big on the blue line, led by Shields, and they've hammered the Louis-Riel forwards down low.*

*Fifteen minutes left. Shields has it, clears the puck to safety, back comes Peltier-Lévesque-LaFrenière, he's been everywhere tonight, and he's rocked by Shields! The Rebels bench is irate. Screaming at the refs for a call. They feel Shields got an elbow up high on their captain.*

*The Rebels have the Tigers hemmed in their own zone. The Tigers are sitting back a little too much for my liking. They're happy to just preserve the lead. The Rebels are playing keep-away, a little tic-tac-toe. Quick shot! And it's in! The Rebels, somehow, come away with a goal! Blackwood and everyone else here in the St. Boniface Community Centre thought he had the puck, but it trickled through and the Rebels found it and put it away.*

*7–7.*

*Eight minutes left.*

*The Tigers have woken up. They're playing with more urgency, more aggression, looking for the win instead of settling for one, not that they can do that anymore. It feels like the next one will seal it.*

*Shields breaks up the ice. With speed. He winds up and claps a hard shot off the goalie's blocker, a nice save. But now it's on for the Rebels, a three-on-two. Shields rushes back to break up the play, the Rebels make one too many passes, and Peltier-Lévesque-LaFrenière goes down. The ref has his hand up. It looks like Shields will go to the box for tripping. It looked to me like Peltier-Lévesque-LaFrenière stepped on the stick of Shields and that's what caused him to fall. That's really unfortunate. A late penalty in what's been an exciting back-and-forth game. You hate to see games decided by the referee's whistle. Let them play. Let it be decided on the ice, both sides at full strength. You might call that a makeup call for the headshot earlier that went uncalled.*

*Two minutes left. Face-off in the Tigers' zone.*

*Another draw won by the Rebels. That's been the story all night. Quick, short passes around the outside, waiting for the Tigers to give them an opening. The Tigers stay tight in their box. Active sticks.*

*Sixty seconds left. Peltier-Lévesque-LaFrenière feeds a pass across the ice. A shot! Blocked by Whiteway! He put his body on the line and the crowd salutes him for it. But the Rebels have it again.*

*Thirty seconds left. Peltier-Lévesque-LaFrenière wrists one through traffic.*

*Where is it? Chaos in front of the net. Sticks. Bodies. Sprawled out. And it's in! The referee is pointing to the goal. The Rebels score! Heart-*

*break for the Tigers! Their coach is furious, purple-faced, leaning over the bench, giving the officials an earful, and they'll eject him. He shouts the whole way to the dressing room.*

*You hate to see it end this way. But that's how it'll end. The seconds trickle away. The Tigers are noticeably dispirited. They gave it everything. The Rebels bench is celebrating.*

*Final score: 8–7.*

# ziigwan

*tannyce shields*

THE OTHER DAY LITTLEFEATHER, WHO HAS BEEN SUGGESTING places we should visit or live or do yoga even though I don't like the feeling of being stretched, convinced me it was time to return to the place of my birth. Winnipeg. She said this after I showed her the email from Tomahawk. "He needs you," she said, taking my head in both her palms and giving me a gentle kiss on the forehead. "It's time we go out that way."

She said we would go together and that we would go through the States, because the highways up this way are to be avoided. Highways, and roads beside bodies of water. Water where bodies are found wrapped in garbage bags and weighed down by rocks, all pale and bloated. We wouldn't stay forever.

We would see Tomahawk, Asemaa, Koko, and together we'd be a family again for a little while, and we'd take off again whenever we wanted because Littlefeather doesn't trust all the bad bodies of water around Winnipeg. There's too much water there. Too many places to sink, to float. We could go anywhere after that. I suggested Los Angeles, because it's warm and sunny all the time and I'd really like to be in a place with lots of Indians. She nodded and said she loved that for us. She said Los Angeles is a place full of all sorts of Indians with big dreams, but that it's still the homelands of the Tongva, Tataviam, Serrano, Kizh and Chumash. She said we would live there, together, for as long as we wanted because we have the right to, and that if the officers at the border try to say otherwise, all we have to do is tell them we're Indian and this is our right under the Jay Treaty, an agreement signed in 1794 between Great Britain and the United States that made it so that we Indians could travel and live freely on either side of the border, and that's what we would say to the officers. But before we do that, she said, we would make a quick stop in a place called Riverside and pay our respects to the stolen children buried at the cemetery of an Indian boarding school there. And then after we would wander Hollywood and pretend we're celebrities, Indian celebrities.

But Littlefeather isn't status, she doesn't believe in status, and to my knowledge neither am I, and so the other day she went to the library and forged and signed band letters for the both of us in case the border officers give us a hard time. They, meaning the border officers, want to see our blood, what's in it, the *quantum* of it, Littlefeather says, see how much Indian we really are, and they would peel back our skin and look at us if they could.

WE'RE ON THE ROAD before the sun bathes the mountains in orange. Just as the birds begin their morning songs outside my bedroom window. We're on the road on our feet, walking to a nearby car rental place where we've booked a small car that will take us to where we need to go. Littlefeather waited for me outside as I left the center, this time for good, smoking and drinking coffee from a Styrofoam cup. I packed a small bag of clothes in a little bag designed like a baseball, covered in pretend red stitches like with the stitches on real baseballs, that I purchased from Value Village, no, borrowed. To be honest, I stole it because inside was a tag that said "Property of Willow Harper, Cowichan Valley" and I felt it was my duty to return this bag to its original owner and I spent a whole week at the library trying to look up a Willow Harper in Cowichan Valley but could only find obituaries, and so I gave up after feeling that Willow Harper would want this bag to go to a caring owner and I could be that person.

At the car rental place the agent behind the counter, a boyish-looking man wearing some sort of animal tooth around his neck, proudly displaying tattoos of random fir trees on both his forearms, gives us a strange, confused look when I tell him we're going to Winnipeg through the States, taking advantage of the safest roads and highways available to us so as not to become yet another number in a long list of numbers, and that we'll return the car there when we get there. We go with a compact sedan. Littlefeather, behind me, asks, "Did he say how many miles the car has? We should make sure he's not giving us a shit box." I relay the message, saying to the man, "She's wondering how many miles the car has?" and he looks at Littlefeather all confused again and says, "It's brand new with a little less than a hundred I think." He smiles. I sign the papers and take the keys.

"Why do you think that boy was acting all weird with us?" I say, tossing my bag in the back seat and swinging the door shut. "Looking at us all weird."

"Just sizing us up," Littlefeather says. "Doesn't trust us. Thinks we're thieves. Happens all the time. Can't even go to the bank without someone thinking we're robbing the place."

I lean up against the side of the car and a sort of peacefulness washes over me. I feel as though things are better. As though my life is about to change *for* the better. I'm glad to be taking this step and when I reach the end of this long road things will be different. The sun has its way of taking care of things.

"You drive," Littlefeather says.

I don't protest and this is because I enjoy driving.

On the road we don't talk much at first. I like Littlefeather. I do. I like her company. But sometimes I become irritated because I find it's always me who speaks first, forces the conversation. We drive with the windows open, smelling the salty breeze, feeling it on our faces. I have one hand on the wheel and the other floating all limp outside the window. In the seat next to me, Littlefeather tilts her head, not exactly out the window but just enough so that her perfect brown hair blows all over.

"What shampoo do you use?" I ask, feeling tired of the silence.

"Same as you." Her eyes are closed as she says this. "Pantene. Sometimes I mix different brands together if I'm running out."

"How is it so perfect?"

"How is what so perfect?"

"You," I say. "Your hair. How is it so perfect?"

"Nimisenh," she says, pulling her head away from the window. "Nothing is perfect. Nobody is perfect. We live in the most imperfect of worlds. But we make the most out of what's been given to us. The only exception to all of this, Nimisenh, is obviously my hair." She laughs.

I laugh, and then it's all quiet again.

She likes to call me her older sister, even though I'm not sure which one of us is older or younger. I've never asked Littlefeather her age, never cared. She certainly looks younger than me, fresher in both mind and body. She has a special fire inside of her that rages when she needs it to, but then settles to something like glowing embers, rising again. As for me: if that fire was ever really there it died a long time ago. Nothing's left but ash. It's been Littlefeather keeping me going, making me feel alive.

"Okay," I say, eyes fixed on the road. "But what about your skin. So perfect. How do you do it?"

I can see she's looking at me, covering her face from the sun. "I don't use soap."

I give her a look, like I know she's messing with me.

"Seriously! Ever since I was a little girl. My mama never made me use any soap. Fuck. I couldn't anyway because she never bought any. She always said water is all you need to clean yourself, and I believed her. Soap sucks, basically. It's another predatory industry."

I take my hand off the wheel for a moment to pull down the sun visor and my heart pumps faster as the car rolls over the rumble strip on the edge of the lane, making the tires vibrate all alarmingly, but I catch it before veering any further. "Are you saying I should quit soap? Don't you feel all dirty? I don't want to feel dirty. It's not a good way to be."

"Not ever. If dirty feels and looks this good then I'd rather be dirty. I'm not saying quit soap, I'm just telling you my experience, and my experience is dirty is beautiful. Holy that's wicked. I should trademark that, hey?" Before I can respond she adds, in a performative voice, like she's the star of an infomercial: "Quit soap, use this special clean water instead. For as long as we still have it. Use it. Quit soap."

I look at her and her eyes are closed again. We found out early in our friendship that we both enjoy car rides without the radio on. Enjoyed the silence. This is how we drive now, without music and without the annoying DJs.

When I'm able to I look at her and admire her again. Her eyes are closed. She may be sleeping, and so I choose not to bother her.

The highway gets busier as we get closer to the border and I wonder what business all these cars have on the other side. Where they're going. What they'll do when they get there. Littlefeather sleeps. She snores loud, just like me, or so Littlefeather says. I have no idea if this is true.

A small hatchback dives in front of me without signaling and continues cutting through traffic super fast and for a second its back lights blink furiously. It happens again, and then again. Similar cars all. Something is wrong, I say to myself. Something here is trying to tell me something. I follow them, pushing ever hard on the gas, and after my first sharp maneuver I can see Littlefeather's sleeping body get thrown against her door and she wakes.

"What's going on?" she says. "What's happening? Slow down."

"Something's not right here." I jerk the wheel to the left and then quickly to the right, around a tour bus. "Something's following us. Telling us something."

"Nimisenh," she says calmly. "Slow down. You're going to kill us. Nimisenh."

"I can't," I say. "They're going to get away."

"Who's getting away?"

"Them! These fucking assholes following us!"

She sits up, shifts her seat forward. Looks out at the road around us. "Where are they?"

I look up the road. The cars that passed us are no longer in sight. "They were just here."

"Slow down," she says, pausing between the words. "Calm down. You could really kill us. Do you want both of us to die and never see your family again? Isn't that what you want? To see your kids again."

I let go of the throttle. I take a big breath but still I feel uneasy.

Littlefeather relaxes in her seat again, lets her immaculate hair hang behind her and it's so long it almost touches the floor of the back seat. And after about five minutes she's back asleep.

THE LINE IS SHORTER than expected at the border for this early and I think to myself that soon we'll be in Washington State.

"Littlefeather," I say, shaking her leg. "We're at the border. Wake up so they don't think I've kidnapped you."

She rubs her eyes and stretches her arms above her head. "If anything, they'll think I'm the one kidnapping you. I'm the muscle in this relationship."

"Everrr," I say, though she's probably right.

I pull into one of the lanes leading to one of the border agents. Turns out to be the slowest lane but I stay put.

"Why do you think they made the Jay Treaty for us that long ago?" I say, feeling the warm sun on my arm out the window. "The settlers hated us more two hundred years ago than they do now. Why respect our right to travel freely across this make-believe border. This arbitrary colonial concept."

Littlefeather yawns. "Because sometimes even a blind pig finds a truffle."

The border agent waves us down and I pull ahead and stop when he tells me to.

"Hello," he says. "How are you today?"

"Good," I say.

"Passport."

I offer him our forged band letters and he accepts and studies them. "We're treaty Indians seeking to exercise our Jay Treaty rights. These letters show our blood quantum meets the requirement of at least fifty percent Indian blood."

He looks at me quizzically. "So you don't have a passport on you?"

I shake my head.

"Do you have any other photo identification? I'm also going to need your long-form birth certificate."

I reach into my wallet and offer him my expired driver's license, which nobody at the car rental place ever notices. Either that or they don't give a shit.

"No birth certificate?"

"Not on me," I say.

"Tell him I'm a freedom baby," Littlefeather says. "We don't believe in government birth certificates."

I turn to her and say, "Shh."

But I turn to the border agent anyway and say, "She's a freedom baby. She doesn't have a birth certificate either, or a passport, or Canadian citizenship. She doesn't believe in participating in these colonial institutions and systems. I'm on that path as well."

He looks even more confused, mouth a little open. He gazes over at Littlefeather and back at me. "Give me a minute." He looks away from us and picks up his phone and begins chatting to someone on the other line and after a while hangs up and says to us:

"This is going to take a little more time to process, but we're going to get this figured out." He steps out of his booth and points down the lane. "Just drive up here, take a left, you'll find a parking lot, park there, and go inside and someone will be in there to help you. We'll get this all sorted. Thanks for your patience."

"Prick," Littlefeather says. "Doesn't know the fake fucking law of his fake country. Typical."

I nod at the man and pull away with a fake smile on my face.

Inside the office I go up to one of the booths and through the glass a plump woman in a horribly stiff, probably hot, probably unbearable uniform tells me someone will call me soon and so I slump back into my chair and wait.

After almost twenty damn minutes a door opens and a beautiful young woman, younger than me at least for sure, calls my name and leads me down a hallway to an empty room with only a table and two chairs on either side.

I take a seat. Littlefeather sits beside me.

"Ask her why we're here. How long this'll take," Littlefeather says. "Remind her of our rights."

"I'll get to it. Just stop running your mouth."

The beautiful young woman sits across from me. She opens a small notebook to a blank page and clicks open a pen. "Can you confirm your name for me?"

"Tannyce," I say.

"Last name?"

"What do you plan on doing with this information?"

"It just helps me remember things. So I have everything correct. I want to make sure no mistakes are made."

"Shields," I say in almost a whisper, watching her write it down in the small notebook.

"Where are you from, Tannyce?"

"Manitoba originally. Coming from Vancouver."

"Where in Manitoba?"

"The capital." I assume she doesn't know Manitoba's capital.

"So you're from Winnipeg."

I nod. Surprised.

"Are you from any particular First Nation?"

I shake my head. "I grew up in the city."

"So what's this, then?" She holds up the band papers for me and Littlefeather. "So you're from Winnipeg, grew up there. You're not from a First Nation. But your band is supposedly somewhere in British Columbia. Is that right?"

"You see a problem with that?"

"I'm just curious."

We lock eyes for a moment and it makes me feel uncomfortable.

"My name is Juju," she says, leaning closer to me, elbows on the table. "I'm Puyallup. I'm a member of the Puyallup Tribe. But I grew up on the Muckleshoot Reservation. My mom is Swanky and my dad is Donny. But he's an asshole. Mom is lovely."

"Where is that?" I ask. "Your reservation."

"Pretty close to Seattle." She leans back in her chair.

"Is it nice there?"

"It is. It's beautiful."

"But you don't live there anymore?"

"No, not anymore. I live not far from here."

"Is it nice where you live now?"

She chuckles. "It's not home. I'll say that much. Nothing is. Doesn't matter where you go. Don't you think?" She rests both her palms on the table. "But what about you. Do you ever think about going back home? Not Vancouver. Your other home."

"Always," I say, nodding and smiling slightly. "All the time. In fact, that's where we're headed."

"So you're driving through the United States. On your way to Winnipeg. Your family there?"

"Yes," I say. "They are."

"How exciting. They must be excited. *You* must be too. You been away long?"

I nod, embarrassed. I can't say for sure how long it's been. I wonder if I'll recognize their faces. If they'll remember mine.

"That's wonderful. They'll be happy I'm sure."

I look to my right at Littlefeather and she shakes her head, like she knows what I'm about to say next. "My son," I say, turning back to Juju. "He needs me."

She's studying me more closely now. "Can I ask you something?"

"Go ahead."

"Can I ask you who your friend is?" She looks in Littlefeather's direction and then back at me, offering a gentle smile.

"I'm Littlefeather," Littlefeather says. I look at her all mean, wishing she'd stay quiet this one time.

"Please," I say.

I know Juju can't see her and I know she probably thinks I'm fucked up, a fucking crazy bitch, because I would too, they all do, but I say anyway, "Her name is Littlefeather."

"That's . . . that's a very nice name," Juju says, and I hear Littlefeather thanking her for the compliment. "How long have you been friends?"

"Long," I say. "Long time. For as long as I can remember." She nods at every word I say.

She slides her notebook over to me and on the page, I see that she's only written down my name and the city and province I'm from. "So look, Tannyce," she says. "You're not traveling with a passport. You weren't able to provide a birth certificate. You also don't appear to be carrying any sort of tribal identification or passport that would demonstrate your tribal affiliation. Your band letter looks fine. But answer me this, if I call this councilwoman who's signed at the bottom here, right now, is anyone going to pick up?"

"Just tell her yes," Littlefeather says. "Just tell her yes. Band offices never answer anyways. Tell her they're all lazy shits."

I turn to Littlefeather. "But it's made up. It's all made up. She knows we're lying. We didn't want to use others for our own lies. Don't you remember?"

I turn to Juju. "Nobody will answer. Nobody will answer ever." My hands begin to shake. "I'm sorry."

I see her look of concern. I know what it looks like by now, and I know the feeling I get when I see it. It feels like I'm slinking away to a place, no, not just any place, a dark place, like maybe a hole or a deep pit dug for some sort of foundation, and I'm there, in that darkness, being built over. Hidden away. It's where they hide us monsters. Underneath the living. As they move about the world built for the people allowed to live.

"Can I ask you to do something for me?" Juju says.

I say, "What is it?"

"Write down the name and number of someone you're close to, right there on that paper." She reaches across the table and offers me a pen and I accept it. "Someone you trust."

I do as she asks and she thanks me without smiling and tells me she'll be back in a minute, but before she leaves the room I ask her:

"Can I use the washroom?"

She waves me over to her and leads me down a blank hallway, blank as in there's nothing decorating its walls except a boring paint that makes me feel nauseous, no flags, no paintings, no portraits of their president. She shows me to the washroom and tells me to go straight back to the room when I'm done and to tell anyone who asks that I'm there to wait for her.

I don't like looking in mirrors. My room at the women's center doesn't have one, because I unscrewed it from the wall on my first night there and left it in the hallway and it was gone quick. But I look at myself now, in this moment. I'm disgusted, no, sickened, no, repulsed, no, horrified, by what I see. All those words. I'm thin and drawn out. Everything about me looks jagged, like I'm sucking in my cheeks, or my cheekbones are jumping out of my face, but I'm not and they're not. The harsh fluorescent light gives a greasy shine to my dirty dead hair and a texture to my rumbling, pockmarked cheeks. I see the white of my scalp, there, where hair should be, where it used to be, where the follicles that were once there left me along with my sanity. I look weak. I feel weak.

"You're beautiful," Littlefeather says, behind me. I didn't see her come in.

I wet a paper towel and dab my face and look at myself no further. "Maybe this was too soon."

"Too soon for what?" I say.

"To leave. To get away from here. Maybe we're not ready."

"Will I ever be ready?"

"I believe so. I do." She rests a hand on my back. I feel it, yes, I feel her touch.

I turn away from the mirror and look at Littlefeather. I fear for our friendship, for the day it will end, wondering when that day will be, like she always said would happen. She smiles her beautiful smile and turns and walks out the door and when I get back to the room she's sitting quietly in the chair next to mine.

I take my seat. After a few minutes Juju comes through the door and says, "So I just got off the phone with Beatrice at the women's center. She said she was worried when she didn't see you this morning. Said you two had plans."

"She's always worried."

"Sounds like a good friend. She's on her way down to help you get back home."

"Back to Vancouver?" I ask, before adding, "She's not a friend. She just works there."

"Winnipeg. I told her you want to see your son. She said, 'I'll take her myself.'"

I turn to Littlefeather and smile and she smiles back. Because we both know it's true. Beatrice is always trying to drive me places, always offers, even though I almost always say no.

"It's always good to have people looking out for you. Trust me." Juju sits on the edge of the table but only for a moment, on her feet quickly like she forgot something. She moves to the exit and turns to me before opening the door. "Water or coffee while we wait?"

I tell her both. She leaves, the door closes gently behind her, and when she returns with two cups of coffee and two bottles of water we talk some more. We talk until it's time for me to go home.

## pete mosienko

IF YOU HAD AN OFFICE IT WOULD PROBABLY BE IN THE PRO SHOP. Not the refrigeration room where you keep a small bed for nights when you'd rather sleep here than at home, and certainly not the garage, which opens up to the outside, making it colder than out there in the middle of winter and your least favorite room in the whole rink, but you're hoping that changes when the Zamboni comes in. You haven't ordered it yet but you're planning to, which is to say you're thinking about it because sometimes thinking is as good as working or moving your feet. You roll up the security grilles to the pro shop when you arrive at the Memorial Arena in the morning, and take a seat at the small desk in the corner of the shop. Tonight is the Tigers' fifteenth game of the season. After this there are only eight games remaining. You hope they win. You hope they win every night, but tonight feels especially winnable. You're also starting to hope and pray they're around next season, but from what you've heard that seems unlikely. You'd hate to change the Tigers' logo encrusted beneath center ice because it's been there for ages and you don't know what else you'd put there. You dream about a sponsorship deal. Maybe Coca-Cola or the more Indian-friendly Pepsi. The possibilities are bittersweet because losing the Tigers will break your heart, because if you could, you'd go back to high school and finish your years with the team in a second. But on this morning you're going over the books, and you're there, it is in ink: you finally have enough to bring an ice resurfacer to the Memorial Arena.

On your laptop you browse an online marketplace called All Star Zambeauties Trader and open a listing you've been window-shopping for some time. It's a 2006 Model 525 with two thousand hours under its belt. According to the description, the machine is fuel-powered and has been "fully serviced and calibrated and is in excellent condition" and is "rink ready," and can be shipped in a matter of days. The owner, an arena in Guelph, has also installed a new seat and steering wheel and ordered a fresh coat of paint. The asking price is thirty thousand dollars, which you find steep, and from the research you've done on these machines over the past few months on both old and new models there may be no way to talk them down. You think about it for a moment. You look around you and then out toward the lobby, where golden light floods in from outside, which has a way of making the dust floating in the air look beautiful. Your doors, your floors, your windows, there isn't much that ain't cracked or bruised or broken, including you. Not much here is beautiful. It doesn't take you long to click on a link that takes you to a sign-up page that takes you to a page where you can contact the seller. You fill in your information, who you are, where you're from, the name of your rink, the address of your rink, what ice-resurfacing model you drive now, which you ignore, and in the comments box you write, I want to buy this Zamboni at your earliest convenience.

YOU'RE IN THE PRO shop when Kelvin walks into the arena. He's late but you don't say anything because he's been late almost every day recently, a habit that has gotten worse and worse over the last two weeks or so, and even you're tired of the way you sound when you're reprimanding him, the way a mother sounds trying to discipline a spoiled child who both know nothing will come of it. You're not used to it, and you keep reminding yourself that he's not your responsibility, that he can fuck up his own life if he chooses. But you will say something about his footwear.

Kelvin, you say. You need boots out there. I can't keep telling you.

When you get a good look at him you see the redness in his eyes. He's high. He's also thin, which you notice more now, as if his face and body are being sucked in, pulled tight against his bones. You want to tell him to go home, cuss him out for thinking you're an idiot. But you need him.

He looks down at his feet and shrugs and that bothers you. Sorry, he says. I'll be careful. And then he continues on to the garage.

You sigh and return to your computer. You're scrolling on Facebook, a small ceremony. You're annoyed about the boots, which you helped him pick out because he asked for your help, and so you went together during your lunch hour to a men's workwear store and watched him try on several pairs. He's on the tall side, and though you'd never admit it he's probably taller than you, but he has small and narrow feet for his height and this made the outing easy, and afterward you joked that had it been a shopping trip for you, you would've been out all day because you've been burdened with impossibly wide feet made flat from age and a life of honest toil. He laughed and teased you, saying someone should start a shoe company for all the Bigfoots out there because that shit's discrimination.

You search Kelvin on Facebook, which you've never done before, and a profile comes up named Kez Whiteway Sinclair, and from the profile picture you know it's him. In his photos, many of which are black and white, he looks mean and is clearly trying to come across as tough, but to you he just looks worried and concerned and frustrated. You find one posted in the time you've known him. He's standing on a deck somewhere and it's dark and he's smiling big, like when you both joke and tease each other, and on his feet are the boots you chose for him, and you look up from your laptop and there's Kelvin, hauling two big garbage bags out the door and they're heavy because he looks like he's doing a farmer's carry. When he comes back inside he goes into the restroom, either washing his hands or stoking the chemicals in his blood.

He comes out and you wave him over and you stand and say, Let's go get a coffee. We need to celebrate. You come out from the pro shop. Plus, it looks like you could use it.

He looks excited and you know he knows what this is all about because you've been talking about it for a few weeks now and you decide it's not your place to mention that he smells terrible. Right on, he says, and he follows you out of the arena.

At the Robin's you order for both of you, a medium black with half a sweetener for you and a large triple-triple for him, and when the lady behind the counter hands you the coffees you carefully transfer one of the cups to Kelvin, and then you turn to the rest of the café and find a table by the window.

You both sit and stare outside. The snow is almost gone, leaving behind all the dirt, dust, rocks and trash that hibernated beneath it through the winter. You hate this time of year. Everything feels bleak. The city looks washed out.

You turn to Kelvin, who is looking out the window, and say, Cheers, and you raise your cup and he looks at you and raises his. We had a Zamboni once. One of the first ones. Didn't last long.

Can't believe you've lasted this long without one, Kelvin says. His eyes clearer now.

For a long time I always preferred the old ways, not that there's anything special about breaking your back with a shovel. I guess it was special to me. Thought it meant something.

Kelvin looks outside again and so do you. Two people—a man and what appears to be a woman—wearing fluorescent-orange vests are cleaning the sidewalks and street corners and gutters with long garbage pickers. You wonder if they're former prisoners doing their community service. Kelvin returns his attention to you and says, Sometimes change can be good.

You nod and sip your coffee. You're not sure your grandfather would agree with that but you do. You pick at the sleeve on your cup and say what's been on your mind, You've been coming to work late, Kelvin. I can't keep having this talk with you.

He rubs his eyes with both his palms. I'm trying, Pete. I'm trying my best.

I hired you because I thought you deserved a chance. I think we both deserved a chance. But for this to work, I need you to get to work on time, and—you look him down—not like this.

I need this, he says. For a brief moment there's panic in his eyes and then he's composed, and you think to yourself that that's a talent.

You can talk to me, you say. I know how hard it can be. This city. These streets.

He scoffs and shakes his head and you're surprised. You've always known what you were, never doubted what you were going to be, he says. Fucks like me are dealt a different hand every shit-ass day, and usually each one is worse than before.

You don't say anything. Because you're not sure he wants you to say anything, and so you sit there until your coffees are finished.

So, he says, composed again. I think I should be the Zamboni driver. I think I have Zamboni driving in my blood.

You smile. We'll see. You say it like you have no intention of revisiting the topic.

I get it, he says. It'll be your baby. Shit, at least teach me how to sharpen skates.

I can do that, you say.

THAT EVENING, AFTER THE Tigers' fifteenth straight loss of the season, which you mourn with a can of cheap beer while sitting in the garage, taking a measuring tape to the space where the Zamboni will live for the rest of its life and yours, and after Kelvin finishes scraping the ice, you invite him into the pro shop for the first time since you've known him and show him the ropes, the science behind finely sharpened skate blades. He's a bona fide natural, which you keep to yourself at first so as to avoid that cocky laugh of his but then, after he cuts one of his soft, uncalcified fingers and bleeds everywhere, you decide to tell him anyway and the laugh through mild pain is just as unbearable. You're both there late, celebrating what's to come.

## *kelvin whiteway*

KELVIN HAS THOUGHT ABOUT THE DIFFERENT WAYS HE CAN GET closer to Clinton. Working at the Memorial Arena has helped, but real success has been slow. He has thought about being the brother who fist-bumps the little brother before the little brother steps onto the ice before games and practices. He thought about going up to the coaching staff of the Tigers and asking the head coach who can't stop screaming throughout every game and practice if he can help by filling the water bottles or passing the sticks to the players as they leave the dressing room, but that would be one of the more embarrassing things he's ever done. Plus, Hurricane attends every game and would see him and surely tease the hell out of him for acting as water boy and stick manager. He wouldn't be able to stand it, because Hurricane still makes fun of him for the time he sang karaoke during a class Christmas party at St. Croix and he sang every word that appeared on-screen, including *instrumental break.*

Pete hasn't helped much either. Pete sees everything. He likes to remind Kelvin that he sees everything. That's another reason Kelvin doesn't stand around the dressing room, waiting to deal the sticks and the water bottles. His boss's eyes are everywhere, eager to order him to the pro shop in his stead or to mop up the bloody-looking remains of a fumbled cherry Slurpee. There's always more work to do, more than last week or the weeks before. Pete trusts him to do it. And the trust bothers him. It comes with so much scrutiny.

Kelvin thinks about these things at home. Because it's Saturday.

He doesn't work at the rink on Saturdays and Sundays, and whatever extra time he has in the morning before work or in the evening afterward he devotes to the hustle with Moose and Hurricane. But he doesn't do anything on Saturdays. He reserves this special day for the couch and reruns of old shows and cartoons and—around noon— ordering heaps of noodles and fried rice from the Asian place down the street that he suspects has been there since before treaty days because the lady who runs the place told him she was a descendant of railway workers and that the Chinese invented gunpowder and money.

When his stomach starts to ache he gets up from the couch and finds the landline in the kitchen. On Friday nights he allows his phone to die and he doesn't charge it back to life until the follow- ing evening. He dials the number to Amazing Chinese Kitchen and Linda's son, Savva, answers and tells him that their delivery driver has hurt his neck in a fender bender and that today is pickup only. Kelvin orders anyway, deciding that he'll walk there to scoop his order because he couldn't find anything to watch on TV. He hangs up the phone and takes a shower. He blow-dries his hair and flosses his teeth. He goes into his room and makes the bed on the top bunk, and around him the room looks the same as the day Clinton left, including his brother's bed. He dresses and in the bathroom he slicks his short hair back with some mousse, something his mother used to do on him when he was a kid. When he walks out the front door he takes the trash from the kitchen with him.

There's a fresh-smelling breeze. The grass is somewhere between brown and green. He wears a hoodie that he bought before serving his sentence and notices a stain on the right sleeve, coffee or burger grease, that wasn't there before he left and that could only mean Clinton borrowed it. He walks across every intersection he passes without any regard for traffic lights and their respective hues and the pedestrian signals, forcing cars and trucks alike to brake for him and only once does a driver honk the horn.

At Amazing Chinese Kitchen the door opens to the sound of jingles dancing overhead. He greets Savva with a nod.

"It's almost ready," Savva says.

"How's your mom?"

"Still in the hospital. She's ineligible for surgery because she's high risk."

Last week, doctors discovered Linda had a problem with her heart, something about her valves not opening and closing the way the Creator intended. Last Saturday, Savva told Kelvin over the phone as he ordered his usual that they tried medicine to no avail, and Kelvin told Savva that he would pray for her and then didn't but he kept her in his thoughts. "I'm sorry," Kelvin says.

"We're praying for a miracle," Savva says. "But the doctors say there's not much they can do. We're on the fifth floor of the Health Sciences Centre." Savva heads for the kitchen and returns with a tightly tied plastic bag and hands it to Kelvin.

"I'll go see her," Kelvin says. "Later."

Savva smiles.

KELVIN HATES HOSPITALS. AS a child he spent too much time in them. Aunties and uncles dying. Friends recovering from failed suicide attempts. Uncles and aunties in dialysis. He hates the bland color of the walls and the uniforms the nurses wear and the waiting rooms with their terrible children's toys. He makes for the elevator without asking anyone for directions and when he lands on the fifth floor he turns left and looks inside each room he passes. He reaches the end of the hall and has to turn back, checking the hall on the other side of the elevator. He walks by a dim lounge area with an old square television playing something barely audible. In front of it sits an elderly man in a wheelchair, the only living thing on the floor. He sees a room a short distance away with piles and piles of flower bouquets and a few helium balloons reaching for the ceiling and when he gets there he takes a couple steps inside and sees Linda on the bed. She opens her eyes and smiles. He tries to smile back.

"How you feeling?" he says.

"I'm fine," she says. "Did you talk to Savva today?"

"Saw him." He pulls up a chair and sits at the foot of her bed. "He'll be lost without you."

"He'll be fine. He works hard."

He looks around. There's even more flowers in the room.

"I heard you're working hard, too."

"I'm trying," he says. "Might have to quit soon. It's been almost too much."

"Don't do that," she says. "Never works out."

"I have other things going on."

She sighs softly and closes her eyes and folds her hands.

She looks much older than last week, the creases on her face more pronounced, and this is the first time he's ever thought of her as an elderly woman. She's the same small and wiry woman who used to run after him at impressive speeds for stealing fortune cookies after school, and when she couldn't catch him she'd call his mother and minutes later she'd be at their apartment. "What would you do?" he says. "If you had someone like Pete working you to death."

"Same as me," she says. "Wait for a miracle."

He hugs her before he leaves the hospital and she tells him, "Be good." Linda visited him in prison more than anyone in his family. She brought him noodles and fried rice.

He cries on the drive home. He wonders if he's more susceptible to crying because he's hungry and hasn't eaten yet and looks forward to eating what he ordered when he gets home.

He parks in front of his apartment building and sees them—Moose and Hurricane—before he turns off the engine, standing around like a couple of creeps at the door. They see him too. He gets out and walks over in a casual way, like he's not bothered that they've shown up at his door on a Saturday.

"What's good?" he says.

Hurricane, smiling, bobs his head up and down.

"Why aren't you answering your phone?" Moose says, and Kelvin can tell he's annoyed about something.

"It's dead."

"Charge it, then," Moose says.

"What is it? I'm not working today."

There's an unsettling silence. Hurricane and Moose look at each other. "You tell him," Hurricane says.

"X wants to see you," Moose says.

"Now?" Kelvin says.

"Nah next week," Moose intones. "Yes fucking now," says Hurricane. Without saying anything Moose turns and waddles, his knees pointing in opposite directions, toward his car on the street and Hurricane shrugs and follows him.

Kelvin stands there and thinks for a moment, sparing a thought for food and his grumbling stomach, and then he goes with them.

XAVIER, THE MAN THEY work for, lives on a quiet street in a big house with a family of seven and three black Labs. In one of the richest parts of the city. Kelvin sits in the back seat, and he's annoyed because usually Hurricane rides back there when Moose is driving. He looks out the window. Even the trees look greener and wealthier than those in the hood. They welcome you on both sides of the road and hold their long, distinguished branches out to cover you from the sun. The streets are wider. There's more space for dogs and kids and hammocks and mock teepees. Some streets become cul-de-sacs, and they turn onto one. Moose points with a finger over the steering wheel to a white house with a garage big enough for three cars and a tree in the yard so wide Kelvin wonders if it could upset the foundation of the property. "That's his."

They park on the street. Kelvin gets out of the car and looks up at the house. He'd only ever seen it at night and it looks much bigger in the daylight.

Before they can ring the bell the door swings open and there is Xavier, wearing Jordan gym shorts and a plain white shirt and suede slippers. Kelvin hears kids screaming from inside the house and down a long hallway he can see children running around the backyard in colorful cone hats.

"It's my kid's birthday party," Xavier says, like he's glad for the distraction that Kelvin and his two colleagues offer him. "We'll talk downstairs."

They follow him down to an enormous basement with what looks like a theater room occupying one half of the wide-open space— a projector screen and a couple rows of plush leather chairs—and on the other side a games area, consisting of a pool table and a hanging dartboard and a bar with bottles of booze that wink like jewels.

He tells them to sit at the bar and from behind the counter he pours them shots of vodka. Moose and Hurricane gulp down their glasses with ease. Kelvin takes his hesitantly.

"So how's life in the trenches?" Xavier says. "Make any trench babies yet?"

Hurricane laughs.

Moose pushes his shot glass forward for a refill.

Kelvin shakes his head.

"You have to keep climbing. This house was built by fighting through that shit. That's how I made it out."

"You built this place?" Hurricane says, admiring the sconces.

"Nah," Xavier says. "We rent it."

Kelvin looks down the bar and none of them are making eye contact with their boss.

"It's my kid's birthday," Xavier repeats. "I got him a pricey drone that looks like the Millennium Falcon. He's three today. The lady thinks he's too young for it. What do you think?"

"Three's a good age," Hurricane says.

Xavier turns his attention to Kelvin and fills his glass. "Is three too young?"

Kelvin drinks and shakes his head. "It'll be a good bonding experience."

"That's what I said." Xavier looks pleased. "I like doing fun shit with my kids."

Xavier refills all their glasses, and as they down them a magician appears at the bottom of the stairs and approaches the bar.

"This is my son's magician," Xavier says.

The magician, a fat man drenched in sweat, glances and smiles at all three of them.

Xavier pours the magician a shot. "Have you seen him before?" He points to Kelvin.

Kelvin feels a sudden dread, something pulls down on his stomach. He's never seen the man before.

The magician drinks and nods. "Yeah."

"Where?" Xavier asks.

The magician stutters nervously, before completing, "The Memorial Arena there."

"I've never seen this guy," Kelvin interrupts and feels a nudge from Moose beside him.

"Quiet," Xavier says. "What was he doing there?"

The magician shifts his eyes back and forth, at Kelvin and Xavier. "He looked like he was working there."

Kelvin shakes his head, face red.

Xavier reaches into his shorts and pulls out a roll of money and counts the bills and hands a small stack to the magician. "Thanks for today," he says. "Loved the new tricks."

The magician says thanks and nods and turns away to climb the stairs.

"X," Kelvin says. "I've never seen him before."

Xavier sighs in an irritated way and rests his hands on the bar. "I've known him for years," he says. "He's a good customer."

"I've known you long, too." The words barely leave Kelvin's mouth.

Xavier smiles unconvincingly. "Come over here," he says, hustling out from behind the bar and toward the dartboard.

Kelvin stands from his barstool, and from his peripheral he sees Hurricane pouring himself another shot. Moose keeps his elbows on the bar like a lonely patron.

"Put your hand up there, palm facing me," Xavier says, shuffling darts in his hand. "I'll give you five hundred for a nick. A thousand if it goes through."

"X," Kelvin pleads.

"Hand up."

Slowly, Kelvin moves beside the dartboard, and, not without imagining himself running upstairs and back to the North End, he lifts his hand and holds it there, covering the bull's-eye.

"Darts is an underrated sport," Xavier says. "One of my favorite things to watch on TV."

Kelvin stares directly at Xavier, he feels calmer looking at Xavier rather than at his hand. "I helped out the old man that runs the arena a few times," he says. "That's it."

Xavier, practicing his stroke over and over, says, "Then are you still working there?"

"No," Kelvin says, and after lying again he suddenly feels ready for penance and steels himself.

The first dart sticks between his thumb and index finger and Kelvin, flinching, eyes shut, hears Hurricane gasp with excitement.

The second bounces off his middle knuckle, producing a trail of blood down his hand and forearm.

The third and final dart sticks into the soft tissue on his palm and stays there and he wails and falls to his knees.

"Fuck!" Xavier cries. "That didn't go through, did it?"

"No," Kelvin grits. He pulls out the dart and is surprised by how easy it was.

Xavier walks to him and throws him a towel. "Listen to me," he says, intending for both Moose and Hurricane to hear. "I lend you product instead of paying up front because I like you. Because you're my boys. You're like sons to me"—he laughs—"But I expect the money on time. And when I hear you're fucking around at some hockey arena instead of getting me my money, then that makes me think something needs to change. Maybe make some changes to the roster."

"X," Moose says, turning his chair around. "We'll fix this." And Kelvin feels thankful for him saying something.

Xavier collects his darts and squats down close to Kelvin. "Quit your job," he says. "Get me my money."

Kelvin nods.

Xavier stands. "Okay," he says, his tone light. "Next item on the agenda. The little brother."

Kelvin regards him to let him know he's heard him.

"It's tough to find young talent these days. It's time to bring him in."

"He won't," he says, the words resistant.

"You can scare a boy into doing anything, even the smart ones," Moose says.

"You do this and maybe we talk about a promotion. I'm thinking I make you my right-hand man. Learn how the sausage is made." Xavier moves to the bar and pours a glass of something honey-brown and drinks it all. "You'll be my Lord Chancellor."

"Your what?"

"Assistant to the King." He looks around with big eyes. "The King of Winnipeg. Howah! Aho!" He laughs.

Kelvin feels like the magician, imprisoned in fat and sweat, but without the tricks. He looks at the bar. Hurricane is laughing away: "I'm a knight, me." Moose is stone-faced.

"But you gotta get this done. Bring the little brother into the family."

Kelvin nods and Xavier is satisfied enough with that response.

"Okay," he says, in a cheerier voice. "Go eat some cake."


AT HOME, KELVIN GETS high, as he always does when the invisible wall stops him from going where he needs to go. He gets higher than he's ever been, trapped in a haze of disappearing lines and fates and destinies, and he knows, deep as knowing goes, deeper than the lake that surrounds his heart, that he's trapped.

And in his high he grabs his gun from the table, quiet and deadly and chromed, and puts the barrel in his mouth. He pulls the trigger and it makes an empty click. It's just practice. It would be quick. Painless, so says the internet. But how would all those alive people know? They don't. Nobody does. He knows, however, that life isn't painless. Kelvin doesn't need the internet to tell him this.


HE LINGERS FOR HOURS outside a 7-Eleven the following day. Usually his buyers come to him, at home or someplace they've agreed on. But on this day he feels like standing and waiting and biding his time before the workweek begins. Memories come to him: his days hustling as a corner boy, fresh-faced and clueless. He ignores every call from Moose and Hurricane. He makes only a single transaction with a local drunk who tries to underpay him. Kelvin grabs the man by the hair and pulls him to the concrete and holds a mini Swiss Army knife to the man's neck and swears in his face. The man cries and begs. The cashier inside the store sticks his head out the door and says he's calling the cops. Kelvin takes back the eight ball and keeps the money and walks away. On Monday morning he goes to work at the Memorial Arena. He puts in his shift. Continues his high in the restroom. He scrapes the ice, mops the floors, takes out the trash. It's a Tigers game day. In the evening he helps out in the pro shop sharpening skates and selling stick tape and clear tape.

Clinton shows up. Presents his dull skates to Kelvin and says, "Get smithing." Kelvin brags, "I'm a magician now." Clinton leaves to get ready for the game. The Tigers lose. Kelvin doesn't see Clinton after. But he sees a man who sees him, too. Xavier's magician, leaving the arena. Fat and damp in normal clothes. He pretends not to remember him but it's no use. Pete asks him for the first time, "Can you close up for me?" Kelvin accepts the keys and his trust. He's alone. He turns off the lights. He wanders around the dark arena. He sits atop the bleachers and looks out at the surface of the rink in front of him and it's impossible to tell that there's cold ice there. It's empty. A void. He feels scared. Something about the silence frightens him. His wounded hand hurts. He looks up the price of a skate-sharpening machine on his phone and figures he could make almost as much if he boosted it. He paces the lobby, wall to wall. He's tired. He believes in ghosts, and believes there's one inside of him screaming, cursing him. He gives up. He goes into the pro shop and finds a heavy wrench. He comes out with it and stands before the arena doors. And then he swings.

## *woman with a dog*

THE WOMAN WALKING HER DOG FEELS SAFE AT NIGHT. SHE BELIEVES that her dog will do anything to protect her from an attacker or a wild animal or both, like the polar bear that escaped from the zoo last summer and then wandered downtown and fought a bum in the streets, a tilt that left both dead once the cops and their lights and their guns arrived. But she carries bear spray attached to a key chain she wears around her neck. She walks a five-mile route and tells her grandchildren to check on her via text every once in a while. But she feels safe because there's usually no one on the sidewalks at night, just cars and their bright lights. Every now and then a police car rolls slowly with the window down and an officer asks her if she's okay and if she needs help and she says she's fine and wonders if they've ever seen a lady and her dog before. The neighborhood comes alive at night. Things are happening. The lights from every home lighting scenes like movies. Parents on their porches laughing. Kids inside screaming. Teenagers somewhere scheming. There aren't any streetlamps to show the way but she enjoys walking. As she walks by the Memorial Arena she hears a sound. Glass breaking. The kind of shattering that sounds like trouble. She knows the man who runs the arena, or at least she used to know him, back when he was a hard-ass but she liked that about him because kids these days are too soft. She hears he's still the same. Back when they were young and dumb and love felt like a storm neither of them could survive. She pulls out her phone and calls a recently dialed contact, and the teenage boy on the other line answers immediately.

"Tomahawk," the woman says.

"Yeah," he says. "Is everything okay?"

"I'll be home soon," she says. "But can you do me a favor?"

"What is it?"

"Call Pete Mosienko. Do you have his number?"

"I have it," he says.

"Good, because it's an emergency."

"Just call the cops."

"Use your head."

"Fine, then. What do I tell Petey?"

"Tell him there's someone breaking into his arena."

## pete mosienko

YOUR PHONE RINGS AND VIBRATES IN YOUR POCKET AS YOU CLIMB the wobbly steps of your porch. It's a number you don't recognize. Not surprising because pro shop customers call you all the time even after hours. But they almost never call you this late. You stare at the number, feel the phone shake in a sort of manic way, and decide to answer. This is Pete. A boy on the other end says, Petey, and you say, Yes, and he says, This is Tommy Shields, a surname you do recognize and like an old photograph summons memories of great detail. My koko says something's going on down at the arena. You ask what's happening. The boy says, I guess she was walking by and called me to tell you that someone's breaking in or something. You say in a confused way, She was walking by and someone's breaking into my arena, and after a moment of silence and phone static, the boy says, Yeah, she walks her dog around there sometimes I guess. You pull open your rickety screen door, and before hanging up you say, Thanks, I'll handle it. Tell her I say thanks.

You go inside your house and stand there in the entrance in the dark. On your phone you press the numbers that would bring a police car or two outside the doors of your rink but you don't make the call. You've never had someone break into your arena. This is a first. And that alone, a beautiful streak ruined, upsets you more than the breaking and entering itself. Without meaning to or wanting to or believing you would do it, you go back through the door and down the steps and into your car and turn the keys and start the engine and before you even have time to think about what you're doing or to know whether it's right or smart you're driving down your dark and quiet street.

It's dark around the Memorial Arena when you get there. The streetlamps are off, because sometimes they're on and sometimes they're not, and if they're on a schedule you're not sure what it is. You drive around the parking lot and find Kelvin's car parked beside a side door that leads into the garage. You park out front. On the floor of your back seat you find a spotlight you carry with you in case your car breaks down. You step outside and shine the light at the arena's front doors and the ghosts of the night disappear and shadows take their place. The windows on your entrance doors are smashed and the safety glass is strewn all over the ground and you think they look like diamonds. Violence piled like sand. You go inside and hear something moving and it's loud and heavy. You illumine the pro shop and standing there behind the counter is Kelvin. When the light finds him he grimaces and turns his face away like he's looking at the sun and holds his hands in the air.

Kelvin, you say.

Holy fuck, he says. I thought you were a cop. I was ready to meet the Creator.

You're not sure what to say. You're not sure what to do or what you're *supposed* to do. He's wearing your work gloves and a black toque.

This fucking thing's bolted on here pretty good, he says.

He's talking about the skate sharpener, which is fixed to the workbench it sits on or at least it was when you left for the night. You don't believe what you're about to say but you say it anyway, You think I wouldn't think it was you.

He grabs both ends of the sharpening machine and lifts it in the air about an inch or two, testing the weight of it, a short grunt as he does so, and then rests it back down on the bench.

I'm sorry, Pete, he says. I wanted to be different.

Then what is this, you say loudly and your voice echoes throughout the rink.

You never asked before you hired me, maybe you already knew, but I had just got out before you met me. From Headingley.

You didn't know this. I don't care who you were before.

When I came home I wanted to do things different, he says. They always say you'll be different when you're done, that you'll be reworked like Play-Doh after doing the time. You'll come out a better person. I guess I felt different there for a little bit. But then when it ends you go back to being normal.

This isn't normal, you say.

For me it is, he says.

You take two steps closer to him and think about a third but hold back. To be honest, Kelvin, I don't care who you're going to be either, you say. But this isn't you. There's still time.

You don't understand, he says. There isn't. I don't have any more.

You turn off the spotlight and let your eyes adjust to the dark. Slivers of light from your car outside bleed in through the broken windows. Just leave, you say. I didn't see you. I won't call the police. Just leave.

I'm not leaving without this fucking thing, he says. Get out of the way—he gestures for you to move away from the door—I don't want to beat your ass.

You say and mean it, You'll have to kill me for it.

You can see the frustration grow in his eyes. Move, he says. Please.

You take that third step forward. You're not going to hurt me, Kelvin.

He grabs something and throws it hard at the wall above your desk, leaving behind an arrow-shaped hole. I have to do this, he shouts.

Leave, you say. And everything will be okay.

He rests both his hands on the counter and after a moment he straightens up. He's calm. As if he wasn't just screaming. He removes your work gloves from his hands and lays them on top of the skate-sharpening machine and walks. As he moves closer to you, you can see his face more clearly. His eyes are watery but he's not crying. He stops just before the doors and you both look at each other without saying anything. When you see him in the light you want to forgive him. He looks defeated. He looks like you. Your look after every season the Tigers go winless. Because you know, if they won just once, you'd feel joy, the kind that feels earned and therefore more euphoric because you waited for it, and you'd feel a part of it, because it would

290 · small ceremonies

belong to you too. He looks like you after every birthday that arrives with no one to celebrate with. You want to take him in your arms and tell him it will be okay and there's still time and that you're sorry for something you shouldn't really be sorry for to make him feel better. But you don't. You won't. You watch him push open the door. You hear the crunch of trampled broken glass. You watch him disappear like he was never here.

## *errol whitecloud sinclair*

### APRIL 1, 2012

I sweat yesterday for the first time since my release, and it felt good to experience a smothering darkness like that. The prison lodges weren't that dark, as I've said. This lodge in particular is in a yard behind where I'm staying, a men's residence. The eyes serve no purpose during those hours, like you're floating in a space with no stars and all there is to do is breathe and pray and feel lost with the other men drifting across that starless space. But there was a moment where I thought I saw spirits, a face maybe, through all that dark, maybe trying to tell me something.

### APRIL 5, 2012

I don't know why I'm telling you all this. Maybe I'm writing this all down because I hope it will somehow help you to learn from my mistakes. I don't know. I wish I had something better to pass on than mistakes, but at least it's something. All my dad taught me to do was drink, and I'm okay admitting now that I learned his lessons well.

## *kelvin whiteway*

THE LINE TO THE MOUNTIE AND THE TWO LADIES UNDER THE CAN-
opy is long. The morning sun smolders above them, and the moon,
big and round and demanding, sits to the east like a bone-colored
replica. It's Treaty Days. Which means everyone is waiting to get
their annual five dollars for the lands they ceded to the government
way back when five dollars meant you were either a king or a sheikh
or a band councillor. Living large. Rich as can be. After parking his
car, he hurries across a couple busy roads and finds himself in The
Forks, outside, the green returning to the trees, and the feeling is
different than when he's normally here. Neechis are everywhere,
waiting to be five dollars richer, and when Neechis are collecting—
welfare, GST, kid tax, any free sum—the atmosphere is different. He
can't quite put his finger on it. Possibilities emerge.

He walks through a crowd and finds Hurricane and Moose in
queue and they see him and wave him over. He apologizes for being
late. There was a line even for the parking lot. But neither of them
say a word. They go about the conversation they were having before
he arrived.

"Right there," Moose says, pointing toward the Mountie and the
two ladies under the canopy. "That's when you do it."

"Do what?" Kelvin says.

"Moose," Hurricane says, annoyed. "It's too risky."

Kelvin looks where Moose pointed. The Mountie, in a chair
behind a table, leans over to his side, and, when he straightens, he's
carrying a fresh envelope filled with fives. He gives it to one of the
ladies, who counts the money in front of her like a bank teller and

hands whatever sum is needed back to him. He then hands a bill, sometimes more, to the next person in line and follows it with a handshake and fake smile.

"Do what?"

"You take it, brother," Moose says, quickly lifting his sweatshirt to reveal a handgun strapped to his torso in a brown leather body holster, which he loves to show off but is often teased for. "Take it all for yourself."

"Put that shit away," Kelvin says, but Moose does so before he speaks.

"Too risky," Hurricane repeats. "I read somewhere that if you go to a bank and hand the bank person a note saying something like, 'I got a gun, give me your money,' that they have to give it to you, because it's bank policy. I'm saying that sounds like a better plan here. Hand the boy a note telling him what's bout to go down if he don't cooperate. Fuck, I bet that boy never once had to pull out his piece in the line of duty. I'm betting he gives those fivers to you."

"Because they don't want bitches getting hurt in the bank?" Kelvin furrows his brow, questioning why he referred to bank goers as bitches.

"Brother, this isn't no bank," Moose says. "Does this look like a fucking bank to you?"

Hurricane takes another look around. "Could be an outdoor bank."

"Fuck outta here."

"What's the difference between this and a bank?"

"Banks don't give people free money," Kelvin says, and Moose nods agreeably.

"That's right. He knows. They're parasites."

Kelvin thinks he knows the answer but says anyway, "Ain't he a cop? He'll be carrying."

"A shoot-out, in broad daylight, here," Hurricane says, shaking his head, "ain't the plan."

"He'd have one between the eyes before he could move if he tried anything," Moose says, kicking his sneakers into the brown grass. "If this were a bank, fine, give the pig a fucking note, some Valentine's Day toddler shit, but this isn't a bank."

"What fucking toddlers are professing love to other toddlers," Kelvin says.

"Plus, how many toddlers are out there robbing banks?" says Hurricane matter-of-factly.

"Shit. You boys ain't ever used the internet, then."

The three of them go quiet, and Kelvin wonders if they're all thinking about the same thing: the absurdity of the Mountie's knee-high shined leather boots.

"He won't be carrying," Moose says. He's been closely studying the table ever since Kelvin arrived. "They there for show, in those gay hats and boots like it's Halloween. Basically ain't real cops. I mean, probably he is. But when they're handing out five-dollar bills they ain't."

Hurricane crosses his arms and gives a look of deep concentration and Kelvin snickers at him because rarely is he this serious about anything. "But how do we know for sure?"

"Now. How much for either of you to pop the kid? I'm asking. Doesn't have to be here. But that's even better work."

Kelvin looks nervously back at the Mountie. He's boyish, red cheeks and sandy hair. Probably has never fired his weapon. Likely he patrols in some lonely, remote place instead of an urban area with bountiful beauties and KFC, a privilege generally reserved for officers of higher rank. "I'm no cop killer," he says. "I'm the city's most notorious bank robber. *Awsh yeah!*"

"Hurricane," Moose says, turning away from Kelvin with a sudden flare. "How much for this work?"

"A grand?" Hurricane proposes, uncertain.

"A grand?"

"Two grand? Three grand?" His eyes shift to Kelvin and then back at Moose.

Kelvin watches him intensely.

"Tell you what. Since you're my boy this is yours"—Moose pulls a wad of bills from his sweatpants and holds it up to Hurricane—"if you go over there right now and point your piece in his face. Just put the fear of God in his eyes, make him a man, but make sure you get our treaty money. Meet us at the car."

Hurricane looks over at the Mountie again and back at Moose.

"Hold up," Kelvin says, conscious of the scowl that has appeared on Moose's face. "I have eight years or some shit to collect."

"Fuck's sake, just get one of those envelopes," Moose hisses. "Make Kezzy here happy."

"How much is that?" Hurricane says, pointing to the roll of cash. "For real?"

"Ten." Moose rests a hand on Hurricane's shoulder. "When have I ever lied to you?"

"What happens if I get locked up," Hurricane says like it isn't a question.

Moose laughs. "I'll bail you out. Get you a good lawyer."

Kelvin feels anxious. Jittery. Everything is a joke. Nothing is a joke. Hurricane is quiet, and beside him Moose is smiling. Sinister. Hurricane mumbles something, which to Kelvin sounds like, "Okay then," and takes a shaky step forward. But before he can move any further Kelvin grabs hold of his biceps, digging his nails into the fabric of his bleach-stained sweatshirt and when he releases him his handprint stays there like memory foam.

"We're not doing this," Kelvin says. "We're not fucking around like this."

Hurricane looks back at Moose.

Moose spits on the concrete, because they're no longer standing on grass. He looks pissed, but also relieved, as if Kelvin spared him the inconvenience of being possibly, partially responsible for someone else's death, be it a rookie cop or Hurricane.

"I'll be in the food court," Moose says, before turning and walking away, moving with his whole body. "They can keep their money. You know I'm good."

At the table one of the ladies asks them for their treaty numbers, which they provide without hesitation, without looking at their Indian status cards. The table is draped in a Canada flag, the maple leaf splayed over the edge to cover her legs and the Mountie's, and those of a lady whose purpose here eludes Kelvin. The woman who took their numbers types and clicks for a moment on a laptop and then, pointing to Kelvin, says:

"Forty for this gentleman." She points to Hurricane next. "Fifteen for this one."

The woman next to her pulls a thin stack of bills out of an envelope and does a quick count before handing the money to the Mountie. Kelvin and Hurricane follow their compensation from person to person like a fancy buffet.

The Mountie, smiling, holds out the bills with his left hand and reaches for a handshake with his right. The name card in front of him says "Constable Dusty."

Kelvin offers both hands and the feeling is awkward. The officer's grip is firm but forgiving once he realizes Kelvin has no interest in squeezing back. He sweats through his uniform. His breath is wretched. The bills are smooth, fresh from the printers.

"Miigwech," the Mountie says, which surprises Kelvin. He wonders how the cop knew he was Ojibwe, if it was just a wild guess, whether he learned how to identify tribes and nations based on physical appearance. Surely, they take some half-assed course on Indians. Lesson One: Brown, Curved Nose, Cro-Magnon Brow Ridge, Long Hair, Almond Eyes, Lack of Facial and/or Body Hair, Points With Lips. Proceed With Caution.

Kelvin nods without saying anything. He takes a few steps from the table and looks back for Hurricane, who has somehow sparked a conversation at the table.

"Have you ever killed anyone?" he asks the cop. Kelvin knows he's messing.

The cop smiles like he's embarrassed, saying shyly, "Top secret."

"Damn, son," Hurricane says, bouncing away. "Wear it with pride at least. Bend the tips of your badge or something after each scalp. We know how you do it."

KELVIN MET HURRICANE ON his first day of school in the city. Hurricane, true to his name, was a walking, breathing, blood-pumping Category Five. Kelvin grabbed the desk behind him and Hurricane turned around and recited a line from *Billy Madison*: "Last year was super easy, but man, I'm so nervous, I think this year is gonna be really tough!" On Hurricane's desk Kelvin could see that his pencil had been chewed and snapped into four pieces and with one of those pieces he had been sharpening the splintered wood by vigorously rubbing it against the edge of his desk.

"Chill."

"Can I borrow a pencil?"

Kelvin looked over Hurricane's shoulder and observed the pieces of his broken pencil once more and Hurricane noticed this but didn't appear at all embarrassed. Kelvin sighed and reached into his bag on the floor and pulled out a flat, unsharpened pencil and, hesitating an instant, handed it to Hurricane and said:

"I don't have a sharpener."

"How did you get that one sharp?"

"I just said I don't have a sharpener."

The teacher, who was now standing from his chair, stood at the front of the room and for about five seconds said nothing, expecting his students to take the hint and quiet down at the sight of him. "Eyes forward," he said, having decided it was time to flex.

Hurricane was still smiling at Kelvin and laughed. Kelvin was confused, unsure of what was funny or why he was now caught in a staring match, and so he looked around the room. There was a sharpener somewhere deep in his bag.

"Mr. Hurricane." The teacher's voice grew louder and impatient. "Eyes forward."

"I'll give it back after class," Hurricane mumbled, turning to face the chalkboard.

To Kelvin's surprise he got his pencil back once class ended, just outside the classroom door where Hurricane waited for him, still unsharpened, cratered by what appeared to be teeth marks.

Kelvin took the same bus as Hurricane to get to school and they were together again on the same bus after the day was up. For two weeks and three days they saw each other every morning and every afternoon and never exchanged a word or acknowledged the other. Kelvin had become quiet, almost mute, since landing in the city and always believed deep down that making new friends was a skill he didn't possess anymore. He had friends from back home, and now they were somewhere scattered across the plains, in big cities and small cities and good towns and grotesque towns, but mostly they immigrated to shitholes, good shitholes and bad shitholes and somewhat livable shitholes, waiting to return to the life they had before they were told to leave.

The morning bus was always on time, never a minute late, but on that morning it wasn't. It didn't show.

Hurricane approached Kelvin. "You got the time?"

"Ten after."

Hurricane's eyes went big, and then he smiled wildly and laughed. "Shit's not coming."

"Day off I guess. They can't blame us."

"Yo. Where you from?"

"From here." He could feel Hurricane studying him.

"No way."

"How would you know?" The defense was halfhearted, knowing he'd already been made.

"City Indians and Rez Indians are easy to spot. You Rez Indians look lost out here. Scared of everything and everyone. Like you haven't learned to talk yet. City Indians are out here like we belong here, because it's the only way of life any of us know. City Indians be more talkative. Anyone can walk these streets, but talking keeps you walking." Hurricane laughed again. "I just came up with that."

"I can tell you like to talk."

Hurricane laughed again. "You ever been to White's?"

Kelvin shook his head, feeling as though he'd already failed some sort of test. He took the question to be an invitation and quickly tried to change the subject. "So why do they call you Hurricane, then?"

"That's my name, my real name," Hurricane said. "Really."

"You're lying." Kelvin laughed, and he felt a joy for the first time in many days.

"For real," Hurricane pleaded. "If you don't believe me, look." He reached into his pocket and pulled out his St. Croix student card and handed it to Kelvin.

"Damn," Kelvin said, still somewhat in a state of skepticism. "Hurricane Spence."

"That's me."

"Wicked."

But it wasn't so wicked, because every fucking stupid name usually has a fucking stupid story. Hurricane had heard two different accounts about how he got his name as a kid. He had a mother, you see, a mother who didn't want to be a mother, and so she considered the moment she gave birth to an eight-pound, thick-dark-haired baby as the moment some sort of natural disaster tore up her life and body, everything around her uninhabitable. She left the hospital without a name for her newborn, and several miserable weeks later, mere hours before the government's procedural process would refer to the child as Baby Boy in the record books, she had an epiphany; thy name be Hurricane. The other story was similar, but different in key ways. Hurricane's shoomis told him his mother had been going through a depression, and perhaps wasn't herself when she said that motherhood was the devil. But his name, according to Shoomis, came from all the crying he did as a baby, and that all his howling made her crazy, pushed her to the brink. He was born with a tongue-tie, which made him unable to latch on to his mother's breast. This struggle to feed made him hysterical, a bomb that went off every day. Some days he would finally get it and other days not, and this made him wild and unpredictable like a hurricane; hence his given name. His dad also lived in the city, a fact he learned later in life, and he sometimes spent weekends with him. His dad had four other kids with a different woman, two half-brothers and two half-sisters, and if there was anything in life that he truly hated it was being the "other son" and all the teasing that came with it. Hurricane grew up in the city and was expelled from every school he attended for fighting. He scrapped for no good reason, claimed to each and every principal that the other boy made some quip about his unorthodox name or scrawny, malnourished physique, which was never true nor believed by the authority figures overseeing his case, and they were fights he never won. He never once raised his hands in victory on the playground. He took beating after beating; left the schoolyard bloodied and bruised and with hematomas around his eyes, nose and forehead. But Hurricane prided himself on the beatings he took, because he always stayed on his feet, was never separated from his consciousness by way of fist, knee or skull. He kept coming, and if any brave warrior had the courage to settle the score once school was

out, be it in the confines of a dusty alley or behind some obscure foliage, then Hurricane would have his opportunity. Because Hurricane,
as his name would suggest, never tired, never took his foot off the
gas until the job was done; he wore his opponent down no matter
how disfigured he became. He settled down slightly when he landed
at St. Croix. He had a teacher—who he referred to only as Teach—
who noticed his scrappy tendencies after Hurricane clocked another
student in the middle of class who referred to him as Leatherface, a
reference to the scar tissue that marked the terrain of his face like the
stripes of a tiger. Teach, a former semi-pro boxer, conferenced with
Hurricane and his mom and suggested that her son might benefit
from learning the sweet science. Hurricane's mom agreed, as did he;
anything to learn how to fight. That's how it started. Hurricane and
Teach trained together in the school gym every morning. For a time
it helped. Hurricane fought less, so as not to disappoint his mentor.
But he had a pain inside of him that only lessened when he was
hurting on the outside. He was a hockey fan, played with his cousins and friends at the outdoor rink, and decided to join the Tigers
hockey team. He played and fought on the ice and led the league in
penalty minutes over two seasons and on more than one occasion
illegally removed his helmet and gloves in an effort to amplify the
brutality. "Skooo! Den! Fok!" he shouted, his fingers waving. Other
teams wanted him banned, expelled from the league, but he was
allowed to stay, probably because he was more of a burden than a
momentum changer for the Tigers. He liked the game, but he liked
the fighting more than anything and this didn't sit well with Teach,
who threatened to stop training him if he kept picking fights, but he
never did go through with it, because he couldn't live without the
training either. Up to this point Hurricane lived comfortably with his
tongue-tie; that is to say, he wasn't able to stick his tongue out. Like
his friends he couldn't laugh loudly with his tongue out all wild, and
when he tried it would never extend further below his pinkish brown
lips. It didn't bother him much but he tried stretching it, clamping
down on his tongue with tongs and pulling so hard his eyes watered
from the pain, dreaming about what it would be like to one day lick
the tip of his nose. Around this time though, girls were everywhere
and everything, and sex was happening, and he began to worry that

the thick band of tissue tethering his tongue to the bottom of his mouth, thereby restricting its movement, would hinder his ability to eat pussy when the time came. Not that girls were interested in him. His neighbors thought that he might turn out to be a rapist or killer or otherwise a complete nutcase who would spend his life in and out of prison. When girls were raped or killed or reported missing after walking home, Hurricane was often thought to be the culprit, though police had no real reason to question him. He was the neighborhood nutcase, the scary kid down the street who you were scared to fuck with, because you never knew what he would do. Hurricane knew people were afraid of him. He knew what they thought about him. But over the years, after he left St. Croix without a diploma, people treated him differently. Men respected him, feared him, moved out of his way. He became a viable candidate for women attracted to truly bad men. The kind of bad that couldn't be tamed. But before any of this would come to pass, the biggest stress in his life was his tongue. He stressed about it for a long time. Doctors always told him his tongue could be fixed and so he decided it was time. The day after his sixteenth birthday he went in for a short, successful procedure to free it from its constraints, and for days afterward he constantly licked his nose and chin and it dangled from the side of his mouth when he picked fights on the ice. A few months later Teach killed himself; hung himself from a tree just outside the city. For Hurricane it was the summer between grades ten and eleven. Hurricane learned things about Teach, gossip mostly, that he didn't know before his death. It was said that Teach, real name Barry Peltier, suffered from depression, that his foster father had raped him growing up, but to Hurricane he always seemed so cheery about everything; he enjoyed holding up the mitts for his protégé. Afterward Hurricane told his mother that he wasn't going back to St. Croix, and she didn't object; she didn't care. He still watches the Tigers play and rarely misses a game, and when Kelvin was locked up he spent most of his time at the rink, watching kids rush back and forth. He didn't go back to school, didn't try for a GED, and he doesn't regret it, though sometimes he misses Teach and the moments they'd spar together and Teach would make him swear to never tell anyone about it, because he could lose his job for hitting a student. Back then Hurricane couldn't stick out his tongue. Now all he does is smile, tongue out when the moment calls for it.

KELVIN DOESN'T BLAME ANYONE for how things ended up for himself. Not his mom. Not his dad. Not even the flood that covered his community in a swampy, unsustainable pool. Even when he thinks about his life, how he ended up here, a so-called gang member, a criminal, a technician of theft and violence, he has trouble recalling the events as they happened. One day he was in school, failing all of his classes, and the next he was breaking into ATMs, selling on the street full-time, and working with Hurricane and Moose. He did his time, was considered a "wishful, however naïve, societal project" by the judge who sentenced him to his rehabilitation, and thanked him for his leniency, as instructed by his lawyer. He believed in the importance of the judicial system despite its flaws. Still does. He wasn't innocent, even though he considered himself to be a victim of the world. He didn't think about the future, didn't have dreams or aspirations.

They make their way back to the car at the edge of The Forks; Kelvin in the driver's seat and Hurricane in the back. It's Monday, hot for May, and the AC doesn't work. In the back Hurricane blows a small, electric fan on his face and moans out loud.

"Did I tell you I went to a psychiatrist the other day?" Hurricane says.

"And?"

"They say I'm depressed." Hurricane laughs, but Kelvin notices that he's not overdoing it like he normally does.

"Shit. I could've told you that."

Hurricane doesn't respond. It's unusually quiet in the back, save for his fan.

"They have you on medicine? Maybe check out a healer or some shit."

"Nah." Kelvin detects something uncertain in his voice, and through the mirror he thinks Hurricane looks mostly the same, but perhaps more tired than usual, maybe a little sleep deprived. More concerned with himself than he usually is. "Drugs like that fuck with me."

Kelvin tries to hide his limbs from the hot sun and uses his phone as a fan to waft cool air in his face and doesn't take the conversation any further.

"Are you going to the game Friday?" Hurricane asks.

Kelvin stares ahead, out the windshield. "What game?"

"The Tigers. Their last game of the season is Friday. I got a feeling the Curse ends this week. It's gonna be a special night for us St. Croix alumni."

Kelvin hasn't been to Memorial Arena in weeks. Can't face Pete. Can't face himself.

"Neither me or you graduated. Pretty sure that doesn't make us alumni."

Hurricane laughs. "Same shit. I still wear Tiger pride. Thinking of getting a Tiger face inked across my chest."

Kelvin shifts in his seat so that he's leaning on his right shoulder and staring back at Hurricane. "You mean your man titties?"

They laugh loud until they hurt their ears from the noise. "I've been working out. I'm going to be looking like Brock Lesnar next summer."

"Sad if you ask me."

"I didn't really care before, but I care harder now after I heard the league isn't letting them back next season. Guess we sucked too hard!" Hurricane laughs. "Just kidding. You know how it always is around here."

Kelvin gives a confused look. "What are you saying?"

"Boils down to the white man hating on us Injuns. Like always."

Kelvin nods. He can see Moose walking to the car, about a football field away.

"You should come. See your little bro play. The last games are always a scene. Maybe we muscle around some white boys, get them scared. Punch some dads out."

Kelvin thought about the Memorial Arena, and by extension Pete, and how he probably wouldn't be welcome back there. He hadn't told anyone what went down, just that he quit. No cops came after him, which meant Pete kept his word. He thought about the final game, and how at these things there was no security, no admissions table, no poster with his face on it with BANNED in bold red letters to give him a problem. "Yeah. I'll come."

"Me, I'll be doing some scouting with Moose," Hurricane says, waiting for Kelvin to look back at him, which he does. "For some potential new recruits."

The passenger-side door opens and Moose slides into the car, and immediately glares at both Kelvin and Hurricane in frustration.

"I said meet me at the food court."

Kelvin doesn't recall him saying anything of the sort, and takes a corroborating glance at Hurricane that tells him he's just as perplexed. "We weren't hungry."

Moose sighs.

Kelvin's phone vibrates and somehow he already knows what it's about. It's a text from Xavier: *Think of this as a two-minute warning. No brother no promotion no future.*

Kelvin thinks, debates inside and writes back: *He's in.*

*Bring him to the house Friday after the game. We'll celebrate.*

"What is it?" Moose says.

"Just some white bitch," Kelvin says, depositing his phone in his pocket. "Feeling hurt."

"Careful with those white broads," Moose says at a leisurely pace.

"That's why I don't bother with white chicks, me," Hurricane says proudly.

"'Cause they're scared of you," Kelvin says.

They all laugh. Moose slaps the car roof in tune with his gunshot laughter.

But Kelvin is the first to stop. He grips the wheel, making that squeezed-leather noise and regret fills his lungs and veins, fills him solid. He notices how old his hands look, which he notices about his face every day. He's young but already rusted. Scrap metal left out in the rain. Them too. Hurricane and Moose. *All of them.* Clinton too, if only because they're blood.

And then he starts the car.

## *errol whitecloud sinclair*

### MAY 10, 2012

It's been a long while. I feel I can only revisit these pages when I know what it is I want to say and half the time I still don't know for certain, and for the past four weeks or so I wasn't quite sure what more to share. As I write it is spring, or *ziigwan.* Or at least it's trying to be out there.

I don't know if I intend for you to read this letter. If you are reading this maybe I'm long dead. I don't know. I haven't planned it out. The truth is, I'm not as courageous as I used to think I was. When you go to prison the expectation is that you'll reenter society afterward a changed man. But you leave not knowing how it's changed you, whether in good ways or bad ways. You never know. If you need to know, don't get caught. Or better yet don't be sinful. I don't drink anymore, which Art tells me is a good thing, but I want to all the time. The urges are still there. And how is this any different. Am I just pretending to be changed? I don't know.

But I will say this. I think I saw what the religious doctor was talking about a few months ago when I saw your little brother at White's. I saw him, but I also saw you. Good gosh you boys look so alike. I saw the same little boy playing with his toys in front of the TV, *Jeopardy!* on mute. I realize now that I have trouble remembering how your face looked. But I remember noticing the scar above your forehead and admiring how it parted your hair to the sides as if it were natural, from that gash the doctor glued shut after you rolled off the tree just past our steps. You were a robustious little menace, once warning a hairdresser trying to give you a cut, "Don't you touch me, bitch." Bad words were about the only thing I taught you, and if you're a big swearer I blame myself. You were at ease most with all your toys, telling stories to yourself and me only by my advantageous location in the living room. And there you were, asking me to explain my life's toughest questions. And so I got scared again, and ran. I didn't have the answers and I'm not sure when I will. Art would tell me all the time that that's okay. And I want to tell you that the same goes for you.

Because we keep on searching.

Maybe one day we'll search together.

## *tomahawk shields*

BY MAY THE TIGERS WERE WINLESS. TO HIS SURPRISE TOMMY HAD gone eighteen games without being knocked off his feet, and to do it one more time would be a two-burger victory. His stability was no doubt owed to his daily regimen the previous summer, but also he'd undergone an unexpected growth spurt since the beginning of the school year, and he had the stretch marks on his back to prove it. A whole two inches taller. He was big, strong, with a short torso and long arms and legs. Intimidation was now part of his arsenal. It was built in.

It was a holiday of sorts, a holiday for Indians of the state. Tommy and Clinton spent the morning at The Forks. Clinton, a Treaty Indian, collected his five dollars from a souped-up Mountie while Tommy, a cardless Indian, stood in line at a candy store inside an old train car and afterward they walked along the Red River and halfway across the esplanade to St. Boniface. They paused to look out at the city. To the west of them was The Forks and the tall buildings of downtown, as well as a large, unfinished structure intended to be a human rights museum.

"How many dead bodies you think are down there?" Tommy said, peering over the bridge.

"Too many."

"How come they don't float to the surface?"

"The Manipogo takes care of it."

"Actually?" Tommy was genuinely startled. He learned in grade ten biology that human DNA is basically the same as that of a banana, and so he was inclined to believe that everything, including mythological beasts that existed mostly in the mind, was on the table.

Clinton, studying the half-done museum, said quietly, "That museum should be sick."

"What museum?"

Clinton pointed to it.

"I wonder if they'll talk about the bodies in the river."

BACK HOME TOMMY AND Clinton mused about the possibility of starting a business together. One of Tommy's cousins was driving for a food delivery app that donated a portion of its revenue to a fund that helped inner-city businesses. Tommy thought it genius. He loved the idea of being his own man, calling his own shots, the two of them bouncing around ideas for hours on a gloomy afternoon.

"What's one thing you think Neechis in this city need?" Tommy said.

"Rehab."

Tommy pinched the bridge of his nose, trying to conjure ideas.

"Honestly, I just want to get out of the city sometimes," Clinton said. "Look at the way they look at us, how this league is treating us. Some days all I want to do is sit in the middle of a lake somewhere and fish, be alone for a little bit. Doesn't matter if it's summer and I'm on a boat or it's winter and I'm trying to keep from freezing to death in a small fishing shack, although I kind of prefer being out on the ice. Less chase. It's almost like they're choosing you. The fish, I mean. That's what my shoomis used to say, that they gave themselves up for us and that they weren't stupid like people think and only stupid people think earthworms live in the water. Did you know Manitoba has the most lakes in the country? One hundred thousand. Crazy, hey? All this land, all these lakes, and here we are."

"Yeah, but they say the city has character."

"I'm sick of character."

"Do you ever miss your family?"

"Sometimes," Clinton said, and then he smiled. "Back on the rez, Kelvin would always turn on the lights in our room while I was sleeping and be like, 'You awake?' He was obsessed with the northern lights. He watched the weather channel every day just to see when they'd be out. He'd wake me up and we'd go lay on the grass or snow outside and watch them. He used to try to tell me they were the sign of the apocalypse, that they were the land taking its last breath. Just to scare me. He was always so full of shit. When we were out fishing he used to tell me that suckers lived off human blood and for years I believed him and told everyone what he told me like it was some interesting factoid and was afraid to go swimming." After this his smile disappeared. Replaced by something more resentful of the memory.

Tommy didn't say it, but he only partially agreed with Clinton. The city, though he'd never been anywhere else, never called another place home, deprived him—deprived him of himself. Leaving the city, reconnecting one's spirit with the land and reclaiming culture and place, as the textbooks argued, was essential to decolonization, the mission they'd heard so much about. As much as he was inspired by the notion he also knew it was a lie, something that looked good on paper and sounded right in a lecture hall. Most Natives were now Urban Natives and to suggest an urban exodus was to reveal one's own privilege, for not all of the boys and girls he knew had the luxury of spending a day or two embracing culture and ceremony out on the land, not even for a weekend. Where would he go if he could? He thought about that a lot, thought of all the possibilities, pulling up Google Maps to look at the little towns he'd never been to, learning their histories, their giant animal statues. A sharp-tailed grouse in Ashern, a mosquito in Komarno. He imagined what life would have been like if he had been made there instead of here. Most of the Tigers were from somewhere they had never been. Clinton was one of the few who could say he lived on a rez, while the others came from families that collected their treaty money once a decade, their annual five dollars accruing in their absence, waiting for them to return to the rez they supposedly belonged to.

But they were all from the same place. Tommy never doubted that about himself. They all belonged to the North End.

## clinton whiteway

THE CROSSWALK TIMER HIT ZERO. I WAS ON MY WAY HOME FROM school, to Tommy's house, when he ran up behind me. Class hadn't let out yet but I had a spare. Napping had become part of my afternoon routine for no reason other than I felt tired. There was no scientific motivation behind it, no desire to increase my lifespan or do it the way the hockey pros do it. I had a spare, I was tired and was heading back to Tommy's place for a nap to beat the after-school rush. It was Thursday, my birthday, the day before our final game.

"Don't you have biology?" I said.

"Mr. Singh loves me," Tommy said. "I don't think he'll care. But who knows. Teachers always acting like they're friends."

Tommy stopped and swung his backpack in front of him. I could see it was heavy.

"I got you something," he said. He unzipped the front pocket and pulled out a square thing in Christmas wrapping paper, which had a small image of Santa on his sleigh all over it like polka dots. The wrapping was poor, half-assed. He used too much wrapping paper. It was crinkled and crumpled and bunched together under one side, and when he handed it to me he purposely displayed the prettiest side of the packaging.

"Christmas already," I said.

"It was all I could find in Koko's closet."

"You didn't have to." I tore it open on the spot and discovered a box of corn flakes and at first thought it was another one of Tommy's pranks but inside was the hardcover of *The Big Book of Animals,* heavy as a ten-pound brick.

"I know how you hate scuffs."

The gesture was appreciated, and I felt like telling him I loved him in a completely platonic brotherly way. "So that's why the cereal box was missing. It all makes sense now."

We kept walking. We were halfway home when at a stop sign a black Sunfire with illegally tinted windows pulled up beside us. It was filthy, its lower half smeared in dirt. It was covered with deep scratches along its entire length, that could have only been done by a key or knife or rock.

The passenger's window rolled down and sitting there was Moose. Across from him, in the driver's seat, was Kelvin, smoking, looking ahead like he didn't care enough to look at me or be a part in whatever was happening, a hand out the window, another on the wheel. I could see Hurricane in the back seat, smiling in a way that was both friendly and creepy and insane, leaning forward just enough so that we could both see each other.

"You boys need a ride?" Moose said. He wore sunglasses that looked like they were meant for a marathon runner and for the first time I noticed the face tattoos that lacked a true professional's hand and in doing so my memory of his face changed. He was big, too big for the car he was in, like a clown on a motorcycle. His black hair was long, shaved fresh on the sides, but still thick and long enough to come down into a ponytail. His teeth were white as Caribbean sand.

I looked to Tommy and then back at Moose and said, "We're good."

"Let's go for a ride. Chill a little bit. Kezzy misses you. Ain't that right, Kez?"

"I think we're good," Tommy said. He looked uncertain about his words, unsure if he was allowed to speak.

"Let's go make some of this," Moose said, holding up a rolled wad of cash.

I looked at Tommy again but neither of us said a word. Moose began reaching for something that I couldn't see through his open window, eventually raising a bottle of water to his lips and taking a swig.

I thought Tommy might speak but he didn't.

"Let's take a ride," Moose said again. "Young men like you need to be able to support your families. We can show you how to be entrepreneurs. Just like us."

"I'm not," I said, with a slight crack in my voice, "down for that." I bent down slowly, scared at first that I might tip over and face-plant onto the sidewalk, and looked through the window and as I did my eyes instantly watered. "Stop coming around here, Kelvin."

I could see Tommy change his focus from them to me, with the new knowledge that this wasn't the first time I'd encountered the three of them like this: me on the street and them in the Sunfire, offering a ride. A ride that was always more and less than just a ride.

"Boy," Moose said, giving an offended performance on Kelvin's behalf. "Don't be like that." He laughed, and it was the first time I'd ever heard him laugh. "We'll party like last time. Get you some girls. Turn you boys into men."

Surely he was referring to the time Kelvin beat the shit out of me in a drunken stupor. I shook my head. "I don't think so."

Moose peered through the side mirror, wincing from the strain it required to get a clear view. The Sunfire was blocking two cars and Kelvin pointed toward the road.

"We'll catch you later, then," Moose said, and as he said this he raised his right hand and rested a shiny chrome pistol, which was either never touched before or freshly polished, on the dashboard in front of him. "Soon."

They skidded away. The crunched pebbles underneath the Sunfire's tires sounded like hot cooking oil. The volume of the exhaust was obnoxious and left behind a rotten, noxious smoke that hung in the air like a ghost covered in the ash of the recently dead.

"What if his gun falls?" Tommy said, waving the fumes away from his nose.

I didn't respond, pretended not to hear him. Because this time I knew they were serious.

## *tannyce shields*

WE ARRIVE IN PORTAGE LA PRAIRIE, A TOWN, MAYBE A SMALL CITY, I've always loved simply for its name. The prairies on the way in were lush with wheat, green and vast and full of life. It's prettier and perhaps flatter and perhaps bigger than it used to be since I was last out here, as if there's more cars and trucks and roads and towns with things to see and places to eat and drink and get gas. Here distance plays tricks on you, like you can almost reach out and grab the sun and stars and half-moon and whatever you want. We're almost there, almost in Winnipeg. We stop at an Indian gas bar and slots where two teenagers, a friendly boy and a grumpy girl in fluorescent orange vests, take your money at your window and pump the gas for you. Beatrice gives the boy her treaty number and then looks at me and says, "I'm going in. You want anything?"

"No thanks," I say.

"You should let them know we'll be there in an hour." She passes me her phone and I take it in my hand.

"Okay."

Beatrice doesn't know that only Tomahawk knows I'm coming, although even he doesn't *really* know I'm coming. She knows that I sort of told them I was coming home, making my long-awaited return to the city, and by them I mean only Tomahawk, emailed him back in December that I would be coming and now it is May and here I am, in Portage la Prairie.

Truth is, I am afraid. Afraid of what they'll think of me. Afraid that they won't remember me, that they'll open the door and turn me away like someone selling them Jesus.

I dial the only other number, apart from Beatrice's, that I have memorized. It rings. Koko is usually slow to the phone. It rings some more. Forever ringing.

"Hello?" It's the voice of a girl.

"Hello." I can feel something swelling inside me. Closing. Locking.

"Who's speaking?"

"It's . . ." I choke. "It's Mom."

For a moment I hear nothing but my own breathing, and then:

"What do you want?"

"I'm in Portage," I say. "I'm coming home, Asemaa. I told Tomahawk. He knows."

She makes a sound in her throat, a quaver and then a sort of growl.

I feel my heart pounding, my jaw tightening, everything, my body, starting to feel more and more restricted, like I'm not me and it's not mine. Littlefeather said this would happen. She told me to make a fist and breathe, bite it if I have to. "But maybe it's not the right time," I say.

"How dare you get his hopes up." The vitriol smacks me in the face.

"Please don't tell him I called."

"I'm not doing anything for you. Tell him yourself."

"Uh-huh," I say, unable to think of anything else. Words elude me.

"Don't come back here," she says calmly. "I don't want to see you. None of us do."

I hear the punch the phone makes as she hangs up and the distant, echoing absence of a disconnected line.

I get out of the car and walk to the edge of the road and wish Littlefeather was here. She stayed behind. She said I had to do this on my own. Plus, she called Beatrice "a lot." Me, I enjoy Beatrice's company, and she knows all the interesting fun facts about every little town and city, which has made the long drive more enjoyable. But maybe she cares too much, and is always in your face about everything.

"You okay?" Beatrice says, kicking up dust from the gravel lot of the gas bar.

"I don't think I can do this," I say, and I feel the tears urging forward, blurring the burning sunset.

"You don't have to," she says, resting a hand on my shoulder. I embrace her touch. "We don't have to do anything."

I say, "Do you think I'm a bad person?"

"Never." She squeezes me with her other hand.

"Up until now the only people I told about me coming was my son. I didn't even fucking tell my mom or my daughter."

"Tannyce!" she says, laughing with her whole body. "Boy you!"

I smile with her, all wet-faced, tasting the saltiness of my tears.

"You'll know when you're ready."

"How will I know when I'm ready?"

"It'll be like when you're a child and your mom calls out to you to come home and you do it not because you want to or have to, but because you need her and she needs you and together you're safe. Because that's what home is. Safe."

We stay there for a moment, listening to the crickets sing in a field of wheat, like a billion gilded trophies dancing to a sweet breeze skimming the earth for miles.

We head back to the car when the grumpy girl in the orange vest waves us down and yells at us about Beatrice's car parked by the pumps. Beatrice throws me the keys and says I can drive if I want and I say yes. We walk back and get in and I start the engine, feel its breath and hum and rumble, and turn it around until the hood faces west and, with every intention of returning, just not now, but when I'm ready, we drive back the way we came.

*pete mosienko*

THE ZAMBONI IS THE MOST BEAUTIFUL THING YOU'VE EVER SEEN.
Better than the sight of a newborn baby or the flesh of a beautiful young woman. This is truly better, this hulk of steel and rubber. With the right care it will live longer than you, and you'll be proud to leave it behind when you're dead. You run a hand across the glittery red paint, the white stripe running along both of its sides. You climb into the cockpit and admire the leather seat and steering wheel, big enough for two if you wanted it to be. It's so beautiful you cried when it arrived yesterday aboard a flatbed truck, which surprised you slightly because you imagined there to be some sort of unboxing, but still you can't remember the last time you cried—in this case it was the driver, who removed his hat out of kindness and offered you a tissue from his pocket. It's so beautiful it makes you reconsider the idea that humans can fall in love with people when you can fall in love with this. You don't want to have sex with your new Zamboni but you can see how someone might want to get up in there. It's so beautiful you think your grandfather would be proud, because your grandfather wasn't proud of many things except for the woman he married and the woman who took him in when he landed in this country and raised him as Anishinaabe. Your dad would've wanted to be there for the first ride. Mom would've at least been glad you're hanging up your shovels.

You arrived at the rink today before noon. You arrived cleaned-up good: shaved, shitted, haircutted, the works. You cleaned the ice, watched first graders learn how to skate, cleaned the ice again, watched figure skaters work on their axels who never used to book the rink because of the quality of your playing surface, cleaned the ice again, watched a group of childhood friends who were now retirees who booked the ice every Friday to scrimmage for an hour or until one or more of them went down with a sore hip or knee, cleaned the ice again, then laced up your skates and pulled on your gloves and gripped your stick and went out there to shoot and dash back and forth until you could no longer breathe. You're down ten pounds. Because you've been skating every afternoon for half an hour. Later in the evening you planned to talk to Olga Shields, reintroduce yourself after all these years. The Tigers will play their final game maybe forever and this, apart from showing up at her door, which you'd thought about on several occasions, would be the last way to bump into someone and make it seem organic. You locked up and went down the street for a late lunch at a nearby deli and when you came back you double-checked every shower and toilet throughout the arena and mopped up vomit behind the bench left by one of the retirees who hadn't skated since his twenties. At three-thirty you took a shower, brushed your teeth and used mouthwash. At four you opened the pro shop and sat at your desk and made some edits to a job opening you're planning on sending around to employment websites. You're on the market for a new assistant, because you liked having Kelvin around—the help, the company—and as you finalized the draft your attention drifted to the arrow-shaped hole he left behind on your wall, which you haven't gotten around to patching. You reminisced. You never found the wrench he threw. You don't obsess over your finances as much anymore, don't need to, because the future looks brighter, and you can see the lights, just over there. Then you sharpened skates, prioritizing those of the Tigers.

It's five and you start the engine. You feel the hum and the vibration and the swirl. She's breathing and you're thinking of naming her Martha, after your mom. You take her out of the garage and begin your pregame flood and from your high vantage point you can see the whole arena, nearly every corner of it, and you see the fans and parents and ancient descendants of the community piling into the lobby and clustering in the stands, the oldest wrapping their legs in blankets and youngest using their youth to stand and watch. Outside, beyond your new glass-paned doors, which you found time to fix,

there's the scraggy men in caps and out-of-season beanies with cigarettes in hand. There's kids in a mixture of professional and minor
league jerseys, just behind the glass encircling you, hustling back and
forth in a ferocious game of tag. Every now and then someone chants
something unheard and unfamiliar, and someone whistles and claps
and shouts and it all sounds more rhythmic than you'd expect. You
go around in circles beginning from the boards, the circle getting
smaller and smaller as you get closer to the center until you finally
cut the whole sheet in half with a slow drive up the middle and now
there's two patches of unfinished ice and not just one, and then you
continue around in circles, picking off blemishes, until the whole
thing glistens and not a single sliver of debris from blades and sticks
remains.

You wave to the crowd. Some clap for you. And as you take your
final turn around the rink you see Olga sitting in the stands beside
a young woman that looks like a younger version of her, a turquoise
star quilt over both their legs. They're laughing about something, and
the chemistry is evident, but Olga is clearly the dominant one, while
the younger woman seems eager to orbit her, her shield. You drive
by them, catch yourself staring. And that's when you see him, with
a sourish and edgy look on his face. Maneuvering his way through
the crowd, rubbing shoulders and sleeves with men in slick track
jackets, getting in line for concessions. Kelvin, and the sight of him
shakes you, offends you. You park the Zamboni in the garage and
rush down and shovel the slushy excrement it leaves at the edge of
the ice. You march out into the assembling crowd with a burning
inside you and you feel the heat and comfort of their bodies, their
reveries and their desperations. You scan the area for Kelvin. You
bump into a referee and say you're sorry. The crowd and the noise
are dizzying, the patterns and social cues complex. You search and
you can't find him, and think to yourself that maybe you don't want
to. You've lost him. But the truth is, he's all of them—tramping and
tumbling and hoping, here to watch the game.

## *clinton whiteway's hockey night in "kkkanada"*

THE FINAL GAME OF THE SEASON WAS AT HOME IN OUR SHABBY, depressed arena that some of our rookies, perhaps out of career-shortening resentment, took to calling the Tigers' Den, even though tigers don't live in dens. Neither do lions, I discovered while reading *The Big Book of Animals.* A part of me felt terrible for our young cubs, who would likely not see the ice next season. A crowd of students, parents and alumni packed the bleachers on one side of the rink, while fans from Trinity High School occupied the other, a mostly white school from the south that adopted the logo of the New Jersey Devils, only their logo was blue instead of red and they called themselves the Blue Devils. Such a turnout wasn't abnormal—season finales attract a lot of faithful supporters, eager to see the Curse be broken. By then news of the league's decision to reshape the league, us relegated to a state of nothingness, had reached the Native public and local press, magnifying the raucousness of the event.

I stretched and jogged and performed high knees in a quiet corner of the rink. I could see Floyd sprinting back and forth along the stands, trying to rile up the crowd. Through the glass and across the fresh ice I saw Tommy near the entrance of our dressing room. He squatted low in skintight shorts, stretching his groin, attempting to put on a show for the ladies. Signs poked through the atmosphere: "Save the Tigers!" and "Hockey Night in KKKanada" and "Skoden!" and students and parents and teachers alike stomped their feet and clapped their hands to the rhythm of Queen's "We Will Rock You." They were Tigers, and we were them. I finished warming up and walked back to the dressing room, taking in the crowd, embracing the moment.

I laid out my gear in fine order and hung my ragged sweater on the hook behind me, displayed with a hanger like they did in the pros and left our crowded room to find an empty one with a vacant bathroom. I walked down the hall and passed who I assumed to be a coach from the other team who was entering his squad's dressing room and I caught a glimpse of their royal blue sweaters and socks and pale faces and the mood was relaxed, much like ours—the Blue Devils, despite making the playoffs and having won some games, were beatable and we knew it. If ever there was a chance to upset the order of things it was now, this game. I found an empty room a couple doors over. I needed peace when I relieved myself, visualizing in-game scenarios and reacting accordingly. I sat in the cleanest stall, detoxing my body, cleansing my bowels, shitting in peace and silence. Sacred, as Floyd would say. Then the dressing room door opened and I heard voices as it was shut and locked securely behind the chatter. Unaware that I was occupying one of the cans in an alcove devoted to lavatories.

"Obviously it looks better if they lose," I heard a man say. He had an older voice, the kind of raspy quality that made talking sound like it hurt. "There's a lot more eyes on us today."

"Then we could point to a talent problem," a younger man added.

"Let it get scrappy out there. Those St. Croix kids love a fight."

"Sure. Sure. Okay. Alright, then."

I heard footsteps. Coming closer. To the alcove with the shitters and a couple urinals. I lifted my feet, tried to peer through the cracks between the door and wall but couldn't see where they were. Then I heard pissing. Like two hoses spraying a wall.

"I've done a few of theirs," the younger man said. "Easily provoked those boys."

"You should see some of the reserve teams we deal with." The raspy man coughed and sniffled and pulled phlegm into his throat and released it into the urinal by the sound of it.

Their voices cautiously became quieter and to hear better I put my ear to the wall. Soap was dispensed, the sinks turned on. I thought: Good for them for washing their hands.

"If anything it'll justify a suspension," the raspy man said. "Zero tolerance, etcetera."

The voices grew distant and the door opened again and the sound of fans and music rushed through and I quickly wiped my ass and pulled up my pants and ran out the room and peered down the hallway and saw the backs of two men, one in regular clothes and the other in a referee sweater, black and white like the stripes of a zebra. The voices likely belonged to them, but how could I be sure? I couldn't. I saw nothing but heard everything. I walked slowly back to my teammates, processing this new information, asking myself if I'd heard it wrong, trying, failing at trying, to convince myself it wasn't the sounds of match fixing, but rather two adult men sharing a harmless piss and casually discussing Indigenous people when we're not around, and when I got there I said nothing and put on my uniform.

## *kelvin whiteway*

KELVIN STANDS AT THE ENTRANCE OF THE MEMORIAL ARENA AND waits and smokes and cracks a can of pop, telling himself he'll loiter there until the game is about to start before going inside. He's come out to wait for Hurricane, but whether he'll show up like he said he would is unclear. He may already be dead. He could be taking his final breaths this very moment. He's known for a long time that Hurricane has wanted to kill himself and it's a weird thing to know, to feel so sure about. But it's true. Hurricane, his whole life, has been struggling with a great, unbearable sadness and Kelvin could see he was hurting, the pain getting worse. They never talked about death or suicide, at least not together. But they knew it was real, that it affected them both, like they shared some sort of twin telepathy even though they weren't blood. Instead, Hurricane opened up in Facebook posts. About his struggles, depression and worsening addictions. Then yesterday Hurricane posted: "Fuck this shit . . . Can't take much more . . . Over it . . . Not worth it . . . Going to end my life now . . . </3" Kelvin saw it eleven minutes after it was published, didn't think much of it, kept scrolling, kept searching for nothing in particular. It wasn't the first time he'd seen virtual suicide notes on Facebook, not just from Hurricane but other Facebook friends. Now he regrets the scrolling, the search for nothing. This morning he went searching, checked out Hurricane's place, knocked for several minutes but no answer. He checked with Hurricane's favorite auntie, who hadn't heard from him either but saw his post. He thought about calling the cops but around here wellness checks kill more than they save. And so now he stands outside the Memorial Arena waiting,

waiting for a ghost. Every now and then someone he knew from high school walks up to him, says hello, shakes his hand, asks about his mom and little brother. He learns of others he once knew who have passed on and feels an awful shame for feeling comforted by this. He says hello to Sam Shields and her koko Olga, who he hasn't seen in ages and the old lady tells him to "take care" and "be good" and he scoffs on the inside. He greets Moose, who's clearly drunk or high or both and flashing a wasted smile, as he stumbles over the whole parking lot, and asks if he's heard from their companion and Moose says "probably being silly" before going in without him. Kelvin waits a bit longer. But Hurricane doesn't show. Doesn't show his face. It's a memory now, he thinks. Memories fade like the body. The game is about to start. He crushes his cigarette into the ground and heads inside.

*slap. shot. bang.*

ALL THINGS CONSIDERED THE TIGERS HAD A STRONG STARTING five. Enough firepower up front to give their goaltender, as well as themselves, a fighting chance. A product of street hockey, Jonah was obsessed with making the "highlight reel save," and Tommy was not alone in believing he purposely found himself out of position in order to achieve the same. Tommy took his usual place on the blue line with his rookie partner Leo Keeper, who everyone called Keepee, while Floyd, who with Clinton would be their only rotating centers for the night, their Hail Mary, was flanked by the Martin brothers on the wing. Fostered by a Filipino family—and often mistaken as blood due to their dark brown skin and almond-shaped eyes—that considered them too dirty to sit on the couch, Colton and Casey were fast and could spot danger before it spotted them.

When the puck dropped the pace was frenetic, both teams absorbing the crowd's energy. The first period ended scoreless, highlighted by Floyd jumping out of the Tigers' bench with such grace and poise and splitting the Blue Devils' defensemen after receiving a cross-ice pass from Tommy, only to be denied trying to go five-hole.

There was no time to recuperate between the first and second periods or let the tension fizzle away, and that meant the roughness of the affair escalated in the second. After a Blue Devils forward recklessly barreled into Jonah, Colton dug into the boy's unprotected spine with the shaft of his stick, snapping it in half. The boy fell to the ice, wailing. When Colton took his seat in the penalty box he was shamed by the white audience behind him. Coach Johnson screamed from the bench at the top of his lungs, his face red and sweaty, over missed calls, and the head referee came over with a warning. "Keep it clean, Coach," he said, "or I'll ask you to leave."

The referee was young, with a messy beard and sandy blond hair that floated under his helmet like wings. Clinton sized him up. He was about as tall as the man he saw outside the locker room.

"Then make a fucking call! Sticks ain't weapons."

The horn blew and the two teams headed off. Tommy waved through the glass at Sam and Koko, sitting at the front of the stands, a patterned quilt draped over their legs. If it were any other game he'd only be hearing Koko's *oohs* and *ahhs*. She had the tendency to scream after every play that showed promise, and "C'mon Toooomaaaa-haaaawk!" even if he wasn't part of it. She gave the games a horror movie thrill. At the top of the bleachers he spotted Kelvin, standing with a thicket of men who all had the same spotty, thin facial hair, because that's all they could sprout. Beside him was Moose, swaying like a tube man outside a gas station.

The Tigers sat around the room, puddles of sweat and thawed snow formed beneath their tired bodies. The smell was awful.

"Keep it up, boys," Floyd said.

For a moment they sat in silence. Then Tommy broke it by saying:

"What the hell is a Blue Devil?"

"It's a comic book character, and also an old-ass French battalion," Clinton said.

"Bunk-ass name," Jonah said.

"Was this the team that used to call themselves the Hawks, and ripped off the Blackhawks logo?" Casey asked.

"That's them. Must've changed it," Colton said.

"It was in the news," Clinton said.

"Fuck the news," Floyd said. "Shit's bleak as shit."

"Well, someone needs to fire whoever's been making their logos," Casey said.

"It's a Christian school. Maybe they thought a red devil would scare the kids," Tommy said.

"They got their colors all fucked up over there," Jonah said. "They probably still think Jesus was white." He squirted water from a green bottle into his mouth. "I personally don't see color. *Hayguh!*"

"What?" Colton said.

"He means Jesus was probably Black," Clinton said. "No offense, Floyd."

"S'all sacred," Floyd said. "Devil's probably a white dude anyway."

"Y'all think the Creator was red?" Tommy said.

"But we're not really red," Clinton said.

"I get close in the summer. So brown I scare people."

"Looking like a dark Cree isn't the same as being red."

"Yeah, but imagine."

"Boys—"

Before Floyd could tell them to cease yapping Coach Johnson came through the door and took the center of the room, surrounded by a fortress of hockey bags.

"Gentlemen, they're getting nervous. Keep getting pucks deep, deep, deep. Keep pressuring, sooner or later they're going to make a mistake, and when they do we'll be ready"—he scanned his notes, trying his best to decipher the mess he put on the page—"But we need cool heads going into this. They're going to come, and it's going to get choppy. So we need cool heads, cool heads, cool heads. This dipshit ref ain't calling anything, but we need to stay disciplined. Let's play our game, be smart. We give ourselves a chance by not letting all this other shit get to us. Forwards, listen up, help out your defensemen—backcheck hard, get the puck out of our zone and then get off, quick shifts. When we keep it simple we limit our mistakes." He turned for the door but stopped before he got there, remembering one last piece of advice, and said:

"Oh, and Jonah, stop flopping around out there and just make the easy save. You look like you're fucking the ghost of your mother, fucking jumping for nothing. We have twenty minutes to break the Curse."

A scoreless Tigers game after forty minutes was already history, Tommy thought. And even if they didn't win, even if they found a way to lose, he knew if he could stay upright for twenty more he'd have something to brag about. They sucked, sure. But for a time he could say he alone reigned, strong and big and standing over bodies. The man.

*maggie mary taken alive*

AT INTERMISSION AUNTIE MAGGIE ORDERS A COFFEE FROM CONCES-
sion and adds cream and sugar at the far end of the counter and
takes longer than usual to stir her drink just so she can take another
look around. The arena is loud, far louder than during any game all
season. Everyone is talking at once, and it's beginning to hurt her
ears. She spots a cute baby in a stroller dressed in pink and wearing big earmuffs and resists the urge to say hello, which she would
have done if Jonah hadn't told her earlier that week that if a baby
ever goes missing in their neighborhood she'd be the first suspect.
"You're the only baby I need," she said in response, and he laughed.
There's a news camera and a female reporter pulling people aside,
asking if they'd like to be interviewed, and she assumes they want
to ask passersby about a certain controversial topic she has taken
to calling "Tigergate," but most people are shaking their heads and
walking away. She has to pee, but the restroom is in the direction of
the camera and its broadcaster and she doesn't want to be bothered
by them and their questions—she watches enough news on TV to
know that reporters will do their damnedest to get the answer they
want out of you. Then, out of nowhere, a young girl approaches her,
introducing herself as Clarissa Walkman from the St. Croix student
newspaper. "I'm asking members of the community their thoughts
on this final game," the girl says, with confidence and healthy posture
and a notepad and pen in her hands. Maggie, annoyed, looks at her
and then to the fire escape, and says, "I don't speak English." She
walks back to her seat in the stands, feels the cool air of the rink on
her face as she leaves the lobby, and waits for the third period to start.

She hasn't watched much of the game, covers her eyes when things become too much. But earlier, when a player from the other team crashed into Jonah, which he was slow to get up from, she jumped to her feet and shouted until her lungs hurt: "That's my boy! You can't do that! That's a penalty! Make the damn call! Make the damn call! Make the damn call!"

*errol whitecloud sinclair*

**NO DATE**

I arrived at the rink just before the third act and I noticed you straight-away, standing there high in the stands. By that I mean I got to the arena just as the third period started and the chants were loud. The whole place lively. I was watching hockey on TV a night or two earlier and one of the commentators referred to the third period as the "third stanza," and I thought: Wow, that's beautiful, referring to the game as something like poetry. Which I guess you could say it is, judging by its beauty. I think I prefer "act" over "stanza" only because it reminds me of something like a performance, which can be different each night, never the same. Always surprising. Shocking. Spectacular. Boring even, ever boring. Heartbreaking too. We hate it when it's boring and dull and appears neither side is trying but when we're winning we don't care much. Isn't that funny? Life can be like that sometimes too. Boring and stagnant, as if you're going nowhere but to your grave, and then suddenly exciting all over again. Like you're a kid again. But as I say I arrived to the game late, before the third act. This is because I hadn't planned on coming. Well, that's not exactly true. I wanted to come, had planned on it. But then I got scared. I was afraid to see you and your brother both in one place, and so I chickened out. That's the plain truth. I'm not proud of it. I'll admit that anywhere. I'm not afraid to admit I'm scared of things anymore, not even to others, and I credit that to Art's teachings. But, as I say, I was at home, flipping through channels, settled on the news of a deadly tornado in Kansas, when I found the courage to peel my ass off the couch and come over and there you were. And there I was, and that's when it happened.

# *ebb & flow*

THE THIRD PERIOD, AS COACH JOHNSON SAID IT WOULD BE, WAS choppy. Both teams rushed back and forth exhausted, their rudimentary strategies similar enough as to make them identical, two partners in a choreographed dance. The Blue Devils had resorted to cheap taunts—they yelled out Indian whoops they'd heard from old westerns, and their chirps ranged in subject matter from the Native man's dependency on welfare to the burden all those handouts put on the hardworking taxpayer, even though every Native boy in the city would eventually yield to the taxman. Others were subtle and required a racist intelligence. "Send me a receipt for your broken twig," one boy said to Colton, with a wily grin.

"Tell your mom to send me one too."

Such comments weren't original. The Tigers knew that hockey was an arena where all the illusions Canadians convinced themselves to be true evaporated along with the moisture in their breath, a wound that still hadn't been tended to, blood gushing.

Nine minutes remained and the Blue Devils iced the puck. The next face-off was in their end.

Floyd went up to Tommy before puck drop, covering his mouth like a catcher checking in on his pitcher. He told him to post up at the top of the circle and pounce when the moment came. Tommy accepted his captain's orders.

Floyd found his position at the dot, flanked by his teammates. When the referee dropped the puck he pushed the Blue Devils' center backward like an offensive lineman. The puck sat there, untouched, as if frozen in time. There it was, and Tommy went for it. He raised the blade of his stick to the sky, made contact and fell to his knees. The blast exploded the goalie's Gatorade bottle like a water balloon hitting a wall. The crowd cheered, arms raised, and his teammates jumped on him. Victory was close.

In the stands Koko raised two fists and clapped and whistled and Sam rose to her feet in celebration. Auntie Maggie's coffee tilted onto her lap but she didn't care. Kelvin smiled, arms folded, stayed cool. Moose shouted his praises, slurring curse words and unfinished sentences.

Tommy and Clinton watched from the bench as the game grew out of control. Players on both sides were pushing and shoving. Boys collapsed on each other long after the whistle. Late hits sent them to the ground, flat, the air knocked out of them. The benches heckled. Parents yelled angrily, at each other and at no one in particular, as if trying to cast spells with their curses. The three referees shared grins, inclined to let it all happen without consequence—the best seats in the Tiger's Den.

"This is a mess," Clinton said.

"This is bush league."

"Bush league is better than this."

"I bet."

"This is what the league wants."

"What?"

Tommy and Leo Keeper jumped onto the ice for their next shift and so did Floyd and Clinton—Coach had decided to stack his lines in the final minutes. Tommy was intent on letting nothing and no one get within five feet of his goaltender. He dug the puck out of a maze of feet and handed it off to a streaking Floyd and a second later, in front of Jonah, a burly Blue Devil with red cheeks and a nose that resembled that of a pig's took Tommy out from behind, knee-to-knee. Clinton looked over to see Tommy's head bounce off the ice, and, without hesitation, he charged forward and sent the kid flying backward. His crumbling fat body took the noise out of the arena. The blond referee sprinted over and grabbed Clinton by the jersey and escorted him away.

"What about him?" Clinton protested, staring back at the boy who knocked over his friend, who lay there in the care of Jonah. For a second he let himself think about the bet and then pushed the thought away. "This shit is rigged. You're a white piece of shit."

The man's eyes went wide and big. "I could care less what happens to you fucking dirty Indians!"

Clinton wanted to fire back but the air was sucked out of him. Everything slowed down.

Casey heard those familiar words and sprinted over and knocked the referee on his ass, and when the man went to grab him, like a monster with his claws out, he swung his stick around as if chopping down a tree and shattered it across the man's head and his body went limp.

The benches cleared. Helmets unclipped and fights broke out on every corner of the ice. Floyd sidestepped a diving assailant and kicked him in the face with the toe of his skate and the boy spat teeth. Jonah helped Tommy to his feet and then went off to exchange hooks and uppercuts with the opposing goaltender, knocking his braces loose. Colton took on two guys at once, dragging them to the ground before Casey joined in and knocked them out cold. Rubbish rained from the stands. The Tigers could fight, and even though they enjoyed it, it wasn't the violence itself they enjoyed. They knew the world thought less of them because they were willing to fight, to draw blood. But they weren't just exchanging fists. A fight wasn't a fight until there was something to overcome, and they knew that better than most. If that meant a few white boys got their faces rearranged, swell.

The coaches managed to separate the players after what amounted to half a boxing match. The squared circle was a bloodied sheet of ice.

There would be no restart, no broken Curse to ruminate around campfires and retirement porches. The game was called off. A loss for both teams.

*olga shields*

KOKO OLGA, WITH HER ARMS WRAPPED AROUND ONE OF ASEMAA'S, made her way to the lobby of the arena. There was shouting, lots of it. At one point a parent pushed another parent and that pushed parent screamed back, threatening to call the cops. Mean words were hurled from every direction. Olga flinched every time she heard someone end a sentence with: "These God damn Indians." In the lobby she paused in front of a trophy case with gold and silver statues and cups mostly dating back to the eighties and seventies and Asemaa gave a gentle pull.

"Koko," she said. "We should wait in the car. It's crazy in here."

"We should wait for Tomahawk and Clinton—Klik."

"I'll come back for them," Asemaa pleaded.

As she said this a young woman near the doors that led to the bleachers was pulled down by the back of her hair and landed face-first on the hard rubber floor. The young woman, who Olga assumed to be a student, was quickly tended to by a friend and as she got back to her feet her nose gushed with blood and her assailant, along with two other young women, whom Olga also assumed to be students, ran out the main arena doors.

Olga gestured toward the exit. "Okay," she said.

They walked outside and into the parking lot and still there was more shouting and rowdy hollering, and the voices sounded distinctly younger and brasher than the ones they heard indoors.

Olga took the passenger's seat of Asemaa's car and looked up at her granddaughter, hovering above her outside. "Go make sure Tomahawk doesn't do anything stupid."

"I'll get them," Asemaa said, closing the door for her koko and turning back toward the arena.

Olga wasn't that worried about Tomahawk. Not him specifically. But she knew how boys behaved in groups. And so she knew, or felt she knew, that they were capable of any manner of things. She'd heard about the stories, sometimes in the news. No she wasn't worried about Tomahawk. She was worried about what this situation could do to him, what it might make him do. She could hear noise still from inside the car. She locked the door.

## *tomahawk shields*

IN THE DRESSING ROOM TOMMY ICED THE BACK OF HIS HEAD AND bottom lip. He'd eaten a stiff jab. Coach Johnson and assistant coach Dale Ducky and team manager Patti Klassen deliberated in a corner about what should happen next. The rest of the arena had descended into chaos. Students fought students. Parents had their own contests. The coaching staff offered no thoughts on the brawl. Expressed no criticism or disappointment. What happened happened, and now their priority was getting the Tigers out of the building safely.

The plan was to leave their heavy bags behind and exit the building quickly, one by one. The coaches would collect their things later. Clinton was near the front of the line, Tommy further back.

They opened the door to the room and Tommy marched forward, his hand on the shoulder in front of him, which belonged to Floyd, who lamented on the result of the game. "So close," he'd say every few seconds for all to hear, shaking his head. "This is bad medicine."

To avoid another clash with the Blue Devils they avoided the narrow hallway and took the path along the rink's boards and bleachers. Blue Devils faithful populated that side of the arena but reconnaissance suggested they likely had nothing left to throw. When they stepped into view angry ladies with white mom hair shouted from the bleachers. "Shame on you!" A tribe of Trinity students sang that stadium anthem reserved for losers, the one that ends with "Nah nah nah nah, hey hey, goooooodbye." Their snaking line came to a halt before Tommy could get through the lobby doors. He peered over his teammates, but saw nothing. He waited for a minute, checking over his shoulder to catch anything before it turned into a surprise.

The arena sounded like a theme park and had the same frightening excitement. Screw it. He broke the chain and squeezed through the doors and paused again when he noticed Clinton a few feet ahead. And just beyond them, at the center of the frenzy, Kelvin and a man in a backward trucker hat jawed at each other, testing the other's toughness like pro wrestlers in the ring. An older man with a big grey beard and camo hat barked from the sidelines: "Get him!" Like a cornerman with a limited knowledge of the sweet science, willing to let his fighter go out on his shield, die an honorable death.

## *clinton whiteway*

I GOT CLOSER TO KELVIN, SHOUTING, THINKING I COULD CALM HIM down.

"Listen to him," the man said, looking over at me.

"And if I don't?" Kelvin said. "You ain't gonna do shit."

"Then I guess you'll find out. I'm glad they're kicking you filthy fucks to the curb."

"Good one. You look like you roll around in cow shit and you call me filthy?"

The man's face turned red. His fists clenched.

"Let's go, then."

I tried to step forward but felt a strong hand on my shoulder pull me back and turned to discover that it was Moose, whose eyes looked possessed, and he quickly positioned his big body in front of me. He looked me over and like a bouncer at a club said, "No."

To my left I noticed another man approach and assumed that he, like me, was about to alleviate the conflict. He was tall and intimidating, mostly because of the numerous scars etched across his face, and behind him, hanging low, was a thick braid that became thinner the lower it went down his spine. He looked familiar but I couldn't remember where I'd seen him. He walked slow at first, hesitant, but then fully committed to the intrusion, arms out to create space between Kelvin and the man, and said:

"Boys. This isn't going to solve anything. Let's calm down."

Kelvin glanced at the braided man. Like me he appeared startled, surprised even, by the man's face. I thought: Maybe they're friends. Maybe this is what he needs right now.

"Who the fuck—" Kelvin said, pausing at the sight of the situation's newest player. "Get the fuck out of here. You're not needed. Never were."

Kelvin's eyes grew sharp, his expression turned into one of bitter rage, and then, with surprising force, he pushed the braided man's chest with both hands and I followed the man's trajectory like a shooting star, as he tumbled onto the floor, crashing into the feet and hands of nervous bystanders.

"Kelvin!" I shouted. I watched him, wondering what was going through his mind, why he pushed the braided man, but he moved on from it, the change in his attention instantaneous. He squared up again with the man in the trucker hat, his main opponent. But the hatefulness was still there, hadn't left him.

He reached behind his back and pulled out a silver pistol and pointed it at the man's chest and the man moved back and put up his hands. "Just take it easy."

I pivoted and peeled around Moose's wide frame and leapt toward Kelvin and swung my arm down in a big chopping motion. "Kel! Stop!"

## *tomahawk shields*

THERE WAS A LOUD POP AND TOMMY'S EARS RANG. BOY DID THEY ever ring. For a moment he was afraid they were done, broken, that he'd never hear again. He dropped to his knees, hands on the floor. He covered his ears, expecting further blasts. He glanced up at Clinton, Kelvin and the man in the trucker hat and saw that their eyes were swollen. Big and fleshy. All he saw was their eyes. Nothing but eyes.

Someone, a young woman, behind the man in the trucker hat crumpled to the floor, and in an instant the entire room piled toward the exit. Someone with heavy boots stepped on his hand and he moaned in agony but he couldn't hear himself for all he could hear was ringing, his ears dying, singing their swan song—*eeeeee*. He was pushed and shoved but fought to his feet. He saw Moose scramble, and then vanish. Kelvin clawed his way through the pack and disappeared. He saw them in that moment, all of them—Kelvin and Clinton and Moose and Hurricane and Jonah and Floyd and Petey and Sam and Koko, everyone—their lives culminating, crescendo-ing, the final useless passion.

Tommy bounced off the stampede, trying to push forward, trying to get close to his friend. He spotted Clinton, looking back, near the doors. He looked scared. Tommy didn't want him to go but he felt something holding him back, keeping him in place, and then he felt an ache deep in his belly, removing the hunger he had felt after the game. He felt light, like if he tried to move he would float, float in place. He didn't speak or shout or cry. He didn't have room for words. He was either light or heavy, with every breath heavy or light.

But then an unseen something moved in his legs, a tingle, a vibration. His muscles felt like waves. He'd worked so hard to be strong, to be strong in the right way. He readied himself, found his balance, preparing to launch forward.

But then he heard a voice, a voice calling out to him, booming, silencing the ringing. Saying his name. The long version. He felt a hand, a familiar and loving touch, and it's her, his grandmother, holding him, returning him to a world of sound. His eyes fizzled with tears, sending out less sight, and he knew then what this meant, what it prevented him from doing.

He searched for Clinton one more time. Found him. They exchanged glances, and then he was gone.

*pete mosienko*

YOU HEARD IT TOO. YOU RUSH INTO THE LOBBY FROM THE COOL-ness of the ice rink and notice a wounded woman up against the wall, leaking warm blood on your floor. You think: Holy fuck. What do I do? You replay the day, the game, the night, the plan in your mind. You sat in the garage all game aboard your Zamboni, too nervous to come out and show your face and so you missed your chance with Olga Shields, and when it was all brought to a terrifying halt you told off several fans for vandalizing your ice with chucked root beers and orange sodas, slowly becoming one with the frozen surface. You scanned the bleachers for Kelvin, and thought you saw him galloping down the steps, bickering with anyone willing to step up to his ghetto strut. And now you run to the wailing woman, get down on all fours, place your hands on her, on her wound, just below her ribs, and you tell her it's going to be okay even though you're not sure if it's true or a lie, but you tell yourself that you're telling the truth, because you're whatever this place needs you to be. It's true, always has been. You're the heartbeat of this community. And right now it needs you to help this woman. Your vision's blurry. You wonder if it's the adrenaline. Or if you're scared and crying. You're pushing, pushing hard but not too hard, applying pressure, holding the life in her body, seeping through your fingers and on your clothes, stains that won't ever come out, not really. You're praying, praying for her life, praying you won't be too fucked up after this, pushing and praying.

## *clinton whiteway*

I RAN. I RAN AFTER KELVIN. MY BROTHER. HE DITCHED HIS CAR, THE adrenaline made him forget he had a car. I caught up to him within three blocks of the arena, just as he was lifting up the lid of a trash bin and tossing the gun and rearranging the garbage bags inside. His skin was damp and glossy, his eyes like pitch-black marbles, removed of their normal brown. I'd never seen him so shaken. Scared even. I wondered for a moment if that's what evil looked like, but then reminded myself that we were kin, are kin, and if he was evil then what did that make me? Evil's younger evil brother.

I gasped for air and said, "Kelvin. Are you fucking crazy! Stop."

"Run away, little brother," he said, refusing eye contact. "They're going to be looking for me."

"Turn yourself in." I tried to find his eyes. "It was an accident."

"I'm not doing that," he said. His eyes began to water. "I'm not going back. Run away, little brother. You gotta get away from me." He paused and looked at me as if he hadn't seen me in a long time. "You gotta get away from me."

"What are you gonna do?" I felt I was being too loud for the moment.

He didn't say anything.

"What are you going to do?" I said this quieter.

He smiled. "Remember when Mom took us to that ice fishing derby back home and nobody was catching anything? The fish weren't coming out. But you stayed out there, were like the only one out on the lake. Probably one of my most favorite days out there.

Sunny. Ice had this greenish look like stained glass. You stayed out there, didn't care, determined as shit to catch something. Finally, after like five hours, you caught a whitefish, and they gave you that mini ATV as a prize. And then, remember, first day of spring, when it was good enough to ride around, we totaled the fucking thing off a ditch jump and you flew off and almost hit your head on a drainpipe. Mom hated me since."

"She didn't hate you. Doesn't hate you."

He gave a slight shrug. "It's all good."

"Kel," I said, my voice cracking. "Don't run. Don't do this."

There were sirens somewhere in the distance, though neither of us could be sure where or of what kind.

"Get away now, little brother," he said, turning and moving down the sidewalk in a light jog. "I won't tell you again."

I went after him and heard him shout over his shoulder: "Go home!" His voice echoed so that I heard it twice. But I kept going, keeping pace. The streets were lit orange, we were caught in it. Could feel the heavy weight and energy of each tall lamp, fueling us like they did our mother. Her sun and her sons. I could no longer hear sirens. He stopped up at a slightly busier intersection with stop signs and two or three cars waiting for their turn to pass through. Kelvin assessed both directions and then calmly made his way to the other side of the road. I stopped too, looked both ways. The car approached me from behind, slowly, made almost no noise. I picked out the hush breathing of its engine just as it crawled to a stop. I turned and looked at it, looked over to Kelvin, looking at me, and then its lights turned on, blue and then red, there and not there but always there, in another place.

"Run!" I heard Kelvin say. "Run! Run now!"

I ran. I dashed through the intersection, followed Kelvin. The cop car followed, sirens on, ordering us to stop. Kelvin was fast, was always so fast, even as a kid he'd come announcing he'd run the 5K faster than the rest of his class. He jumped the front fence of a small white house and continued toward the backyard and hopped another fence and I did the same, though less gracefully, and together we were in a narrow alleyway and he stopped and waited for me. Heaving. Catching our breath before resuming our run. We came upon two separate paths, one forward and the other to the left, both similar back lanes.

Kelvin coughed harshly and the sweat on his face and around his eyes made it appear as though he was crying. "Go left," he said, a subtle pause between each word. "Go left. Go back to the arena. I'll keep going. Go home. Don't tell anyone you saw me."

I didn't object. I stared down the dark lane, then at the ground, then at my dirty white sneakers. He stepped toward me, wrapped a hand around the back of my head and higher part of my neck, his fingers deep into my hair, and pulled me to look at him. Somehow he didn't look like a monster, he'd found a way to turn it off. Hide it from others. He was changing shapes, blending into his environment. He wasn't the vampire that came home nearly a year earlier, sucking up the life around him. I thought I saw his eyes turn brown again, speckled like the coat of a deer. And they stayed that way when he released me and kept running.

I went left and shortly after I could hear the sirens again, getting closer. I looked behind me and there they were, following me. On me. The lights blurry, swelling in the darkness. The car braked hard and the tires screeched loud and two men got out, hustling toward me. I kept running, as fast as I could until it felt like I could no longer feel the ground, like I was flying, learning to fly, and after three long minutes it became clear it was a dead end. I quit then. I started to feel it again. I started counting. I reached into my pocket and held my red pen and tapped its cap. Something in me was trying desperately to leap out of my skin. My run turned to a walk and I turned around and only saw white lights and flashing lights and the silhouettes of two human men.

I felt a sharp smack, as if the wind was taking out its revenge for attempting to defy gravity. A hole burned through me, through my stomach. The wind left me. I felt another, through my chest, and then another, through my stomach. And then another, though I can't remember where. I fell, fell backward. I didn't want to, but the fall felt right, couldn't help it, I couldn't stop it. And in the time it takes for me to get there I wonder where I'm going, where I was, why I can't stay here just a little bit longer.

I'M ON THE GROUND now. It's hard and cold and warm and soft. I try to move but I can't. I tell myself it's okay. It's okay not to move, and I feel a gladness at not having to move anymore. I blink several times. Tears I can't wipe. I tell myself that I need to move, I need to keep going, keep moving. I move one finger ever so slightly, then another, then another, then my thumb, then my pinky, then my whole hand and wrist, then my whole arm and shoulder and I pull my limb back to my chest and reach inside and hold my heart in my hand and there, in front of my wet eyes, it beats. It's big and beautiful. It looks like a painting by some fancy artist. It tells me it's time to rise and so I put it back and I move my other arm and I turn over and press both palms on the hard ground and with all my might, along with a loud painful roar, I rise to my feet and when I do I'm standing on the beach back home, back on the rez. The sand is a beautiful white. I'm in clean clothes and dirty sneakers. I inspect my abdomen and chest and the holes that were just there are now gone. My clothes are clean, and smell of the same detergent Mom used to use on us. The powdery kind. I'm small again. A young boy on the rez. There's people in the water, swimming and splashing and wrestling. Like they used to. This is before the flood, before we moved to the city. Has to be. The water looks like crystal, just like stained glass, just like Kelvin said. A young boy and young girl run past me, playing tag, in their bathing suits and the young boy turns to me and says, You coming? And I say, I don't have trunks, and he says, Who cares, no one's going to see you. I watch them run through the shallow shoreline before diving into the lake's deep drop. They rise and laugh and splash. I smile and laugh like I'm part of it. I take off my clothes and shoes and begin my run in my underwear and I dive and immediately shiver from the cold. But after a minute it's okay. I swim to the boy and girl. Both have long hair and when I mention it they look at me oddly and say, So do you. And I do. I remember now having long hair before I moved to the city and got shy about it. Mom was sad, cried that day, when I asked to get it cut short. The boy is Little Red Bear and the girl is Mayheve and I know them once I see them up close. They lived here on this rez when it was a place you could live.

I look around and study every face hovering above water. Somehow I know them all. We all come from here. This place. This place that once existed but which I know for a fact was pulled under years ago. I ask, Why are we here? and Little Red Bear points down the lake and says, We're here to go there. It's a setting sun, sitting beautifully just above the horizon, far in the distance. Again like some beautiful work of art. Its beauty terrifies me. I ask, Why? and Mayheve says, Because they're calling for us. I look toward the shore and wonder if it's not too late to swim back and there he is, Kelvin, ass in the sand, feeling it between his toes, and I turn to Little Red Bear and say, What about him? and he says, It's not for him just yet. We're no longer swimming but being pulled by the waves, heading for the sun. I resist at first but then let go, I let go because I have to. I let go because my heart is telling me to. I hear my name being called out. I hear my koko and my shoomis. Telling me it's okay. Leaving is okay. I hear all the kokos and all the shoomises. They sing. They await us. There on that other side. I'm in my clothes and shoes again, walking. We're walking on ice, the lake is frozen solid, but it's a warm summer day. Everyone from the water is with me, walking. We're walking, together we're walking, but we're in no rush, and over there, beyond that bright sun, they're waiting for us.

# miinawaa biboong

TOMMY STANDS IN A BARE AISLE OF A SUPPOSEDLY DISCOUNT HARD-
ware store. The whole store is empty of other people, due to it barely
being noon on a Monday. It's winter again, the next winter after
the last one, a real winter's winter, and in the cart beside him he
has procured the cheapest auger he could find, a large white pail,
and a scooper. He's trying to choose between a selection of fishing
rods, and wishes now that he'd done some research before this sudden trip to the hardware store, but he'll go with the cheapest option
regardless—a rod that apparently offers maximum grip and flex and
power, and can be used on light, medium and large "species"—and
laughs to himself as he collects it. He laughs because that's what
everyone's been calling him: Cheap Guy. And he lives up to it daily.

It started with the parties he, Floyd, Jonah, Casey and Colton
went to after they all graduated from St. Croix in June and turned
eighteen. When parents and/or foster parents and/or auntie(s) were
out of town. He'd bring the cheapest beer and cheapest snacks, which
in the world of such consumables usually meant the worst kind possible. "Boy you're cheap," Floyd started saying. "The Creator gave
us options for a reason. Good and bad ones. Kind of like women.
Cheap Guy." It stuck. At the bar he never bought rounds, usually
left early, accused his employer, an NDN grocery store, of paying
too little, even after promoting him to supervisor four months into
the job, which none of his friends believed. Truth was, he was saving, still is. He turned eighteen a month after airing his graduation
cap and considered himself an adult man, though he was an adult

man who still lived at home with his koko and sister. A house, he thought, while stocking chips one afternoon at work. Yes. He'd save for a house. He'd have land to himself, yes, somewhere nice, perhaps just outside the city where the sky is big and endless and the prairies never end.

He pays for his things and in his car, which he's only renting for the day, he opens his phone and checks his email. He's looking for a reply from his mother, who's doing better, who claims to be better, and who he's been exchanging emails with for several months, mulling the possibility of visiting each other, either here or there. But nothing. There's another message from a reporter doing a story on the lost lives at the hands of cops and wishing to speak to the people who knew them. He's not sure how the journalist got his email address and doesn't care much, but deletes the request anyway. Another in the bin.

THE NEWSCASTER SAID TWO cops chased Clinton down an alley off McGregor and eventually cornered him, nowhere to go. At that point, the officers claimed, he turned on them with a red ink pen, the same one he used in class—much to the disapproval of teachers—to stand out and because he liked the color, and they had no choice but to hit their target seven times in the torso. It was him or them. An internal review cleared the officers of any wrongdoing and a month later they were back to work. Word circulated through the neighborhood, perhaps originating from the mouth of Kelvin, that Clinton went after his brother, his only brother, and when he found him they ran. The sirens were out, pulling over drivers on streets the whole force had highlighted on a map, the bad ones. Kelvin slipped into a backyard and hid in the weeds. Still as concrete. He was apprehended a day later down south near Saint Jean Baptiste. His flair for the dramatic lured him to the Red River and into an unlocked canoe. The judge referred to it as a foolhardy getaway with only one conceivable outcome.

Tommy decided early on he'd never believe the police's story, but wasn't sure the truth would come out one day either. He hated the idea of being one of those people he read about in the news. Those people who mourned and loved the dead, who could testify to who they really were. Who would believe him if he tried to explain to the chubby white guy with the balding head and a notepad just how sweet that boy was? NDNs like him, NDNs of the same NDN blood, were shot for less, and now they were less because of it.

Instead he went on with his life as if nothing happened, as if the city had rinsed it from memory. He graduated, took pictures wearing a suit in front of the fountain at the legislature, went to prom, split a limo with the other graduating Tigers, kissed his date Eliou McKay on the dance floor during a slow song, hugged his friends, teachers, mothers serving as chaperones, drunk fathers cosplaying as chaperones, friends who were closer to strangers than actual friends, friends he suspected could be cousins, cousins, cousins he didn't know were cousins, his enemies, his enemies that were now almost like friends, at one point the DJ, at one point Principal Goodstock and Coach Johnson at the same time, and, of course, Eliou McKay, who decided later in the evening that they were probably just friends, because a fancy university in Montreal beckoned.

The email from his mother arrived a week later, the first in a long time.

Hi my boy,
　　How are you? Are you well? I know it's been a long time but I hope you're well, doing well. I did the math: you're almost 18, which means you graduated? Or about to? If so. Congratulations! I'm proud of you. If not. Then I hope you keep trying. Because trying is better than nothing. I have some good news: I'm seeing a doctor, staying at a place where they have doctors. It's sort of like a cozier, friendlier hospital, with more gardens and outdoor spaces to sit and chat to others. It's been good. I feel good. It was hard at first, but like anything you get used to it. I thank my friend for helping me, encouraging me to make this choice. Beatrice her name is. So me I'm doing good. My other friend, I think I mentioned my other friend Littlefeather to you before, she wasn't so

sure about it at first, a little upset with me for not seeing her always, but she came around. Again. Hope you're well. Hope Koko and Sam are well too. I hope this is the first of many.

Thinking of you,

Mom

He responded to her, told her everything, told her what happened to Clinton. He told her about the protests that followed, the severe lack of accountability and the protests that followed that too, the trial of Kelvin, his sentencing. That Koko was there, pulling him to Sam's car amid the dizzying panic. They kept writing, all throughout summer. In September he got his driver's license and enrolled in business classes at Red River College and thought maybe he'd start a car-share company after discovering how much it was to rent a vehicle, even just for the day. It was about time all those whining cabdrivers had some competition, he thought. Maybe it'll be my way of helping. They all had a role to play.

Sam left for England at the end of summer. She sold her car, reasoning that by the time she returned home she'll have earned herself a new one, one that isn't consistently invaded by rats. The day before they took her to the airport Tommy mentioned to her the state of their mother for the first time since Sam told him she didn't want to hear about her and her emails.

"She's doing better," he said, throwing himself on his sister's bed.

Sam was finalizing her suitcase. "Good," she said.

"She's at a hospital. With gardens and places to sit and chill."

She didn't respond.

"She asked if I wanted to come out. See her, see the city. Maybe next summer. Maybe sooner. Like January or February. Who knows." Tommy rolled onto his back. "What do you think?"

"That could be nice. I guess. That's good for her though." She zipped her suitcase closed. "Don't get your hopes up."

Tommy sat up and retorted, "What do you have against her? Seems like she's trying."

Her breathing grew intense. Her shoulders and arms went limp, as if dragging a burden. "She tried to come out here. Back in May. She called. I told her it wasn't a good idea."

Tommy felt breathless, his eyes burned. But nothing could surprise him anymore. He thought his own heart and lungs and veins ought to live outside his body as a nod to the suffering, to survivance, and all the things that could no longer hurt him, numbing him. He filled his lungs. "She's doing something at least."

"Good. Good for her. How am I supposed to feel about someone I haven't seen in years? My mother, *our* mother, the person who's been here for us, taking care of us, sacrificing for us, doing what a parent is supposed to do, is downstairs." She moved to her open door. "I'm happy for her. I am. But for now. Leave me out of it." And then she left.

She was right. He knew she was right.

At the airport they hugged long. She cried and Koko cried, and then she turned around and walked to security. But she would come back. She said so herself.

HE PULLS AWAY FROM the hardware store and heads for the city limits. When he passes Warren, a town that looks like it consists only of grass, grain and trees, he's officially the farthest outside the city he's ever been. Been there a few times for games. The world outside is flat and white. As far as you can see. He keeps going, northbound on Highway 6. Past a town called St. Laurent and another called Lundar, its giant goose statue greeting those arriving and leaving. He turns off at Eriksdale and goes down a small road that gets thinner and thinner and eventually turns into gravel until he reaches Lake Manitoba.

He parks and gets out and spots a fishing shack painted red in the distance. Nothing else around but white and blue sky. He tosses all the things he bought from the hardware store on a sled he brought from home, the same one he uses to whip down Garbage Hill, and when he reaches the shack he realizes he doesn't need the auger. There are holes already dotting the lake and he cracks one open and scoops out the ice, and for a few hours he sits there on his pail and he's alone the whole time and he knows, deep in that large scarlet part of him, his friend would have loved it, waiting for whatever swims beneath to choose him.

# acknowledgments

I couldn't have done this without the love and support of my big and beautiful family. To my mom for making me who I am and being there no matter what. This couldn't be done without you. My brothers River and Sage, for their love and laughter and stories. Koko Valerie, for making sure I grew up loving books and art. Shoomis Edwin, for his wisdom and teachings, and raising me like a son. Koko Emma, for always reminding me to be proud. To love who I am and where I come from. For being an example of strength for us kids. Auntie Deanna, the deadliest of deadly aunties. Uncle Dean and Sabrina and Clan, for always feeding and clothing me. My two boys, Dostoevsky and Leo, the best writing companions a man could ask for. Those who walked on and who I wish were still here: Randy, Kimmy, Leonid, Dennis, Karen, Raymond. Miigwech to my cousin Tommy for letting me use his name, the long version, still the deadliest in the game. Sincerest miigwech to all my relatives and relations back home on the Lake Manitoba First Nation and the Ebb and Flow First Nation, and big miigwech to the Ebb and Flow chief and council for supporting me through college.

There were many people who helped make this book what it is. From the bottom of my heart, miigwech to the Stanford Creative Writing Program and the Wallace Stegner Fellowship, for giving me the time and space to write this novel. Adam Johnson, for believing in the importance of the book when it was nothing more than an idea. Chang-Rae Lee, for his careful reads and honesty. Elizabeth Tallent, for making me a better student of the game. All the Stegners, from whom I learned so much. Sterling HolyWhiteMountain, for being one big supportive Indian. Miigwech to my PhD family at the University of Southern California, without whom I am just another broke-ass writer. For being some of the coolest people around. Percival Everett and Danzy Senna. For their support and mentorship. My editor Joe, for being one of the first to read the short story that this book came from and loving it, and believing in it so much that he bought it with the promise I'd make it a novel. For work-ing with me every step so that it became what it is now. My editor, David, for everything he's taught me as a writer and teacher and advisor and friend and for making the book better. Stephanie Sinclair, for being the best former agent a boy could ask for, and everything she's done for me as my Canadian pub-lisher. My agent Ron Eckel, for having my back and supporting this book when it needed someone like him. Everyone at Pantheon. Everyone at McClelland & Stewart. Shout-out to Winnipeg, that crazy and beautiful place I hold dear. Shout-out to the precious gift that is hockey.

Lucky is the man who gets to write this.

*a note about the author*

Kyle Edwards is a Provost Fellow at the University of Southern California. He grew up on the Lake Manitoba First Nation in Manitoba and is a member of the Ebb and Flow First Nation. He lives in Los Angeles.

*a note on the type*

This book was set in Minion, a typeface designed by Robert Slimbach and produced by the Adobe Corporation in 1990 specifically for the Macintosh personal computer.

Typeset by Scribe, Philadelphia, Pennsylvania

Designed by Betty Lew